T0279393

Praise for Book One of the

ABOVE THE BLACK

fantasy trilogy!

★"A skillful blend of action, suspense, and comic relief. After each airship battle, readers can barely draw breath before political intrigues turn the story on its head."

—*Kirkus Reviews*, STARRED REVIEW (*Sky's End*)

★"Teeth-clenching and gory battle scenes, complex and well-developed characters with constantly evolving relationships, found family, loyalty, and a hint of romance."

—*Booklist*, STARRED REVIEW (*Sky's End*)

★"A dazzling setting reminiscent of *Treasure Planet* and 'Attack on Titan,' where vast lore sets the scene for complicated ethical and cultural questions. . . . A great read for anyone who loves fantasy and dystopian fiction."

—*BookPage*, STARRED REVIEW (*Sky's End*)

AMONG SERPENTS

Published by Peachtree Teen
An imprint of PEACHTREE PUBLISHING COMPANY INC.
1700 Chattahoochee Avenue
Atlanta, Georgia 30318-2112
PeachtreeBooks.com

Design by Lily Steele
Composition by Six Red Marbles
Edited by Jonah Heller

Printed and bound in November 2024 at Sheridan, Chelsea, MI, USA.
10 9 8 7 6 5 4 3 2 1
First Edition
ISBN: 978-1-68263-706-7

Library of Congress Cataloging-in-Publication Data

Names: Gregson, Marc J., author.
Title: Among serpents / Marc J Gregson.
Description: Atlanta, Georgia : Peachtree Teen, 2025. | Series: Above the black ; 2 | Audience: Ages 14 and Up. | Audience: Grades 10–12. | Summary: At the behest of his tyrannical uncle, sixteen-year-old Conrad embarks on a secret mission to turn the tides of battle and defeat the monsters devastating his world.
Identifiers: LCCN 2024023675 | ISBN 9781682637067 (hardcover) | ISBN 9781682637074 (ebook)
Subjects: CYAC: Quests (Expeditions)—Fiction. | Monsters—Fiction. | Fantasy. | LCGFT: Fantasy fiction. | Novels.
Classification: LCC PZ7.1.G74165 Am 2025 | DDC [Fic]—dc23
LC record available at https://lccn.loc.gov/2024023675

EU Authorized Representative: HackettFlynn Ltd, 36 Cloch Choirneal, Balrothery, Co. Dublin, K32 C942, Ireland. EU@walkerpublishinggroup.com

NEW YORK TIMES BESTSELLING AUTHOR

MARC J GREGSON

AMONG SERPENTS

ABOVE THE BLACK

PEACHTREE Teen

To Hazel, Ivy, and Vera, my sweet,
quirky children whose laughter fills
our home with love, joy, and big dreams.

—MJG

CHAPTER 01

MY SISTER STANDS OVER AN UNCONSCIOUS MEMBER OF MY crew.

Ella's white hair flies in the wicked evening wind, and blood dribbles from the end of her dueling cane. I leap from the hatch and step onto the deck of my skyship. She rotates on her heels, and her fierce eyes find mine.

"He was being insubordinate," she hisses.

"What have you done, Ella?"

She glances at Declan. And spits.

My stomach twists at the sight of the man beneath her boots. The green pin of Swabbie shines on his jacket. Declan of McDougal. He's an aged veteran, honorable. Keeps the deck clean, the laundry scrubbed, and the corridors clear.

Blood stripes his forehead.

A jagged streak of lightning cracks behind Ella, illuminating the other ships in my squadron. Ella's lips curl as she stares at me.

My late father's voice creeps into my mind.

Take her cane before she hurts you, too.

"Ella." I breathe to slow my raging heart. "On my ship, Declan doesn't have to follow your commands."

"I am the Princess of the Skylands."

"So?"

Her mouth shuts, and her eyes narrow. "You are the *Prince*."

I meet her gaze dead-on. Being delicate doesn't work with her.

"Uncle gave me that title, but my crew follows me because they respect me." I take a step toward her. "Princess or not, this is *my* ship. You are not a Hunter. You have no right to attack my crew. Step away from him."

She squeezes her cane dangerously and remains in place. I almost scowl. It's always a challenge with her. We finally reunited after Uncle tore us apart for six years, and I thought we'd go back to the way we were when we were rich Highs in Urwin Manor. When we'd steal cookies from the kitchen and break windows and leave mud pies under the blankets of our guests' beds.

But we've outgrown such things. Uncle poisoned Ella's heart, turning her into the angry thing that stands before me.

"Ella." My voice rises. "Step back."

"He is *untrustworthy*, Conrad."

"Declan's an old man."

"He was talking to someone." She jabs at the empty night sky around us. The three other skyships in my squadron float nearby—but not close enough to hear anyone aboard my ship. "There's no one on deck, Conrad. Who was he talking to?"

"He talks to himself," I growl. "Whispering. Laughing. Singing. He's weird, but he's a great Swabbie. And my crew loves him." My voice tightens with frustration. "Now, get back."

When I approach her, she readies her cane. So I snatch it, quick as a snake strike. She nearly topples. I tap the button on the side of her cane, halving its length to three feet. The cane was our mother's.

It was supposed to be Ella's path to learn a better way. Instead, it has emboldened her warped sense of power.

"Give it back." Ella crouches, hands outstretched like some wild thing about to jump me. "Now."

Brutally cold wind blows between us. I stoop over Declan and press my fingers against his neck until I find a steady pulse. He still needs medical help.

"This is not the way, Ella," I whisper.

"This is Meritocracy, Brother. The Highs rise, and the Lows fall."

"It is not the *right* way."

She pauses. Considering me with her icy green eyes. Some claim Ella's the worst of my family. Worse than Uncle, even. The Father part of me, the part that wanted me to learn the world's hard, brutal lessons, demands that I teach Ella the hard lessons, too. Beat her with the cane she used on Declan and humble her.

But the Mother part of me believes in another way. One of compassion and growth through experience.

"Attacking my crew is unacceptable," I say. "Physical conflict is not the Hunter way."

She scoffs. "You can't tell me to act like a Hunter, then forbid me from hunting with the rest of the crew. I killed three prowlons. By myself."

"Prowlons are not five-hundred-foot gorgantauns, Ella. You're not ready for sky serpents."

"I'm ready for more than you know."

My head shakes. What the hell am I supposed to do with her? It's been three months since our reunion, and I'm exhausted from the battles. She fights with my whole crew. She sneaks around the ship and eavesdrops on everyone. And despite being the Princess, she has a penchant for stealing.

Roderick's still missing weapon plans.

Beat her down, Father's voice whispers again. *Humiliate her. Ensure she'll never challenge you. Because deep down, you know she wants what you have. She wants to be the heir.*

I study her. She has too much of Father in her. What she needs is more of Mother. But I can't be her mother. All I can do is teach her in the ways Mother taught me.

"Conrad," Ella growls. "Give me the cane."

The stag of Hale shines at the end of Mother's cane. Beating Ella won't fix her. No, she needs something Uncle never gave.

So I toss her the cane.

Ella snatches it and blinks, confused. But, after a breath, she starts toward the hatch.

I cut her off and point at Declan. "He needs to go to the medical room. You owe that to him. And when he wakes, you'll apologize."

"Urwins don't apologize. I'm not your servant, and I'll not drag him anywhere."

She tries to side-step me, but I block her path again.

"*Move*," she says.

"Hit me."

"What?"

"Hit me, and you'll be excused. You can do whatever you want for the rest of the night."

She hesitates. If she were all rotten, she'd have already done it.

"Hit me once, Ella, and you're free to go."

She eyes me, licks her teeth, then crouches into her dueling stance. "Have it your way."

I frown. "Your posture's too low."

"Birdshit."

I sigh. Ella hasn't faced true challenge yet. Sure, Uncle forced her to hunt prowlons, and she fared in that trial better than I did. But when Uncle threw Mother and me out, I survived by dueling in the Low pit and enduring nights with hunger gnawing away at me while listening to Mother's hacking coughs. For six years, that was my life. Then, on this very ship, I rose from the boot-waxing Swabbie to Captain.

Uncle's teachings cannot replicate real experience.

"Stand straighter," I say, circling around her. "Raise your cane."

"That's not how Father taught me."

"*Father*? Uncle is *not* your father."

"Might as well be. Uncle didn't abandon us. He didn't leave us."

"*Leave*?" I take a breath to swallow my anger. "Ella, Father was *murdered*."

"He was weak—not the true leader of Urwin."

My voice grows bitter. "You sound like Uncle."

"That's because I *am* like Uncle."

I stop. I'm on this cold deck, the gales chilling my skin, standing in front of the person I dreamed of rescuing for years. But all I feel now is an empty heart.

"Ella," I say softly. "I was on your path once, too. I was a paranoid, irrationally angry person who ate alone in the cafeteria and refused to engage in meaningful conversation with anyone. It got me nowhere. But being better than what the world intends . . . that got me where I am now."

"It made you Prince?"

"No, it made me Captain of this ship, and that's what I care about more than being the heir."

She eyes me skeptically. "Being better . . . who said that?"

"Mother."

Ella considers this, then shrugs. "Hardly knew her."

I glower. "Fine. Use what your '*father*' taught you. Strike me with the cane once and you're free to go."

"Your cane's in your cabin. I'd rather duel. It's not a fair fight right now."

I laugh. "Fair? This world is *never* fair. But I'm sure you've learned that lesson. What you need," I pause, "is the lessons Mother taught."

She studies me. "What lessons?"

"Compassion. Mercy. Proving that true strength comes not from weakening others but building them up. True leaders lead powerful people."

"That's ridiculous."

"Do you think I'm weak?"

She doesn't answer.

Bitter wind blows between us again, and a gentle rain peppers the deck.

"Use all that Uncle taught you." I wave her toward me. "C'mon."

She spits, then crouches in her too-low stance again. The next instant, she's swinging her cane at me. Fast, her eyes wild, movements agile.

But I'm nimbler. Her attacks hiss past my head, my shoulder. Strike air instead of my gut. She swears with frustration. Ella has Uncle's sensibilities in dueling. Uncle never likes a duel to last more than a minute. To become King, he challenged King Ferdinand to a duel and killed him in under ten seconds.

Her cane grazes my skin, but I slide away before she can get me. Ella continues jabbing. I step back, giving her an open path to the hatch. She studies me, then marches for it, her eyes gleaming with victory.

But I cut her off.

She scowls and furiously charges me again. I duck away and pivot around her. She keeps on the offensive. Swinging wild, frenzied attacks. Finally, her cane nearly strikes my cheek, but her momentum sends her sprawling and she hits the deck, chin-first.

If I'd listened to Mother's lessons only, I'd rush to her. Maybe let my guard down. But Father taught me to never trust a downed foe, especially one who needs a whole damn gallon of humility.

Ella's rolling in pain. I watch her and wait for the act to end. Eventually she snaps upright, brushes herself off, and seems ready to shout at me. Her body's shuddering with frustration.

My fingers twitch, preparing for another attack. Instead, she leans on Mother's cane and takes a long, calming breath. She looks me up and down.

The rain's falling thick now. Making her white hair stick to the side of her reddened face.

"What does it mean?" she asks softly. "What does it mean to be better than what the world intends?"

A sudden hope blooms inside me. This isn't a breakthrough, not much more than a flicker of a candle, but it's something. For months, I've been looking for an opening just like this.

"Help me take Declan belowdecks," I say, "and I'll tell you."

She considers me, stands straighter, then retracts her cane and clips it to her belt.

"Fine."

My chest swells a little. Maybe I've just discovered the secret to getting Ella to listen to me. She respects strength. And perhaps through that vessel, I'll teach her and finally become the big brother Mother would want me to be.

We walk to a small control panel, recently installed by Roderick, and tap a button. The deck cracks open in the center and the munitions platform rises. Harpoons, mobile launchers, flak cannons, and shoulder cannons rest in the crates atop the platform.

We catch Declan's collar and gently drag him onto the platform. After another touch of the button, the platform descends us into the bowels of the ship. While the attached chains rattle, I feel Mother with me as I begin explaining to her daughter the lessons she never had a chance to pass on herself.

CHAPTER 02

I INJECT DECLAN WITH MEDS. WITHIN A FEW MINUTES, HIS groggy eyes open. Ella leans against the white walls of the medical room, watching the man wake from his stupor. He slowly sits upright, and I cram another pillow behind his back.

Declan's still touching his forehead and taking in his surroundings when Ella breaks the silence.

"I am sorry." Her words are rigid and unfeeling.

Declan coughs. He reaches into his mouth, touches his bloody gums, and winces. "You attacked me, Princess."

"Yes, and I just apologized."

He looks at her. "An apology is simply noises if there's no remorse behind it."

She glances at me, irritated. Then repeats her apology with false sweetness.

"*Ella*," I growl.

"Pardon me, Captain," Declan says. "But an apology means even *less* if it's forced."

"She doesn't know how to apologize," I say.

He raises an eyebrow, perplexed.

"It won't happen again, Declan," Ella says.

He stops, perhaps realizing this is the best he'll get from her, then nods. She's been taught, like all Urwins, that people apologize to us, not the other way around.

"Ella, you're dismissed."

She looks between us and leaves without another word.

Declan massages his gray jaw. He appears exhausted, with bloodshot eyes. I pat his shoulder. He's a sixty-year-old man among my crew that ranges between sixteen and eighteen. Was a Captain of his own ship, earned a lot of money. Amazingly, after forty years of being a Hunter, he's still in one piece. Many Hunters have lost limbs, or worse, while taking out gorgantauns.

His silver uniform hugs his thick, muscular forearms. Like all Hunters, he has a black jacket draped over him, gloves, and heavy magboots. A pair of wind goggles rests over his neck, just above the harpoon insignia on the chest of his uniform.

I drafted Declan to the *Gladian's* crew because he wanted this to be his final hunting tour. He wanted to pass on his knowledge to the next generation of Hunters. After his six months end and the next Hunter draft arrives, he plans on retiring and working on the docks at Venator or, if he's lucky, teaching at the Hunter Academy.

"Why did she attack you, Declan?"

He exhales. "She wanted to duel. I told her physical conflict is *not* Hunter's way. She kept insisting, so I told her I wouldn't duel a little girl. Next thing I know, I'm here."

"Were you talking to someone else on the deck?"

He blinks. "I was the only one up there until the Princess arrived."

I exhale and touch his shoulder again. "I'm sorry."

"Least you understand how to apologize." He slides his legs off the bed and grunts. Fortunately, the meds work quickly. Developed by Scholar Doctors. Still, he needs to take it easy.

"Get some rest," I say, "and take tomorrow off to recuperate."

He nods and ambles toward the door but pauses. "Captain . . . I've met a lot of people, but rarely have I met ones that feel broken." He looks back at me. "Like something inside them is wrong."

I stare at him, my mouth hesitating. But I keep my face passive, even though my skin goes cold.

"Good night, Declan."

"Captain."

The door shuts. And after a few seconds, I lower onto the edge of the bed, feeling the weight of my responsibilities. Uncle's poison has gone beyond Ella's heart; it's in every part of her. And the worst thing is, Ella's only one of my concerns. Only one of the things that has torn sleep from me and filled my skull with pressure headaches.

The war.

I exit the medical room and walk the quiet, dark corridors. The *Gladian's* engine gives off a persistent, living sound. I walk beyond some of the rooms of the crew. Past my friends, Pound and Roderick and Keeton.

And then I pause at one door.

Bryce's the one we need in this war more than anyone, but I'm worried about her. She's not sleeping. Turning paranoid. She's been waking the crew in the middle of the night to face phantoms on the deck.

Pound claims she's losing her mind.

I sigh and head to the Captain's cabin. Once inside, I see Ella's already lying on the bed down the hall. When she came aboard my ship, I gave her the bed while I got the couch. This works better for me anyway because I'm often up late.

A stack of papers rises over the desk—plans from Pound, our Strategist, for the next hunt. We face so many dangerous beasts in these open skies. Things like acid-spitting acidons and skull-ramming orcons. But they're not nearly as dangerous as the class-eight gorgantauns we've been seeing more often.

Killing those creatures helps the Skylands. And returning their carcasses to Hunter outposts earns me money—money that I've been using to pay off this ship so that it's mine and can never be taken away from me.

I glance at the board where I've been tracking how much I've earned: three hundred thousand coins so far, seven hundred thousand to go.

My eyes itch with exhaustion. I'll worry about hunting tomorrow. I'll read Pound's plans then.

I lower onto the couch and kick off my boots. Gentle rain patters against the window. The calmness of it eases my tension. Then I clutch the soft blanket, lower onto my side, and shut my eyes.

A sudden crack of lightning erupts outside. I turn away, trying to ignore it, trying to get comfortable. But another clap shoots my eyes open. I roll back and stare at the three Hunter skyships hovering near mine. They're obscured by the wet window—nothing more than dark shapes.

Those ships are under my command. Uncle wanted to give me more responsibility. So now I'm out here, in the middle of the open skies, helping protect the fragile supply lines from sky serpents. Each of those ships is built of pure gorgantaun steel. Sleek and silver—they're mirror images of the *Gladian*. Harpoon turrets line their decks, and their pointed bows, like the edges of a sword, skim through the clouds. Several of their windows glow red from the warmth of their heatglobes.

After another streak of lightning, I growl and kick off the blanket. Can't sleep when it sounds like a battle out there. Can't sleep when I'm thinking about the war.

I sit up.

Three months ago the people of the Below exploded into our lives, surprising us with their existence when their greatest weapon left hundreds of thousands dead. The Below created the terrible beasts of the sky. They infiltrated our Meritocracy, our Trades, our islands. And, if there's something Bryce has taught me about her people, it's that they prefer to strike at night. When it's dark and cold.

My body sinks into the cushions again. Just a few seconds of rest, that's all. I'll let myself get a little weightless, let that tempting embrace of dreams drag me away. Oh, the blanket feels nice. Soft. Wrapped so gently around my torso, warming my legs.

My breathing gains a gentle rhythm.

✦✦✦

My communication gem explodes with light, and a voice shouts, "Alert! All hands on deck!"

I leap to my feet in a daze.

Ella shouts from down the hall. "What is it?"

My heart races as I quickly regain my senses. "Stay, Ella."

"Like hell!"

"Stay!"

My gem lights up again with Bryce's voice. "Battle stations!"

Fear clutches my heart. We're under attack. I shove on my boots, slip on my jacket, and race into the hall. My dazed crew's shouting in the corridors. I climb the ladder and push through the heavy hatch onto the deck. Readying myself for war.

The Below has come for us.

CHAPTER 03

ANGRY CLOUDS SWELL AROUND US, AND WIND LASHES MY body while Bryce stands at the bow, pointing frantically at the sky.

"Alert!" she cries into her comm gem. "All hands on deck!"

I snap on my goggles and hurry to her side.

"Bryce? What's happening?"

She's got a mobile harpoon launcher mounted on her shoulder, and her frame becomes a silhouette against jagged lightning. "They're coming."

Rain blurs my goggles. I snatch the spyglass from my belt and scan the sky: my ships and the living sky swirling around us. But no enemy ships. No beasts. Nothing.

"Where, Bryce?"

Suddenly, my comm gem lights up with the voices of the other ship's Captains. They're reporting empty skies, too. Still, their crews mount mobile harpoon launchers on their shoulders.

Bryce clutches the back of her neck, winces, then screams, "Battle stations!"

"But there's nothing out there!" Captain Joo Won of the *Securis* says over the comm. "What are we looking at?"

My crew comes above. The Master Gunner, Roderick, has bed-face, his muttonchops sticking up on the right side. He stares at Bryce, an irritated eye twitching. This is the third night in a row she's called an alert. Keeton follows him and catches his thick arm before he charges Bryce and explodes.

Behind them, Drake, the Navigator, rises from the hatch. His eyes are puffy with exhaustion. We've been pushing him too hard lately. He nearly fainted during our last hunt. Arika trails him. The teal badge of Cook shines on her jacket.

Then comes the biggest birdshit out of them all: Pound. He's a scowling bald giant at seven feet tall. The frightening thing is, he's only seventeen and just a little older than me.

He might grow more.

"Where the hell are they this time, Bryce?" Pound demands. "You woke everyone again for nothing, didn't you? *Didn't you?*"

"Just look, Captain," Bryce says desperately, lifting a finger toward churning clouds of gray. "*Look.*"

I sigh and turn back to the clouds.

Several of my crew stop beside us. We peer through our spyglasses. The storm rages almost like it's a living organism. Bryce stabs impatiently toward the clouds, and a pair of shadows dance inside. My eyes narrow on the shadows, until I realize they're only a small island floating in the storm.

I exhale, lower the spyglass, and gently clasp her shoulder. "Bryce, you need sleep."

"No, Conrad."

"You're exhausted and not yourself."

"No!"

I tap my comm gem, sending a message to every ship. "False alarm. Go back to bed."

A series of curses follows. The squadron's already upset because we lost a ship a few days ago. A whole crew. I pause, recalling their shouts as a gorgantaun coiled around their ship and crushed it. Some of them leaped overboard. We flew after them, but they dropped into acid clouds because we couldn't—*I* couldn't—get my ship to them in time. The toxic clouds ate them.

I shut my eyes and push the *Hastus* from my mind. Must focus on the people I can help now. My squadron needs sleep, but they're not getting any because Bryce is losing her mind. As Quartermaster of my ship, she's supposed to be the stable one. The organized one. If Keeton weren't such a phenomenal Mechanic, I'd wonder if maybe Keeton should be the Quartermaster again.

The worst thing is, I fear the other Captains are suspicious of Bryce. If they discover her true origins . . .

"Pound," I say. "Take the Quartermaster belowdecks."

"No!" Bryce yells.

"I'm injecting sleep meds in her," Pound says, towering over her.

She backpedals. "No one's listening to me."

"Bryce," Keeton says gently, "we *are* listening. But you keep waking everyone for nothing. This is for your own good."

"No," Bryce says. She raises her fists. "Stay back, Pound."

He stops and stares at her. She's vicious as hell. Won't go down without someone getting a broken nose. Pound looks at me.

I massage my brow. What am I supposed to do? Trap her in her room, maybe? Until she rests?

Finally, I nod at him.

Pound reaches for her, but she swipes away his hands. Pound shakes his head. When he lunges for her again, a sudden explosion cracks the sky. The world lights up. A burst of heat slams into us, and I'm rocketed across the ship. I shout and tumble into the railing net that surrounds the deck's edges. My head's spinning. Voices buzz in my ears.

I roll out of the net and struggle to my feet, my vision bouncing. Blood dribbles down my cheek.

Then I see fire in the sky.

Holy hell! HOLY HELL!

The nearest skyship, the *Mortum*, is blazing with golden flames. A great fissure splits the slender ship in two. The bow topples forward and after a groan, the metal rips, and the front half of the ship sinks.

People fall.

No. Not again. NO!

The crew of the *Mortum* shouts in panic over the comm. We've got to help them. Can't lose them, too. Won't lose them!

I crank the magnetics in my boots to high. "BATTLE STATIONS!"

My heels snap onto the deck.

Pound and Roderick race to the turrets. They leap atop the seats and strap themselves in. Bryce fires a harpoon at nothing but sky. Arika runs for the munitions platform to collect weapons. Keeton hurries to the hatch, going belowdecks to manage the engine. And Drake dashes for the helm tile to fly us for the *Mortum.*

"Save the crew," I shout over the comm. "Save—"

I stop. Something appears in the clouds, close to where Bryce's harpoon flew. It's the head of a giant beast. Brown metallic scales on a silverish shell, and a round beak. Almost like . . . a turtle?

"What the hell?" Pound says.

"Just kill it!" Roderick shouts.

They rotate their turrets and launch thick, black harpoons at the beast. Meanwhile, Drake leaps onto the helm tile. A glass bubble slides out from the platform and whooshes over him, encasing him inside.

Suddenly, a fissure of light grows in the giant turtle's mouth.

"Fly, Drake!" Bryce shouts.

The monster sprays a beam of electricity at us. Drake throws the helm strings forward. We launch and wind slams into my chest. I bend my knees to keep from toppling over. And the jagged streak of light skitters past us.

"The monster's gone!" Pound roars, swiveling his turret, scanning the sky. "Where'd it go?"

I lick the rain from my lips. The back half of the *Mortum* is still afloat.

"*Securis*," I say to another ship over the comm. "Rescue the *Mortum* crew."

"On it."

The *Securis* zooms for the remains of the *Mortum* while my crew and the *Titus* watch the sky.

"What the cuss is this creature?" Roderick asks.

"It's a torton," Bryce says breathlessly over the comm.

"Torton?" Arika says. "Hunter never trained us on these."

"That's because they weren't here," Bryce says. "Until now."

"How do we kill it?" the *Titus* Captain asks.

"When it reappears," Bryce says, stuffing a harpoon into her mobile launcher, "aim for the skull."

We soar in circles, protecting the *Securis* as it drops ropes to the panicked *Mortum* survivors. Their lifeboats were destroyed, and their ship's still sinking. Worse, the *Securis* reports some of the *Mortum* crew are stuck belowdecks.

"IT'S BACK!" Bryce launches a harpoon. It slides just over the torton's shell and shoots into open sky.

The giant turtle sends another jolt of lightning at us.

My eyes widen. "Drake, mo—"

The blast strikes the helm bubble, making the whole ship buzz. My ears hum.

Roderick and Pound roar and fire at the beast.

Drake convulses as electricity shoots through him, his eyes wide. His whole body shudders and smokes. Then he tumbles. The helm rings slide from his fingers. He topples off the platform and hits the deck.

I run for Drake. My legs ache from the magnetics in my heels. I slide and crouch beside him. Arika joins me in a panic.

Drake's still shuddering. Twitching. Half his face is charred. Blood seeps from his mouth where his teeth bit through his tongue, and the rain sizzles against his burning skin.

Finally, his convulsions end, and he goes still. Arika lowers onto a knee, checks his pulse, then frowns at me.

I stand, hardly feeling anything at all.

Arika slides Drake's body into a railing net so we won't lose him.

Suddenly, my gem lights up with cries again. The *Mortum* sinks. A trio of the crew made it to the deck, but the ship's sinking too quickly toward the acid clouds. The *Securis* dives for them, dropping ropes again.

I snap out of my daze and rush to the railing. About to shout for us to go after them, but no one's flying the *Gladian.* The *Securis* desperately tries to get the trio to catch the ropes. But it's too late. The *Mortum* crashes into the black clouds, sending plumes of toxicity into the sky. My comm glows with the screams of people melting away.

Then all goes silent.

"It's back!" Bryce yells. "Starboard!"

She races to leap atop the helm platform. Within seconds, the *Gladian* revs to life. The torton reappears on our starboard, almost out of thin air. Pound and Roderick launch harpoons. Meanwhile, the *Titus* and *Securis* swoop in, shooting their own harpoons at the torton.

Light glows in the beast's mouth.

My teeth grit. This bastard monster! I lift a mobile launcher from the munitions platform. Rest the giant weight on my shoulder and peer down the reticule. Then, I squeeze the trigger. My shot darts into the stormy air. It flies right into the turtle at the base of the neck. White blood gushes, and the creature screams and vanishes again.

"Nice shot, Conrad!" Pound yells.

Hardly hear him because I'm loading another harpoon, my skin tingling with rage. Then, just as the turtle reappears again, another blast streaks across my deck. Pound ducks before nearly getting decapitated, and Bryce launches us forward again.

We swerve into the sky and zoom between the *Securis* and the *Titus*. Toward where the turtle was. Wind lashes against my enraged face.

But the creature's gone. It keeps vanishing before we can hit it hard. It's got some type of camouflaging system.

"There are people aboard," Bryce says. "Inside the torton."

"Inside?!" Pound says. "Like, swimming around in its gut?"

"No. There's a chamber in the shell." We jerk left. Then right. In a wildly sporadic motion. But I get the sense she's following something. Somehow, she knows where it is. Or has an idea.

"Bryce, you're flying like a drunken lotcher!" Roderick yells.

The *Securis* and the *Titus* follow us. Trying to replicate our erratic motions.

I keep one hand on the railing to steady my balance. Suddenly, Bryce pulls the strings back to her hips, and Pound nearly slams his head against the turret's controls. He swears at her.

The other ships stop.

Another surge of torton electricity blitzes toward my ships from our left. This time at the *Titus*, but the ship swerves, and the attack merely grazes the stern.

We make a hard left turn.

"Flak cannons," Bryce says. "It'll help us see them."

Roderick and Pound kick another lever on their turrets, changing their barrels. A new enhancement Roderick made to our weapons. Soon golden flak glitters in the sky like fireflies. All three ships are firing. Sending off blasts of gold everywhere. But the rain makes the sparks fade quickly. Roderick and Pound keep it going. Firing wave after wave. Suddenly, the golden sparks bounce off a rounded shape: the torton's shell.

The monster reappears and faces us. Its mouth opens and a light grows inside.

"Bryce, dive!"

She shoves downward and the *Gladian* plummets. Wind slams into my face. The electricity surges above us and crashes into the *Titus*. And I stare in horror as the ship erupts in fire.

"The *Titus*!" Arika cries.

The ship ruptures in two. Holy hell, the *Titus*! But I can't help them yet. We have to kill this damned thing or it'll get us all.

Roderick rains flak on the torton, revealing it again. Pound kicks another lever, and his repeater turret rapid-fires harpoons. They streak into the torton's shell as if it were made of sand.

"DIE!" Roderick bellows.

Arika and I stuff harpoons into launchers. My shoulder thrums after I fire and my harpoon cuts through the storm. It sinks right into the bastard's eye.

The groaning beast begins tumbling. This torton can throw a mean punch, but sure can't take one worth a damn. Now it's falling while the *Titus* still burns, and my comm is filled with the shouts of the dying. Can't save both.

"*Securis*, go for the *Titus*." I shout over the gem. "Bryce, after the torton! The people inside may have information we need!"

Bryce shoves the strings, and we pitch forward, tipping after the torton.

"Roderick," I say. "The clawgun."

"Got it."

The wind slams against my goggles. I hold the railing, focused on the falling beast. We rocket after it. Wind lashes through my hair. The torton's body spins, flippers flapping in the storm.

Roderick clicks another lever on his turret, and his harpoon barrel switches to a clawgun. The claw at the end of the chain will latch into the torton. But we'll be tethered to it, and if the torton weighs enough, it could take us down with it. Got to take that chance. This damned thing destroyed two Predator-class vessels in minutes.

Roderick rotates the turret and peers down the barrel. After a steadying breath, he squeezes the trigger. The clawed hook ripples after the falling beast. It catches a flipper, or leg. Or whatever the hell this thing has. But the clawgun rips the limb free, and the torton continues tumbling.

"Bryce!" I yell.

She shouts, arms shaking, as she pushes us after the torton. Rain blurs my vision. Roderick desperately fires the clawgun again, but the torton slips into the acid clouds. A swell of acid rises. And the clouds eat through the beast, shell and all.

Bryce curses and pulls back on the strings, leveling us just above the reach of the acid barrier.

Pound slams his fists against the turret. "Damn!"

My stomach churns with disappointment, and I shut my eyes. Two ships gone. Drake gone. A casualty list certain to come, and we lost the torton.

I'm quiet, leaning forward, my hands on the railing. My crew's silent. Roderick pauses, noticing Drake's body. Pound does, too. Then, in melancholy, Bryce turns the ship and shoves us toward the *Titus* above. It's billowing with flames. Some of the crew have evacuated on the bobbing lifeboats nearby.

The *Securis* collects them.

I don't even know what to say as we come to a stop beside the ships. The heat blazing in my eyes. This is on me. Bryce was right. Something was out there, maybe following us for days, and I didn't believe her. People died because I didn't listen.

The *Titus* begins a slow descent. No way to stop that now. At least the *Securis* saved the crew. But now my squadron, originally composed of five of the most advanced ships Hunter has to offer, has only two left.

I watch the *Titus* sink.

"Bryce," I say quietly over the comm. "Are there more tortons nearby?"

She slowly shakes her head.

I drop my launcher, and it clangs hard against the metal. The rain chills my skin. Don't know whether to cry, or scream, or both.

Bryce steps off the tile and leaves the platform. If I weren't so broken, I'd march over to her right now. Demand to know why she hasn't told me about the torton. Or why she hasn't told me anything, really.

Pound unbuckles from his turret, looking ready to confront her himself. But he pauses, perhaps recognizing the look in her eye. Complete and utter exhaustion. She takes one wobbly step, then falls forward and hits the deck.

"What the cuss?" Roderick says, unbuckling from his seat.

I hurry to kneel beside her. Roderick stands over my shoulder, concerned. My fingers touch Bryce's neck. She's still breathing. I lift her from the deck and Arika follows me. Arika's the Cook but has a bit of medical training.

Pound carefully pulls Drake's body from the railing net. Drake was the youngest among us. Competed in the same Gauntlet where we learned to be Hunters. He'd been the Navigator on another ship. Now, he's gone.

Bryce is light in my arms.

There's so much I want her to tell me. How did she know the torton was here? It's almost like she could sense it. But how? Or maybe it's not the beasts she senses. She did mention there were people in the torton . . .

While I'm holding her, the *Titus* falls. It's a thrashing flame that sinks with the storm. The ship hits the acid clouds with a splash, and for a moment a blaze glows inside the black clouds. Then, nothing. Gone.

Roderick clenches his eyes shut. We all stare at the black clouds—the barrier that separates us from the Below.

Suddenly, Pound breaks the silence. His deep voice sings "The Song of Falling." It's a tender ballad for those who have suffered the greatest fall. The notes a reminder that no matter how powerful we think we are, in the end we are all equal in death's embrace. The song spreads to the rest of my crew. And soon, to the *Securis*. It latches into my heart and pulls out pieces of me.

My voice cracks as I follow Pound's lead.

No one speaks after the last chord, and perhaps it's because we all know this won't be the final time we sing for those we've lost.

CHAPTER 04

I LOWER BRYCE ONTO HER BED AND SIT BESIDE HER. SHE'S sleeping soundly—first time in days. I grip her hand, hoping the girl I know will return when she wakes.

If another torton attacks while she's out . . .

Her round window provides a glimpse of hard rock. After the battle, we slipped into the crevices of an island for the night. It's less exposed.

I squeeze her hand a little tighter, and I'm not sure if this is to comfort her or myself.

"My squadron has fallen apart."

Three ships gone. Drake gone. And other honorable men and women—experienced Hunters specifically chosen by Uncle—all gone. Just a week ago, my squadron was cutting through the sky. We worked with unmatched efficiency, taking down sky serpents. We even took turns towing gorgantaun carcasses back to Hunter outposts so the other ships could continue hunting. The supply lines were clear. We were earning coin.

A lot of it.

The squadron was happy.

Now?

My head sinks. Earlier tonight I told Ella that the strong lead because they're meant to lead. But how can I claim that I'm strong when I'm leading ships to their demise?

I exhale and glance around Bryce's simple room. Once, she shared a room with Keeton, but Keeton decided to bunk with Roderick. Now it's all hers. A clay sculpture rests on Bryce's desk. Before she started acting so strangely, she'd spend her off time carving a face into the clay. The sculpture's a face of some teenage boy with short pointy hair and hard eyes. I can't help but feel a twinge of jealousy whenever I see it. I've noticed the way she gazes at it. It's someone she loves.

But Bryce seems at ease when she's working with clay. Once, she told me she didn't want to be a Hunter. She wished she'd been Selected by Art. So I wasn't surprised when, after we split the coins from our first kills, she bought art supplies: oil paints, clay, stencils, and even an easel that Roderick bolted to her floor.

I breathe out.

All my energy and coins go toward paying off the *Gladian*. In the last three months, I've paid nearly a third of it. Even though I'm the Prince, this isn't technically my ship. It belongs to my Trade. I'm only permitted a year free of mutiny. So if I fail to pay it off nine months from now, and my crew decides I'm a terrible Captain, I could lose my position.

My eyes shut. After tonight, who could blame them for demoting me? Maybe I'd become the Swabbie again. If that happens, Uncle will disown me. Still, it's not likely my crew would mutiny; many are my friends, but Meritocracy is treacherous and turns even the best person cruel.

I pull Bryce's blanket up to her chin and touch her shoulder.

Soon, I'm walking the corridor. Should head to my cabin, go

straight to sleep, but Ella's probably waiting to demand I explain everything about the torton fight.

Besides, I still need to speak with someone else. Someone I hate. So my boots clang on the stairs as I descend into the lowest level of the *Gladian*. At the base, I follow a path of soft crystal lights. Food crates and spare water tanks form walls around me. This is the supply room, the ship's largest room. Right now, the crates are mostly empty because we need to resupply.

I despise this place. It's cold, quiet, and still reeks from the treacherous person we kept locked in the brig nearby.

Sebastian.

His plaque-covered grin still haunts me, and the last words he spoke to me almost echo off the walls. *Someday, our paths will cross again, and I'll be the one to ruin you. It will be the joy of my life.*

I stop outside the bars of the brig and glance at the torn mattress where he hid his knives. Glance at the toilet he clogged with fabric. This is the one part of my ship Ella rarely visits. Perhaps she's afraid of it. Or perhaps it's because there aren't usually people to spy on. It's the one place I can be assured she won't eavesdrop on a conversation.

I peer back at the stairs to be sure there's no lurking shadow, then lean against a wall of empty crates and sink to the cold ground. My fingers play with a small crystal, a special comm gem Uncle gave me. Anytime I get information that could be helpful for the war, I'm supposed to contact him immediately.

My legs tuck close, and I sit in the cold darkness. Suddenly, Drake's shocked face burns in my head. Drake of Norman was young. One of the best fliers I've met. Now he's gone. Just like that. Another victim of the war.

My head taps against the wall.

When I was a Low and my gut begged for anything, even moldy bread, I yearned for everything I now have. Power. Responsibility. Respect.

But now?

My crew looks at me like I have the answers. Like I know what I'm doing. But I didn't know a thing about the torton. And Bryce . . . Dammit, Bryce, why didn't you tell me earlier?

My eyes grow warm.

Mother's tender voice slips into my mind. *Never lock your feelings away, Conrad. They'll make you noxious, and one day they'll all explode from you and end up harming the ones you care for most.*

Her words, once a warm hug, leave me cold and empty. This is Meritocracy. Can't reveal I'm weak. Still, I pause.

Maybe I'm not cut out to lead.

I imagine sharing that thought with Ella. She'd never take me seriously again. And Father? He would break the doubts out of me. Like the time he circled me in the Urwin Square, holding out his dueling cane.

"Look at you, a pitiful sobbing mess," he spat. "You must show no weakness, Conrad! Get up. Face me. Show me the Urwin inside you."

Father had forced me to duel him ever since I was three. For a few years, the duels were playful things. But once I had become adept enough at holding a practice cane, once my balance was nimble enough to pivot and dance in the arena circle, he'd let loose.

And he'd leave me bloodied on the ground.

"There you are."

A person appears on the stairs. I quickly turn away, wipe my cheeks, and straighten my back. The figure pauses for a moment, watching me, then her expression softens. She strides toward me, her silver Hunter uniform shining against the meager light. The white badge of Mechanic glimmers on her black jacket.

"You always disappear and isolate yourself when you're upset," she says softly. "Usually, it's the deck. But the *Securis* might watch you through their spyglasses. Am I right?"

"Not now, Keeton. I need to contact the King."

Keeton stops beside me. Black locs fall over her shoulders. Her silver sleeves are rolled up, exposing her dark brown forearms. She folds her arms in that stubborn way of hers. "You never contact him."

"He needs to know about the torton."

Keeton rests a hand on her hip. "Okay. So tell him. I'll wait."

I say nothing.

"Why are you hesitating?" she asks.

My mouth remains shut.

She exhales and slides down beside me. Not a lot of people can talk to me this way, but we have a friendship that goes deep. When we first boarded this ship together for Hunter's Gauntlet, both desiring to become Captain, we were competitors. But I saved her life. And when the Below attacked, she returned the favor.

It's because of our friendship that she agreed to stay on as Mechanic when Bryce got Quartermaster again. Well, with them getting equal pay, of course. That's how all my crewmembers are paid—all taking a cut of my pay so we make the same amount.

Maybe it goes against Meritocracy, but I don't give a damn. They're important to me, and I don't want to lose any of them to other ships.

Keeton's shoulder is warm against mine. She glances at me. I hate knowing she's reading past my stoic, stiff posture. That her eyes are scanning me and pulling out my weaknesses and leaving them bare on the floor.

She bites her lip, like there's a thought on them. Then, slowly, her hand reaches forward and curls around mine.

"You'd rather be alone."

"Yes."

She chuckles.

"What?"

"You're so blunt. You'll be the grouchiest old man ever."

"If I live that long."

She punches my shoulder. "We're all going to grow old. Bryce, Roderick. Even that birdshit, Pound. All of us. Our little children will spend their days dueling one another, bleeding and crying in the hot arena sand."

"What a dream."

She laughs. "Really, Conrad." She squeezes my hand again. "We'll make it."

My mouth shuts, and I try to not calculate the odds.

"I think this is the curse of being Prince," Keeton says, sighing. "Meritocracy tells us that we should rise and gain power, but once we do—we don't find joy at the end."

"No, we find responsibility."

Silence falls. She doesn't have to remind me that we live in the Meritocracy. What I did months ago to win the Gauntlet doesn't bring the dead back to life tonight. She has every reason to question my leadership. Still, she squeezes my hand again. Affirming our friendship runs deeper than the system.

"I packed up Drake's rock collection," she says. "I know you wanted to do it, but you need to learn to share the load. You can't do everything by yourself."

"I killed a class-five gorgantaun by myself."

"You got lucky."

We look at each other. She's got a playful twinkle in her eye. And somehow, we laugh. It cuts the tension in my shoulders.

My voice softens. "How did Bryce know the torton was out there?"

"Conrad, she might be the most important person on this ship—in all the Skylands. As far as we know, she's the only defector from the Below."

"So, what am I supposed to tell my uncle tonight? If the *Securis* discovers who she truly is . . ." I pause. "She'll be killed. Simply for being her."

"You want my advice? Don't tell your uncle a single thing about her. I don't trust him."

"But the Skylands are desperate for information, Keeton. The Trades are all in disarray. Not even Scholar knows what will happen next. The gorgantaun pods are more organized—and there are constant rumors of attacks in far-off regions. Ships and crews disappearing. The skies themselves acting strangely. Uncle even hinted to me that someone made it through Sky's Edge."

She scoffs. "The cloudwall in the East? Impossible."

"Just what I heard."

She frowns, then stands. "Until we know more, don't say a thing about Bryce. She'll tell us when she's ready." She notices my skepticism. "Conrad, Bryce turned on her own people—there's no going back from that, and we're her friends." She pats my shoulder. "Good luck."

Once her steps vanish up the stairs, I twirl Uncle's crystal between my fingers again. There's not a man alive I despise more than him. That bastard took everything away from me. Murdered my father and made it seem a suicide. Threw Mother and me out into winter's chill and kept Ella as his own.

Uncle only made me his heir because I proved myself "worthy." Only let me reunite with my sister because of that.

Suddenly, the crystal illuminates on its own. An incoming caller. My eyes shut.

The comm continues flashing. I hesitate until I remember when the capital island, Ironside, fell from the sky. When the Below attacked and the five-thousand-foot gigataun came through a gap in the acid clouds beneath us. And nothing, not an entire Hunter fleet, not Order carriers, not a dozen battlecruisers, nor thousands of sparrows could stop the beast from digging into Ironside and eating the island's heart.

I can't afford to not speak to him. So I tap the gem.

"Yes?"

His voice is sharp and angry. "Why didn't you contact me immediately?"

"Hello, Uncle."

He goes quiet. "You will address me as 'King.' And you have disobeyed a direct order from the Highest High. You, and you alone, were meant to contact me once we learned crucial information. This torton creature is *crucial* information."

"I was carrying an unconscious crewmate to their room."

"That's what the Swabbie is for, *Nephew.*" He pauses. "You're not using your tools properly. The Captain of the *Securis* contacted me after the attack because he knew you wouldn't do it. Not quickly enough, anyway."

My skin flushes hot. Joo Won and the *Securis* undermined my authority? My hold over the final remnants of the squadron is evaporating.

Uncle's next words carve into my deepest insecurities. "This hunting tour of yours is over."

My eyes dart around the darkness, like they'll find a good response. "This is my ship, and I'll be damned if I don't pay it off—"

"Stop," Uncle growls. "You're losing valuable ships. Crewmembers can be replaced. Skyships cannot. Furthermore, you have Ella with you."

"But—"

"You have been a disappointment, Conrad. If you don't improve, I'll cut my tether to you. Then you can enjoy worrying about paying off your little ship all alone and hoping your crew doesn't betray you in a mutiny. I'm coming in three days to collect Ella."

My whole body freezes. "What?"

"Your sister's not safe with you. You have failed. The Princess is better off with me on the *Dreadnought.*"

Gooseflesh prickles my skin. My breaths are shallow. I sought Ella for six years, and now he's going to take her away from me? He'll undo any progress I've made with her in the last three months. He will inject even more of his vicious poison into her.

"Once we meet, I'm giving you a mission," he says. "It will be your last chance to prove yourself worthy of your title."

"I already proved myself to you, *Uncle*."

"You think your position is permanent? Power fluctuates all the time, Conrad. New Dukes and Duchesses almost every month. The war hasn't stopped Meritocracy or the duels."

My teeth gnash. "What mission?"

"We can't discuss it over the comm. It's too sensitive."

"I could just fly away."

Uncle laughs. "Don't think I don't know you, Conrad."

Suddenly, there's shouting over my comm. Pound's yelling about approaching ships. I stand. And before I can formulate a plan, something thuds against the ship. Maybe the clang of hooks attaching themselves to the *Gladian*.

"Captain!" Pound cries. "We're being boarded."

My brow furrows and I race up the stairs.

"You were a rodent for six years," Uncle continues as I run. "Always trying to squeeze out of trouble. Just living off what you could. I'm not stupid. You'd flee with the only other heir I have left. You'd destroy the legacy of Urwin simply because of your selfishness. But I'm taking a more hands-on approach in molding you. You will either become the proper heir and bow to my authority, or . . . Well, you know what I do with people who no longer serve a purpose."

Then the comm goes gray.

My heart's throbbing. Once I reach the top level, I climb up the ladder and push through the hatch.

Multiple hooks hang from our railings—tethering us to an enormous white Order carrier that has pulled behind us, near the cavern's entrance. My mouth is dry. It's the flagship of Order. The *Triumph* is filled with hundreds of one-manned fighters, called sparrows, and a deck covered with soldiers and cannons.

A gangway connects the *Triumph* to my deck, and a tall, thin woman with an upright posture stands above me at the hatch. Several Order cruisers hover in the sky behind her.

She nods. "Your Majesty."

I climb to my feet.

My crew stares at the Order people aboard our ship. Pound looks ready to punch someone. Keeton and Roderick stand together, whispering. Arika's scowling at the tall woman standing before me.

"I am Addeline of Lewcrose," the woman says. "The Master of Order, the Highest Admiral of the Skylands. King Urwin has sent me here to escort you back to Venator personally."

My veins go cold. Uncle sent Order's leader to collect me.

And to take Ella away.

CHAPTER 05

"LOOK, CONRAD," ELLA SAYS, STABBING A FINGER IN MY FACE, "I'm not interested in your life lessons. You're only four years older than I am, and you act like you're some wise old Scholar."

She paces the command room, stamping over papers—Pound's hunting plans which she threw to the floor earlier.

"The strong rise," she says.

"You don't care that we'll be separated again?"

"We haven't earned the right to be together."

I lean on the table toward her. "Listen to what you said. Repeat it. *Aloud*."

She folds her arms.

Oh, she's difficult. She's Her Royal Stubborness of Urwin. Always must have her way. Always so focused on her goals that nothing else matters.

I take a breath. "Let me tell you more about your mother."

"She abandoned me," she says. "Why would I care about her?"

"Abandoned you? Ella, Uncle *exiled* her. He murdered your father and left Mother and me to die in the Lows! And you can't claim you don't care, not when her cane hangs from your hip!"

"This is temporary. I care nothing for it," she says, shrugging. But I know that's a lie. I've seen her polishing it, making the cane's black stag shine. "Uncle promised me my own cane if I survived the prowlons. Well, I did. But I haven't been back to him because I've been stuck with *you*."

The room goes quiet. She stares at me, perhaps waiting for me to erupt. But I'm blinking, suffering through the knife of her words. Slowly, I lower into the soft chair. I can't keep battling her. Can't be giving 180 percent toward this relationship, especially when she only gives five back.

"When we get to Venator," I say softly, "and when Uncle comes, we may not see each other again. I want you to know, Ella, that despite our differences, I still love you. And that I'm sorry I wasn't there earlier for you. I failed you."

Her voice lowers. "Conrad, you usurped me."

"Usurped?" I meet her gaze. "Do you think I wanted to be the Prince? This ship—I *earned* it because I wanted you in my life. And now this ship is my home. My crewmembers are my friends, my family. I care about them. I never wanted Prince, but if power is what I need to protect my family, then that's what I seek."

She stares at me.

"Ella, you didn't just lose a father when Uncle took over. You lost Mother. You lost your grandparents. Your brother. You lost everything. I was in rags, but you—you lost the things that made you who you *are*."

"And you want to help me get them back?"

"I can't get them back for you if you don't want them back."

She goes quiet. Her fingers trail the cracks that graze the surface of Mother's cane. Perhaps trying to read them and hear Mother's story. She bites her lip, and I'm hoping she'll finally open up. But then she holds her head up and starts for the door.

And like a true Urwin, doesn't even look back.

As her steps retreat down the corridor, I sink deeper into melancholy. I worked for years to get her back into my life. Now I'm wondering if I wasted all that time and energy on a lost cause. Uncle's venom has gone too deep. And not even her own brother can pull it out.

✦✦✦

"She's still sleeping, *Elise*."

Pound's leaning against the wall outside Bryce's room, his stupid eyes watching me approach. *Elise*. He sometimes calls me by my mother's name. He used to think it was an insult. Now I think he uses it in an endearing way. I have my own name for him.

"Good morning, *Asswood*."

He wipes his nose with his huge forearm. "Go away. This is Bryce's first sleep in days."

"You're standing guard?"

"Keeton put me up to it. We both knew you'd try to wake her at some point. So I'm standing guard because of you."

"Since when did you become so altruistic?" I pause. "Wait." I grin a little. "You care about Bryce. She's your *friend*."

"So?"

"So I thought Atwoods don't care about anyone but themselves."

"Eat my phlegm, Elise." His thick brow furrows, wrinkling his bald head. "We need her. She's the only one who knows about the Below."

"Comm me when she wakes?"

"She eats first."

"Never expected you to be someone's nanny, Pound."

He roars and his cucumber fingers try to snatch me, but I duck and slide back. We stare at each other, our fists tightening for an instant. Then I shake my head and we chuckle like idiots.

Dumb bastard.

Later in the afternoon, as the *Gladian* is towed through blue skies toward Venator, Keeton excitedly pitches me her idea to make the ship even faster. We stand in the white engine room. Control panels, nozzles, and pipes surround us. A tall tube of reinforced glass, braced against the wall, houses our engine crystal. The skull-sized crystal pulses with life, giving the ship energy.

"If my estimates are correct," Keeton says, "we can get the *Gladian* flying at three hundred percent of her normal capabilities."

I stare at her, dumbfounded. And in the next instant, I'm lost as Keeton fills my head with a series of carefully concocted calculations. I understand the basics of crystallic engineering, but Keeton's expertise far exceeds my own.

Finally, I raise an exhausted hand.

"All right," I say. "I trust you."

"I can try it?"

"Of course. But you do realize we'll be grounded on Venator in a matter of minutes, right? We won't even have access to the ship."

She nods. "I'll get started right away. Shouldn't take me long. I—" She pauses. "Well, I already got started on this."

She watches me, perhaps expecting me to be angry for her not following procedure. But autonomy doesn't bother me. My crew needs to be able to make decisions without me breathing over them.

"Hope it works, Keeton."

She beams and immediately turns to focus on the engine.

Once I'm back in the corridor, I turn the corner, and a figure stands outside the laundry room. I stop. Her hair's spikey like yellow grass, and her face is set with concentration as she jots onto her notepad. Inventory. One of the many duties of the Quartermaster. She closes the laundry room door and turns toward the stairs.

"Bryce."

She goes rigid.

"Captain," she says quickly, turning from me and walking away. "Sorry, I'm a little busy. Behind on my work."

I hurry to her. "Wait . . ."

"I need to know what we're low on when we make port on Venator," she says, starting up the stairs. "We need to restock."

"Bryce."

She stops. Her eyes meet mine, sinking me into blue water. A little stitch tightens in my chest. My first instinct is to demand everything she knows and be furious that she didn't contact me once she woke. But that's not the way Mother taught me.

"H-how are you?"

Her eyes narrow. "That isn't what I expected you to ask."

"Well, it'd be rude to ask anything else first."

"Ah. So merely a platitude." She grins, posture relaxing a bit. "Since when have you cared about being rude?"

"I'm never rude."

We smile, but it's short-lived because reality closes in on us. Bryce knows something. And she knows I'm desperate to learn about it.

"Bryce, I'm sorry I didn't listen to you, but I feel like you're not telling me everything." I breathe. "And I thought you were going to contact me when you woke so we could talk."

"Am I supposed to tell you every time I do something?"

That cuts me. My voice quiets. "I'm worried about you."

Her boots shuffle, and she scratches the back of her neck.

"Bryce, how did you know the torton was out there?"

"I had a hunch, okay? That's all. Call it instinct. I know my people. All right?"

"I thought you were on our side."

"I'm not on anybody's side."

I stop.

"That's not what I mean," she says, exhaling and wiping her face. "I'm just—look, you just have to trust me."

"Bryce, I can't just—"

She touches my arm. "Please."

I sigh, recognize the warmth of her touch and the sincerity in her expression. She smiles gently. Oh, I wish I could trust whatever she tells me. It'd be easier that way. But I haven't forgotten the last time I caught her in a lie. She jabbed me with a needle, and I was paralyzed for an hour while she escaped.

After that, the gigataun came.

"Bryce, we need to know."

"Conrad, drop it."

"But—"

Her eyes go fierce. She looks ready to spit something, but a voice comes over our comm gems.

"Attention, Your Majesty and his fine crew," Addeline of Lewcrose says. "We have arrived at Venator. Please collect your things. You will be disembarking once we reach the dock."

I close my eyes.

Then, before I can say another word to Bryce, my mouth shuts as I realize I'm standing at the base of the stairs, alone.

CHAPTER 06

MOST OF MY CREW'S STANDING ON THE DECK UNDER THE early evening light. We're breathing Venator's humid air as we approach the massive, green island in the distance. The home of Hunter.

Bryce stands at the stern, talking quietly with Keeton. I consider approaching them, but cornering Bryce never leads to anything productive. Besides, I have other concerns.

I search for Ella. Haven't seen her since our fight. She didn't even return to the cabin to sleep. I worried that she'd left the ship and boarded one of Order's vessels. But she reappeared on the *Gladian* for a few minutes this morning when the crew and I discussed a plan to escape Venator.

Pound and Roderick guffaw about something stupid near the starboard, and Rod laughs when Pound finishes the punch line. Later Arika of Gupta arrives with Declan. Their luggage is already packed.

She smiles at me.

Arika's long, black hair frames a big grin against her tan face. She's the Cook, a rank just above the Swabbie, but she mentioned when I interviewed her at the Hunter draft that cooking is her passion, even if it's not the most respected thing in our Trade.

Ella finally arrives. She stands near the hatch, considering everyone, her eyes narrowed with suspicion. I've seen the expression before. It's the look all Urwins make when they're studying an opponent. We Urwins have been taught, since we were little, to distrust others because people expect things from us.

I step toward her.

Together we lean against the port's railing as the first stars dot the sky. My mouth opens, then shuts.

"You didn't return to the cabin last night," I say.

"I was busy."

We go quiet.

"I love Venator," she whispers.

I follow her admiring gaze to the approaching island and try looking at it the same way she does. The island shines under the late afternoon light. In another context, maybe it'd be easy. I learned to become a Hunter on Venator. Perhaps Ella sees opportunity here, or the happy place where she'll reunite with Uncle.

But as I notice all the Hunter skyships patrolling the island's perimeter, and the anti-G batteries stationed on the mountainsides, and the walls that surround the Hunter Academy, I don't see opportunity.

I see prison.

Two Order cruisers drag my ship like it's their latest kill. Addeline's carrier, the *Triumph,* looms behind us.

Ella identifies the classes of all the nearby Hunter vessels. There are Titanium-class ships, Predator-class, even some from the defunct Orion-class. She only struggles with the ancient wooden ones, flown by masts. But most of the ships, like mine, are built from molded gorgantaun steel and run by clean crystal energy.

"Ella, I'm sorry."

She stiffens at my apology. "Why?"

"I couldn't get through to you."

She squeezes the railing. "You trying that reverse thinking Scholar birdshit?"

"This is genuine. Wherever the wind takes you, Ella, I hope it brings us together again. Good luck to you."

Then, I turn and walk away.

"Conrad?" she says.

But I don't respond. When we were separated, she could've slipped out of Urwin Manor anytime. Could've had a High carriage bring her to the Lows. Could've done anything to reunite with me, to help Mother. We could've escaped together, the three of us. Gone off to another island.

But she never came.

If she wants me to be part of her life, she'll have to show me. I have other important people, too. I've got a war to fight. Perhaps I'm failing Mother by leaving things like this with Ella. But I can't continue bickering with my stubborn sister as the world falls apart.

I lean against the stern, not far from Bryce, Arika, and Keeton. Then I focus on the island ahead. Venator greets us with its familiar junglescape striped with white waterfalls.

Suddenly, Addeline of Lewcrose speaks to me over the comm. "Your ship will be held at the Academy docks. You will not be permitted to board until the King approves."

My jaw clenches, and I breathe in to relax my anger.

The High Admiral stands on the *Triumph* nearby, stoic. Addeline is Order's new Master—accepted the role after the last High Admiral turned out to be an infiltrator. I don't know much about her. She's had minor victories since the war began. A skirmish here and there. From what I've heard, she's incredibly honorable, and many respect her. But maybe the tales of her honor are wrong because when she glances my way, she gives me a smug grin.

I don't bother responding to her.

The *Securis* breaks off and leaves to dock at the Venator's shipping docks. Its departure is the final stinging reminder of my hunting expedition's failure. My guess is I'll not see that ship or their crew again. But I'd already lost their respect. Unfortunately for the *Securis*, Uncle will likely blame their Captain for my failures to keep the Urwin name clean.

Uncle's a bastard.

We soar over the shipping docks and fly above splashing rivers to the Hunter Academy. Soon, dockworkers catch our chains and hook us to a massive ring. Once our gangway drops, Ella strides off with her luggage. A little tremor in my chest worries I made a mistake. But as she's descending the gangway, for the faintest moment, she looks back.

That's the thing about Urwins. We're taught to always look ahead.

A group of Order guards surrounds her, walks her through the crowded dock, and marches her toward the grand Academy doors. She disappears—as quick as the moment when she vanished from my life years ago.

My crew gathers around me, their luggage in hand.

"Everything okay?" Keeton asks.

"Never better," I say.

"Typical Urwin birdshit," Pound rumbles. "Always drama."

"We're more complicated than the Atwoods."

"You've got that right," Pound says. "You all talk too much. In my family, we resolve our problems with our fists."

I stare at him. "Not sure you can punch your way back into your family's good graces, Pound."

"We'll see."

Soon we're treading down the gangway toward the wooden docks. When my boots hit the planks, I almost smile. Solid ground feels strangely still without the engine's hums beneath my feet.

The Hunter Academy splays out before us. Vines drape a series of pastoral-looking buildings carved from stone. The buildings spread on and on, covering the cliffs and mountainside. But I'm not focused on the buildings, nor the dozens of grizzled veterans rushing down the dock. I'm not even focused on the sky serpent alarm that suddenly blares, telling us that gorgantauns have been spotted nearby.

My attention is on the person standing in the center of the dock among a group of Order guards—her gray hair flittering in the wind. She's the person who Selected me to Hunter. The person who pushed me to become better and once considered making me her protégé.

She's one of the most powerful and influential people in all the Skylands: The Master of Hunter. Koko of Ito.

✦✦✦

Master Koko motions me to walk beside her as we sweep through the Academy doors.

"Send your crew for rec time," Koko tells me. "Tell them to go to the pubs, the baths, or get an early dinner at the restaurants. We need to talk. Alone."

I pause. Not even the Master of an entire Trade can order the Prince around. But without her, I'd never have been Selected to Hunter, never have risen to Captain, nor proved to Uncle I was worthy of being an Urwin again. I'd have been another lonely victim of Meritocracy. Incapable of working with others or trusting anyone.

So I give the order to my crew.

Pound and Roderick laugh and hurry away. Declan goes in another direction, perhaps off to visit friends. Meanwhile, Keeton, Bryce, and Arika glance at me before reluctantly going after Pound and Roderick.

My eyes follow Bryce. She's the one I shouldn't leave alone. Fortunately, she stays tight to the others. And there's no reason for anyone on Venator to know her origins anyway.

Master Koko gives Bryce a quick glance, before focusing on me. "This way."

She moves ahead, making me follow. A trio of Order guards trails us at a distance. When anyone could be an infiltrator from the Below, precautions are necessary.

"Your hunting expedition was a disaster," Koko says. Her gray-and-white hair sways by her shoulders as we start down the packed, stone corridor. "At first I was impressed. You were killing beasts. But this last week? Three ships. Gone. Just like that."

Young trainees cram the space, all staring at Master Koko in awe. They hurry out of her way. She doesn't care about their expressions, nor does she care that her boots are dropping dried mud onto the stone floor. They're so awed by her they don't even realize I'm beside her.

"And don't spit any excuses to me," she says.

"It was my responsibility."

She stops. The guards do, too. Then she peers me up and down. "Careful, Conrad."

My mouth shuts as I meet her gaze. Her eyes do all the talking. Telling me that maybe she appreciates my honesty, my admission of my failures. But I should not admit to them in public. Maybe *she* can be critical of me, but *I* shouldn't be critical of myself.

We pass a couple of guards and push through a door, leaving the crowds behind us. She leads me up a dark, winding staircase—up into an area I've never been. Master Koko, despite her advanced age, isn't even panting as she continues her criticism.

"You are the Prince now, Conrad. I don't have authority over you. I am unable to punish you. But if you were under my authority, I'd take the *Gladian* from you."

"Master . . ."

She turns to face me. Her eyes cold, serious. "We need *people*, Conrad. And you've lost many."

Heat flushes my cheeks.

"Your family is the talk of the islands again," she says. "But for all the *wrong* reasons. The Skylands have had no victories over the Below. Just a rising death toll. They are bleeding us, and we don't even know where the next attack will come from." She watches me. "Nothing to say in your defense?"

"I'm not going to make excuses, Master. And I'm well aware of the issues facing the islands."

"Oh good. You're *aware*. Now the war will turn in our favor."

We pass another pair of guards and step out onto a quiet, mostly vacant floor that overlooks the Academy grounds. The wide windows provide glimpses of a river cutting through the jungled hills, and a flock of multicolored birds soaring nearby.

This is the floor of the Master and the Master Trainers. It's an enormous privilege being here.

A woman stands ahead of us—looking vaguely familiar. She holds a clipboard.

"Ah, my assistant," Master Koko says. "Conrad, this is Teresa of Abel."

Teresa's black hair is tied back into a bun. She stands erect in her Hunter uniform and nods stiffly at me.

"You'll remember that she's the aunt of your former crewmember, Sebastian."

I swallow my disgust.

"Yes," Teresa says, eyeing me. "Sorry about my nephew trying to kill you." She speaks bluntly, without a hint of remorse. "The Gauntlet causes a lot of . . . stress."

"Teresa," Master Koko says, taking the clipboard from her and signing a few papers, "when are the new Selections arriving?"

"New?" I ask.

"You haven't heard?" Master Koko says without looking up. "We're Selecting four times this year. Maybe five. We need more people to replace the losses. Didn't you notice how young some of our trainees are?"

My mouth shuts.

"The next set will be arriving tomorrow morning," Teresa says.

"Good," Master Koko says, returning the clipboard to her. "Carry on, Teresa."

Koko leads me to a door at the end of the hall—the one emblazoned with beautiful woodwork depicting a raging gorgantaun locked in battle with a skyship.

"Your room," she says.

"Let me guess," I say. "The King's keeping me locked in here."

"Locked? No. But you are grounded on Venator until he arrives."

"What about my crew?"

"They have their own rooms. They're grounded, too," she says. "I stand by what I warned you about after the Gauntlet: crewing your ship with friends, rather than the best people, is likely why your hunt went so poorly."

My voice becomes stern. "They *are* the best people."

She smiles a little and pats my cheek. "There's that fire in you again."

Koko stuffs a key into the lock and shoves the door open to reveal an expansive room inside. It's ten times as large as my cabin on the *Gladian*. She strides forward and lowers onto the couch near the window. The room's connected balcony peers over Venator's rushing waterfalls and jungle cliffs. Hunters are not known for glamorous accommodations, but apparently, when they're hosting the heir, that changes.

A small chillglobe throbs in the center of the room. The white orb sends chilly pulses that break the tropical air. A posh bed, overflowing with pillows, calls out my name. But I feel too sour to rest.

"Your sister changed you," Koko says. "When I first met you, you had an insatiable desire to rise. But you've grown too comfortable."

"I am *not* comfortable, Master."

She continues. "You wouldn't let anything stop you. You were the wild boy who ran the length of a gorgantaun. Ripped the beast's eye from its own socket. Even let his own ship get swallowed by a class-eight so he could fly out through its heart. Now, look at you, dragged back like a lost puppy. What a fall."

I scowl.

"You have rings of exhaustion around your eyes, Conrad. You're thin—are you eating? I'm guessing you were focused on your sister instead of your last hunt. Tell me I'm wrong."

She sits with a self-satisfied look on her face. And that, more than anything, irritates me because I can't argue with a single thing she's said.

Master Koko's hard as stone. But as she watches me, perhaps she notices the anguish on my face, because her voice softens.

"Sit, Conrad."

When I lower onto the couch, it's like the weight and burden of everything I've been carrying presses me into the cushions. I'm so tired. Always chasing something. Never getting a moment to rest.

"Master, those ships were my responsibility." I pause. "Drake of Norman died . . ." I reach into my jacket and pull out an envelope with the seal of Urwin. "A note to his family. I thought he'd fly my ship for years."

She frowns as I lower the envelope into her hands. "Conrad, many Hunters don't last for long. When you first came to this Academy, you flew solo. Distrusted everyone. Now you're making attachments to your crewmembers in mere weeks. How well could you have known Drake?"

My fists squeeze. "Just because I didn't know him well doesn't mean I'm content with his death."

"Conrad, you won't be able to lead if you look back. You must look forward. People die in Hunter. This is partly why I suggested you get a crew that didn't include your friends. It's easier saying goodbye to strangers."

My cheeks burn. "My friends are *not* going anywhere, Master

Koko. I'm tired of this suggestion. Don't mention it again. My crew is safe with me."

"Like Drake?"

I stand. I'm about ready to lose it. Maybe it's because she's needling into my insecurities and I'm afraid she's right. But I've spent so much of my life without anyone except for my mother. And when I finally find some people who care about me, people I care about, I'm told that they shouldn't be with me?

Critique me? Fine. Tell me I've been a miserable failure of a leader? Go for it. But to suggest that I push away the people I care most about?

That crosses the damned line.

"We are at war," I say through gritted teeth. "My crew and I were stalked by something never encountered by anyone. And we destroyed it. The Skylands now know how to take down a torton. They're all aware of the Below's method for spying on us."

She stares at me.

"What I care about are the people who have helped me rise. And I will NEVER abandon them. So I'll say this for the last time: *back off.* I'm willing to learn from you, but I'm not willing to give up my friends—my family—to do that."

Master Koko considers me a moment, then leans back. "Very well."

We go quiet. It's awkward until a school of pishon sails past the window. The peaceful, fishlike creatures are not much longer than a man's hand. Their metal-coated bodies dive toward the jungle to munch on leaves.

Suddenly, Koko stands and touches my shoulder. "I push you, Conrad, because in all my years as a Hunter, I've never met one with so much potential. I originally Selected you because of your family. A nudge by your uncle, and I was curious how an Urwin would do in Hunter. But, even with those expectations, I still think you're capable of more."

I don't respond.

She lowers beside me. "Conrad, tell me everything you know about the torton."

I exhale, turn to her, and explain what we learned.

She's quiet a moment. "So, flak will reveal them?"

"Yes, but the problem is, you won't know they're there unless you're constantly firing flak."

"And you believe Bryce can sense them?"

"Somehow, yes."

"She needs to tell us more."

"That's my next task."

"She's not being entirely forthright," Koko says. "Watch her."

"She already betrayed her people, Master. She won't return to their side."

"Can you say for sure? If the war continues its current trajectory—who knows?"

I stiffen. Could Bryce really betray us?

"Conrad, when she speaks, you tell me as soon as you're able. We need any information we can get." She pauses. And I sense a growing exhaustion in her. Master Koko was supposed to retire—I was someone she hoped to become her heir. But now, she's got a war to fight. "Every day Hunter's losing more ships. I've got three assistants, beyond Teresa, running Selections on all the major islands. We're training more than ever. But these young people we're bringing in . . . they're malnourished Lows. They're the weak ones who haven't had a full meal in months because the supply lines are constantly under attack. The problem is, the young people who are eating well? The Highs? They're not joining the Selection. Those lotchers are hiding in their manors. Or taking their enormous ships and evacuating to the farthest airs—as if they can escape. Worse, the gorgantauns are no longer attacking in their sporadic ways. They're . . ."

"Strategic."

She closes her eyes and nods. "The Below can control them. Somehow, those bastards can control them."

We gaze out into the blue sky. Several skyships fly toward the Academy docks in the distance. We need more ships. More than that, we need people. We don't have enough of either to fight off both a fleet of Goerner's stolen ships and the beasts the Below created.

"Conrad," Koko says, "I have a new Navigator for you."

"I'm not interviewing candidates?"

She frowns. "This came from the King."

"Ah. He's dropping a spy onto my ship."

"This person's an incredible flier, and you won't regret having them aboard." She pauses. "Conrad, I wish we'd have met again under better circumstances . . . that we could've expressed happier sentiments." She pauses. "But your family's in trouble."

I wipe my face. Of course it gets worse.

"Your uncle has been challenged to two duels in the last three months. He met each challenge personally."

"He's getting challenges?"

That bastard never tells me anything.

"Yes. Rumors have spread that King Ulrich challenged King Ferdinand to purposefully weaken the Skylands before the Below's attack."

"That's preposterous," I say, before realizing how irritated I am by having to defend my uncle.

"Despite the flimsy logic, it's still a damaging rumor," she says. "The Skylands are getting impatient. Even a dueler as seasoned as Ulrich of Urwin cannot meet every challenge. These aren't simple challenges, either. These are coming from Archdukes and Archduchesses. Some of the most powerful, well-trained people of the sky. Furthermore, I've heard a rumor that the strongest dueler in the Eastern Airs is considering a challenge."

I stop. "Sione of Niumatalolo? But he's a High. Not an Archduke."

"Sione's famous. If he makes a public challenge, how could your uncle decline? It'd make him seem weak. Sione's also a mercenary. Dueled in the place of many lotchers—all for a hefty price. He's defeated several Archdukes and Archduchesses simply because he disliked their leadership. He kills his target and gives the title to someone else. Sione loves dueling—not leading. He's dueled seventy-two times. Never lost."

I blink at this information—just considering the idea of dueling that many times and not losing once.

She pats my leg. "For now, you're safe. But know that even Venator has its dangers. I will, of course, do what I can to ensure your safety." She stands. "This room's yours until the King arrives. Whenever you leave your room, you will be followed by an armed Order escort."

I sigh and nod.

She pats my cheek. "Get some rest. You look terrible." She catches the door, then looks back. "By the way, an old friend of yours pleaded to see you. One of your former crewmembers."

My heart leaps a little. "Eldon of Bartemius?"

Master Koko smiles, then she's gone.

Eldon's back? We didn't always connect on a personal level, and we often found ourselves in disagreement, but the way he flies . . . The strings are his paintbrush, and the sky his canvas. He's a wonderful Navigator.

Suddenly, there is a knock at my door. I hurry to yank it open. The new Navigator. It must be. But as I peer out into the corridor, my face falls. It's not Eldon. It's someone I haven't seen since he tried to kill me.

And my fists shake as he smiles that yellow grin of his.

Sebastian of Abel.

CHAPTER 07

SEBASTIAN BOWS. "YOUR MAJESTY."

"*You*," I snarl. "You're my new Navigator?"

"Your Navigator?" He laughs, getting spittle on my face. "I'm a terrible flier. That'd be preposterous. What made you think that?"

I wipe my cheek with my sleeve, disgusted. "What are you doing here? I thought you were tried by the Hunter Tribunal."

Sebastian's my age and frail figured. Black hair, pale skin, and pink lips. He glances at the Order guards behind him. Their hands remain near their auto-muskets. It's shocking that Master Koko allowed him to come to my room without issue. Then again, she's never tried to protect me from challenges. And perhaps Sebastian having a close family member as Master Koko's lead assistant has its perks.

"The Tribunal?" Sebastian says with a dreary look. "A completely boring affair." He raises his hands and makes them talk to each other in a deep voice. "'Therefore, it is the ruling of this Tribunal that Sebastian shall be spared, in part due to the growing enemy threat, but also the belief that he shall serve a better purpose alive than dead.'" He lowers his hands. "The irony is that while war takes lives, it spared mine. Hunter is losing so many people they decided to keep me around. Unfortunately, I'm grounded on Venator. Like you." He scratches his neck. "So, I heard your hunting excursion was a miserable failure. How many people died because of you?"

"What do you want, Sebastian?"

"I'd like to come in."

"I'd rather rub pepper seeds on my eyeballs."

He laughs. "Dramatic as usual."

He pushes past me and strolls into my room. A guard outside makes a move, but I sigh and raise a hand to stop him. The guard squints, then relaxes against the wall.

I shut the door.

Sebastian's already on my bed, tossing grapes to himself. The bastard misses several times before finally catching one on his tongue. He laughs happily and bites down, letting the juices dribble over his chin and onto the pillow.

"What do you really want, Sebastian?"

"To see my friend."

I fold my arms. "Ah, yes. Great friends. Remember all the good times we shared, like when you broke Samantha's neck, or when you tried to turn the crew against me, or when you tried to murder me?"

"You talk too much," he says. "Open your mouth."

He tosses a grape. It hits my lip and falls to the ground.

"That would've gone in!" he exclaims. "You've always been such a miserable birdshit, haven't you?"

"You tried to use Bryce's secret to force her to kill me," I say. "I should throw you off the balcony."

He snorts. "I told everyone about Bryce being from the Below, by the way."

I stare at him.

"Well, not *everyone*. But it's pretty hilarious going up to random people who don't know me, don't know Bryce, and telling them she's an infiltrator. They don't know how to respond."

My hands ball into fists. "Are you trying to get her killed?"

His eyes twinkle. "That's kind of the idea. She's a traitor."

"She's on our side."

"Oh, Conrad. There's no *our* side. These are the Skylands. Only one gets to be Captain. Only one gets the crown. The rest of us? We get the scraps."

Don't want to listen to this snake any longer.

"I know all about the Below," he says. "I've been learning, Conrad. They're called 'Lantians.' Did you know? They live in colonies dug beneath the rocky surface. Some people are calling them 'dirt-eaters.'" He chuckles. "*Dirt-eaters*."

My brow wrinkles. Sebastian knows nothing. Then again, Bryce hasn't been exactly forthright about much, so how can I contradict him?

He plucks another grape from the bowl. "I'd never let any harm befall you. We are linked, you and I."

"I should call for Pound."

"Not the guards?"

"They wouldn't be as fun."

He hops off the bed. "Oh, that's right." He taps his chin. "You and Pound have that little romance going. You both betrayed your families by becoming allies and all. I've heard about the Atwoods. They rose to High without him, and they're aiming to challenge a Duchess." This makes him giggle. "Pound has no chance of being welcomed back into that enormous, shitty fold."

"Is there a reason you're here, Sebastian?"

"I want back into your crew."

"We don't need another Swabbie."

He laughs, but his eyes are cold. He slides off the bed and strolls to the window, his back facing me. His reflection on the glass stares at me with an evil, unhinged look. "Oh," he whispers almost to himself, "you who occupied the crystalline manor atop Holmstead Island. The boy born with a dueling cane in hand, and the strings to any skyship ever devised. How terrible your life has been. No one has ever seen greater pain."

I've had enough. "Get out."

He turns to me, grins, and wipes his greasy hair from his face. I advance on him, but he raises his hands to stop me.

"Okay, the real reason why I'm here," he says.

I keep moving toward him.

He speaks quickly. "I've come to give you a warning: your dear uncle's sending you on a *mission*. I'm afraid if you take this mission, you'll not come back."

I freeze. How the hell would he know about our mission? The King won't even discuss it with me over the comm.

"*If* you somehow make it back," he says, "many of your crew won't. It'll be a catastrophe."

"What mission?"

His green eyes study me through his bangs. "Do you remember my promise, Your *Majesty*? I promised I'd be the one to ruin you. Well, if you go on this mission, I may never get the chance."

I snarl and catch him by the back of his thin neck. He winces, and his boots kick around as I slide him toward the door. But he's laughing. The bastard's laughing.

My teeth grind.

Then I toss his small body into the hall. He hits the ground before the guards' boots. They stare at him, wide-eyed, and reach for their auto-muskets.

"This disgusting serpent's never allowed near my room again," I growl. "Understand?"

The guards nod quickly.

I slam the door as they start dragging him away. But even with the door between us, Sebastian's muffled voice reaches my ears.

"You will regret going, Conrad. You will regret it."

Then he laughs. And laughs.

CHAPTER 08

MY CREW GASPS AT THE RIDICULOUS SIZE OF EVERYTHING in my room. It's completely unlike typical Hunter accommodations. The *Gladian's* one of the most advanced ships in the fleet, and when we first boarded it, Hunter stocked it with rickety beds in the Low quarters on purpose. But this room?

Pound leaps onto the plush couch. It makes even him look small. Roderick plops onto the loveseat. Keeton stares at the beautiful vista through the window—the green jungle, the waterfalls. And in the far-off blue sky—outlying islands.

Exotic birds rest on the balcony, eating seeds from inside the stone mouth of a tiny gorgantaun.

"I'm ready to be the Prince," Roderick says, lifting a silver dome and exposing a stack of sweet bread drizzled in fresh cream. "So, they bring you food? Like, all the time?"

Arika takes a bite of the sweet bread and nearly goes cross-eyed. "Oh, this is wonderful. The Cooks here really are spectacular."

Pound ignores the plates and utensils and snatches a huge chunk of bread. He stuffs the whole thing into his mouth, spilling crumbs everywhere.

Arika watches him, frowning.

Declan of McDougal enters the room, too. He lowers onto a couch and watches us, as he usually does. Just an old man observing. Interjecting little bits of wisdom from time to time. Sometimes, I think he falls asleep with his eyes open. I've not been able to prove it, though.

We wait several minutes, hopeful for two more guests. But I can't wait much longer because in a couple of hours, I'm supposed to speak to the trainees. Master Koko's organizing a new Gauntlet—and the trainee crews aren't going to the Hornthrow Isles to hunt. This time they're going southeast to Greenrye Island. The home of the Trade of Agriculture. Apparently, gorgantauns have been encroaching upon several of the produce islands, the ones that provide much of the food for the Skylands.

"I still don't understand this plan," Declan says suddenly, scratching his graying beard. "We're grounded here. What does escaping Venator accomplish other than getting us in trouble with the King?"

"We're at war," Pound rumbles. "Venator might be full of infiltrators."

Declan scoffs. "Venator? Infiltrators? This is one of the most secure islands, Strategist. The Below would be foolish to attack here."

"We're simply discussing plans, Declan," I say. "Just in case."

The old man wrinkles his nose and nods.

"Is Bryce coming?" Keeton asks.

"I tried contacting her twice," I say. "No response."

"She's probably catching up on her sleep," Roderick says. But he doesn't look convinced.

Wisely, none of them mention my sister's absence.

We wait a few more minutes, then begin. I come up with a code word I hope Ella will understand and share it with the rest of the crew, a signal in case something goes south. Then, for the next hour, we discuss plans. Apparently, after we disembarked, my ship was moved back to the main shipping dock. So we decide that some of us will distract the guards near the *Gladian*. Meanwhile, another pair of us will steal a lifeboat and fly it to the *Gladian* while the guards are busy. They'll take the *Gladian* to Eastdock, the tourist side of the island, and the rest of us will meet them there.

It's not a perfect plan, but it could work.

After we finish the details, Keeton promises she'll speak with Bryce. Apparently, they were given adjoining rooms directly below mine. Then I say good night to them.

Once they leave, I zip up my Hunter jacket, tighten my boots, and exit into the hall. The Order guards follow me. Soon we're outside, walking under the late, humid sun and approaching a familiar place: the Learner Building.

Once inside, I find Madeline de Beaumont, the woman who trained me on being a Hunter, leaning against the hallway wall.

"Were you waiting for me?" I ask.

She frowns. "Not even a greeting?"

Madeline wears an assortment of medals on her black Hunter jacket. Her dark brown hair, turning gray, flows past her shoulders. She pushes off the wall, walks straight up to me and stares me in the eye, then hugs me.

"You're stronger," she says, squeezing my shoulders. "Even more hardened, too."

"Killing gorgantauns does that."

"It does." She frowns and steps back. "So does fighting new beasts. Like the torton I've heard about."

Madeline walks me through the halls. We pass Hunter flags bearing the harpoon insignia of our Trade. As we walk, small trainees, carrying flight manuals, gape at us.

"Master Trainer," I say, "are—"

"You don't call me that anymore. Madeline will suffice."

I nod. "Madeline, is Hunter really choosing trainees younger than sixteen?"

Madeline sighs and nods. "Dropped to thirteen. Too many lotchers in our society. We had to go younger to make up the gap. But even though these recruits are little, they are strong and determined."

Her assessment is infinitely more positive that Koko's.

We approach a mousy boy. He stares at me, his mouth falling open, and nudges a friend. Madeline and I sweep past the pair and enter the dining hall.

Suddenly, I'm brought back to all the times I spent in here. Sebastian, Eldon, and Samantha arguing about gorgantaun origins. Master Koko telling me I wasn't good enough. Bryce asking me to go on a walk with her. And even waiting to get drafted after losing in the Day of the Duels, and Pound choosing me as his Swabbie.

The whole room stands as I enter. I climb to the top of the platform to join all the Master Trainers and Master Koko. After some brief greetings, Master Koko steps to the platform's edge and leans over the balustrade.

She begins to introduce me.

I'm not exactly sure what Master Koko wants me to tell the trainees. But I have an idea, because she knows the fire that burns in me. And when I came here, I wasn't expected to win. Just like all these trainees now. They're not all expected to win, or even survive.

After she finishes the introduction, I walk to the edge of the platform. I stand, looking over the young faces below. Public speaking has never been my strong suit, but this is nothing compared to the horrors I've faced. As I study them, I decide to tell them the story of how I became Captain. The moment when I ran the length of the class-five and ripped out his eye with a mini clawgun and shoved a small explosive in his eye socket.

I tell them this because they need to know that despite the worsening odds, we can always win.

Always.

It's a message that maybe I need to hear, too.

✦✦✦

I stir awake. The moon peers through my window, and a gentle breeze chills me through the open balcony door . . .

Wait, that door was locked. I checked it just before I slipped under the covers.

My stomach tightens. Someone's inside my room.

My dueling cane's strapped to my luggage on the other side of the room. Stupid. Should've kept it closer to the bed.

I breathe out as if I'm still sound asleep. Then I peer through half-closed eyes. Fear lumps in my throat. A shadow's crouching in the darkness by the balcony door.

It watches me.

My skin goes cold. Scenarios play in my mind, each turning deadly. I clench my fists under the blanket. Readying for a fight. But the motionless figure does nothing. They're not actually watching me, just focused on the door to the hall. What the hell are they doing? Well, if the figure's not going to make a move, I will.

I hurl a pillow.

The figure tumbles back. Within a blink, I'm in the air. Leaping at them. Don't know what they have on them. Doesn't matter. I'll fight with all I have. I've got one life; it's mine to protect.

Our bodies collide, and we hit the ground. My fingers reach for their neck. I'll choke them out. But just as my hands coil over their neck, two quick jabs rattle my ribs.

I cough and fall back.

"You idiot," she snaps.

My ribs sting and sparks fly in my vision. "Bryce?" I wheeze. "What the hell? Why are you sneaking into—"

Her hand clamps over my mouth, and she raises a finger toward the door to the hall. "They're coming."

"Who?"

It's too dark to make out her face. She drags me toward the bed and crouches behind it. She peers over the pillows toward the hall door.

"Go back to sleep," she whispers. "Hurry."

"Go to sleep? Who's coming, Bryce?"

"Trust me, Conrad."

"That's the thing, Bryce," I whisper, "I'm not sure I can anymore."

She growls. "Conrad, get in bed and under the blankets or we're both dead."

My fingers twitch. I glance toward the hall door and suddenly, a shadow blocks the sliver of light beneath it.

"But the guards are outside," I whisper.

"They're dead."

I pause, considering my options. Then I hop into bed. "You better know what you're doing."

I pull the thin bedsheet over my face. It obscures my gaze. Seconds later, the hall door clicks open, and light invades my room. The door hinges squeak gently, and three indiscernible shadows stand in the doorway.

My mouth goes dry.

Can I trust Bryce? She's saved my life before . . . but she still hasn't been completely honest with me. She's hiding something. What if she—

The door gently shuts, enveloping the room in darkness.

My breath's hot beneath the sheet.

The trio of shadow assassins creeps toward my bed. Quiet as a pack of prowlons. Muscular frames. It takes all my willpower to not rip off the sheet and charge them. Beat them into the walls. But they probably have weapons.

What the hell is Bryce's plan? Getting me killed?

The shadows stop before my bed. Their obscured faces stare down at me. Maybe they have knives. And for several horrible seconds, I imagine a blade sliding into my gut. Imagine the cold steel burrowing deep and these shadows leaving me to bleed out. Death by a stomach wound is said to be one of the most painful ways to die.

Suddenly, Bryce leaps onto the closest man. In an instant, he's down. Shouting. She attacks his gut, knees his face. Knocks him out. The other two shout and back up.

But I'm up, too.

I hurl the bedsheet at the nearest assassin. He tumbles backward, wrapped up inside. Then, I leap at another man and smash him into the ground. All my rage lets loose in a series of vicious punches. I'm better with the cane, but I've brawled plenty in the Lows with desperate people who had nothing to lose.

He smacks my jaw. My vision spins. But I don't fall back. Won't fall back, because if I do, he'll free the knife from his belt. He'll gut me. So I go to absolute war on his face. Punch it until my knuckles feel warm liquid—his blood, or mine, I don't know. Don't care.

Finally, he goes still.

The other man rips the bedsheet free, but Bryce dives into him. Her fists, like furious viper bites, pulverize his ribs. Making him falter. Oh, she's fast. I watch in amazement as she works a man twice her size into the wall. Dodging his big arms. Ducking and juking. Finally, she punches him in the groin.

He leans forward, moaning. Then, she grapples his neck with both hands and slams his face into her knee.

He falls unconscious. For a flicker, she stands over him with a terrible expression. One that fills her face with pained wrinkles.

"I should kill him," she says, breathing hard. "All of them."

"They won't hurt anyone right now," I say, wiping my knuckles on the bedsheet.

"I'm not worried about that." She pauses. "You know what will happen to them, Conrad. They'll be tortured. Their arms will be lopped off, and they'll be thrown over the side of a ship."

A traitor's death. I reach for the scar on my shoulder, given to me by Admiral Goerner. He was the Master of Order. But turns out, Goerner was from the Below, and he was going to cut off my arms and toss me overboard after Bryce exposed him.

Fortunately, I got away with my arms intact.

"Bryce, are you a Lantian?"

She stares at me. "Where did you hear that word?"

"Are you?"

Bryce nibbles her lip. "Yes, I'm a Lantian."

I blink. Sebastian was telling the truth. That birdshit. But I can't worry about that now because more assassins are likely to come. Instead, I snatch my cane from the luggage and take my comm gem from the nightstand and slap it onto my wrist. "I should call for Order. Alert the island."

"No. The comms aren't trustworthy tonight. While you were planning with the crew, I was uncovering this plot."

My eye twitches. "How did you know about the plot?"

She turns toward the balcony. "Venator's heavily infiltrated. We never should've come. After we leave the island, we'll warn Master Koko."

I catch her shoulder. "Bryce, how did you know they were coming? How do you know there are so many infiltrators? Talk to me."

"You're good at climbing, yeah?" She shrugs me off and approaches the balcony. "Let's go."

"Bryce!"

"Conrad," she snaps. "This is NOT the time."

I stare at her, hands on my hips. "You're irritating the hell out of me, Bryce."

"Yes, well, you do the same to me. The corridor will be packed soon, and more Lantians are coming. Get changed into your Hunter uniform. It'll help you blend in. We'll need to pull up your hood."

"Your hood isn't up."

"It's not my face I'm worried about."

My brow knits, but I flip open my luggage. She turns away as I get dressed. It's not long until I pull the jacket's hood over my head and clip my cane to my belt.

Shadows appear outside the hall door again. Bryce and I quickly exit onto the balcony. The door clicks open, but we're already hanging by our fingers from the balustrade. Our legs dangle beneath us into the open air.

The Lantians enter and speak in alarm as they check over the unconscious bodies. But these killers are the least of my concerns because I'm hanging over a dizzying drop. This building rises over a jungle cliff.

Powerful wind sweeps over us. My stomach clenches with nerves. Only minutes ago I was sleeping peacefully. Now my heart's in my throat as Bryce gives me a look. She lets go and drops onto the balcony below.

This is insane.

The Lantians approach my position. Dammit! I release my grip and drop. No way this is our escape plan. I land silently onto the next balcony. The drop stings my shins and makes my knees wobble. But I make it.

"We need to reach the bottom," Bryce whispers. "They're in all the halls."

"Bryce, that's like ten floors."

"Eleven. C'mon."

She drops to the next level, and I've no choice but to follow.

"What about my sister?" I whisper on the next level. "And the others?"

"We can't use the comms, Conrad."

"I'm not going without my sister," I say. "You know that."

"If Ella wants to come, she'll come. She knows you have a plan to escape the island. We all talked about it on the *Gladian*. Besides, you don't know where she is. She'll have to come to you."

I pause and scan the neighboring buildings. Some windows expose rooms illuminated under soft, crystal light. She could be anywhere.

"Ella doesn't know we're leaving tonight," I say.

Bryce touches my arm gently and meets my eyes. "Conrad, she wants to be with your uncle."

"Would you give up on your family that easily?"

She exhales and massages her brow. "Fine. Warn her and the rest of the crew. But we need to go now."

I breathe out and tap the comm gem. "Ella, the mud's on the floor."

Bryce stares at me.

"We used to get mud around Urwin Manor," I explain. "It's the best I could do. The crew will understand. C'mon."

We climb over the balustrade and drop again. But we still have nine more levels to go. Nine more chances for something to go wrong. A fall from here, and our bodies might not be found for days. Maybe never because a pack of boarlons could drag them off into the jungle.

We drop again.

And again.

Finally, we reach the ground floor. My shins are screaming from the impact. My feet are buzzing. And sweat pools my forehead, stinging my eyes. I crane my neck to see how far we've come.

Holy hell.

"C'mon," she says.

I glance over the bottom balcony at the ridiculous cliffside that drops directly beneath us, then turn to follow her.

We open the balcony door into the room. People sleep on all four beds. We slip inside and breathe softly. The floor creaks beneath us, but the people keep snoozing. Before long we slide into the quiet corridor. A few people walk about, carrying on hushed conversations. Bryce snatches my hand, her grip fierce.

"Whatever happens," she says, "you need to listen to me."

A horrible thought creeps into my brain. Bryce has all the power over me right now. Everything. She could give me to the Below. Could give me to Admiral Goerner. But as our eyes connect, I remember the girl filled with compassion. The girl who came to the Above not to destroy, but to save lives.

That's always been her goal: saving lives.

So I pull my hood down again to cover my face, squeeze her hand, and we start down the corridor.

CHAPTER 09

BRYCE AND I PEER AROUND THE CORNER OF THE HALL. WE need to get out of the building. That's what she keeps telling me. But a quartet of Lantians guards an exit, their faces twisted with scowls.

Bryce yanks me back.

"Do you feel that?" a man says.

"The hall."

"Brutus. Go."

Footsteps approach us, but we turn back and run. Soon we're racing down an empty hall with the wind against our faces.

"Faster," Bryce hisses.

She runs ahead, legs eating up ground. I push myself to keep up with her. My heart attacks my ribs.

Bryce slides to an abrupt halt and raises a hand to stop me. I lean on my knees to breathe. Then she tugs me toward an open doorway. I wipe my forehead and remove my hood to let my skin breathe for a few precious seconds. She pulls it up again.

This enormous room is filled with displays of beast organs. One tank contains the giant, translucent heart of a gorgantaun. It's as big as my ship.

We scuttle past it, climb a platform, and approach a window. Sealed shut. And even if we broke it, it leads right over the edge of the cliff.

Damn.

We enter an attached room and jog past stuffed beasts: mashtauns, prowlons, and lupons. Then we exit into a hall that leads to a new foyer. Above us banners of Hunter hang between two columns, and portraits of Hunter's previous Masters adorn the walls. The Masters' eyes judge us.

Fortunately, the foyer appears empty. A glass door there exits into the dark jungle. We hurry toward it. We're going to get out, we're going to make it. I can only hope that my crew got the comm and that Ella took the hint. We continue toward the exit when Bryce touches her neck, then pulls us another direction.

"Bryce, what—"

"Quiet! Quickly now."

I growl, and we start jogging again.

"How many are there, Bryce?"

"Thirty. Maybe more."

I almost stop breathing. "On the island?"

"Not the island. The *building*. They'd infiltrated this place long before I came above." We stop, and she peers around the edge of the next hall. She nods and we creep around the corner.

"Thirty people in a single building." I repeat the number, astounded.

"Yes, they've likely planned this moment for a while."

I bite my lip. "Do they know about you?"

"I betrayed them. What do you think?"

My mouth shuts. I can't stand this. Can't stand being pulled along as though I'm helpless. She glances back at me, and her expression softens. She squeezes my hand.

"We're getting you out, Conrad."

We slip into an atrium garden and maneuver around splashing fountains. It's a beautiful area, but eerie around the shadowed trees and bushes.

She suddenly yanks me behind a gray column.

I shut my eyes and exhale. Don't know how much more of this I can take. Our bodies come together behind the column. She pulls something from her pocket, a slab of metal, and holds it against the base of her neck.

"Bryce?"

"Shh."

Through the atrium's glass doors, two women slink inside. Their steps click on the cobblestone until they stop on the other side of our column. My body freezes. Breathing slows. I lean against the column, trying to make myself small.

"That fussock is here," one whispers. "She's here."

Bryce winces as she presses the metal deeper against her neck. My fists tighten and my jaw clenches. Can't stand here and do nothing. I'll knock these women out quick—before they can alert anyone. Drag their bodies into the bushes.

But Bryce grips my wrist, and her eyes tell me to stay.

The women move around the atrium. They check the bushes, look up a tree, and peer at the open sky above us.

"She's not here anymore," the other woman says.

"Did she sever?"

"No. Must be back in the corridors."

"Once I get ahold of that traitor . . ."

"Goerner wants her alive."

"Accidents happen."

Bryce and I breathe close to each other, our skin radiating in the humid air. As the women slip into the corridors, I'm trying not to think about how many people the Below sent. But my thoughts become scrambled when Bryce leans closer to me. And suddenly, I'm trying not to think how close I am to her, and that her chest is pressed against me. And I'm really trying not to look her in the eyes.

Bryce keeps the metal slab on her neck, checks the door, and pulls me away from the column. We hurry from the garden area and finally find an unguarded exit out of the building.

Once outside, I suck down air and pull the hood off again. The evening air's cool on my sweaty body. My hands are shaking. And my thoughts won't stop spinning—won't stop displaying images of those I care about, facing assassins in their own rooms.

"C'mon," Bryce says.

We run down a path lit by glowing crystal lampposts. The ground taps under our heels, and my knees still ache from the balcony drops. Finally, we leap over a railing and rush through the jungle. Bryce races ahead, pushing branches away from her face.

"Stay behind me," she says. "Always behind me."

The canopy rattles under the wind. Moonlight dots our path, reflecting on the dew-covered undergrowth.

"We have to get to the *Gladian* and fly out of here," I say.

"It's under guard."

"We'll figure out a way."

We leap over a mossy log, and the mud sucks our boots in. My leg muscles grow warm from exhaustion. Insects chirp in the distance, and the eyes of strange beasts, hanging from the trees, watch us as we run.

Finally, we slosh through a puddled path and exit the jungle.

We step into the gentle glow of the colorful lamps of Westdock and lean against a stone wall, breathing hard. A side ache throbs in my gut. Around us, a few pubs, built right above the docks, explode with laughter from boisterous drinkers. Waiters hurry about, distributing vino and hot pepper rice.

The view of the pubs provides a bit of security and safety.

Bryce wipes her forehead and tries to run again, but I catch her hand.

"Running attracts attention," I say. "Are Lantians around?"

Her forehead wrinkles with concentration, and she scans the numerous nearby buildings. They rise along the jungled hill with gleaming light through their windows. Suddenly, a trio of people turns the corner of the path. They approach us, but Bryce doesn't tense.

"Hunters," she whispers.

Perhaps they're veterans returning from a successful hunt. One of them laughs as he considers all the coin they got.

"Class-six," he boasts. "Three hundred thousand coins split between the crew." He sees me and chortles. "This guy knows what I'm talking about."

The other guy's eyes widen. "Wait, that's the Prince!"

Bryce snatches my hand, and we part between the men. They watch us, stunned, before continuing.

"We can't be this out in the open," Bryce says. "You're too recognizable on Venator." She pulls my hood up again to obscure my face. "C'mon."

We follow the fringes of buildings, careful to keep our faces down whenever someone approaches.

"There," I say, pointing ahead, "just around the bend is the dock, and the rendezvous point."

"Rendezvous?"

We pause by some barrels and peer around the street.

"The crew and I agreed on it when we met earlier without you," I say. "An escape plan."

"Oh. Well, we can't stay on Venator long."

I stare at her, trying to read her. "Bryce, are they going to attack the island?"

"It's likely."

"Then we must tell Master Koko, even if it's dangerous."

"Conrad, the Lantians want you. That's why they're here. Their number one priority is to capture you. I don't know why."

I go quiet. This revelation leaves me twisting with guilt. I'm the reason they're here.

"Once we're off Venator, we'll contact Master Koko," she says. "Until then . . . we can't risk it. C'mon. Let's check the rendezvous point. If the crew's not there, we leave without them."

"No way in hell."

My skin feels hot from the suggestion. Pound, Roderick, Keeton—they're my friends. Arika and Declan are valued members of my crew. And there's no way I'm leaving Ella here alone.

Bryce tugs on me, but I don't move.

She exhales. "Conrad."

"We aren't leaving them."

"We will give them time. A few minutes. But you must understand—this is war. The Below wants you. We can't let them have you."

The suggestion of leaving everyone behind cuts me up inside. I stand, remembering the night when the gorgantauns attacked my island and my ill mother was left alone. I couldn't get back to her in time. The feeling of unbearable guilt. I wouldn't be able to live with myself if I lost my crew, too.

But she's right that we can't stay on Venator. Not forever.

"Bryce, the torton that attacked us . . . bothered you in the sky for days. It wasn't trying to destroy us, was it?"

Her voice lowers. "No."

The torton was meant to turn my hunting expedition into a disaster. Force me and my crew back to Venator. They knew they couldn't catch me in the open sky; my ship was known to fly at an elite speed, even before Keeton upgraded the engine.

This is why the Lantians are on Venator. This is their chance to try and take me.

Bryce and I hop over a small wall, and the dock splays out before us. Westdock is enormous. Dozens of skyships from every island and Trade float and bob under the gentle wind. The *Gladian's* out there somewhere.

The rendezvous point, the Hunter armory, stands ahead of us. My body tenses. What if the crew doesn't show? How long can we really wait? But as we draw nearer, I spot someone under the crystal light near the entrance. A giant with a shining bald head.

I almost laugh.

Until I see Pound's bleeding arm, and that he's carrying someone who's hurt. Someone small with white hair.

My gut falls.

And then I start to run.

CHAPTER 10

NOT ELLA. NOT AFTER MY LAST WORDS TO HER WERE SO cold. I press my ear against her chest, hoping she's okay. Hoping my failures aren't the reason she died on Venator.

A slight thud—a heartbeat—greets my ear. And I almost collapse with relief. My lip trembles, and I grip her in my arms.

"How?" Bryce asks Pound. "What happened?"

Pound winces, holding his bloodied arm. "After Conrad's message went out, I saw Ella being chased. She was fighting. Had her cane out, took on four people at once. But one had a spear—some electrical thing."

Bryce eyes widen with alarm. "Did the spear hit her?"

"Almost got me, too." Pound seethes as blood dribbles between his fingers. "But I bashed the bastard against the wall and hurled him out the window. Cut my arm on the glass."

"Let me see her," Bryce says.

Pound lowers Ella to the ground. Bryce kneels, and her fingers delicately tap the back of her own neck.

My eyes narrow. "What are you doing?"

"Quiet," Bryce says.

The hair on her other hand rises. The tips of her fingers spark, and she presses her palm against Ella's chest and closes her eyes. Pound and I glance at each other, perplexed. Suddenly, Ella's body jolts, and she bursts upright. Breathing hard.

"Ella." I rest my hands on her shoulders.

Ella blinks as she looks around. "Where am I?"

"You're safe," I say.

"I was being chased. I tried to fight." She notices Pound and her eyes bulge. "*You*. You saved me."

"Yeah," Pound says gruffly. "Don't expect it to happen again."

She considers him, and I can almost read the calculations on her face. In the world of Urwin, there's no such thing as a selfless act. And worse yet, he's an Atwood.

"The King will pay you," she says, brushing off my hands and standing. "Then we'll be even."

Pound's face hardens. "I didn't save your life for money, *Princess*."

"Then why?"

"Because you needed help."

"I would've fought them off."

"So, if I hadn't been there, you would've been fine?"

"Yes."

Pound reddens in anger, but he bites down his tongue and turns to Bryce. "Electric spears that send people into paralysis. Jump-starting them back to life with a touch. What was that? What the hell kind of technology do your people have?"

"Technology designed for war."

We go quiet.

Suddenly, four shadowed figures approach from around the armory's edge. Bryce and Pound flash an anxious look. I stand and quietly unclip my cane. Ella gets hers out, too. Pound raises his fists. Bryce slinks back to stand beside me, tightening the dueling braces on her forearms.

"They can't have you," she whispers.

We gear ourselves up, all ready to fight and claw. These bastards brought the war to us. Well, we're going to give it back.

A figure ambles out of the shadows and into the light. I squint, and then Pound booms with laughter.

"YOU!" Roderick shuffles out of the shadows, smiling a relieved, goofy grin. He's followed by Keeton, Arika, and Declan. All have a few nicks and bruises, except for Declan.

My whole body relaxes. Then, I laugh, too, shaking my head.

Roderick shoves Pound playfully, winks at Bryce, then catches me in his thick, Master Gunner arms. Nearly breaks my spine, too.

"They didn't get you," he breathes.

"Rod," I grunt, "you're crushing me."

He lets go. "Sorry." His smile shrinks a little. "They're after you." A bit of blood drips from his face. "They were going to use us against you. They know about you and me, Conrad. They know we're friends."

Keeton and Bryce hug. But Bryce stops, noticing a cut on Keeton's chin.

"Are you all right?"

"Me?" Keeton scoffs. "You should see the woman who attacked me."

Arika glances back to where the jungle meets the edges of the street. "We need to get off Venator."

Declan's eyes narrow. "Leave Venator?"

Pound growls. "You don't expect us to sit around here scratching our asses while we wait to get attacked again, do you, old man?"

Declan frowns.

"Heard the infiltrators talking." Roderick massages his bruised, bloodied knuckles. "They're going to escalate the war again."

"Escalate the war?" Pound says. "How—"

But then he pauses. We all do—perhaps all of us trapped in the memory of the attack on Ironside. When the island fell and thousands perished.

"The gigataun," Bryce whispers.

We shift uncomfortably.

My brow furrows and I raise my comm gem. Don't care that the lines are compromised. I have to warn Master Koko.

"Conrad," Bryce says, "what are—"

"People will die if I don't."

Her mouth shuts.

I tap the comm, switch the colors, and rotate a dial until I come to the short-range frequency Koko gave to me. I swallow a deep breath. "Master Koko, Venator's under assault. An attack may be imminent. Prepare your people."

We stand, waiting for a response. But my comm gem's light fades.

"Maybe they got to her," Roderick says.

Declan glances around the armory's edge and looks toward the Hunter Academy above. "We should go back for her."

"Did someone punch your head really hard?" Pound says. "The Academy's swarming with infiltrators."

"She's the Master of Hunter," Declan says. "If we lose her, the whole Trade could fall into shambles."

"We warned her," Keeton says. "Now we need to get the heirs off the island."

Everyone falls silent and looks at me and Ella.

"It's your call, Captain," Arika says.

I scratch the back of my neck. Hate leaving Master Koko, but she's one of the toughest people I know. Anyway, if going back for her is too crazy for Pound, then it's way too crazy for the rest of us.

"We'll go to the *Gladian*," I say. "Follow our original plan."

Declan is aghast. "We're just going to leave her?"

"She's the damned Master of Hunter," Pound rumbles. "Not some yippity, defenseless lotcher, Declan."

"But why the *Gladian*?" Declan asks. "It's locked down. If we're going to retreat like cowards, then I know several ships that'll be easier to get aboard."

We stare at him.

"The *Gladian* is what we know," Pound says.

"Keeton made it the fastest in the fleet," Arika says.

"And," Keeton says, "if we're stuck in a fight, there's no ship I'd rather be on."

"But it's guarded," Declan says. "The King locked it down. How—"

Suddenly, an alarm screams in the distance. Loud enough that I wince. Then horror spreads across the faces of my friends. A wave of terror ices up my back.

The sky serpent alarm.

Gorgantauns.

✦✦✦

Venator becomes chaos. We run along the crowded dock. Dozens of skyships from the Academy soar overhead, launching toward the approaching threat.

The long, undulating gorgantauns fill the sky with their metallic scales and golden eyes of death. It's a pod of thirty. The biggest I've seen. And worse, they're arctic gorgantauns. How the hell did they come this far west?

"C'mon," Bryce says. "We can't stop. I can feel"—she pauses—"infiltrators."

She snatches my wrist. And I see her face, the fear and concern, the same look of panic she had when we were attacked by the torton. These gorgantauns . . . they're another ploy to get me out in the open.

I grip Ella's sleeve and tug her after me. Bryce leads the way through the terrified crowd. But as the snakelike gorgantauns approach the island, the mob turns primal. They shove one another and completely lose their minds in a mad rush for the jungle or for cover.

The nearest gorgantauns' mouths open, exposing teeth longer than my whole body. Arctic gorgantauns are half the size of the southern variety, but still three hundred feet long.

Dozens of ships soar out to greet them, and whistling harpoons begin stabbing the air. Anti-G batteries from atop the Academy walls send blue explosives that set the sky alight. The reverberations nearly knock us over. But we can't stop. We push through the horrified masses, fighting against the current.

A couple of trainees tumble before us, crying, and Pound hoists them to their feet.

"Go," he shouts. "Into the trees. Go!"

They scramble off.

"The *Gladian's* down this way." Arika points. "I saw it when I took a walk after dinner."

"How far?" Pound asks.

She grunts after a person runs into her. "It's going to take a while. A few hundred yards, maybe."

Adrenaline shoots through me as I study the people we pass. Any of them could be an assassin. An attack could come at any time.

Ella grips her cane as tight as I clutch her sleeve.

In the distance the skyships and gorgantauns battle. One serpent chomps off the bow of a Predator-class vessel while another beast crushes a Titanium-class under its coils. But more gorgantauns thrash and howl as they're assaulted by weapons from all directions. One writhes as harpoons burrow past its icy defenses, and soon it's drifting motionless into the sky.

People rush to the docks and more skyships launch, some escaping the island entirely, but many to join the battle.

"Get the hell out of our way!" Pound roars at the people pushing toward us.

"Quiet!" Bryce yells. "You're attracting attention."

He grumbles at her, then shoves people aside, creating a path for us until we reach a four-foot-tall wall that's beside the path. The stone barrier spreads hundreds of feet and blocks off the jungle from the dock. We climb over it, and my feet hit the soft dirt on the other side.

I'm breathing hard. My mouth's dry. We all stop to recover, crouching or sitting against the wall.

"Captain, I know another ship," Declan says, kneeling beside me. "A friend's ship. It's close." He motions me to stand with him. We carefully peer over the top of the wall, and he jabs a finger at a thick, dark beast of a ship with scars striping its hull. Carnivore-class. It's wider than the Gladian, but not as long. "We can make it, Captain. Then we'll come back for the *Gladian* once this is over."

Declan's ship seems like an effective vessel. Ten years ago, the Carnivore-class was top of the line for Hunter. Still, there are few in my circle that I trust. And I'm not planning on expanding that right now. Not while we're under attack.

"We go to the *Gladian*," I say, and lower again.

Declan exhales.

"We're not far, Declan," Arika says. "We can make it."

We stay crouched and creep along the wall, flinching at the shrieks of gorgantauns. Panicked trainees leap over the wall, nearly landing on us, and hurry across the grass into the jungle. I glimpse Ella behind me and notice the cold, dripping dread in her expression. She peers at the curling mass of gorgantauns in the sky. She's never faced gorgantauns. Not like this.

The Skylands weren't ready. Even after losing the capital, we're still a disorganized mess. Easy targets for the Lantians.

"Halt," Bryce says. "Quiet. Everyone freeze."

We sit, our skin clammy, while Bryce presses that metal piece against the back of her neck again.

Pound's brow knits. "What the hell are you doing, Bryce?"

"Shh," Bryce says.

We bunch together while Bryce rises slightly to look over the wall.

"There," she whispers. "Look."

I rise slowly and spot two men among the crowd. They're standing off to the side. Not running. Not panicking. Just watching the people run past.

"Lantians," Bryce whispers.

Roderick squints at her. "How do you know?"

"I can sense them."

"Sense them?" Pound says. "How? I don't get it."

She gives him an annoyed look before we lower again.

"All right," she says. "Follow me."

"No," Declan says.

We look back at him.

His face is red. Flushed. "We won't make it to the *Gladian*. Do you all have a death wish? We need to get aboard a ship. Right now. What if that—that gigataun thing shows up? Eats the island's heart, and the whole island falls? We need to get aboard my—"

"Oh hell," Pound grumbles.

"Declan, we're not leaving the *Gladian*," I say, my voice agitated. "I won't say it again."

Bryce leads us along the wall for several minutes. I glance to the left, at the jungle. Maybe Lantians are in there, waiting for us if we choose to run into the trees. More explosions and shouts from the battle continue. More skyships zoom over us, spraying us with wind. Finally, we reach the wall's end, where it meets the bricks of a supply building.

Bryce peers over the top of the wall. "Arika was right. The *Gladian's* just ahead."

A candle of hope ignites in my chest. We've almost made it. Within a few minutes, we'll be aboard, soaring into the sky. We'll have our turrets, our weapons, and one another.

Suddenly, Roderick shouts. It's a strange, pained cry. I whirl back, and he topples forward with a silver dagger in his back.

Horror floods me.

"Rod!" Keeton roars.

Before I can blink, Declan shoves past me. He leaps at Bryce with another blade, ready to stuff it into her eye.

"No!"

I catch his legs, and his dagger slices her thigh. He smacks the ground. Bryce yells in pain. Pound roars and reaches for Declan, but the old man kicks free of my grip, smashing my nose. Sparks fly in my vision. Hot blood travels my face. The old man rolls away from Pound and rises to run.

Pound gives chase. "Traitor!"

"Here!" Declan cries as he runs for the jungle. He's speaking into some metal cube device. "The heirs are here!"

Roderick's moaning, lying on his stomach. Keeton's stemming the blood in a panic. Ella's helping. Bryce is holding her cut leg, seething as red trails her calf. And I don't know what to do. This can't be happening.

Can't be.

Pound dives at Declan, but the old man ducks away. Arika, fast as birdshit, catches Declan. Actually leaps onto his back and starts throwing hell into the back of his skull. But Declan weighs twice as much as she does, and he elbows her chin. She drops onto the mud, coughing. Then Declan leaps onto a boulder beside the trees and climbs above. Once there, he shouts into his cube again, waving his arms above his head.

"The heirs are here!"

I kneel beside Roderick. See the terror in my friend's eye. Bryce straps her belt over her thigh, then hobbles to us. And while Roderick struggles, and as I stare at the blade still stuck in his back, an uncontrollable rage fills my heart.

Declan continues to shout and wave.

My eyes narrow. Every part of me grows hot with trembling fury. I want to catch that old man by the neck and slam his face into the rock. But he's an agile bastard. So I snatch a stone. And while he's still signaling, I hurl it. The rock spins through the air and smacks him right between the eyes. Declan pauses a second. Dazed. Then he falls forward off the boulder and lands awkwardly, headfirst, into the earth with a sickening crunch.

Pound dives after Declan like a prowlon that just caught lunch. He lifts him and Declan's head hangs limp. Pound checks Declan's pulse, then discards the bastard into the mud.

"Dead."

Arika and Pound march back to us.

Maybe I should feel something besides rage when I look at Declan's body. But he betrayed us. Worse, somehow a Lantian infiltrated my crew. How did Bryce not know about him? Wouldn't she be able to sense him, too?

"I told you he was talking to people on the deck," Ella hisses at me.

"He must've severed," Bryce says breathlessly. "Or didn't have one. I didn't know. I didn't know."

"Severed?" Pound says. "Didn't have wh—"

Our attention snaps back to Keeton's panicked voice.

"Rod," she pleads, patting his shoulder. "Rod, stay with me."

Rod gurgles and blood spills from his lips. I kneel beside him and go numb. My hands trembling.

"We've got to go," Arika says.

"We're not leaving him," Keeton says, her voice going shrill.

"Well, we can't stay here!" Arika yells.

I grip Roderick's hand. Feel his strength weakening. He's trying to speak, but it's all sputtering.

"C'mon," Pound says. He lifts Roderick gently from the ground. "We need to get him meds on the *Gladian*."

I'm all cold as I stare at Roderick's paling face. Can we make it in time?

Before long, Bryce leans on me and Ella as we climb over the wall. The war in the sky continues. Several dying gorgantauns are sinking, their final bellows echoing in the distance. But one, an ice-white monstrosity, approaches the dock. It's unconcerned with the harpoons that crash into its icy side. The beast slides its maw across the dock, consuming dozens of screaming people and broken wood.

Then it sees us.

"Go! Go! Go!" Keeton yells.

We run for the *Gladian*.

The scattered crowd races for the jungle, clearing our path. A skyship zooms overhead. It goes straight for the gorgantaun and gushes flame from a turret. The golden heat strikes the beast. Melts through its icy exterior and exposes the weaker scales beneath. And then come the harpoons. The gorgantaun thrashes and roars so loudly that people drop to cover their ears. The beast whips its sharp tail at the ship, but not before more flame hits its face. And then a timely shot from an anti-G battery explodes the serpent's face, sending white blood spraying onto the dock.

We almost cheer, until we realize the beast's momentum keeps it hurtling toward us.

"It's going to crush us!" Pound sprints ahead, even with Roderick in his arms. "MOVE!"

But I can't run any faster with Bryce hobbling like this. So I roar and lift her. Feel her weight attack my lower back. But my adrenaline takes over. And while her arms wrap over my neck, we race. Race so hard I fear my heart will burst.

The dead gorgantaun crashes into the dock. Splintering wood. Crushing people. Destroying docked ships.

We keep running.

And finally, the carcass slows, grinding to a stop just feet from us. About a quarter of its body still floats, presumably because the gas was still trapped inside the coils.

I cough and lower Bryce onto her good leg. My body begs to rest, to just breathe.

The massive beast glows with white, and the ice from its body slowly spreads frost on the wood.

"Don't touch the ice," Bryce breathes to Ella. "It's contagious."

We continue toward the *Gladian,* some of us crying. No matter how many breaths I take, I don't feel like I'm getting enough. Finally, my ship appears again through the rising dust. It's the best thing I've seen all day.

But my hair rises at the sight below it.

A dozen bloodied Order guards lie by the chains that attach my ship to the dock. Their shocked, dead eyes stare upward.

Bryce gives me a wary glance. She touches the back of her neck, and she's about to say something when a group of men appear down the empty dock. The crowds have cleared, leaving only us and them.

"The heirs!" one of them shouts.

Electric spears glow in their hands, and they charge.

We sprint up the wobbly gangway onto the *Gladian*. Got to fly. Got to get Roderick belowdecks for meds. But as we reach the deck, we realize our horrible mistake.

Fifteen men with spears stand on the deck, waiting for us. And the others on the dock, they start up the gangway, blocking our escape.

I unclip my cane, ready to fight. Take them all down. But a young woman parts the group of Lantians with an auto-pistol that she aims at my skull. Her dark hair's tied in a bun, and she stands in the rigid way all Order soldiers do.

Alona of Mizrahi.

"Conrad of Urwin," she says with a tight smile. "This time, you're not getting away."

CHAPTER 11

MY FRIENDS ARE DRAGGED ELSEWHERE INTO THE BOWELS of the ship. But even as I'm hurled onto the floor of the *Gladian's* cafeteria, and even as swift boots dig into my gut, I'm thinking of Roderick.

"Please," I say.

Alona laughs. "Look at him. Raised to meet any challenge. The heir, and the winner of the Gauntlet, blithering a plea."

"My friend," I say. "Roderick needs meds."

Her face sours. Disgusted that I could be thinking about anything but the pain. She waves six men forward. The assault's merciless. They stab my ribs. Pummel my face. Stomp my back. At one point they lift me to my feet and make me fight back. But my balance is dizzy, and when I fall, I'm greeted by more boots and fists.

They haven't asked me a single question. Haven't demanded anything. This is nothing but hate.

Once I'm blinking in and out of consciousness, Alona snaps her fingers. Her men stand back like dogs and fold their massive arms. One massages his split, bloody knuckles.

Alona crouches beside me. Her dark eyes meet mine. Alona won Order's Skywar. Defeated all the other competitors to be first in her group and become one of Admiral Goerner's most trusted Commanders. The Skylands were excited about her, what her future held.

Before she and the former High Admiral of Order revealed who they truly were.

"We're taking you," she says, "to Goerner."

Goerner. The traitor who set the gigataun upon the capital of Ironside.

"If you don't help us," Alona says, "Goerner will finish what he started with you."

She presses a finger into the scar of my shoulder. Then she smiles. Can hardly see her through my puffy left eye. I'm a pile of stinging, red pulp. Might have a broken rib, or three. Even so, the thought of a traitor's death jolts dread into my veins.

"Rest well," she says, running her fingers through my curls.

Then she stands, and her crew follows her out of the cafeteria. The door slams closed, and a locking bar slides across.

I lie pitifully on the cold floor in my own blood. The ground's sticky with it. My head's swimming, ears buzzing.

Is Roderick still alive? Could the others help him without medicine? Arika has some medical experience. Maybe she could keep him alive for a couple hours.

Please . . .

And what about Bryce? She has a bad gash on her leg, and it could get infected if she doesn't get treatment. Worse, what will they do with her?

If they touch Ella . . .

My hands slap against the floor, and my arms wobble as I push myself into a sitting position. I breathe, trying to ignore that my swollen ribs are sticking into my lungs. After several minutes, I stand. Then I take a few steps and stumble to my knees.

The sky outside the window is shooting past. Venator, the ships, the battle. All of it is behind us. Suddenly, I'm thinking about the Hunters and Master Koko. Did Koko survive? Did the Hunters stave off the attack?

Got to get out of here. I stand again and hobble toward the kitchen area. Pain shoots up my legs, and my magboots feel heavier than normal.

The kitchen drawers are barren. There's nothing left except crumbs. The freeze box is the way we left it when we docked: empty. I gingerly kneel beside the air vent. It's narrow—much too narrow for me. Still my fingers search around the edges, seeking a weakness. But it's screwed down tight.

I check my sleeve. Comm gem's been stripped.

My side throbs as I limp toward the door. Muffled voices from the corridor filter in. They're the grizzled, scratchy voices of Alona's men. What could Goerner want with me, anyway? Ransom? Capture me as a trophy?

My fist feebly strikes the door. "Let me out."

No response.

So I pound again and again until my hands sting. Finally, a man in the hall shouts, "Quiet!"

I don't.

"You itching for another beating, *Prince*?"

I keep pounding.

Finally, the bar slides across and the door opens. Two men scowl at me. Their faces splotched red. I raise my fists. I can take two. Easily. But the next instant, I'm on the ground, coughing. My pathetic attack struck the first man on the jaw, but it had no power behind it. And once I'm on the ground, they spit on me.

"Quiet!" they say.

Then they leave and slam the door shut behind them.

This time I don't have the strength to get up.

✦✦✦

A day passes, and my bruises swell. A black splotch covers my ribs. My stomach's gurgling nonstop. Alona's people haven't fed me, so I drink extra water from the sink just to feel full. Fortunately, I managed to find a chunk of bread near the heating station. It's old and crusty, but I've had worse.

I save it for later, just in case.

Now I sit by the window. An island appears in the distance, and a pack of orcons pick at the rocky underside. It's the most interesting thing I've seen in hours. Orcons are one of the rarer beasts—outcompeted by the gorgantauns. Still, they're intelligent pack hunters. These white, metallic beasts measure fifty feet in length, have thick teeth, and rotate two powerful flippers that they use to maneuver and make quick turns.

They ram their thick heads into the island's underside, loosening chunks, and revealing sheltauns beneath. Sheltauns are like giant, metal crabs. One sheltaun scurries about and snaps its thick, steel pincers at an orcon. It's a big sheltaun, ten feet across. But the orcon slams into it twice, dazing it before swallowing it whole.

Orcons fetch ten thousand coins a beast. Not nearly what we'd get for gorgantauns, especially the largest of the southern breed, but still a good price. If the world hadn't gone to birdshit, if I'd been able to be a real Hunter, I could be off hunting things like them. Now I'm feeling like the helpless sheltauns getting pulverized.

Before the orcons turn and spot us, whoever's flying the *Gladian* shoves the strings forward and we launch away at an incredible speed. The floor shakes beneath me. Keeton's engine enhancements really are working. Even if Uncle, or any of his people, know we've been taken, we're impossible to catch.

My head drops.

Hours pass.

The guards outside argue about something. Can't understand much through the door, but they're complaining about having "searched everywhere." A few seconds later, the door cracks open, and a woman tosses two apples right into my stomach. Then leaves.

My forehead wrinkles. They're giving me food? More likely it's poison. No. That doesn't make sense. If they wanted to kill me, they could come right in and finish the job.

Something about the apple's sweet scent awakens my hunger. I chomp off a bite. Oh, it's good. Crispy and cold. The sweetest thing I've ever tasted.

My stomach cries for the other one. But I force myself to put the spare apple on the kitchen counter beside the bread. Then I sit and stare out the window.

✦✦✦

For hours I watch passing islands and creatures. At one point I observe the undulating forms of a trio of gorgantauns. Later I spot a fleet of ships. They're outdated but powerful. The decks are blanketed in cannons like they're porcupine quills. These ships came from an era when mobility was less important than raw firepower.

I squint at them.

Pirates, maybe? No. Their flags, whipping in the wind, display . . . a lightning bolt. Hope swells in me. These are ships from the Stonefrost Armada. Commanded by the Duchess of Stonefrost, an ally of my uncle and the Urwins. It's the most powerful collection of skyships in the whole world that's not run by the King or a Trade. It's built to protect the northern islands from gorgantaun threats.

The ships seem to focus on us. Perhaps, they're contacting us over the comm. Demanding that we identify ourselves. But the *Gladian* rockets away, and soon they're nothing but specks in the distance.

I sink to the ground and seethe as I hold my ribs.

At least I know where we are. Passing the Stonefrost Armada confirms we're traveling far into the Northern Airs. The neighboring islands are blanketed in white. And as I'm watching the skies of my youth, I'm considering that Uncle's intelligence was wrong. They told him that Goerner was in the East somewhere, but Goerner's been hiding among the arctic gorgantauns.

A worrying thought stabs me. What if Goerner's on my island, Holmstead? A new Archduchess took Uncle's place when he ascended. What's she doing with my island? Does she have any idea about Goerner? If only there were a way to warn her about potential Lantians in the area.

Worse, something tells me that the closer we get to Goerner, the more likely my friends will be murdered. Maybe the Lantians need me or Ella alive. But they don't need Pound, or Roderick, or any of them, really.

And they have every reason to dispose of Bryce.

My head leans against the wall, and I rest until something knocks in the kitchen area. A gentle tap. I stand. The sound comes again.

My voice is soft. "Hello?"

No response.

I cautiously start toward the kitchen. Peer around the edge of the heating station and toward the freeze box. But no one's there.

"Here," a voice whispers.

I nearly jump. In the next second, I'm crouching by the air vent, staring at the grimy, sweaty face of my sister.

"Ella," I say, breathless. "How?"

"Shh!" She raises a finger to her lips. "Loud noises travel in the vent."

My heart springs with joy. Just seeing her alive. Just seeing another friendly face.

"Where are the others?"

"In the brig below," she whispers. "Well, most of them."

"Are they okay?"

"I think so. Pound fought back, and I escaped before they could lock me in. I've been squirming around the vents this whole time—but they're loud, and I got lost and wasn't sure where you were." Exhaustion rings her eyes. "Can you let me in? My arms are killing me."

"Okay," I say. "Together."

My fingers grip the vent's grill, and I brace my boot against the wall. Despite my stinging ribs, I yank with all I've got, and Ella shoves.

A screw comes loose, but it's not enough. So, we try again. I clench my jaw, my forehead perspires, and my arms shake. We keep fighting the vent until finally, I fall back as the grill tears from the wall with a huge bang.

A voice in the corridor shouts. "What's going on in there?!"

"Back!" I hiss at Ella.

The bar outside the door slides across.

Ella slides deeper into the vent's shadows. I replace the grill, scurry away, and lie on the floor as the door opens. The guard peers inside and stares at me.

I raise my head. "Where are my friends?"

He scowls, scans the room, then slams the door. The bar slides across again.

Once the guards are murmuring outside, I return to the vent and pull off the grill. Ella climbs out. She's completely covered in dust and grime. Mother's cane dangles from her belt. I squint. But how? We were all disarmed. Ella stretches her arms and walks around, wincing as she cracks her back.

"You look terrible." She stares at me, gently touching my chin to turn my face. "They did this to you?"

I nod.

"Bastards." She reaches into her pocket and takes out a half-eaten cookie. "You need strength. I saved this for you. Stole it from Alona's room."

I almost laugh. "You snuck into Alona's room?"

"While she was sleeping in the Captain's cabin. Thought about killing her. But it was too big a risk. I was the ship's only hope. They're trying to find me, and they're furious because I keep taking things."

I watch her with admiration. Our relationship has been unsteady at best, but this common enemy unites us.

"I stole this from the Captain's cabin, too." She climbs back into the vent, grunts, and brings something else out. My mouth falls as she drops it into my hand. And I almost can't believe it. It's a long black rod of wood, capped with a steel Urwin eagle at the end.

My dueling cane.

This cane is legend. Passed down from generation to generation. Something about holding it reminds me that I'm still alive. And that in my blood flows the strength of Urwin.

"You should eat the cookie," Ella says.

"I just had my last apple and a chunk of bread. You need the cookie more than I do."

"I've been eating this whole time," she says. "I've stolen all sorts of food."

"Wait, you've been stuffing your face this whole time and all you brought me is half a cookie?"

She grins. "I wanted the other half." Then her smile shrinks. "Though, to be honest, I don't think they have much food left. The ship was low on supplies when we docked at Venator, and Alona's people only brought enough for whatever journey they're taking us on."

I nibble the cookie's buttery edge. The sweetness is so comforting. "Have you checked on the others since you escaped?"

Ella bites her lip. "I don't know what they did with Bryce."

My eyes shut. They want to kill her. Planned to kill her the last time they captured her.

"Is she still aboard, Ella?"

"I . . . I don't know."

I can't help but visualize a terrible death for Bryce. Arms gone. Tossed overboard. Screaming.

"But Roderick's alive," she says.

"He is?!"

"I stole meds from the medical room and got them to him. But the brig's filled with guards. They were furious Roderick survived. They wanted him to die in his cell and rot, but Arika kept him alive long enough for me to get him meds."

Ella looks me over, studying my bruises again. I've seen my reflection in the glass. It's not pretty.

"Are you well enough to fight?" she asks.

Ella, the cookie, and this news about Roderick spurred some life into me. I squeeze the cane of my ancestors, feeling the cracks in its surface.

"Last I heard, we're supposed to meet Goerner tonight," Ella says. "They're planning on stripping the *Gladian* to find me once we get there. If we're making a move, we need make it now. So, can you fight?"

My heart starts to pump. Adrenaline courses through me. Everything Father taught me in the Urwin Square returns, fresh.

I grit my teeth as I meet her eyes. "Yes."

CHAPTER 12

"CONRAD!" ELLA HISSES. "LOOK!"

I stop pounding on the door. My sister's pointing at something outside the window. She pulls a spyglass from her belt—must've stolen that, too—and we take turns peering at the specks in the distant sky.

The *Golias*, Admiral Goerner's ship, hovers above a blanket of dark clouds. Enormous cannons rise over the black ship's wide deck. It's a Battlecruiser-class, and it'd been Order's flagship for a decade until Bryce revealed Goerner as an infiltrator. Carriers with vast hangars, and other battlecruisers, and a flock of sparrow fighters encircle it. A few tortons float around, too, their flippers directing them in the air.

A tower rises over the *Golias's* deck, one that seemingly attracts the creatures that surround it. Including the worst thing of all: gorgantauns.

"That tower must be how they do it," Ella breathes. "How they control them."

These gorgantauns are of the southern breed, and they're gigantic class-fives or larger. Many are bulls with thick crests around their furious heads.

We rush back to the door. I've tried pounding for twenty minutes to get the guards' attention, and my fists have gone raw.

Ella and I take turns attacking the door. But the men outside continue chatting casually.

Finally, Ella whispers, "I have to go out there."

"Not without me."

"You won't fit through the vent."

"But you don't know how many are out there. We're doing this together."

"Conrad," she says, meeting my eyes, "we don't have a choice."

I stare at my little sister and her flowing white hair, and I'm reminded of Mother's calmness. The trust I held in her. But Ella's only our mother in appearance. There's a different kind of resolve in her eyes. The kind that Uncle put in her.

Uncle's strong. And he's forged Ella in his image.

Not sure how much I can trust Ella, but we have the same goals right now. And either this works, or we'll both be swallowed in Goerner's grip.

"If there are too many," I say, "you return, and we come up with a new plan."

She nods, but it's too quick. She's an Urwin. She plans to go out fighting. It's better to be taken in, covered in blood, than on your knees and unbruised.

Ella crouches over the vent and squeezes inside. While she squirms away, I pound the door and shout until my throat hurts. I shout so loud that the men roar back at me. But I don't stop because any distraction could cover Ella's approach.

The men talk loudly, trying to drown me out. Suddenly, there's commotion in the hall.

I stop.

And then comes the crash of a dueling cane against the sparks of an electric spear. Voices yell. Ella shouts. Boots shuffle around. People grunt. More steps—maybe from behind her—block off her escape.

I slam my shoulder into the door. C'mon, dammit. Open! Open!

The fighting intensifies. Ella's yelling—the men are yelling.

I feel rotten, ashamed that I'm stuck here. Worse, what if one of the Lantians sends out a comm to the others? The whole crew will come running. And Ella will be overwhelmed—no matter how talented she is with her cane.

Finally, the sounds stop. My shoulder screams in pain. My chest heaves. Breaths are tight.

"Ella?" I say, voice timid. "Ella are you there?"

No response.

"Ella?"

Something shuffles in the hall. The sound of them dragging her away? Off to take her to the brig, or worse, to Alona? This can't be happening. We'll be hauled before Goerner to be tortured or held for ransom. Goerner probably thinks that if the gigataun by itself wasn't enough to make Uncle surrender, the threat of losing his heirs might be.

A pair of steps stops outside the door. The bar slides across, and the next instant, the door cracks open. I'm ready to dive at them. Beat them into the ground and leave their wreckage at my boots. But my mouth drops as I find Ella alone, huffing and sweating. She wipes someone's blood from her cheek with her forearm.

"They didn't get a comm out," Ella says. "At least, I don't think so."

Four men lie on the ground behind her. Full-grown men. Ella can't weigh more than eighty pounds, and she took all of them.

"Are you injured?"

She scowls as if the very notion is offensive. "We need to find Alona. Take back the ship and fly it out of here. We don't have much time."

"Alona's guards have auto-muskets," I say. "We'll need to even the odds."

We drag the men into the cafeteria. After we pull in the last one,

Ella crouches over an unconscious man and laughs as she reaches for his belt.

"What?" I ask.

She raises the brig key. I smile. That'll help us even the odds.

"How many soldiers does Alona have aboard?" I ask.

"Twenty," Ella says. "Maybe more."

Okay, so maybe we won't be able to even the odds. But we'll have surprise on our side. Just so long as—

"The Princess!" a man shouts into his comm device. He's standing in the doorway. "We've found her. She's—"

My cane flies from my hand, and the eagle hits him directly in the forehead. He drops like a sack of grain. Two Lantians appear behind him, and before Ella can charge, I march before her.

My rage ignites. My body's racked with it. I catch my cane from the ground. My body's beaten. I've got a limp. Broken ribs. But the surging adrenaline masks some of the pain. And soon the two men, charging with sparking blue spears, meet my cane.

The dim cafeteria lights up with sparks.

I wince as I smack away the man's attack and jab his chin. Then I crack his chest and send him spinning into the wall. The other man hesitates.

I don't.

His unconscious body crashes before my boots, too, his spear crackling. I kick it away. Another man appears and attempts to slam the door shut, but Ella tosses a spear. It hits him in the throat. He falls, shuddering and coughing. I dive into the hall. My teeth gnash as aches throb through me. But I was taught, as a boy by Father, to fight through pain.

Three more Lantians wait for me in the corridor. I dive through them like a bird of prey. I crack their shoulders, their skulls. And once the last one falls, splashing into his unconscious neighbor's blood, I turn away and retract my cane.

Ella watches me. "Where did you learn to move that way?"

"Father."

"But"—she falters—"but you're hurt. The way you were moving—it was as if you've never lost a duel."

A voice echoes over the communication cube near the closest man's fingers. "Status?" Alona demands. "Did you capture the Princess? Where are you?"

Ella and I stare at each other.

Alona's voice comes again. "Answer me!"

I grab the cube. It's not like our gems. My fingers fiddle around it. No button. Nothing to rotate or press. The hell? Worse, what am I supposed to say? If I stay silent, Alona will send her troops. They'll probably have auto-muskets.

I mutter a few words under my breath, trying to capture the accent of the Lantians. The subtle way that Bryce speaks and gently avoids hard *r* sounds.

"We have the Princess," I say, holding the cube to my lips and hoping it'll send my voice. "She's unconscious. Where should we bring her?"

The cube goes silent. Did Alona buy my accent? Did the message even go through?

Finally, Alona's voice returns. "Bring her to my cabin. We're nearing the *Golias*, and they're preparing their hangar for us. We'll be docking inside in thirty minutes. I'd like to have a chat with her before then."

"We'll be there shortly," I say.

Ella and I smile. Oh, we'll be there shortly, Alona. But we won't be alone.

✦✦✦

Ella and I sneak down the stairs to the darkness of the lowest level. We scurry through the shadows of the crates while my crew sits quietly inside the brig. Pound's enormous silhouette blocks most of the view.

I rise to look over a crate. Even if we get everyone out, we're still outgunned. Six Lantians guard the brig, and one has an auto-musket. They're leaning against the wall, chatting. Laughing about Ella being captured and wondering what Alona's doing with her.

Ella peers at me. I nod.

We pounce from the shadows. The next instant, the woman with the auto-musket hits the ground at my feet, shouting. Roderick and the others stand. I kick away the auto-musket. Then Ella and I work with cruel focus, beating down the Lantians until, finally, I'm facing the last one.

But he's smiling because he's got a comm cube in his hand. Readying to speak. I toss my cane, but he leaps backward. The man prepares to alert the ship over the cube until he realizes he's backpedaled right into the bars of the brig.

Pound's massive arm catches him, and the man yelps as Pound savagely yanks him against the bars. Pound cups a hand over the man's mouth, swipes away the metal cube, and chokes him unconscious.

My crew's all smiles as Ella stuffs the key into the lock. The door swings open, and Keeton and Roderick burst free to hug me. I wince from my ribs.

"Oh, sorry," Roderick says.

"You're alive," I say.

"What?" Roderick says with his goofy grin. "You think a huge knife in my back would stop me?"

We laugh, but it hurts to laugh.

"Ella," Keeton says, turning to my sister, amazed. "You're so like your brother."

"Right. Just as unlikable," Pound says. "About damn time you two got down here. Any longer, and we would've broken ourselves out and saved you."

Roderick snorts.

Arika limps from the brig's shadows and we all go quiet. Pound reaches out to her, and she grips his big arm. Her eyes are purpled with bruises.

"Arika?" I say.

"They beat her," Pound says, "after we tried to escape."

Arika's face twists into a scowl. "Let's kill these bastards."

Suddenly, the nearby comm cube comes alive with Alona's voice. "Where the hell are you? The *Golias's* hangar is opening. We're docking."

"We had a scuffle," I say back. "But we'll be there shortly."

"Where are you?"

I don't answer.

Suddenly, the *Gladian* stops moving. My body goes cold. In minutes we'll be trapped inside the *Golias*. And there's a whole list of things that must go right, or we'll never get out.

Fortunately, Roderick left some spare weapons down here when we ran out of space in munitions, and we've got a stolen auto-musket, too. Pound rips open the crate. We pull out mobile launchers and stuff harpoons into the barrels. I mount a launcher onto my shoulder while Roderick loads it. These harpoons are meant to pierce a class-two gorgantaun.

"This is dangerous as hell," Pound says, grinning. "Firing a harpoon inside the ship." Then he stomps toward the stairs. "C'mon. Let's hunt."

✦✦✦

I peer around the hall's edge. Four Lantians guard the Captain's cabin. I'm about to give the signal for Pound and Roderick to pivot around me and fire their harpoons, but the cabin door opens. Alona's there. And she's dragging Bryce's limp, bloodied body out.

"I'm done with this one," Alona says. "Where is the damn Princess?"

Something about seeing Bryce that way—I lose it. My blood boils, and dots blur my vision. I roar, slide out from the corner, raise my mobile launcher, and fire. The sound, trapped in the corridor, explodes in my ears. My harpoon flies down the hall. It grazes Alona's face, lifts the man and woman beside her off their feet, and hurtles them down the corridor. They stab into the wall and die with shock in their eyes.

Pound and Roderick spin out from the corner. Yelling.

The guards raise their auto-muskets, and the corridor rings with terrible pangs. I drop to the ground. Roderick's harpoon launches another man into the wall. The last Lantian ducks, dodging Pound's attack. He lifts his auto-musket toward us. But I'm up. Running the last bit of the way despite my aching ribs. I beat the final guard with my cane. And the next instant, I'm at Alona. Striking her down. Spitting on her. Shouting.

Alona smacks the ground. She goes into a daze—perhaps unconscious. But as I glimpse Bryce's red, unmoving body, I don't relent. I'm ready to crack in her skull, until a pair of massive arms coil around me. Lift me off the ground.

"We need Alona alive, Conrad!" Keeton steps into my vision. "Think of all the information she has!"

My legs swing at Alona, and I'm still puffing. "Let me go!"

No one hurts my family. No one!

"Get Alona out of here," Keeton says. "Away from Conrad."

Arika catches Alona's collar and drags her into the Captain's cabin.

"We don't have much time," Roderick says. "If Goerner closed his ship's hangar doors, we'll have to blast our way out. Fortunately, I've got just the thing in munitions. Pound, I'll need your help."

"Elise won't stop squirming," Pound grunts, struggling to hold me.

My heart's still raging, but as Keeton gently kneels beside Bryce, I fall into the coldest, deepest waters. And I'm broken and tired and sick. Pound lowers me, and I drop to my knees.

The crew stares at Bryce's body. Silent.

Arika returns from the cabin. "Alona's tied up. I want to fight."

Keeton breaks from her stupor. "You're hurt. Are you sure?"

"I'm no lotcher," Arika says.

"You're tough as gorgantaun steel," Pound says.

Roderick stares at Bryce. "Is she . . . ?"

"Go," I say. "Get us out of here."

"But . . ."

"GO!"

Keeton touches Bryce gently, then stands. "I'll fly."

The crew splits. Arika follows Keeton toward the hatch's ladder. Pound pats my shoulder and rushes to join Roderick.

But I slide to Bryce's side. My fingers gently press against her cold forehead. Her skin's bruised, broken. Blood in her golden hair. I pull her close and cradle her against my body despite my aches. Ella watches us, quiet.

And then a faint hint of breath on my neck.

Bryce is still alive. Barely.

"We need to get her meds now!"

I lift Bryce, and I stagger forward.

The ship lurches. My legs scream in pain, side throbs, but I push through it. Gotta get to the medical room.

Ella stalks ahead of me, scanning the corridors.

Three Lantians shout and appear before us. But Ella extends her cane and tosses it at the nearest Lantian, who has a raised auto-musket. His eyes widen before the cane smashes his face. Ella dodges as another Lantian fires. She dives forward and snatches her cane. With two quick strokes, she fells the final two with a powerful smack to their skulls.

I'm a soggy mess, struggling to hold Bryce. Ella grabs Bryce's legs. Finally, we step into the medical room and lower her onto the bed. The ship rumbles again, so I strap Bryce down. Ella hurries to the drawers.

"Where the hell are they?"

My heart locks up. Did we use them all? We couldn't have. Not unless the Lantians . . .

"Here!" Ella says.

She tosses me the meds. I breathe with relief even with the explosions outside. Then I pull up Bryce's sleeve and inject them into her arm.

The ship rocks again, and I catch the bed to stay steady. Something outside explodes. I should be above. Should be helping the others. But first, I squeeze her hand gently.

"Come back," I whisper in her ear. "Please."

Before long Ella and I exit into the corridor. We run without slowing until finally, we leap onto the ladder leading to the deck and climb. The ship lurches again. When I push open the hatch, a fiery wind blows heat into my face. An enormous explosion rocks the late-afternoon sky. Somehow, we've made it outside the *Golias's* hangar. Pound's laughing as he squeezes the triggers of the flame turret. Golden flames swirl in the open air, melting enemy sparrows. The one-manned fighters drop from the sky.

Ella and I climb out against the fierce winds.

In the distance the enemy fleet fires, sending explosives after us.

Keeton's already standing on the helm platform, glass helm bubble sliding shut. Ten golden strings, all connected to rings on her fingers, give her command of the ship, and she yells, shoving her hands forward. The *Gladian* responds, launching away with ferocious speed.

Two class-six gorgantauns screech. Their bellows sting my eardrums. They wind up their tails and launch after us, their mouths ready to chomp off our stern and consume our engine.

Keeton maneuvers us sharply to the right, and the gorgantauns shoot past us, roaring in frustration. She shoves the strings forward again with more intensity.

I tumble to the ground from the sudden burst. My exhausted arms shake as I push myself upright. Then my fingers crank the dial on my belt, and my magboots snap to the deck. I try lifting a harpoon launcher but can't get it more than a few inches off the deck. My strength's gone. All of it.

Sparrows trail after us with the gorgantauns. They're shooting white lights that sink into the *Gladian's* metal. Arika roars and launches a harpoon. It stabs a sparrow's cockpit, and the fighter spins wildly and collides with the other.

Keeton screams at the strings, willing the ship to unbelievable speeds. Nearly wipes off my goggles. My feet slide back, even with the magboots at full strength. I slip and fall, and try regaining my feet before I slide weakly into a railing net.

The gorgantauns wail.

Pound laughs. "Can't keep up with us, you bastards!"

More shots sparkle the sky near our stern. But the gorgantauns fall behind. The sparrows lose pace. And soon we're flying into open airs, away from Goerner's fleet.

Once we're free, I roll out from the net and exhale with relief, knowing that the *Gladian* is ours again. And not only did we escape Goerner's fleet, but we know their location.

The King's fleet will be coming for them.

CHAPTER 13

UNCLE'S QUIET OVER THE COMM AS I RECOUNT OUR CAPture on Venator. Once I give him the coordinates to Goerner's fleet, he orders the *Dreadnought* Captain to speed to the Northern Airs. Uncle knows Goerner will be long gone by the time they arrive, but they're coming anyway.

"And your prisoners?" he asks. "The dirt-eaters?"

"Lantians," I say.

"What?"

"They're called Lantians. The people from the Below are Lantians."

"Whatever they are called, what have you done with them?"

I'm seated at my desk in the Captain's cabin, the descending sun glowing gold on my bruised skin. Still aching from my injuries, but I've taken meds, and my ribs have already started to recover.

"The prisoners are locked in makeshift cages. Sixteen of them."

"Sixteen?" He pauses. "Impressive that you managed to escape."

"It wouldn't have been possible without Ella."

"Oh?"

I detail some of her heroic feats.

"Yes," he says, "she has learned well. Remind her that she has earned her first cane. I am bringing it with me."

I say nothing.

"Now," Uncle says. "Interrogate the compliant prisoners but toss the stubborn ones overboard."

I almost cough. What? I'm no executioner. I'll fight in battle, but murdering defenseless people?

"Uncle, I planned to deliver them to a Hunter outpost."

"The Skylands don't need dirt-eaters—particularly ones who offer us nothing in return. They're a drain on resources."

A chill climbs my spine. These Lantians are living, breathing people with families of their own. This feels wrong. No, it *is* wrong.

"Uncle—"

His voice snaps. "What mercy did they provide the Skylands when they brought down Ironside? There is no moral high ground here, Conrad. Take them to your deck. Force them to talk. If not . . ." He pauses, letting me finish the thought for him. "Keep Alona of Mizrahi alive regardless. She's leverage that may prove useful. Understand?"

My skin flushes hot. I've not forgotten the lesson Father taught me when he threw me onto the island with the prowlon. It was either the prowlon or me. But it can't always be that black and white. There must be some gray. There must be a path that doesn't turn me as rotten as my opponents.

Be better than what the world intends.

"Understand?" Uncle repeats, irritated.

My jaw clenches. "Yes."

"Good. Your escape has proven, once again, that you are a true Urwin. Rising is in our blood. So you're aware," he says, "the battle at Venator became a slaughter. After the Below's initial attack, we triumphed. Master Koko was among the targets. They have failed to assassinate her." I sink into my chair with relief. Koko is alive. Uncle continues. "The tales of your escape will inspire some confidence in the Urwins once again."

Then he stops and lets out a long sigh. The comm goes quiet, and when his voice returns, it's tinged with irritation.

"Ironside fell under our watch, but Venator is our first victory—and we need to stay the course. Admiral Goerner must fall. In two days, join us at Holmstead. It's time we return to our island. Once there, I expect a full report on your prisoners."

Then the gem goes dark.

I sit in silence, frozen still. I should be excited about Master Koko's survival, about the victory at Venator, and about returning to where I was born, but all my thoughts are on the murderous task Uncle just ordered.

✦✦✦

Bryce is still unconscious. I sit by her bedside in the medical room, holding her calloused hand while I explain Uncle's orders. I tell her my father taught me to be merciless from the time I was a toddler. That he forced me to duel weak opponents in the Urwin Square. He'd even bribe elderly Lows with a few coins to face me in a duel. And I'd beat them for Father. If I didn't, he'd come at me without reservation.

"I just don't know if I can do this, Bryce," I whisper. "I'm not an executioner."

Bryce breathes lightly. She'd know what to do with the prisoners. I wish I could wait for her to wake, but we can't keep the prisoners here. We don't have enough food for them. Worse, one managed to escape his makeshift cell and attacked Ella.

His mistake. She beat the hell out of him.

"Bryce needs rest, Captain."

I turn around and find Arika standing in the doorway. She's

completely recovered from her beating, and her limited skills have been the closest we have to a Scholar Doctor's.

"When will she wake?" I ask.

"No way to know for sure. Tomorrow? Three days?"

She feels Bryce's forehead. "I understand why you didn't tell me about her origins, Captain. But I'm not an idiot. I knew something was up. From now on," she says, meeting my eyes dead-on, "if you want me to be part of this crew, you don't leave me out again."

I stare at her. Tongue locked. If I were any other Captain, I might scold her and remind her of her rank and that I could easily replace her. But I learned in the Gauntlet how valuable good Cooks are. If you have a terrible Cook, you have an unhappy crew. Food heals.

Arika is a healer.

Furthermore, she's earned my trust. I consider her an ally, and to be honest, I hope we'll become friends over time.

"You are with us now, Arika."

She nods, then perhaps to show there's no hard feelings, grins a little. "Okay, time to go, Captain."

I nod, squeeze Bryce's arm, and stand. Need to talk with the crew anyway, so I call everyone to meet in my cabin. Well, everyone except Ella. I don't want her to have any part of this. A few minutes later, my stunned crew stares at me as I explain the King's orders for our prisoners.

Roderick turns green. Keeton shuts her eyes. And Arika stares at the floor in silence.

"What's the problem?" Pound raises his hands in confusion. "This is war, and they attacked us first. King Ulrich's a bastard, but he's not wrong."

"Don't you have any compassion, Pound?" Keeton asks.

"Compassion?" Pound laughs. "Those dirt-eaters murdered thousands of innocents."

"What the cuss, man?" Roderick explodes. "We all heard that term on Venator. So, you're going to call Bryce a dirt-eater now, too?"

"Right," Keeton says, staring at Pound. "What if some of our prisoners are like her? Good people, I mean."

Pound pauses a moment. "Well, if they were like Bryce, they wouldn't have beaten us when we were defenseless or left Roderick to die in the cell."

The room falls silent.

"Murdering them for not speaking," Keeton says finally. "But we can't just keep them here, either. We don't have enough food. Not enough weapons. We're low on everything."

"More reasons to eliminate the dir—the *Lantians* who don't talk immediately," Pound says. "I'll handle the interrogation myself if the rest of you lotchers can't stomach it."

"Are you really this quick to kill them off?" Roderick asks.

"We're giving those people a choice," Pound says. "They cooperate? They live. They don't . . . ? We can absolve ourselves of any sense of immorality here because they're making the choice. It's not as if we have another option."

"If Pound's so eager to become the interrogator and executioner," Arika says, "then I say we let him handle it. He can have it all on his conscience."

Pound meets her eyes, his face reddens, and he goes quiet.

"How about we leave the Lantians with the nearest Hunter outpost?" Roderick suggests.

"We can't take sixteen Lantians to an outpost," Keeton says. "They'll kill them, too."

Roderick massages his forehead. "We can't let them go, either. Imagine if we let them go and they kill someone. How would we live with that?"

My fingers play with the eagle at the end of my cane. Father's words invade my mind. *When the desire for mercy tries to overwhelm you, think hate. Nothing should stand in your way of rising. Not friends. Not the world. If you let your guard down, even for an instant, it'll cut you to Low.*

And as I recall the moment he told me this, I suddenly realize an alternative. Not a perfect one, and it won't free our consciences completely, but it will leave their fate up to the winds.

My mouth opens, and as I explain my thoughts to the crew, they listen quietly. No one argues—though Arika shifts a little uncomfortably.

It's the only way.

"But can't the Lantians control the beasts?" Pound asks. "They've been controlling gorgantauns and tortons and whatever else they want."

"Not these things, no," I say.

The room quiets. No one's happy about my suggestion, but they're not distraught, either. The mark of a fair compromise is when no one's happy.

"Keeton, Pound," I say. "Go to the command room and check over the maps. See what you find."

Once they're gone, Arika approaches me.

"Captain, the Lantians brought only a bit of food aboard. I'm rationing it for the crew, but there isn't enough for the prisoners. I'll prepare lunch with what I can." She pauses. "Hopefully, we'll be able to keep it down."

After she goes, Roderick stares at me. "This is where we're at, huh?"

My whole weight sinks into my chair. "I don't know what else to do."

Roderick nods, starts toward the door, then stops. "It's going to get worse, you know. We're still trying to hold onto our humanity, but at some point, with the way this war is headed, we'll all have demons following us. I just hope we can recognize whatever's left of us afterward."

CHAPTER 14

THE NEXT MORNING, BRYCE WAKES.

She's sitting upright on the medical bed, spooning the thin soup Arika brought her. It seems to give her energy because I sense strength behind her blue gaze again.

I'm seated on the chair beside her, my hand near hers. It's just us, and there's so many things I want to say. So many things I need to know.

Bryce slurps more of the golden soup. "Where are the prisoners?"

"No hug?"

"You're an Urwin. You don't hug."

"You're an exception."

She smirks, lowers the bowl onto the tray, and turns serious. "Where are the prisoners, Conrad?"

I lean back and tell her that early this morning, we flew to a series of isolated islands. Ones filled with aggressive bears. We gave the prisoners the chance to either talk and stay with us or walk the gangway to the island. Only three of the prisoners decided to stay with us.

She drops her spoon. "You let them go?!"

My body prickles. My voice comes out a little defensive. "They can't control bears, Bryce."

"Of course they can't control bears. Conrad, Lantians can *sense* one another. It's how we're able to gather when we're sent Above."

"I know. But those islands are remote, no reason for ships to go anywhere near them. Besides, I—I didn't want to kill them."

Bryce stares at me. "What?"

Then she goes silent as I explain what Uncle commanded me to do. And as the words spill out of me, her face wrinkles with disgust.

"You are better than your uncle," she says, "but all those Lantians, they'll be found. It's a matter of time. Some might die from bears or hunger, but many of them will make it. You basically freed them."

I exhale with regret. What the hell was I thinking? I should've just kept them around for a couple more hours until Bryce woke up. But they were already making escape attempts and attacking the crew. Our makeshift cells were not permanent solutions.

Bryce leans forward and clutches my hand. She's a little wobbly, and her face is still puffy from the bruises, but she meets my eyes with steadfast strength.

"You are a good person, Conrad. In a sky full of the heartless, you have risen above and proved that not everyone up here is birdshit." She exhales. "This was my fault."

"I'm not letting you take the fall for this."

"If I'd been honest with you, you'd have never let them go."

We sit in silence for a few seconds. She's right about that. So why has she been keeping information like that from me, especially when it risks the safety of our crew? But even if she had told me, what then? I'd just keep a ship full of prisoners and lie to Uncle until I'm discovered? It's as if I didn't learn the lesson Father taught me with the prowlon. It's either me, or it's them.

"Conrad," she says.

I look up, and there's resolve on her face. Her shoulders are slouched. "I need to tell you something."

I stop breathing for a moment. I've been waiting for this. The whole world seems to have gone still. She's going to tell me something big, something that she's kept hidden from everyone.

Her fingers fiddle with the blanket. "This is a secret that every captured Lantian has taken with them to their end. They kept this secret, even as their arms were cut off, even as they were about to be thrown into the sky." Her voice is soft, tremoring. "We've kept this secret safe because if we break it, our families will be put to death."

Her eyes water. "But I don't have a family."

My mouth is dry. I keep her hand in mine to let her know I'm here.

"You wanted to know how the torton found us?" She pulls away, slides down her collar and leans forward, exposing the back of her neck. "Look."

My eyes narrow. A small, pink scar stripes the base of her neck. It's so minor, so indiscernible, that I probably wouldn't have noticed it without her pointing it out.

She rises and looks at me. "I need you to understand why I'm revealing this secret. The Lantians will keep killing, Conrad. The capital was just the beginning. The gigataun will come again and again. My people believe the Skylands will surrender if they drop one or two more islands. That's their hope, because they don't think they can win a long, drawn-out war with the Skylands.

"But your people won't surrender. You are products of your Meritocracy, your merciless desire to rise. In your society, losing means exile. Your uncle exiled you because he wanted you to prove yourself worthy of being an Urwin. Only when you proved that you were strong were you welcomed back. Pound lost his whole family because he lost a duel. The Skylands will never surrender."

I don't argue.

"This is something my people won't understand. We are tough, like you, but we are not so individualistic. We work together for the common good—even though our leaders are often corrupt. We bow to our community leaders—our Council. We trust their decisions, even when some of us starve and die for them. We do what's best for the group."

She breathes out.

"This mark on my neck . . . every infiltrator sent above has one. It's from my symbion."

"Symbion?"

"My people built their entire society around biomechanical beasts. Gorgantauns. Calamauns. Blobons. Pishons. Prowlons. And we have them inside of us, too."

I stare at her, stunned. "You have a living thing inside you?"

"It's not alive, exactly. It's part of me. In the Below, there's no greater honor than being given one. It's like being Select status in your world. You're Chosen for it."

I go quiet trying to process all of this. "And you can sense when others have one?"

"I knew who Admiral Goerner was immediately."

"You told me it was his accent."

"Well, he has one, yes. But do you think I'd tell you, while I was trapped in a cell, that I had a symbion in my neck?" She scoffs. "While your uncle was listening? They'd have experimented on me. Cut it out while I was alive."

My mouth shuts and opens again. "Is it—What does it do?"

"It's better to be shown. May I?"

I bite my lip, uncertain what she means, then nod.

"Don't be afraid." She touches the back of her neck, and her fingers start sparking. "As far as I know, you are the first person in the sky to experience this." She reaches for my hand. "I'll be right with you."

"What do you m—ouch, Bryce! What—?"

✦✦✦

My eyes widen because I'm not in the medical room anymore. Hell, I'm not even on the *Gladian*. I'm standing in a dark tunnel full of craggy rocks.

It's not real, Conrad. It's like a memory, but more.

I whirl around in panic. "Bryce?"

Her voice comes from somewhere distant, as if it's only in my head. *This is an experience.*

I blink in shock at my hands because they're not my hands. They're small and dirty. Fingernails scraped, like when I was a Low, but they're gray, indicating massive malnourishment.

"Bryce, what have you done to me?"

You're in my experience. You will feel what I felt, Bryce whispers. *See what I saw.*

Suddenly, a gnawing ache for food stabs my gut. It's a hunger I experienced when I was a Low. The kind of hunger that makes you dig desperately into garbage. That makes you eat rotten things and swallow long, hard breaths so you can keep moldy bread down.

I start down the rocky tunnel, exploring—but I'm not really controlling myself—because I'm in Bryce's mind, her head. Dirt grits beneath my bare heels as my eyes struggle to adjust to the meager light.

In the Below, Bryce says, *we live in colonies beneath the earth called* Zones. *Like the Skylands, we have our rich and our poor, and like the Skylands, there are those who have corrupted the original intentions of our society.*

I stare at the cold tunnels around me. This can't be real. I'm on the *Gladian*. This isn't my body. I shouldn't be able to feel these things or have someone else's thoughts in my head.

Conrad, you're going to experience something that happened to me more than five years ago.

I continue wandering. Fear in my heart and heat growing in my eyes. Is it my fear or Bryce's? Either way, it nearly overwhelms me. I'm so damn scared, and I don't know why. I'm really worried about a noise. Some chittering sound that's coming from the darkness. An instinct's telling me those dark tunnels ahead of me are forbidden.

It's like I'm gaining Bryce's knowledge along with her experience.

On my eleventh birthday, Bryce says, *my dad told me he was taking me to get a gift.*

Suddenly, I'm blinking in a new place. It's a home, except this is a home carved into rock. I'm standing in a room, the hearth room. It swells with life from a smokeless fire in the center. Connected tunnels shoot into the deeper regions of the home leading to the rooms of Bryce's family.

Somehow, I know these things.

I'm rubbing my tiny, pale hands over the fire when a wrinkled man with spikey blond hair kneels before me. It's Bryce's father: Farlan. He smiles and touches my cheek.

Decrepit furniture surrounds us while a thin broth boils near the fire. A young man in the corner has a sour look as he leans against the rocky wall. His name is Damon. He watches us, unsmiling.

I recognize him. The clay sculpture Bryce has been making in her room on the *Gladian*. It's him. That's her brother.

Damon walks away, following a tunnel deeper into the home. I watch him go until Dad rests his hand on my shoulder, and all my concerns about Damon dissipate. Dad's the protector, the strength. He's the man who kept my family—or Bryce's family—going even after Mom got lung rot. He has Bryce's piercing blue eyes, and her determined jaw.

Dad told me we'd have to walk to the quiet tunnels to get my birthday present. Bryce pauses. *The dangerous ones.*

"Is Damon coming, too?" I ask, hopeful.

Dad shakes his head. "Just us."

"I want Damon to come."

"He has to work."

"He always has to work."

"That's because we need money to eat."

I frown but laugh when he lifts me as though I'm still his tiny girl. I let him because part of me still wants to be his little girl. Back when things were better, when we lived in Zone 7 and Mom was still alive. When we didn't need ration cards. That was back before the Council said everyone needed to sacrifice for some weapon the Designers were making that needed the food. The Council promised that once we used the weapon on our enemies above the toxic clouds, we'd rise.

Then we'd have all the food we ever wanted.

I wanted to be Dad's little girl again because when I was, we didn't live in Zone 20. We didn't live near the unControllables. I almost shudder at the thought of them—scaled monstrosities that live in the crevices of the dark.

The unControllables are the failed creations of the Designers, Bryce whispers. *Try as we might, we haven't been able to get rid of them. We seal off tunnels, but they still come for our Zones, our people. The poor live in the Zones closer to the unControllables, far from the rich. The poor keep the monsters fed and less likely to dig deeper and go for the rich. The rich stay safe, while the poor—they must always be prepared, or they might get dragged off into the darkness. This sacrifice, we're told, is for the greater good. A collective need. Those who live in the first ten Zones? They're the smartest. The strongest. The ones who can contribute the most.*

The poor's contribution is keeping the strong safe. They're also expected to mine in the most dangerous tunnels.

Dad's holding my hand and leading me out the rusty door. Now we're in the tunnels I call my neighborhood. These are quiet tunnels. Glowlons create a moving pattern along the ceiling. The harmless insects glow in light blue. Blinking as they scurry about. They're almost like stars. I wish they were stars. Real ones.

In the distance some merchants sit on the rocky ground, their wares resting on long rugs.

"Farlan," a man says as we approach, "I've got new mining equipment from Zone 2."

"Zone 2?" Dad says. "Why are they sending it out here? Is it broken?"

The man smiles and glances down the tunnel. "Smuggled. Cheap. Real cheap."

Dad tugs my hand past the man. "Not cheap enough."

"It'll get you ahead of the others in the mines, Farlan," the man calls after us. "You'll be able to move your family away from the Deeps again."

Dad pauses for an instant, then he pulls me away. Dad usually ignores the peddlers; he's lost too much money on things that he learned too late had no value.

We exit into the Central Square of Zone 20. The Mayor's home rises over the square—the one wooden building in the entire Zone. A clock tower reaches the rocky ceiling. This area houses several of the Zone's nicest shops—just holes in the walls—but they have windows, and sparkly, cheap jewelry on display. Mostly things that come from the Zones closer to the Council Center in Zone 1.

A massive glass ball filled with glowlons hovers from the ceiling. When I squint at it, it's like I'm glimpsing the sun. Like the best days on the surface, after a rain, when the acid clouds are not as thick.

The butcher, a stocky woman named Sumerset, slams her cleaver against piles of white meat. The meat's carved from beasts created by the Designers. Docile creatures. The kind that need little food to survive and keep us fed even though their flesh is tough and flavorless. Other Zones get the luxury of flavor and texture. When we were in Zone 7, we got real chickens. Not manufactured. The meat was so sweet, so tender and juicy, that just thinking about it makes me almost cry.

We pass the schooling tunnels where I learned our history, such as when we fought the Eagle Empire before they fled into the sky and left us behind. But the Designers sent their creations up, too. So the Skylands created a wall of acid clouds to protect themselves. A wall that was supposed to be impenetrable. We've found ways through, but it's difficult.

There are always theories about how we can take down the acid clouds—because we all want to stand safely on the surface, under the sun, and see the stars. Many Councilors got themselves elected because they claimed to know how to eliminate the acid clouds.

Liars.

Dad pulls me past people in grimy clothing who gather around the water pump. We go down tunnel after tunnel. Farther away from the muffled noises of the crowd. My feet ache from the long walk. The tunnels get darker. Fewer glowlons skitter about on the walls and ceiling.

"Where are we going, Dad?"

"The Deeps."

"The Deeps? But they're forbidden."

He says nothing. My heart bangs against my ribs as we approach a huge gate. Dad steps to the left, taps a control panel, and uses his Miner card to unlock it. The gate cracks open, and a dark tunnel waits ahead of us—like an open mouth that leads into decay and death. Not even the glowlons go past the gates.

"You left my present in the Deeps?" I ask. "Why?"

"Had to smuggle it in from Zone 4," he says stiffly, tugging me past the open gate. "I didn't want anyone to find it."

Warning signs in bright yellow depict strange beasts above us. The unControllables. School taught me to never go past the yellow signs.

"Dad?"

He says nothing, doesn't even look at me. His grip tightens, cutting the circulation in my hand. We slip into the darkness.

"Dad, you're hurting me."

He keeps going. Tugging me along with him. My eyes grow wet. I don't understand. We go on for several minutes, even pass a sealed tunnel where something broke through, leaving rocks scattered on the path.

Suddenly, a shadow dances behind us. Something chitters, and my skin tingles. You don't want to be around anything that chitters.

I was the youngest of four siblings, Bryce says. *Dad had a lot of mouths to feed, and the mining company was cutting back on work. I realize now why he did what he did. But that doesn't make it right.*

Dad stops right in the darkness. Barely visible. Then he bends down to my level and hugs me tight. It's the kind of hug that hurts my ribs. The kind of hug that feels like the end of all hugs.

"Wait here," he says.

"Dad, I'm scared."

"I'll be back. I'm going to get your present. It's too dangerous for us to walk together out here."

"But Dad. It's—"

"Bryce," he says in his stern voice. "*Stay.*"

He starts walking, but I try following him. Even after his commands. Then he runs. Runs without saying anything else to me. Runs at such a pace that I fall and scrape my knees.

Tears well in my eyes.

"DAD!"

He left me. In the deepest of the Deeps.

I hug myself and cry. Call for him. When he doesn't come, I wipe my nose, stand, and aimlessly wander in the dark. My hands blindly feel for the walls. Need to find glowlons or the gate and get back to Zone 20 and get home. Prove to Dad that I deserve to live. I'll eat less. I'll polish shoes. I'll stop schooling and go to the mines with him.

Anything.

I stumble into a new tunnel. A meager bit of light glows at the end.

A single glowlon. My chest swells with hope and my feet eat up ground as I hurry toward it. I must be close to the gate.

Something chitters.

I freeze and slowly glance back.

Suddenly, terror travels my skin as, out of the gloom, a chitleon crawls from the broken seal of a collapsed tunnel. It's a long, pale creature with twelve legs, shiny pincers, and a dozen red eyes.

Frozen horror surges through me.

The creature's sharp head turns in my direction, then squeals like a horrible pig. Its pinchers gleefully snap as it charges.

I run. Run so hard that blood tickles the back of my throat. Run so hard that I hardly realize the rocky tunnel's shredding my bare feet. But as I'm running, I slam into something warm and I hit the ground, shouting.

Something cups over my mouth, shielding my cries, and drags me into the darkness. I squirm and struggle.

I'm pressed against a wall. No, it's going to eat me. Dad left me out here to get eaten alive because I'm supposed to die for the greater good. For the rest of the family. I'm the runt. The weakest.

No. I won't die. I'll claw and fight.

Then a voice whispers in my ear. "It's me. Damon."

I nearly evaporate with relief. My older brother holds me in his protective arms. I want to cry. But I can't—because the chitleon's still out there. Its long, sharp legs clicking against the rock as its antennae search for us.

While we hid, Bryce says, *Damon told me that once we got away, we'd run off together. We'd sneak into Zone 18 or 19. He said he'd take care of us. He was a good miner. A strong miner. For a moment I had hope for his dream because the chitleon skittered past our spot.* Bryce's voice quakes. *But then the chitters returned.*

We run for the light. Damon outpaces me. He's seventeen. A strong boy with long legs.

The chitleon gains. Its legs skittering across the rocks. I glance back and scream as it squeals again. Its pincers snip at me, nearing my ankles. Damon tugs me to keep up. But I can't. Just can't. I'm not strong like him.

That's when something crosses Damon's face. Something I can't describe. The next second, he hangs his Miner key chain over my neck, rips his pickax from his belt, and turns to face the chitleon. He dives at the creature, shouting.

"Damon," I say, sliding to a stop, tears in my eyes. "No!"

"Run, Bryce."

I lift a rock to fight with him. The chitleon, like a horrible centipede, lifts its head and front legs off the ground and stabs at my brother.

Damon swings the pickax against the beast's rusty, metallic legs. "I'll hold it off. Go. Bryce. I can—" He swings again, but the thing cuts out his legs beneath him. Before I can blink, he's screaming. Screaming as the thing rips into him, cutting him into pieces. Shredding him with its legs that are as sharp as swords.

I'm crying. Tossing rocks.

"Run!" he gurgles. "Bryce, RUN!"

I can't leave him. But as his cries weaken, as his fight slows, an instinct takes over. My legs start churning and I abandon my dying brother.

"Don't stop." His dying voice echoes as the chitleon drags him away. "Don't stop, Bryce."

I run with watery eyes. Run until I find the glowlons again. Run until I reach the closed gate. I desperately swipe his Miner key card and soon I'm out of the Deeps and back in the Central Square of Zone 20. People are going about their day, completely unaware of what I just witnessed. An old man looks at me and notices the tears on my dirty face. He approaches, perhaps to help, but I run from him like I ran from the chitleon.

I'm crying and tasting the snot and the salt of my tears. I walk past my home. Past everywhere I know. Just wandering with bloody feet, my arms hugging my ribs. My stomach's knotted with guilt and sadness and anger. I can't help but call out to Mom as if she'll come back to life and find me. She'll invite me to curl into the warm blanket with her. I'll nuzzle against her neck as though I'm still the little girl she kissed at night.

But she's gone. Damon's gone. My family's gone.

Everything is gone.

✦✦✦

Suddenly, I feel a jolt on my hand. Except it's not Bryce's hand anymore. It's my real hand. And I'm snapped back into the medical room of the *Gladian*. Bryce sits before me, body shaking, her eyes red with tears.

I pull her close and hug her tight. There's no words I can say. Nothing I can say to make anything better. Finally, she pushes against my chest so she can look at me.

"You must tell your uncle," she says. "This is how the Skylands can identify any infiltrator anywhere. The mark on our necks—the symbions. This information will alter the war. It means . . . the deaths of thousands of Lantians." She wraps her arms over her legs. "But the Lantians won't stop. They're desperate. There are too many, like me, who were abandoned in the tunnels. They won't stop, because to them killing Skylanders, even innocents, will help the greater good."

"Bryce, are you—"

"Go," she says. "Tell him."

I touch her hand, but she shoves me hard in the chest. And I realize how horrible this is for her. Abandoned by her father. Abandoned by her people. Losing her brother. Never seeing her siblings again.

Then faced with the growing war and more innocent deaths, she chose to reveal the Below's greatest secret. She's choosing what she hopes will help end the war. And I—I'm getting the feeling that she's choosing to trust me.

My heart aches for her. I meet her eyes, then turn and hurry to the Captain's cabin—off to deliver this war-altering intel to the one man I cannot stand.

But as I'm reaching for the special comm gem in my cabin, my thoughts are not on how this will help the Skylands or how it'll help us in the war.

I'm thinking about Bryce, and the little girl she once was.

And I realize I've got tears on my cheeks.

CHAPTER 15

"THIS NEWS ABOUT THE SYMBIONS," UNCLE TELLS ME OVER the comm, "may just save the Skylands."

My fingers drum on the desk while he alerts his advisers of this vital information. They'll soon share it with the Trades and the rest of the Skylands.

"Conrad," Uncle says, returning to the comm, "how many prisoners remain on your ship?"

"Four including Alona."

"Have you begun interrogating the compliant ones?"

"I plan to."

My stomach knots, fearing he'll ask what I did with the other prisoners. It's dangerous lying to Uncle.

"It seems you have disposed of the excess," he says. "We will meet tomorrow at the rendezvous point. You and your crew have earned a rest and a restocking of supplies." He pauses. "However, Ella will return with me."

This news should cut me, or make me burn with anger, but I simply exhale a long breath. "Understood."

"Good. After your short rest, dear Nephew, I'm sending you on a task that will win us this war." I pause, remembering this mission of his. "Until then, I must discuss this news about the symbions with the Masters, the Archduchesses, and Archdukes."

The comm goes gray and I sit, tapping my fingers against my knees. I won't be able to sleep after that conversation. For a moment I consider going to Bryce, but she needs sleep, so I go above and stand under the stars. Chilly wind bites my exposed skin. I zip up my jacket, raise the collars, and lean against the bow's railing. The Northern Skies are bitter cold at night. I'd almost forgotten how wintry their embrace is.

Instinctively, I reach for the gold chain on my neck. Ella's necklace. But my fingers find nothing because I no longer have it. My chest is hollow. That necklace was a promise to Ella that we'd always be together. That we'd rise in this unforgiving world as brother and sister. I returned it to her when we reunited. Does she still have it?

I plummet into melancholy.

Ella and I weren't supposed to repeat the relationship Uncle had with my father. We weren't supposed to battle over being first in line.

My eyes shut. I need more time with her.

The Father part of me says I should ignore Uncle's orders. I should take this ship, fly off into the skies with my sister, and force her to see reason.

But if I stole Ella away, what would Mother think?

While my breath mists the air, I can almost see Mother standing beside me, her white hair whipping in this cold wind as she tells me to be better. Tells me it'd be wrong to take Ella against her will.

Mother's voice has become less defined since her death, but it returns now, clear as the crisp air on my cheeks.

You gave Ella the chance to find a better way, but you can't force her on that path. She must follow her own winds.

She isn't you, Conrad. She is herself.

She wants to go back to Uncle.

Let her.

This realization punctures me. My eyes grow wet, and my head lowers. Uncle ruined everything. Took away my family. Took Mother away from me. My sister. Everything I had. And I can't get Ella back, not the way she was, no more than I can get Father back. Or get Mother back.

I wipe my eyes, exhale, straighten my jacket, and turn to head belowdecks to finally get the sleep my body desperately needs because tomorrow . . . tomorrow I say goodbye to my sister.

✦✦✦

Early in the morning, I'm walking the cool corridors of the third level when Arika's voice comes over the comm.

"I found some food in the storage room, but I need help getting to it."

"Did you say *food*?" Roderick answers over the comm. "I can be there in thirty seconds."

I tap my gem. "Too late, Rod. I'm already halfway down the stairs."

"Ugh. Don't eat it all, you cuss."

I hop off the final stair and enter the shadows of the lowest level. Arika's standing between the aisles of storage crates, away from the sleeping prisoners.

I step beside her. "How can I help?"

Her hands rest on her hips. "Apparently, a box of canned cakes fell in with the surplus harpoons. But I can't lift all these harpoons by myself to get to them."

Together we lift harpoons from the crate, and it's not long until she's laughing as she hoists the box of canned desserts above her head in triumph. I smile a little, but my empty stomach's even happier.

We start up the stairs, leaving the darkness behind us. When we get to the third floor, I consider checking in on Keeton and the engine, but I glance at Arika and realize we've not spoken much since Venator.

"Arika," I say, "I'm sorry about Declan. I know you were . . . close to him."

She's quiet. Perhaps she'll respond with some guarded answer. Many would because of Meritocracy. Afraid of revealing weakness. Afraid that somehow, this information will be used against them, and they'll never be able to rise.

Instead, she opens up. "As much as I've integrated with this crew," she says softly, our boots tapping the stairs, "Declan and I . . . we were the outsiders. This crew," she hesitates, "you are all close. It's not like my crew from the Gauntlet. My former crew—you wouldn't have believed what we did to one another."

"Tell me."

She side-eyes me. "Well, early on, our Cook gave the Captain food poisoning on purpose. A couple of days later, we found our Cook locked in the freeze box, the chillglobe cranked to high. He was frozen solid."

"Damn," I say, grimacing. "Is that how you became your ship's Cook?"

She shakes her head. "I was the Quartermaster, but I secretly wanted to be the Cook even though it's a Low rank in Hunter." She pauses. "In fact, I was supposed to be Selected by Agriculture. Become one of their famous Chefs. Like my parents."

We step off the stairs and walk down the second level.

"My family hasn't spoken to me since Master Koko called my name," she says. "They were all Selected by Agriculture. My brothers and sisters and parents command the cornfields, the beef farms, and the massive restaurants on Greenrye Island." She grins sadly. "They don't know I still cook."

I pause, recognizing her pain. The pain of dealing with unreasonable familial expectations, and the horrors Meritocracy foists upon the young.

"Have you tried contacting them?" I ask.

Her face twists, bitter. "There's no pleasing them. A couple of months ago, I sent them a letter telling them I was a Cook for the Prince. Thought it'd impress them. They never answered."

"Arika, I'm sorry."

She shrugs.

Soon we reach the cafeteria, and I push the door open. The wide windows give us a glimpse of the early sun and golden clouds. She sweeps inside, and I follow her toward the kitchen.

I change the subject. "So, you were on the *Laminan* during the Gauntlet?"

She nods and slices open the box, revealing eight cans inside. Each about four inches tall. She stacks the cans on the counter and tosses the box.

"We lost several of our crew," she says, "but we didn't kill a single gorgantaun. I had no friends on the ship; in fact,I didn't have many in the Academy, either. The only friend I had there was—" She pauses. "Well, she became the Navigator for the *Calamus*."

"The *Calamus*? They almost beat us."

"She and I probably got too close in the Academy if you know what I mean. Things didn't work out. She was chosen by a different crew, and we went our separate ways."

"Do you miss her?"

She pauses again.

"I'm sorry," I say. "I've overstepped."

"No," she says, shaking her head. "It's fine. She and I . . . well, sometimes after you get to know a person more, you realize you're just too different. Even so, you still respect them. Does that make sense?"

"Perfectly."

She grins.

"So, now you're the Cook here," I say.

"And proud of it. I love cooking." She taps cakes out onto a tray. "Don't get me wrong, Captain, I want to rise. But I want to be a Cook."

I raise a skeptical eyebrow.

She laughs and slides the tray into the crystal-heated oven. "The Hunter Cooks of Venator. The Head Chef. They feed hundreds. Usually, they're on the older side, but there are always excellent up-and-comers. That's who I want to be."

I never even considered that was an option. Then again, there are thousands of Hunters on Venator. Master Gunners who devise weapons for the whole Trade, and Mechanics who work closely with members of the Trade of Architect to devise new engines and ships.

"Arika, if you got a job like that, you'd have to leave us."

"That's Meritocracy for you," she says. "We must sail our own winds. But we can always be friends, yes?"

I grin. "Yes. Always."

After she glazes the cakes and slides the tray out under the heatlamps, I tap my comm gem for the crew.

"Arika prepared dessert for breakfast."

Within a minute Pound and Roderick burst into the room and grab a plate.

"You both only get one portion," she says sternly.

Pound scowls. Roderick, who already shoved his cake in his mouth, raises his hands as if he hasn't eaten anything.

I laugh.

"Haven't heard that in a while," Keeton says, eyes smiling as she enters the cafeteria. "You have a nice laugh, Conrad."

"Nice? He sounds like a drunk horse," Pound mutters.

Roderick snorts.

Soon the whole crew enters, except for Bryce, who's still resting, and Ella, who's likely sleeping in. After everyone takes a helping, Arika lowers onto the table beside us and forks in her first bite.

Keeton side-hugs her. "Orange sweet cakes! Can't believe you found them."

I lick my fork, savoring the sweetness on my tongue, and watch my friends guffaw. I don't have a sweet tooth, but I've missed moments like this with my crew. Wish we had more of them, and time for us to just be us, to laugh and enjoy good food together.

I raise my mug of water in the air. The room quiets.

"Thank you, Arika," I say. "For this meal."

Roderick hammers his fists on the table, showing his excited agreement. Pound awkwardly raises his hands toward Arika, as if he wants to pat her shoulders or something. She doesn't quite understand what he's trying to do. And Pound turns red from something that's not anger.

He lowers into his seat.

Roderick and I make eye contact, our mouths hanging open. Holy birdshit! But I give Rod stern eyes. *Don't you dare, muttonchops. Don't you say a damn thing or I'll make you scrub the toilets.*

Ella suddenly enters the cafeteria, takes a cake, then leaves without a word. Seeing her come and go sticks a knife into my heart. But my spirits soar again when Pound recounts the moment in the brig when Roderick kept blowing kisses at the Lantians.

Arika and Keeton laugh.

The *Gladian's* nothing without my crew. My friends. Their voices are what give it life. Still, now that we're together, there's something I need to tell them. Something big.

I clear my throat.

They all focus on me. With Bryce still recovering, it's my duty to reveal the existence of the symbions. So I tell them everything I know. The room falls into deep silence. They stare at me in shock. Disbelief.

"But this means—we could still be discovered," Keeton says. "Right now. All of our prisoners are acting like beacons."

"We freed all those Lantians with the bears," Roderick mutters, wide-eyed. "They'll be rescued by the enemy! What will the King do if he finds out?"

"*I* freed them. The responsibility is mine alone." I exhale. "We don't speak of those prisoners again. Soon we'll be rendezvousing with the King's fleet."

"Wait." Pound blinks at me. "You're bringing your sister back to the King? That bastard? She's already bad enough as it is, Conrad. But she's coming around. She saved this ship. You take her back, and—"

My shoulders fall as he speaks. Keeton squeezes Pound's arm.

"What?" he says.

The warning in her eyes makes his mouth shut. She meets my gaze. Maybe she knows the conflict inside me. Knows that I've come to this myself and I don't need anyone second-guessing my decision.

Pound folds his arms and grumbles. Is it possible he's started to respect my sister?

Suddenly, Ella returns to the cafeteria. She stands in the doorway, watching me. Roderick notices her, clears his throat, and stands and claps. "All right, crew. Back to work."

"Who made you the boss?" Pound says. "You're a Middle, and as Strategist, I outrank you."

Rod gives him a look. Pound glances between me and my sister, then shuts his mouth. They all stuff in the last bites of their cake and slip from the room.

Ella and I stare at each other.

For an instant I consider telling her about the symbions and that she'll soon be back with Uncle. But that's the thing about Ella; I can't keep anything from her. Anytime I think she's asleep, she's listening.

"Symbions, huh?" she says.

I nod.

"It all makes sense now," she says. "Can't believe Bryce told you something like that." She shakes her head. "Roderick told me that you have an uncanny ability."

"What ability is that?"

"Turning people to your side. This crew . . ." She pauses. "They're unusual. They should be focused on rising, and they're all capable of rising, but they don't. But it's not because they're terrible at their jobs. It's because they follow you."

"This sounds suspiciously like a compliment, Ella."

"I only give compliments when they are earned. You turned this crew to your side," she says. "Turned an Atwood like Pound to your side. You turned a *Lantian* to your side. How do you do it?"

"They're human beings, Ella. Not tools. I'm their friend."

"How can we be friends with them when they want the same thing we want?"

"Do you honestly think Roderick wants to be the King?"

She shuts her mouth, ambles over to the table, and sticks a fork into her cake. I almost grin, realizing she was waiting to eat hers with me.

"The world is big enough for all of us," I say. "Not everyone wants to be Highest High."

"Do you?"

"I just want to keep the people I care about safe."

She digs into her cake. While I enjoy the last few bites of mine, I'm reminded of those moments when she and I would hide in the cupboards in the Urwin Manor's kitchen, snickering with chocolatey grins and stolen cookies in our hands.

These cakes, they're not the decadent stuff. They're saccharine and have been filled with preservatives to give them a longer shelf life. The glaze is a little too sour, too. Even so, we finish every crumb.

She pushes her plate away.

"Ella, I need to say something."

"Oh?"

"Yes. I—I'm sorry I didn't trust you earlier."

She goes quiet, then finally shakes her head. "You apologize too much, Brother."

I frown. She's all Urwin. Never got what I had. That was stolen from her, and she doesn't quite understand what she missed out on.

"You still have a lot to learn about dueling," I say. "So don't get overconfident just because you took down like a dozen Lantians." I grin. "Try fifty. Then I'll be impressed."

She smirks, before her expression turns serious. "Uncle will teach me."

"Yes, he will."

The room goes quiet again.

Ella's hand lowers, and she massages Mother's cane. Finally, I sense her looking at me. Hesitating.

"Conrad?"

"Hmm."

"Tell me more about Mother."

My lips part in surprise. I almost lose all my thoughts, but I push through the feeling and force something out.

"She was so strong, as if she could command the winds." My voice almost cracks, like I'm wishing I could transfer all my experience with Mother to Ella just with the tone of my voice. "But she taught me true power isn't holding something over someone. It's about rising the right way. The people who lead should be strong and show everyone else there's a better way."

Ella leans forward, seeming to hang on to my words. "Could she duel?"

"Oh absolutely."

"Tell me."

"She defeated Father once. In the Urwin Square."

"She did?" This ignites a fire in Ella's eyes. "Father was a great dueler."

"So was she." I lean back and close my eyes to visualize the moment. "Father was the best dueler in the Northern Skies. You wouldn't believe how fast he moved. And how intense he was. But

Mother knew his weaknesses. It was just us three in the Square. I got to officiate."

"Where was I?"

"Probably tracking mud in the halls."

"Yes, I was a little rodent."

"Still are."

"No. I'm bigger now."

I stare at her. "Ella, did you just make a joke?"

She grins a little.

I chuckle. "Not bad." Then, I pull myself back into the memory of when Mother and Father dueled. "It was a best-of-three match. One strike, one point. The first point went to Father. He came at her, his cane twisting. And you know Father—it didn't matter that she was his wife. The mother of his children. He was merciless. He went straight at her—got her in the gut with a timely jab.

"But Mother understood him," I say. "And when he came at her for the second round, she knew he'd try to make it quick. In his mind, that was mercy. Initially, this duel seemed playful, but after the first strike, Mother tied her hair back. She motioned Father to come toward her. He attacked, almost blinded with single-minded focus. But he didn't expect her pivot. She predicted his attack, spun around it, and thwacked him on the back."

Ella's eyes widen.

I laugh, just remembering the shock on Father's face. Remembering the feeling of disbelief in me. I'd tried to hit him thousands of times and only had bruises hidden under my collar to show for it.

"Mother didn't cheer or celebrate. She got back into her dueling stance. And she motioned him to attack again. Maybe there was something in the wind that day—something that filled Mother with strength, because when she made eye contact with me before the third round began, I knew. She had him. Father attacked, aggressively as usual. The collision of their canes still rattles my bones. They were so graceful together. Pirouetting around the other like a dance. This was a sudden-death round. First strike would win."

I pause.

"It was one of the times I saw their love for each other. Father was still merciless, but he loved Mother, Ella. Loved her fierce. He was a product of our Meritocracy. When he dragged me out to midnight duels, it wasn't because he hated me or relished making me cry. It was because he wanted to prepare me for the realities of this world. It was how he showed me that he loved me."

I go quiet, thinking of the man.

"How did the duel end?" she asks softly.

I clear my throat and blink the heat away. "Father seemed to have the upper hand, coming at her over and over. But she deftly maneuvered around each attack. And then she went on the offensive."

Ella's mouth falls.

"Father couldn't believe it. He tripped. Mother always professed mercy, but she had victory in her eyes. Before he could roll away, she leaped into the air, howling like a wild beast, and smacked him directly in the chest."

Ella stares at me in utter silence. Perhaps trying to visualize the scene. The stunning moment when Father was defeated.

"What did Father do afterward? Stomp away like a child, I'm sure."

I shake my head. "He congratulated her. And kissed her."

"What?"

"Father loved her, Ella. Anyway, he gripped her hand, and they walked away together, laughing as they strode under blossoming trees toward the hedges of the maze. Hip to hip."

"What happened next?"

"Ella, when your parents give each other eyes like that, you don't follow them."

She stares at me, understanding, but not quite understanding.

Afterward she abruptly stands, thanks me for sharing the story with her, and starts toward the door. For an instant she stops at the doorway. But she's a true Urwin. *All* Urwin. And this time, she doesn't look back.

✦✦✦

The harsh northern sky makes our breaths mist. Keeton, finished with her calibrations to the engine, comes to the deck with goggles on, a scarf wrapped over her face, and in multiple Hunter jackets. With all the layers, she looks almost as stocky as Roderick.

"Look at you, puff ball!" Pound laughs. He's not even wearing his jacket, and he's slid up the sleeves of his uniform. "This is swimsuit weather."

Keeton shivers as another blast of cold wind waves over the deck. "Maybe I shouldn't have volunteered for flight duty."

Pound laughs even harder. "You lotcher!"

Keeton throws him a middle finger parade and attaches the helm's rings to her hands. Once we're on our way, I slide down the hatch's ladder into the ship. Need to check on Bryce. I follow the corridor and stop at her door.

My hand rises, and after a calming breath, I knock.

Bryce's voice croaks, "Who is it?"

"Conrad."

There's a pause. "Come in."

I push inside, and my eyes widen. Bryce is curled in a ball on her bed. Sweat pools down her face, and her skin's pale.

I rush to her. "Bryce?"

She's shivering. Clutching her blanket up to her chin. I hurry to her closet, pull a spare blanket from the top shelf, and wrap it over her.

"Bryce, you're burning up."

"I—I tried cutting it."

"Tried cutting what?"

She rotates, revealing a bloody gash at the base of her neck.

My stomach drops. "Bryce!"

"I—I couldn't finish. I need you to do it."

"What? No. No way in hell."

"Conrad." Her eyes dig into me. "You're the only one I trust with this. Please."

"I don't know the first thing about surgery." My chest aches, seeing her this way, and my voice lowers. "I don't want to hurt you. Maybe Arika . . ."

"No. You."

Gooseflesh climbs my arms. And as I stare at her, so shriveled, so weak, unlike the powerful girl I know, I'm reminded of all the times Mother coughed in her tattered blankets. Or when she vomited black tar while I held her tight.

"Conrad . . . please."

My throat constricts. Finally, I nod. "Okay, Bryce. Okay."

She exhales.

I lift her in my arms, blankets and all. She's light and her head nuzzles under my chin. We go down the dark corridor toward the medical room.

"Your he-heart," she says, teeth chattering. "It's hammering."

"I'm scared."

"Y-you don't get scared."

But today I'm more scared than when I leaped off the ship to face the class-five. I'm almost as scared as the day gorgantauns attacked Holmstead and Mother died. I don't know Bryce as well as I'd like, but the thought of not seeing her, not being around her, not hearing her voice makes my blood cold.

We enter the medical room, and I lower her onto the bed.

"We should've kept you in here," I say.

"I needed a window," she says. "S-something to look at, and I wanted to be with my brother. Thought I could work on the sculpture."

"Can I give you meds?" I ask.

"We're almost out. Besides thi-this is a disconnect. I need to be alert."

"So then . . . you'll feel everything?"

She grasps my hand. "Y-yes."

The next instant, I'm holding a scalpel. Prickles wave up my spine. She chatters through instructions to me. Tells me to cut at the base of her neck where she started the incision herself—before she couldn't do it and damaged her symbion.

"It won't die," she says. "We're cutting it—its tail. That's where it transmits. We c-cut the tail, and it'll no longer be detectable."

"Will it be in pain?"

"It doesn't f-feel pain." She pauses. "But I do."

"Bryce—I'm really not sure if—"

She squeezes my hand fiercely again.

I breathe through the nerves. Must help her. No matter what. Even if that means putting her in agony. So I grip the scalpel, swallow hard, and gently insert it into her neck.

Oh, she trembles. She clasps the bed's bars, and my vision goes blurry. Bryce seethes but doesn't tell me to stop. I can hardly tell if I'm breathing or not. I push the scalpel deeper until it *tinks* against something.

"Now," she says, shuddering, her skin sweaty. "Slice across. Quickly."

I suck in a sharp breath and hold it. My stomach bubbles with nausea. Then I tighten my grip on the scalpel, grit my teeth, and make a quick slicing motion.

She screams. Screams so loud I want to cover my ears. Screams until she loses all her breath and finally passes out.

My head buzzes. I feel sick as I insert tweezers into her neck and pull out the tiny, quarter-inch-long tail. It's a bloody, spiny thing. Coated in steel. I drop it onto the tray, bandage her neck, then roll her over.

Her hair's clinging to her damp forehead. But she's still breathing.

I hold her hand. She's moaning something. I stay beside her for ten minutes. Twenty minutes. Watching her. Making sure she's still breathing.

Finally, her eyes open, and her faint voice says, "You did it."

CHAPTER 16

ARIKA INJECTS THE LAST OF OUR MEDS INTO BRYCE. WE need her alert if we're going to interrogate our prisoners and cut their symbions. Then, after a quick brothy meal, Bryce is on her feet, walking through the corridor with me. Irritated that we had to use the final meds.

"We're getting more soon," I tell her. "We meet with my uncle in less than two hours."

"I would've been fine."

"Not fine enough to interrogate the prisoners with me."

She pauses and drops the argument.

We start down the stairs. I shouldn't have put these interrogations off for so long, but honestly? I didn't want to speak to them. Didn't want to see Alona or the other Lantians. And now I'm thinking I'm going to have to cut their symbions.

Hell. It just feels so wrong and awful.

"You'll need to do most of the talking," Bryce says. "I doubt they'll speak to me."

I nod.

We hit the last flight of stairs when a horrific explosion slams against the ship. Bryce and I tumble, rolling down the stairs. I hit the floor at the bottom, and Bryce crashes on top of me.

She rolls off me, groaning. My vision's soggy. Holy hell. What just happened?

Keeton shouts over the comm. "Captain!"

The *Gladian* shudders again and the hull moans as something rams us.

"They're trying to break through," Pound roars on the comm. "Lantians on deck!"

Bryce and I leap to our feet, horrified. They found us. We should've cut out the others' symbions hours ago!

"Battle stations!" I yell over the comm.

Despite my bruises, I start for the stairs, but Bryce catches my wrist. A trail of blood trickles her forehead.

"They'll try to take you. That's what they want. *YOU.* Stay here."

"Like hell."

I pull away from Bryce's grip. She chases me, but too slow. She's still in a weakened state. Soon I'm climbing the ladder with ferocious speed. I shove open the hatch and climb into a sky full of rocketing harpoons. Two tortons circle us, roaring. Little blasts erupt from openings in the sides of their shells.

The attacks strike us, melt through the hull.

Keeton's caught in a railing net, unconscious, paralyzed by an electric spear. A Lantian man stands near her, his spear gripped tightly.

He smiles at me. "The bears weren't hungry."

My brow furrows. One day. That's how long that man was marooned before getting rescued. A single damn day!

He charges, but Roderick swivels his turret and squeezes the triggers. Harpoons shred the man into red chunks.

"Conrad!" Rod says. "Get below!"

Pound fights four Lantians with his bare fists. They've got electric spears and black armor.

Bryce climbs up beside me.

"You're in no condition to fight, Bryce. Go belowdecks!"

"*Like hell*," she says.

Pound grabs the nearest man by the neck, bashes his face into the railing, and hurls him into the sky. But the others jab him with their spears. He shouts, trembling as electricity shoots through him. Then he hits the ground and goes still.

Roderick roars, swivels the turret, and launches harpoons at the three Lantians. He completely eviscerates them.

The tortons close in. Two more Lantians leap from an opening in a shell and land on the deck. They charge me. Bryce tackles one, but the man kicks her off. He rises above her, ready to stomp her face in until Roderick swivels his turret and sends the man flying into the sky with a harpoon caught in his chest.

The other Lantian lunges his spear at me. But it meets my cane. I jab the eagle into his chin, and he rocks back before tumbling to the ground.

The tortons continue cutting through us. Melting our hull.

Got to move. I clench my teeth and dash for the helm bubble. Another Lantian leaps aboard, but I crush his face with my cane. After he falls I leap onto the helm tile, and the glass bubble slides over me. Then, with the rings on my fingers, I shove forward. The strings resist, but the *Gladian* launches. Pound's paralyzed body rolls into a railing net.

My arms shake. These damned strings fight me. Something's up with the engine, and our Mechanic's unconscious in a net!

Arika arrives and promptly topples over because tortons ram us again. The creatures crash into the hull where their weapons made the metal soft.

But Roderick, and now Bryce, are on the turrets, launching

harpoons into the beasts. The harpoons penetrate the torton shells. Arika fires a shoulder cannon. And within a blink, a torton spirals out of the sky, screeching, plummeting toward the black clouds.

The other torton switches to a shade of the blue sky before vanishing from view.

"Flak!" Bryce yells.

She and Roderick rotate their barrels. Golden sparkles explode in the sky. They fire at random, in every direction as I navigate the ship. The wind howls against the glass. Suddenly, Bryce's flak showers over the invisible form of the torton.

"FIRE!" Roderick says.

But before they rotate their barrels, a bizarre sound fills the sky. A high-pitched squeal from the torton, almost like a siren.

"No," Bryce says breathlessly. "Kill it! Kill it now!"

My arms shake against the fierce strings. I pull my right arm back and straighten my left, and the *Gladian* turns sharply. The bow points directly at the monster. Arika fires the shoulder cannon. The explosion ripples the torton's shell.

I shove the strings after the beast. Chasing it. Just then, Ella arrives on the deck. I'm about to shout at her, tell her to go belowdecks.

"Conrad, slow down!" Bryce yells. "Slow—"

We rock from a sudden collision. My shoulders nearly dislocate from the strings as I slam forward. Bryce and Roderick yell. Ella tumbles as the bow of the *Gladian*, like a sharp axe, cuts the torton in half.

I regain my balance, pull back on the strings, and the split torton falls from the sky. It's dropping so quickly there's no use diving after it.

I sigh. No torton to collect this time, either.

We check the sky for several seconds. Bryce and Roderick continue firing flak. But we find nothing.

"Conrad," Bryce says finally, "we have to leave. It's not safe here. The torton called for something worse."

I push the strings, but they hardly register. "Something's wrong with the engine."

Bryce's face falls. She eyeballs Keeton, and in a second she and Roderick pull her from the railing net. Bryce touches the back of her scarred neck. Her fingers spark, and she jolts Keeton's heart. An instant later Keeton shoots upright.

"We're going to have to fight," Bryce says. "Everyone, get ready."

"Keeton," Roderick says, "are you okay?"

She nods numbly.

"The engine's struggling," Roderick says. "Can you fix it?"

Keeton stands, a little woozy at first, and then she nods. Soon she's sliding down the ladder, heading to the engine room.

Bryce hurries to Pound next. She, Arika, and Ella drag him by his massive boots from the railing net. I should be helping, but I have to stay inside the helm bubble. In case we need to move. Bryce jolts Pound's chest. He leaps upright. Furious. Ready to keep fighting. Not even dazed like Keeton.

Suddenly, a horrific shriek fills the sky.

Bryce whirls toward the sound and races for the turret. "Battle stations!"

Then, against a canvas of clouds, an icy sky serpent undulates toward us. It's a white beast, a class-two. At least two hundred feet. A bull with a thick crest around its head.

And great hunger burns in its eyes.

✦✦✦

The white gorgantaun grows in our vision. His body, encased in ice, cracks as he moves. But the ice reforms, over and over. His electric-blue eyes narrow on us, and he releases another horrific shriek. Even encased in the helm's glass bubble, I grimace. The shriek instantly gives me a headache.

Ella contacted Uncle again. We just have to hold out until he arrives.

I shove the strings, fighting to use whatever power the ship has, and launch us away from the gorgantaun. But the creature's head turns to chase us.

Bryce yells and squeezes the triggers. Harpoon after harpoon slams into the gorgantaun's side. The harpoons clank away against the beast's icy scales, and he bares his ten-foot-long teeth, revealing an enormous throat that could nearly swallow us whole.

We're so damn slow.

"Keeton?" I yell over the comm. "Engine status?"

No response.

With blazing speed, the gorgantaun loops around us, readying to constrict us within its coils. Holy hell, this bull radiates winter. Frost spreads across the deck.

His head dips beneath us.

I grit my teeth and grunt as I lift the resisting strings. The *Gladian* tips and launches upward. The chomping mouth snaps just past the bow.

"Keeton!" I shout into the gem again. "Engine status?"

"I'm trying!"

The bull's head nears again. His open mouth reveals horrendous white teeth. Arika fires a harpoon down his throat. The bull bellows but keeps coming. Roderick swivels the turret and kicks a lever, making the barrel switch.

"Eat it, you cold cuss!"

Liquid flame gushes from the end of his barrel and splashes onto the bull. The monster screeches and sideswipes us with a coil. We go spinning, slamming against icy scales, but the bull dips away, howling in pain while the ice on his face melts.

Bryce attacks. Her harpoons fly past the beast's melted defense and pierce the thin scales. Cold, milky blood gushes into the sky.

"Kill him!" I shout as I turn us back for another round at the head. "While the ice is gone!"

Ella nearly falls over after she sends a harpoon flying. Arika fires another, too. Pound shoots a blast from a shoulder cannon. The explosion ruptures the beast's eye and juicy flesh sprays. It mists the deck as we fly through it.

The gorgantaun shields his bloodied face behind one of his coils, and our weapons clank against ice again. So Roderick lights him up with fire.

"DIE!" Bryce roars as she unloads more harpoons. "DIE!"

We absolutely cut into the beast. Dozens of the harpoons pierce the gorgantaun's scales. Digging into vital organs. He thrashes wildly, his sharp tail dangerously whipping around the sky.

My arms ache, scream for a break. There's just not enough power in the strings. We curve over one set of coils, then dive below a loop. The beast's head dips after us, shrieking. Roderick continues gushing fire while Ella, Pound, Arika, and Bryce work in tandem to blow off chunks and fill the monster with harpoons.

My goggles fog, and it slows me enough that I don't notice the icy loop. Shit. The coil wraps around the deck like a weed. Mashing the railing. And slams into Ella. My sister falls backward, screaming as ice rapidly flies up her boots.

Roderick pours flame onto the beast again, making him retreat.

My heart stops as Ella's lower half goes crusty with ice. Everything goes blurry. And I'm no longer flying the ship. My calves are burning as I race against the wind. The beast shrieks as the fire turret melts its side again. Arika cheers as her harpoons find their mark.

The gorgantaun pulls away, bleeding profusely. Great pools of blood sink into the sky. I dive to Ella's side. She's tucked in a railing's net, shivering. Her wide eyes looking up at me.

"C-Conrad."

Without knowing if the gorgantaun is dead, I lift her. Clutch her against my body, even though the contact transmits the ice to me. The horrible ice spreads across my stomach, stinging my skin, making my vision sparkle with pain.

The rest of the crew's so busy fighting, they don't even realize what's happening.

"What the hell?" Arika shouts. "Who's flying the ship?"

The gorgantaun retreats. But Arika leaps onto the helm tile and launches us after the monster.

Soon I'm holding Ella over my shoulder as I climb down the hatch. The crew shouts above. Still fighting. Cheering.

"The beast's dying!" Pound roars victoriously over the comm. "We got him."

A low moan vibrates through the walls of the *Gladian*. I kick open the door into the medical room. Gorgantaun ice spreads across any surface, and if untreated, will leave Ella and myself encased in blocks of ice.

Her voice weakens, "C-C-Conrad."

I lower her to the ground. Frost rises above her hips and up her abdomen. Sharp crystals stab my fingers as I desperately try wiping the ice off her. It'll be a minute until it reaches her heart. And then . . .

"Ella!" Her eyelids flicker, and her teeth aren't chattering anymore. Her breath expels cold mist. "Ella, stay with me!"

The ice grows over my abdomen, too. My breaths tighten—can't expand my ribs. Suddenly, I realize I might die, too. The only way to stop this ice is to get heat on it. Something incredibly hot. Then I see it, tucked in the corner of the room.

Heat. HEAT!

I scurry across the floor and tap the button on the room's heatglobe. The round device kicks on, glowing red. My shivering fingers crank it to the highest setting. Then I crawl back to my sister and drag her to lean against me near the warmth.

The ice travels across my torso so much that despite the swelling heat, darkness builds in my vision. Can't fight it.

I fall beside the heatglobe, and all goes black.

✦✦✦

I wake to the faces of my crew leaning over me.

"Conrad," Bryce breathes, patting my face. "We didn't know where you went."

My body throbs as though winter breathed into my bones. Bryce taps the button at the base of another heatglobe, and Keeton and Arika wrap blankets over me and my sister.

I sit up. "Ella?"

"She's breathing," Arika says. "But we're out of meds."

Bryce and I make eye contact.

"The engine is dead," Keeton says. "I think the line has a fissure somewhere, but I haven't had a chance to check all the damage yet. We're stuck here."

Roderick helps me stand. Ella's unconscious on the medical bed, her skin pale. Eyelids blue. The red rays of the heatglobes pulse on their maximum setting.

Oh, my dry skin hurts. The ice didn't travel as far across me as it did Ella. But outside of some lingering pain, I'll be all right. Hopefully.

"The heat should keep her alive," Arika says.

My hand gently touches Ella's forehead. All this time, I've fought to get her back into my life because I thought I could keep her safe. And now here she is, almost dying under my watch after just a couple months with me.

"We killed the gorgantaun," Arika says. "But—well—"

Roderick scratches the back of his head. "The ice spread into the ship. The bottom floor. Two of our prisoners—Pound found them. Encased in ice. The third died before we could thaw him."

My gut sinks. "What?"

"We hurled their bodies into the sky," Keeton says. "Their symbions might still be transmitting."

"Who's left?" I ask. "Did Alona . . . ?"

"No, she's still alive," Keeton says.

I exhale.

"But we were lucky it didn't get her," Arika says. "She was holding onto the top bars of her cell when we found her. The ice was climbing toward her. We moved her into one of the other cells. We've got the heatglobes going in the rec room now. Roderick spent the last hour with heatguns, finding and melting ice."

Pound enters without a word. He sweeps past me, checks the pillows around Ella, and places a warm cloth on her forehead. We all stare as he gently tucks in the sides of her blankets. Maybe Pound is used to things like this, being a big brother and having lots of little cousins and nieces and nephews to look after.

"Captain, I'm returning to the deck," Roderick says. "Someone should be on watch. We need to be ready—in case we're detected again."

"No," Pound rumbles, looking up after ensuring Ella's tucked in tight, "what we need is to toss Alona overboard. Let her join her peers. Her beacon's exposing us. We were supposed to get to the rendezvous point with the King. Easy. Except, it hasn't been easy because they know where we are! And now, the engine's not working, so we have to wait until the King comes to us."

We go quiet.

"I'll handle Alona," Bryce says.

Keeton turns to her. We all do.

Pound's eyes narrow on her. "How?"

"By cutting her symbion."

The room's silent. Something about it doesn't feel right, knowing how connected symbions are to their host. Knowing how Bryce reacted when I cut hers. But we don't have a better option, and it's better than killing her.

"Fine," Pound says. "I'll hold her down."

Bryce snatches a scalpel, and after she and Pound leave, Roderick hurries to the deck to keep watch. Keeton, meanwhile, heads to find the fissure in the engine line.

That leaves me alone with Arika and Ella.

"Captain," Arika says gently, "are you all right?"

"Fine."

She studies me a moment, then nods and starts toward the door. She pauses there. "Conrad . . . this wasn't your fault."

I lean against the bed and shut my eyes. All my life, I believed my sister needed me. But now I'm realizing that if I want my sister to be safe, being around me is not in her best interest.

She wants to go back to Uncle. She's better off without me. This thought leaves me feeling colder than ever.

I've lost ships, lost people, and worst of all, I've failed my own family. Uncle let me reunite with Ella because I won the Gauntlet, but for the first time I consider that maybe I don't deserve to have her back if I can't protect her.

I can't protect anyone.

CHAPTER 17

I PUSH INTO THE REC ROOM. THIS PLACE NORMALLY HOUSES equipment for exercise and games, but for now it's a cold, dark brig.

The open doorway casts light onto our final prisoner: Alona of Mizrahi. She raises a pale hand to block the sudden light. Once the door shuts, her hand lowers, and our eyes adjust to the darkness. A bloody bandage dangles from her neck.

"Your fussock cut my symbion," she snarls.

"Yes, well, we couldn't have you telling your friends where we are."

"They already know," she says bitterly. "It was pointless."

"We won't be at these coordinates forever."

"Is that so?" She presses her hand against the floor. "Is that why the ship's not moving?" She laughs, and her dark curls fall over her face. She brushes them back. "You're our number one target, you know."

"I'm aware."

"Well, you Urwins are many things, but you aren't idiots." She limps toward me and leans against the bars. Her eyes look me up and down. "You are powerful. It's too bad we're on opposite ends of the clouds."

The way she looks at me makes me feel queasy.

"You know," she says, leaning back, "we're not that different. There's a reason why my people are desperate to get you and Ella. Two chances to flip to our side."

I cough a laugh. "You think we'd flip to your side?"

Her eyes twinkle. She turns her back to me and stares at the ceiling. "If you knew what I know . . . yes."

I shake my head. Hate cryptic games. Had to play them with Sebastian. Now this birdshit's doing the same?

"Alona, I'm very busy. Tell me something of interest, something that will make me more willing to spare your life. Clearly, you want to live; otherwise, you'd have let the gorgantaun ice consume you."

She doesn't respond.

"But if you keep being cryptic," I say, "I'll walk away right now and leave you for my uncle."

"You're leaving me up to your uncle regardless. It's not like you have a choice."

"I always have a choice."

She looks at me. "That's right. We know all about how stubborn you are, Conrad of Urwin."

"Why would Goerner believe I'd ever flip for him?"

She exhales and paces her small cell. "The Lantian Republic has had a change of heart about you and your sister. The Council has ordered us to give you both a chance."

"And that's why you had me beaten?"

She smirks. "I don't believe you're worth it. So I did the bare minimum."

"Your recruitment is off to a stellar start."

She snorts. "You're funny. It's too bad you didn't get picked by Order. I would've enjoyed competing in Skywar against you. Or getting closer to you. Instead, you were on this weak little vessel, hunting our creations. Did you know my mom was a Designer?"

I sigh. Growing bored of her already.

"Trust me, Conrad. If we wanted you dead, you'd be dead already."

"Your ice gorgantaun tried to kill us," I say.

"Yes, well, shit happens in war. Not everything's perfect."

My eyes narrow on her. "Tell me one reason why I'd betray my people."

"It's not unheard of, Conrad. There are already people turning on the Skylands, even as we speak. Goerner's support grows. Your people follow winners."

She comes toward me, cups one hand over her neck, and reaches her sparking fingers through the bars. Her hand stops several inches from my stomach.

"I have one great reason why you'd consider joining us." She meets my eyes. "Let me share an experience with you. You know about them, yes? I'm sure Bryce has been sharing all of her tragic past." She says everything with a lack of empathy, and it takes a lot to not just stomp away.

Still, I'd be lying to myself if I claimed I wasn't a little intrigued about what knowledge she has that could make me even consider joining them. But getting close to Alona, letting her control my consciousness?

I step back from her sparking fingers. "Nice try, Alona. I think I'll leave you with the King."

She scowls and pulls her hand back. "You'll discover this truth eventually, Conrad. And when you do, it'll drop you from the sky."

I leave her to marinate in darkness and loss. I'd sooner let a prowlon bite me than let Alona into my mind.

✦✦✦

The *Gladian's* stuck in place, waiting to be attacked. Fortunately, in the late afternoon when a group of black battlecruisers appears in the distance and we hear their identity over the comms, we can finally exhale with relief.

The King's fleet has arrived.

Command towers rise over the decks of the battlecruisers. They carry multiple cannons that could rupture my ship in two. Behind them comes a trio of behemoth-sized carriers, each capable of holding hundreds of sparrow fighters.

Behind all comes the King's ship, the *Dreadnought.* It's essentially a small island. Double the size of a carrier. The largest skyship ever built. Thousands of crewmembers, countless turrets, cannons, and multiple hangars capable of docking ships even larger than mine.

Roderick stops beside me. He pats my shoulder as we watch the *Dreadnought* slowly approach.

"We made it," he says.

I look at him. He stares ahead, his muttonchops waving a little in the wind. We don't say much else because we're too tired.

Keeton joins us, too. Followed by Pound, Arika, and Bryce. We all stand together as the crew of the *Gladian.* And something tells me, as the *Dreadnought* slows to a stop before us, that maybe this is the last time we'll be together for a long while. Maybe I'm wrong. But Uncle—he has never appreciated my crew.

And he had to rescue us.

Still, this crew's prepared to fight to the very end. There's no one I'd rather be with in a war, and I'll fight to keep them with me.

As the King's ship stops and we ogle it, all the relief I feel at being surrounded by my friends and the fleet evaporates because I know who occupies that massive vessel. The man who is going to take my sister away.

Pound thumps my back. "Tell the King that he's a cheating birdshit."

Soon the *Dreadnought* encases us in cold shadow. Roderick's mouth nearly drops at the sight. And I've got to admit, it's impressive. Seemingly infinite layers of levels and ladders, all buzzing with crewmembers hurrying along the different platforms.

Even from a distance, I recognize the man standing on the *Dreadnought's* deck above us just by his posture. His salt-and-pepper hair waves in the wind. He's a handsome man. Broad shoulders. Strong jaw. Uncle looks down his nose at me like a falcon as his ringed fingers dance on the railing. Strangely, he's not alone. A woman stands beside him. Close. Almost touching his arm.

But I don't get a good look at her because they step away when the *Dreadnought's* massive hangar doors crack open, revealing a darkened space of platforms inside. Two tow-ships zoom out, shooting toward us like small fireflies. The ships, domed in glass, are about the size of a large lifeboat. But they've got angry crystallic engines that hum with silver fire.

"Your Majesty, please detach your gorgantaun," a woman says into my comm gem. "We'll take it from here."

I nod at Roderick. We kept the gorgantaun corpse for the war effort. The ice glands from northern gorgantauns are particularly useful for building chillglobes or freeze boxes.

Roderick kicks a lever, and the chains pull away, scraping across the deck until the dead gorgantaun is freed. A tow-ship zips around the beast, and despite its diminutive size, fires a chain around the beast's neck and carries it off.

Then the other tow-ship brings us in.

We enter the shadowed hangar. It's dark and ominous. A few platforms reveal workers pushing empty hovering carts toward a well-stocked Hunter vessel. The workers hurry to collect nets full of sheltauns.

"It's like a little city," Bryce murmurs.

The *Dreadnought's* being used like a Hunter outpost, and Hunter's providing the ship with food and other supplies. One sheltaun, still alive, snips its crablike claws at a man, nearly cutting him in half. The man jabs a spear through its eye, and the beast's metal claw topples against the dock.

That single claw could feed a dozen people for days.

Once we dock, Pound drops our gangway, and a group of workers races upward with tools on their belts. Ready to get the *Gladian* back into flying shape. It'll take them a while. My ship is a disaster. Holes in the frame, the deck. Melted metal. Ruined engine line. Potential remnants of gorgantaun ice locked somewhere inside.

Alona of Mizrahi is brought to the deck through the supply platform. She's gagged, and Order guards yank her toward the gangway. She glances back at me with a smile in her eyes. If she talks to Uncle, she'll get to live . . . for a while, anyway. But once you've served out your purpose to Uncle, he'll cut the tether.

After Alona's gone, I stare at all my friends. And my heart sinks as I meet their eyes. Keeton grabs me and hugs me without a word. Bryce joins in. Same with Roderick.

We say nothing.

But this won't be the last time we see one another. I can promise that. Besides, I've brought Uncle a great victory. Because of my crew, we know all about the symbions. That must count for something.

I straighten my Hunter jacket and double-check my belt to ensure my dueling cane is clipped on. Then, with my breaths tight, I start toward the gangway on my way to Uncle.

CHAPTER 18

UNCLE ARRIVES IN THE HANGAR WITH THE SAME WOMAN from earlier. She has long, jet-black hair and hazel eyes. Perhaps a decade younger than him. A silver cane dangles from her hip—topped with a familiar animal at the end.

My eyes narrow.

Advisers from Politics, Order, and Scholar encircle them, all giving Uncle reports. But he waves them off, leaving me alone with him and his female companion.

Uncle looks me up and down. No hug. No handshake. Not even a smile. Just meeting my eyes is enough of an acknowledgment in his mind.

"Welcome to the *Dreadnought*, Nephew," he says. Then he motions to the woman beside him. "This is Severina of Urwin."

My forehead wrinkles. Another Urwin? From where?

Severina's voice is cold. Unfeeling. "I am Ulrich's wife."

I look between them, stunned. Never even met this woman, and she's married to *him*? For how long? And is Uncle's poisonous heart even capable of love?

"We were wedded two months ago," Uncle says.

My face nearly twists into a scowl, but I keep it passive and unimpressed. Uncle talks a lot about Urwins—about our blood. The family. But he doesn't treat his family as *family*. He kills his brother. Exiles his nephew and sister-in-law. And marries without thinking to even mention it to me or Ella.

"It is unbecoming of the King," Uncle says, "to be unmarried."

Since she took the Urwin name, Severina must be the Queen Consort—she's married into the family but is not an Urwin by blood.

The two do not touch, and a healthy gap stands between them. I don't trust her. Everyone's trying to rise—whether that's through the Trades or Selection. Maybe she found a different way. Worse, what if she married Uncle because she actually loves him?

That'd make her even more untrustworthy.

"It is unfortunate, Prince," Severina says, "that your travels have kept you away from the news of our union. But we are together now." She speaks in such a measured tone. "I've heard much about you. The tale of you running the length of a class-five gorgantaun is legendary." She looks over the scratches striping my uniform and the tatters of my jacket's hem. "You'd do well with a bath, some change of attire, and lots of rest." She turns to Uncle. "And you do plan to let him rest, King?"

"We don't rest."

She nods in deference. "Of course. I shall check on the Princess. Prince, is she still asleep in the medical room?"

I nod.

"I'll care for her," she says. "We'll have a family meal, yes, King?"

"Conrad and I have matters to discuss first."

"Whenever it is convenient."

Then she's gone, up the *Gladian's* gangway, and once away from Uncle, she becomes a person of power. She orders people out of her way like a lifelong Urwin.

Uncle focuses on me. "Come."

I follow. We climb steps, and I glance back at my crew. Roderick and Keeton are already in discussion with the repair crew, likely notifying them of the ship's numerous problems. But Pound's face is sour. If there's one person Pound hates with all the fury of the winds, it's Uncle. But he seems just as annoyed with Severina, who's now climbing down the hatch.

Uncle and I leave the echoing hangar, follow a corridor, and enter a guarded elevator that deposits us into an empty hall—well, empty except for the stoic guards staring straight ahead. A red rug flows to the end. We walk in a cold silence. For a moment I consider asking about Severina, but I've got enough on my mind besides concerning myself with Uncle's romantic endeavors.

Finally, we push through a thick door and enter his office. It's adorned with bookcases. A great desk is bolted to the floor near the window, and a table with six chairs stands before a map of the Skylands. The mounted map is marked with places where Uncle and his advisers have presumably been guessing Goerner's location.

Beyond that, the giant window displays the whole of the King's fleet.

Uncle watches me as I stride through the room. Immediately, I leap onto the couch. Oh, I need sleep. And with the security of the fleet around me, this is the first genuine moment I've had to relax in days.

Uncle's gloves squeak. Irritated. "Comfortable?"

"Yes."

"I wish I had that luxury."

"There's another seat there."

His eyes narrow.

Uncle wears a white suit with a gray vest—not unlike an Order soldier. But maybe that's the point. Order's the Trade that'll protect us in the war. And he's the Highest High. Appearances matter. On his lapel rests a pin of each of the Twelve Trades.

"Stubborn *child*," he says finally.

He strolls to his desk situated beside the window and sits. The fleet floats behind him. Scholar ships, an Explorer ship, even Agriculture's giant dairy ships. There probably isn't a safer place in the Skylands.

He intertwines his fingers under his chin. "I have the feeling, Nephew, that if not for your ship's current predicament, you would've flown off into the skies because you didn't want to return Ella to me."

I say nothing.

"I can accept you taking Ella, hunting gorgantauns, and trying to stay strong and prepared while we ascertained where the giga will come next," he says. "I admire your loyalty to your sister. But your loyalty should always lie first with *me*. I am King—the head of Urwin—and I'm afraid to say that I do not trust you to keep Ella safe. Her injury—we are fortunate that she will survive. We now need to consider that the Skylands' importance overrides your desire to remain with your sister. As such, I am taking her from your care from this point forth."

I don't argue.

He blinks a little, perhaps surprised I didn't raise hell. But he views people as tools. Things that he can control. He expects me to view Ella the same way. Well, I've realized I cannot control her any more than he can control me.

"This is not the reaction I expected from you, Conrad." But then an idea forms on his face. He leans back and betrays a tiny smirk. "Oh, I see."

"What?"

"This same thing happened between me and your father. You and Ella realized that being family is impossible. You both want to be the heir. The first in line."

"That's birdshit, Uncle."

"*King*," he corrects. "Come now, Conrad, you don't think that your father and I had an amazing relationship, do you? We are Urwin. Allred happened to be born first." His voice softens and goes emotionless. "But I am here, and he is not."

My teeth grind. Oh, how I'd like to beat this man. Make him lick the heel of my boot after I best him in a duel.

"You still hate me," he says.

"Yes."

He nods. "As much as you irritate me, Nephew, I have always appreciated your ability to express blunt truths. But you are wrong to feel this way. Selfish, even. Did you know, after the Battle of Venator, that Master Koko had to cancel the Gauntlet?"

I stare at him.

"It's true. The trainees were all entered into the Hunter draft. Without training. Because we need people. The Skylands are at war, but that doesn't mean you and I must be."

I don't respond, even though I'm thinking of the implication on Hunter that so many untrained Hunters are in the fleet now.

"Wasn't it a saying of the Hales . . . How did it go again?" He says this coyly. "Something about 'being better than what the world intends'? Well, Conrad, I suggest you heed this advice: 'Be better.'"

My hands ball into fists. This man knows nothing of morality. He's manipulative and dangerous. And he pretends to care about Ella, but he didn't bother checking on her when we arrived. Didn't sit at her bedside and wait for her to wake. He just heard my report over the comm that she would make it and that was enough for him.

Uncle stands, clasps his hands behind his back, and strolls to the window. His fleet splays out before him. Got to admit, it is quite a sight. Grown since the last time I saw it. Which is interesting because the last time I was here, Uncle ordered much of the fleet to disperse to protect the Skylands. Have the islands constructed more vessels in a short time, or has Uncle contracted the forces to keep himself safe?

"The revelation of the symbions has proved highly beneficial," he says. "It may change the course of the war. It is unfortunate Bryce wasn't more forthcoming with this information earlier."

"She doesn't want more death," I say.

"Well, she could've saved many Skylanders if she'd been honest from the beginning. But you were correct about her, Conrad. I'm glad you convinced me of her importance. Just don't let yourself get too close to her. If word got out about who she is . . . about who the Prince has been fraternizing with? It could throw our whole family into question. Whatever you do with her, do *not* get her pregnant."

My skin blazes. "She's none of your concern."

"The Urwin bloodline will never be tainted by a Lantian," he says, turning to stare at me. "I'm skeptical that you are willing to do whatever is necessary to win this war. But you're young. You can still be molded. Me? I am willing to do whatever it takes." He faces the window again and raises his comm gem to his mouth. His expression is cold. Dark. "Do it."

My brow wrinkles. "Do what?"

Then I stare, horrified, as a screaming man falls headfirst past the window. Blood trails after the man, squirting from gaping wounds where his arms once were. Lopped off, so he can't even flap.

Traitor's death.

"The dirt-eaters," Uncle says softly as the man falls, "brought the war to us."

Two more Lantians fall. I flinch as a streak of blood splashes against the window. Then more people drop. Five. Ten. Fifteen. One shouting woman, after a gust of wind, slams into the glass. She sees me for an instant. Horrified disgust oozes inside me. Then she slips away. Another dozen people fall. No, more than a dozen. They don't stop. Mists of red sprinkle the glass.

I turn away. Can't stand the sight.

Uncle observes me as they fall—his face twisted with displeasure—not because of the falling Lantians, but because I can't watch.

The executions go on for several minutes and my throat constricts. The room darkens from the reddened windows. The sun, murky behind the sheet of death, spreads crimson hues on my skin. Almost like the blood's on me. My stomach bubbles and my skin goes clammy. Uncle saved this display for me. He gathered all the Lantians he'd uncovered in his own fleet, then organized a group above to butcher their arms off and toss them overboard just to make me watch.

"You are weak, Conrad," he says. "The dirt-eaters made our people fall. How are we expected to win this war if they do things we cannot?"

We're better than this. Can hear Mother saying it in my head.

We are better than this.

Uncle turns back to the last of the falling people. "Those monsters made our capital fall. But we will make *them* fall, Conrad. You and I. The Urwins. Because we are built of something different. Rising," he pauses, "is in our blood."

Another splash of red hits the glass.

After the last person falls and their cries fade away, the room drops into silence.

An attendant enters at Uncle's request over the comm and takes me across the hall to my suite. My legs are numb and hardly work. Not even sure I'm breathing. But soon I'm away from Uncle, away from the bloodied windows and the red sun. And I breathe, just breathe.

The attendant brings me into a massive suite.

"Your Highness," the attendant says. "This is your room."

I nod without feeling.

The attendant leaves me in the rich suite filled with every manner of comfort. But I'm not in awe of the wide windows, comfortable couches, or trays of food. No, I rush to the toilet.

And throw up.

✦✦✦

After a bath and a sleepless nap haunted by bloody images, I dress in the new uniform Uncle left for me. It's a white suit with a gray vest, covered with pins of the Twelve Trades. Then I'm summoned back to his office. It's been a couple hours since the executions, and my stomach's still squirming.

Uncle's heartless, but there's a war going on, and he has much to tell me.

When I enter, he's seated at his desk, reviewing papers and drinking a coffee. The descending sun shines in through the shiny windows. Not a speck of blood, almost like the executions never happened. Some poor bastards had to rappel over the side of the ship to clean the glass. While Uncle reads, live music projects from the comm gem on the mantel. Presumably, it's music from Art Musicians elsewhere in the fleet, playing entirely for Uncle's benefit. It's a soft, soothing tune.

Uncle doesn't look up, but he motions me to the seat before him.

For several minutes, he leafs through the papers.

"Alona of Mizrahi," he says finally, lowering the papers, "has not been very forthcoming. My interrogators tell me that the only thing she has said is that the Lantians want you and Ella. Do you know anything about this?"

"She tried to share an experience with me."

"An experience?"

"The symbions can transmit memories and experiences through touch, but I don't trust her. I didn't want her in my mind."

He leans back and studies me. Part of me wonders if I should tell him what else Alona claimed. That she and Goerner knew something that would make me flip sides. But Uncle's trust in me has always hung on the end of a plank. Just a little shake, and it'd fall.

"It's fascinating," he says, "how little we know about them. Their tech really is quite remarkable." There's a hint of admiration in his voice. "It is unfortunate that they have chosen this path with us. If they had come above and bowed before me, perhaps the old war could have been forgotten. Everyone could have benefited."

He leans back and meets my eyes. His cold blue gaze digs into me. We're silent for a time. My stomach's still squirming.

"Conrad," Uncle says, regaining my attention. "The gigataun's coming."

An icy hand glides down my back. The giga. That beast's one of the reasons I've struggled to sleep. Many nights I've woken in the Captain's cabin, dripping in cold sweat. My tense knuckles massage my thighs. Horrifying images cloud my mind. We fought the gigataun at Ironside. The *Gladian* flew among a whole fleet of Hunter ships as the giga's bellows quaked the whole sky. Even now, its roar rattles my bones. That beast rose through an opening in the acid clouds. And I'll never forget the look of it: a giant snake with scales red as fire and eyes like blue snow.

"When is it coming?" I ask.

"A week. Maybe less."

"And how will we fight it?"

He exhales and goes quiet.

I know some things. Like that Hunter's offering sacks of coins and a Predator-class vessel as a reward for any Hunter Captain who takes down the gigataun. Order's offering any Commander the position of Vice Admiral. And Scholar's offering unlimited research funds at Dandun University to any Scholar Scribe who manages to uncover the giga's weaknesses.

But against the gigataun, incentives will only take you so far.

"The reality is, Conrad, we don't know enough about it. We do, however, have a plan, one that you'll need to help with." He pauses. "I'm sending you on a mission. You and a squadron of ships."

Uncle stares at me, perhaps considering if he should tell me more now, or wait. Whatever this mission is, Uncle's kept it close.

"Unfortunately," he says, "there's not enough time before the gigataun comes. I can't spare the ships at the moment." His expression darkens with determination. "We're going to fight it."

Adrenaline courses through me.

"We'll give it everything we've got," he says, "and we've got more this time. Order has attached some of their prototype cannons aboard their battlecruisers. Our sparrows have been outfitted with explosives. And Hunter? Master Koko personally designed a new harpoon turret—one that's so large it only fits on their Titanium-class vessels. The harpoons are as thick as a small boat. Furthermore, when the monster attacked us last, it came as a surprise. We had a dismantled fleet. The *Dreadnought* wasn't available last time, either. But this next battle? The beast will meet the entirety of the Skylands' power."

I sit, wondering if that'll be enough. "Do we know where the giga will attack?"

He shakes his head. "Not yet."

We go quiet for several seconds. My brain fires off possibilities. Dandun, the home of Scholar. Venator, the home of Hunter. Greenrye, the home of Agriculture. Maybe even Regnum, the shared home of Law and Politics.

"In the meantime," he says, "we're returning to Holmstead to resupply. It's the closest major island."

I blink.

"I've not stepped on any island since the war began," Uncle says, "and I'd prefer that my next steps are on Holmstead." He watches me. "I'm sure you will be pleased to walk freely among the Urwin grounds again. I have heard it's quite lovely now, under a fresh layer of snow."

My stomach squeezes with a momentary thrill. I'm going home. But a hollow feeling swells inside me. Holmstead Island isn't just home to my best memories but my worst ones, too.

Uncle turns in his chair and gazes at the nearest Order carrier. It's a massive ship, dwarfed only by his own. It was only a few months ago that he offered that ship to me. He'd told me it'd be the only way to keep me safe. I'd have had access to all of Order's weapons. Hundreds under my command.

I turned him down.

"I have spoken with Master Koko," he says. "She has agreed to release you of any of your contractual obligations to Hunter."

"What?"

"You are no longer a Hunter, Nephew. It was a rather unprecedented move on Master Koko's part, but these are unprecedented times, and I need you with a clear, focused head."

I explode out of the chair and reach for my cane. Ready to take this man down. I earned my position in Hunter. I am a Hunter Captain. And I earned that. *I* earned that.

He watches my twitching fingers and glances at the cane on my hip.

"Sit down, Conrad."

I remain standing.

"I do not repeat myself, Conrad."

"I heard you the first time."

He stares at me. Eyes narrowed. "And, because you are no longer a member of Hunter, that little ship of yours is no longer in your possession."

My body shakes.

"You are the heir, Conrad. If I die, Ella isn't old enough to inherit yet. You are all that's left. Do you not understand this?"

"Uncle!"

He stands. "No. You will address me as 'King'! Your things are being moved now."

"Where? To this ship?"

"You will take command of the Order carrier I offered you months ago. But you will not be allowed to leave the *Dreadnought* until I command it."

My blood boils. Every part of me becomes fury. I want to bash this man's face into the desk. Make him crack. Break his ribs. Thunder over his broken, rattled body.

"And my crew?"

He sits again. "Those Lows on the *Gladian*, you mean? They'll not be joining you."

This is a step too far. I unclip the dueling cane from my belt.

He studies me. "Are you going to challenge me, Nephew?"

My hand squeezes the cane. "Those 'Lows' on the *Gladian*," I say through my cracking voice, "they are my *family*."

He frowns. "The thing about you, Conrad, is in some respects, you are undefeatable, but in others, you are a disaster. You are broken and weak. So desperate to find a family. No matter how many people you surround yourself with, your mother will never come back. Your father will never come back."

He rises and steps around the desk. Coming toward me, his cane still attached to his belt.

"You keep seeking a place to belong, but you belong with me. *I* am your place. Your family."

He stops before me. Just daring me to raise the cane. Finally, he steps away, and once he sits behind the desk again, my thoughts burst into a flurry. Exploring potential ways to convince him. My mouth opens, then closes.

The threat of my cane won't convince him.

Something else might though. The thought sickens me. But what other option do I have? He put me in this situation. He has all the power, and it's time to let him know I recognize the power he holds over me.

"Okay," I say.

"Okay?"

"The *Gladian* is my home. And the crew—they're not just important to me, Uncle. They're useful . . . *tools*." I speak in a way that he understands. "They've kept me alive, helped get me and Ella off Venator. Uncle, after we freed ourselves from the enemy's grasp and captured Alona of Mizrahi, my crew fought off an arctic gorgantaun. My crew stood beside me. Bleeding. Ready to die."

He stares at me.

"My crew brought you the information about the symbions." I look down at him. "Respectfully, *King*, the idea that my crew has no purpose is complete birdshit."

His brow twitches. He intertwines his fingers. Listening. Letting me try to convince him.

"King, anything you command, I shall do," I say. "*Anything.* But grant me this one privilege. I earned my status. I am a Hunter—for life, and not just that; the *Gladian* is MINE. I've earned that ship. Maybe I haven't paid it off yet, but no one will take it away from me. If I'm going to die in this war, there's no ship I'd rather be on, and no crew I'd rather fight with.

"All the power is yours, King. You can accept that I will follow *all* your commands—be the loyal heir you've always wanted. Or you can force me to abandon those I care about. Force me to command an Order carrier I did not earn. And make me lose all the things that I fight for."

He stares at me as wind slides across the glass, then licks his teeth. "Your speech sounds suspiciously like a plea, Conrad. Pleas are for lotchers. For Lows."

"Then consider it a demand."

He studies me. "They are making you weak, those people on the *Gladian*. They will leave you the first chance they get."

"Then let me learn that lesson, if it arrives, the hard way. Isn't that how you want to build us Urwins? Make us learn tough lessons and rise above the challenge?"

He leans back and intertwines his fingers again.

"Keep me on the *Gladian*," I say. "It's one of Hunter's finest ships.

Nothing can match its speed. Right now, the islands need Hunter ships and Hunters like me. We're the ones who will bring down the gigataun."

He pauses. "You have passion, Conrad. I respect that. But how far are you willing to go for your crew?"

"To sky's end."

A twinkle forms in his eye. "Very well. You shall prove this. Unclip your cane."

"What?"

He steps around the desk and strides past the couches. "If you can hit me, just once, I will give you your crew, your ship, and your title back. So long as you agree to cut out the stubborn birdshit."

"You want to duel?"

"If you call what is about to happen to you a 'duel,' then fine. So be it."

My mouth goes dry. Uncle's the most prominent dueler in the Northern Skies. Perhaps the whole of the Skylands.

Undefeated.

But that's no way to think. I'm the son of Allred of Urwin and Elise of Hale. I learned how to duel in the Urwin Square. Maybe I can't beat Uncle, but I can hit him.

I can.

I unclip and extend my cane.

The next instant he's unbuttoning his jacket and rolling up his sleeves. He unclips his cane and stands in the open spot in the spacious office, away from the couches, and turns on his heels to face me.

"My new cane has few stories to tell," he says. "Today we will give it one."

His cane snaps as it extends to double the length. It's black and only has a few dents in its smooth surface. A polished silver eagle with outstretched wings rises at the end. Then he gets into a posture that's low, but not too low, and waits for me.

"Let's see if you'd truly chase your crew to sky's end, Nephew."

My heart's thudding. He's going to beat me until I'm soaking in my own blood. That's how Father dueled with me. Afterward he'd inject me with meds and make me do it again the next night.

And the next.

I've only seen one person strike Uncle in a duel. My father. But they weren't fighting for anything other than to spar. To practice and strengthen Urwin.

I'm fighting for my friends.

I rip off my jacket and roll up my sleeves. Soon I'm standing across from him, trying to keep my breaths steady.

In a blink, he's at me. No warning. He's twirling his cane with brutal savagery. How the hell did he get so quick? I pivot back, dodge one swing. I'm fast, too. Been trained most of my life. I block two attacks before his elbow slams into my chin. Dazing me. Then he swipes out my feet from under me.

I hit the ground. Coughing.

Uncle strikes my ribs. My stomach. The Urwin eagle dents me. I roll away. Scramble to my feet. Bleeding from my mouth, my chin.

He comes at me again.

I meet his cane. The collision stings my fingers. Can't just let him attack. He'll overwhelm me with his power and speed.

His form is immaculate. Each motion carefully orchestrated. His balance and posture refined.

I swing. Block two more attacks. Pirouette away from a third. And storm at him. He ducks beneath my assault, then jabs me in the gut. A swift kick sends me onto my back again, and that's when he lets loose.

"How far will you go?!" he roars, saying the words to the rhythm of his attacks. "Until you're dead? When will you give in?"

I roll away. Cough. Everything hurts. Head soggy. Ribs aching. Even so, my shaking arms push me upright, and I use Father's cane to help me rise. Then I stand, facing him. Blinking at the disorienting images in my vision. Three versions of Uncle stare at me. All dancing around, even though he stands still.

Have to hit him once. Just once.

I cough blood. And after a stinging breath, I charge. But I stumble over my feet and fall.

Uncle attacks me. Hits with violent focus. Doesn't stop, even as my quivering arms try to push me upright again.

My arms collapse. I can't even hit him once.

He strikes me until I'm bleeding all over myself. Strikes me until finally, I'm groaning in pain. And that's when he finally retracts his cane and steps back. Stopping only because he needs an heir.

"I gave you an offer," he says, crouching over me, holding my hair in his grip. "Just one hit," he says. "And your ship, your crew. All of it would be yours. But you couldn't even do that."

He shakes his head with disappointment, lets my head fall, and turns to walk away. Perhaps to get meds—just to keep me alive.

I'm broken. Defeated. Could never hope to hit Uncle, let alone beat him. But as he steps away, I glimpse my friends in my memory. Hear their laughter. The time when the crew found out Pound's real name was Evergreen and Roderick wouldn't shut up about it. Or when Arika and I fed our friends dessert for breakfast. Or when Bryce and I stood, looking at the stars together, our hands close to touching. Or when Keeton caught me as I fell from the sky and saved my life.

Can't give up on them.

Can't.

As Uncle steps away, I use my cane to push myself up. My whole body's screaming. Can't see out of one eye. My vision's splotched with dots. And I feel like I'll retch again.

Once I'm propped against the couch, I lift my father's cane. Uncle's forgotten one of the primary lessons all Urwins have been taught: never trust a downed foe.

"Uncle," I rasp.

He turns in surprise.

Then I hurl the cane. Hard as I can before I tumble. When I hit the floor, my cane slams into him. Right in the chest, dropping him to the ground.

"The *Gladian,*" I seethe, "is mine."

CHAPTER 19

I STAND ON THE *DREADNOUGHT'S* DARK DECK, SQUEEZING the railing with excitement because Holmstead Island appears in the distance. It hovers in the sky, a giant mass, almost like it's held up by invisible string. The midafternoon sun highlights Holmstead's thick pine forests bordering the city. A Holmstead eagle soars past us, its pure-white body blending with the island's snowy surface.

I lean against the rail and wince from the sharp pain stabbing my side. My torso's covered with black-and-purple bruises. Uncle only gave me a partial dose of meds. Enough to save me, and enough to hide the bruises on my face—but not enough to forget who's in charge.

Still, I refuse to massage my aching body. Uncle might be watching from the command tower behind me. Despite my pains, I grin a little because I hit him. I hit the bastard. And my ship will remain mine. Best of all, my crew isn't going anywhere.

Holmstead nears.

Suddenly, I'm enveloped in island memories. Soon I'll be able to visit the Middle gardens, where Mother and I enjoyed cherry ice cream. Or sit on the banks of the Holmstead River and listen to the whistling wind between the trees.

But my smile weakens because as I stare at the city that climbs the white mountain, and at the Low shacks that rest at the base, and the walls that protect the Middles and Highs from scavenging Lows, something bitter trickles down my throat. Holmstead was where I lost everything. Where I was beaten in alleys. Where I cried, clutching my stomach because the hunger pains throbbed. Where fake people were more concerned about their damn top hats than giving me and my mother bread.

On Holmstead, Lows are lower than manure. Lower than ticks.

A pair of boots stops beside me. I look Pound up and down. He wears an ugly brown suit with golden buttons and a piss-yellow vest.

"You look like birdshit," I say.

"Speak for yourself. That your father's uniform?" He pauses and leans on the railing beside me.

"Uncle gave it me."

He hocks some phlegm and sends it arching into the distance. "Guess we both dressed for our grand returns, eh?"

Skyships travel to each of Holmstead's major docks, from the Lows to the Highs, and a few even soar to the private docks of some of the island's most powerful families.

"This is a grand return for you, Pound?"

"My family's going to be waiting for me."

I raise an eyebrow. "At the Urwin docks?"

"No, you fool. At their new manor. They're Highs again, you know."

"Ah, yes, I'm aware."

"Rose on the back of my father, Aggress. Great man, my father."

"Great? He disowned you."

His mouth shuts, and he focuses on the various manors near the crown of the mountain. The best, most beautiful homes with long terraces and splayed-out grounds of white, and little forested regions. Pound likely doesn't know which manor belongs to his family now. He hasn't spoken to them since he was rejected for losing a duel to Glinda of Muriel.

The Atwoods are well known across the North, not just for the size of their bodies but for the sheer number of them. Before their fall, some believed that the Atwoods would become so big and powerful they'd overtake the Urwins.

"How do you manage to remember all their names?" I ask.

"I keep a note in my shoe."

I laugh. "You're kidding."

He reaches into his left boot and slides out a paper full of names. More than I thought. Maybe seventy?

"My sisters and aunts love having babies," he says. "My brothers and uncles love making babies. I'm sure the number has grown since I left." He slides the note back into his boot.

"What will your family think?" I ask. "Knowing that you've allied yourself with an Urwin?"

"They respect strength," he says. "True strength."

"Uncle is strong," I say.

"He's also a bastard who has surrounded himself with lotchers. With people he knows will never try to take his role."

"And do you think I'm like him?"

He snorts. "No. But it may not matter what I think. It matters what my family thinks. Do they think you're strong?"

I consider what they'd think of me. "Your family could demand you resign your position on the *Gladian*. Go to another Hunter vessel."

He nods. "It's a possibility."

I pause, breathing through the sting of his matter-of-factness. "Does it bother you?"

"Would you choose this crew over your sister?"

I hesitate, try to answer, then shut my mouth. He smiles in

understanding, pats my shoulder, then stomps away. And as he goes, I wonder why it is Pound, of all people, who has become one of my closest friends. When we're enemies, he bruises me. When we're friends, he bruises me.

Keeton, Arika, Roderick, and Bryce approach. Their luggage is packed and ready. They've all earned a little break while the *Gladian* undergoes repairs inside the *Dreadnought's* hangar.

Keeton's draped in extra Hunter jackets. She dances in place to keep herself warm.

"So," Roderick says, hands on his hips as he gazes upon the giant manor at the apex of Holmstead, "that's where you grew up. Looks quaint."

Arika laughs.

Urwin Manor's a shiny beacon with great balconies, columns, and terraces. A white hedge maze borders the Urwin Square, and beyond that is a steaming pond. The grounds even have a secondary manor, tucked away in the trees near the base of the grounds. That was where Uncle lived before he murdered Father. Now Uncle uses it as a guest house to host powerful allies when they come to visit.

I glance behind me. Uncle, Severina, and Ella stand atop the *Dreadnought's* command tower. Uncle's pointing at the manor, perhaps telling stories to his wife. Severina watches. And Ella's smiling.

"Look at that gazebo," Keeton says, "right on the pond. How peaceful."

"Are there fish in the pond?" Roderick asks.

I nod. "The pond's heated, too."

"Heated?" He stares at me, astonished. "Rich brat. You have fishing poles?"

"I didn't know you liked to fish, Rod," I say.

"I *love* to fish."

I smile. "Well, we have trout, perch, and salmon. You're welcome to fish as much as you want."

Roderick brightens. "Keeton?"

"Catching fish?" She grimaces. "They're slimy, and it's *so* cold right now."

"We don't have to eat them. Besides, I'll keep you warm."

"Right," she says, rolling her eyes. "You eat everything."

"Can't blame him," Arika says. "Fish are delicious. Rod, if you can catch enough, it'd be nice to have a fresh stock when we return to the *Gladian*. I'd love to do a fish fry with some fresh lemon and pepper cream."

Roderick practically drools until he sees Keeton's expression. "Oh, don't be such a lotcher. I'll pull them off the hook for you."

"You kill gorgantauns for a living, Keeton," Bryce says. "You're worried about slimy fish?"

"Hey, I like being tucked in the warm engine room while all of you get drenched in gorgantaun blood."

We stare at her, and then we laugh again.

"So, are you fishing with me or not?" Roderick asks her.

"It's not boring?"

"Not at all! It's super exciting," Roderick says. "You get to sit around, enjoy some snacks, and wait."

Arika and I glance at each other and smirk.

"Okay, Roderick," Keeton says. "Okay."

Finally, the Urwin skydock nears. Groups of workers wait for us. I recognize some of them. They're older people from families who've worked for the Urwins for generations.

Before long, my friends and I step off one of the many bouncy gangways that descend from the *Dreadnought*. We walk along the heated, defrosted dock, followed by a crowd of people from the King's ship. The ground's wet, and mounds of snow form hills beside the dock. A fifteen-foot stone wall blocks us from entering the Urwin grounds. Six Order guards check people in through a station outside the Urwin gate.

"Your Highness," a guard says to me, his breath misting the air, "please lower your collar."

"Excuse me?"

"Orders from the King. No exceptions. Not even for you."

I lower my collar, and his cold hands gently feel around the base of my neck. Checking for a symbion scar.

The guard thumbs me past him. "You're free to move on."

For an instant I'm thinking that Holmstead is safe. No Lantians. But then I look back and notice Bryce has gone rigid. Her face sheet white. My heart plummets while she steps back, out of the line. Keeton, Arika, and Rod watch her, too, their mouths hanging open.

"Go in," I tell Keeton, Arika, and Rod.

"But . . ."

"Go."

They move ahead to get inspected, pass through the gate that leads toward the manor. But they're looking back, heartbroken.

I hurry after Bryce. While the crowd parts for me, Uncle's watching me from the ship above. And he's grinning. The bastard! Purposely ensuring that Bryce will never be able to step onto Holmstead again. Or at least, not in Urwin Manor. He'd never accept anyone with Lantian blood inside his home. Not even if that person is helping him shift the war.

Bryce cuts through the crowd, past Pound who looks at her questioningly, and starts back up one of the many gangways to the *Dreadnought*.

I call out to her. "Bryce!"

How can Uncle expect her to work with us if he treats her as an enemy? He's a damn birdshit. Bryce lived on Holmstead for two years. She went to University here. Had people she wanted to visit—even if it's dangerous for her.

I race up the gangway and find her standing alone at the starboard side, staring at the sky. Her shoulders slouched.

I stop beside her, mouth hesitating. Finally, I settle with lifting my arm and resting it on her shoulder. She shrugs me off.

Neither of us speaks for a couple minutes.

"This world," she finally whispers, "is broken. No damn good. Above. Below. It's all birdshit."

She turns, heading toward the stairwell that leads belowdecks. I call out to her, but she keeps going.

And then she disappears into the cold bowels of the ship.

✦✦✦

After I take Keeton, Roderick, and Arika around the manor and to the manor's guest rooms, I show Roderick where the fishing supplies are. Then, I eat a sandwich for dinner and enter my old room. Uncle left it exactly the way it was. He could've thrown everything out, but maybe he always knew I'd make it back. Or maybe he had so many rooms that it didn't matter if a child's room was left untouched and unused.

I feel so big compared to the small clothes hanging over the messy drawers. Paintings of Order cruisers and battlecruisers decorate the walls. Dust-covered gorgantauns dangle from the ceiling, spinning on their strings. And my closet's still half-open, revealing mountains of unused shoes and boots inside. I grin a little at them. Mother always fought to get me to wear shoes, and every time I claimed I'd lost them, she'd get me a new pair.

So the pile grew.

I plop onto the bed that's almost too small for me, and dust plumes the air. The twinkling stars glimmer at me through the glass ceiling. I lie, practically drowning in memories of this place. Can almost hear Ella snickering in the closet with me as we stuff our faces with stolen treats from the kitchen.

But my happiness slips away because of the glimmering stars above. They're a reminder of the girl with spikey hair who loves the stars. I've caught Bryce just gazing at them so many times. What's she doing now? Maybe she's back on the *Gladian*, even if it's under repair. Perhaps working on the clay sculpture of her brother.

I tap my comm gem and send her a message. But she doesn't respond, and the comm gem turns gray.

I sigh.

Part of me wants to barge into Uncle's office. Interrupt his meeting with the new ruler of Holmstead, an ally of his. As always, placing people he can control in power. And then I'd demand that Bryce gets to step onto these grounds. But I've pushed Uncle too much lately. Have the bruises to prove it.

Still, I'm not going to sit here, enjoying myself, while Bryce is stuck in that steel cage. So I open my luggage, and soon I'm zipping up my Hunter uniform and clipping on my magboots. It's better to be dressed as a Hunter. Less likely to be recognized.

Soon I'm walking under cold flurries, my hood up, and it's not long until I'm climbing the gangway to the *Dreadnought*. A few Order guards patrol the deck around the massive turrets and cannons. One stops me before realizing who I am. Then I descend the stairwell into the carrier's gray corridors, tap the button on the elevator, and lower to the hangar.

Sparks fly from the *Gladian*, and the echoes of shouting workers carry to me.

Once I step aboard my damaged ship, a repairer approaches me, but she realizes who I am and backs away. I slide down the hatch's ladder and walk the dimly lit corridors inside my ship while the walls vibrate from the tools above.

I stop at Bryce's door, staring at it, and raise a fist to knock. But I pause. Maybe this was a mistake. If she wanted to talk, she would've replied on the comm, right? My head shakes. No, I came all this way to see her.

I knock.

No response.

"Bryce?"

Something shuffles inside. After a few seconds, the door yawns open. Bryce stares at me through the crack, her eyes narrowed.

"What?" she says, irritated.

Her jacket's resting on her bed, and her silver Hunter sleeves are rolled up, exposing the clay on her arms.

"Hi," I say.

She watches me with cold eyes, and a sudden heat blooms in my cheeks. This—this is not how I hoped this would go.

"Bryce, you . . . you didn't answer the comm."

"Yeah?"

My mouth hesitates. "Are you okay?"

She exhales. Behind her is an open bag of clay. The face of her brother has been partially destroyed.

"Bryce, I—"

"This isn't a great time, Conrad."

"It always seems to be that way, though."

"Did you expect me to be excited to see you tonight?"

My mouth shuts. Right. Stupid. I shouldn't have come. "Okay." I backpedal. "I'll just leave you be. Good night, Bryce."

She looks ready to say something, but shakes her head and shuts the door. Got to admit, this hurts. But what did I expect? I'm a damn idiot. Fighting gorgantauns? That I can do. But this?

I'm woefully unprepared.

I follow the quiet corridor, clasp the bars of the ladder, and start up. My boots echo toward the hatch. Bryce has a lot on her mind right now. Perhaps she's a little like me in that way. She needs to be alone sometimes. I get it. And she's been through absolute hell. Abandoned by her family. Lost her brother. Sent to the Skylands and failed her mission to rise. Betrayed her own people. Revealed their deepest secret, the symbions.

Of course she didn't want to see me. I'm not used to feeling so embarrassed, but holy hell, my skin's practically burning with discomfort. What was I thinking?

You dumb birdshit, Conrad.

When I reach the deck, I hurry toward the gangway leading to the *Dreadnought's* platform.

But a voice calls for me. I stop and turn around.

Bryce stands just outside the hatch, her arms folded. She came to me this time. That must mean something, I think. Or maybe she just wants to let me know what an idiot I am.

I stop before her.

She licks her teeth. "Why did you come? Really?"

"I was—well, I was thinking of visiting Holmstead."

"You don't need to see me to do that."

"I thought you'd want to visit it, too. But you don't—"

"How?"

I blink, then nod toward the lifeboat and the *Dreadnought's* open hangar beyond. "We fly out."

"Fly? The island has Order checkpoints."

"I'm the Prince. I don't think Order will stop us unless we try to go to the Highs or Urwin Manor. That's where security will be tight. That's how it has always been."

Her hands rest on her hips for a moment. Her face is still tightened with irritation, but finally, she turns on her heels and stomps toward a lifeboat.

"C'mon," she says. "I'm flying."

✦✦✦

Bryce navigates the lifeboat into the chilly open sky. Months ago I paid part of my Gauntlet winnings to purchase enhanced lifeboats for the *Gladian.* Ones with quick crystal engines instead of sails.

The lifeboat soars smoothly among the fleet. I sit just a little ahead of Bryce, gripping the side. It's not long until we're contacted over the comm by the giant shadows looming before the moon—the biggest ships of the fleet. But once they realize who I am, they act exactly as I believed.

With deference.

We shoot past the carriers, and now we're gliding under the stars and among gentle snowflakes. Bryce jerks the crystal engine rod, turning us toward the city.

Our breaths cloud the air.

I glance back at her. She's so focused, eyes studying the white mountain that rises over the island.

"Bryce," I say softly, "there's another reason I came to see you." She looks at me, and I swallow a big gulp of air. "You and I—I've been thinking. I'd like to work on our communication."

She considers me. "You're many things, Conrad, but you are not always the best communicator."

"Neither are you."

"I have always had my reasons for keeping things from you."

I pause, and we go utterly quiet. The icy wind trails over the boat, and Holmstead Mountain grows larger as we approach. For an instant I'm watching the glowing lights of the city, stewing in memories from my lost childhood. Remembering Father and his stoic gaze as he'd look over the city from his office.

But Bryce snaps me back into the moment.

"The King murdered them," she says suddenly. "I heard what happened. People on the *Dreadnought* were talking. Hundreds and hundreds of Lantians dead because I revealed the symbions."

The reminder leaves me queasy. "Bryce, that's not on you."

"How is it not? I revealed the secret knowing it'd happen. I made my decision hoping it'll, in the end, save more lives than it takes." She pauses. "But I have this nagging fear in the back of my mind."

"What fear?"

She frowns. "That the only difference between the Lantians and your uncle is they have a massive weapon, and he does not."

Her words hit me like a fistful of snow.

"Conrad, you must remove him one day."

"Me?"

"You're an Urwin. The Skylands know your family, your family's strength. They'd respect you. There isn't another person I'd trust to be the Highest High."

"But remove him?" I turn to her and wince from the bruises Uncle gave me. She raises an eyebrow as I hold my side. "Bryce, I'm a strong dueler, but I'd never be able to—"

She scoffs. "You're an arrogant bastard, but you lack confidence regarding your uncle? The man who took all you wanted? You want to beat him, don't you?"

"Of course, but—"

"But what? Have you grown soft because you reunited with your sister? Because you have a crew who cares about you?"

"Bryce—"

She stares at me, frowns, then gently rests her hand on my shoulder. I don't respond. Master Koko said I'd gone soft, too.

Am I really getting too comfortable?

A bitter cold wind blows between us. I zip my jacket to the top, but Bryce lets hers flap, ignoring the icy wind that pales her cheeks. She knows Holmstead winters.

Lived them for two years.

A blue galaxy of stars glimmers above us, and we soar above the golden glow of the Highs. I breathe out, slowly so I don't hurt my aching ribs, and push Uncle from my mind.

Suddenly, a pair of Order sparrows zip up to us—perhaps to investigate who we are, but the men inside the ships recognize me and shoot away.

"Bryce, where are we going?"

"My favorite place on this miserable island."

I blink, realizing that if she's taking me somewhere special to her, I think this means she's letting me in a bit.

Maybe.

I lean over the side, eyeballing the High manors of Holmstead. A few of the rich walk the streets under the lamps of waving crystal light, their shiny, uncracked canes dangling from their hips. Giant manors tower over them. The old Atwood Manor, now Muriel Manor, is one of the more grandiose, with arched windows all along its eastern wing.

For an instant we peer through a manor's glass ceiling and glimpse a giant feast attended by Highs. Six long tables stand under fine dining cloths and delectable rich curries, golden breads, and roasted meats.

We sail over the manor, above several floating carriages, and out of the Highs. As I glance back at the retreating manors, I wonder if Pound found his family's new manor yet.

Now we're above the pointed, snowy roofs of the Middles. The brick homes glow with light and laughter. The Middles are the heart of Holmstead. At least, that's what Mother taught me. We shoot over little cafés where people drink late-night tea and laugh while sheltered under patios warmed by the pulses of heatglobes.

In the distance, rising over the Middles, are the great spires of the University. This long-standing institution is run jointly by multiple Trades to help people get Selected. Scholar, Art, Mercantile, Architect. I've even heard Hunter runs a few classes, though I've never been. When I was little, my parents paid for tutors, so I never considered going to the University. Furthermore, Father wanted me to be a dueler, not someone with Select status. After his death Mother and I could barely afford food, so Mother tutored me the best she could. She thought, even if I was going to be a dueler, that I needed to have an education to better understand the world and make informed and more just decisions.

Several University students walk beneath us, carrying their bags. Some chat, and their voices echo to us. The crystal lamps sway below, reflecting beautifully off the sparkly snow. It's so calm and peaceful tonight.

Bryce seems to be breathing everything in. Looking over the University like she's lost in nostalgic bliss.

We continue over the campus. I used to wonder why University was in the Middles and not the Highs. But it makes sense now. The Highs are filled with too many lotchers who don't care about getting Selected. Whereas the Middles are hungry to learn. And to rise.

"I took several Art classes as an elective there," Bryce says suddenly, pointing at a blue building. She then nods toward a red one. "I studied social hierarchies with Scholar, too. But I was sent to the Above to become a Hunter with the hopes of eventually becoming Master Koko's successor. That was my dorm, right there."

We zoom over a plain, bricked building with little stone balconies. Red light from pulsing heatglobes shines from the windows and permeates the swaying snowflakes with crimson. The interiors of the dorm rooms are tiny, big enough for just a small desk and a narrow bed.

We soar past the University, fly over the Middle gardens, and approach a small dock that rises above a street filled with quaint shops and cafés.

"This is it," she says, pulling the boat's rod back, slowing us to a stop beside the planks.

I toss the chain overboard and lock it to the dock, and we climb out. Snow crunches under our boots while we descend the stairs. Our breaths puff, but the night's so calm.

Bryce points at a small chocolate shop across the street. A golden mug rises over the front entry, and the windows beam resplendent light on the slushy path.

"I used to go here with my friends after big tests or long days of studying," she says. "It's open all night."

We stop as a hovering carriage zooms past us, the crystal engine humming in the back. After we cross the street, we enter the chocolate shop, and it bathes me in a warm hug. Chocolates of all types and colors, in shapes of everything from gorgantauns to insignias of the Twelve Trades. Even some crafted into full-size dueling canes.

A few people wait to get items from behind a glass case.

We pass all that to approach a counter at the back. A few University-aged employees chat on the other side of the glass before turning to look at us. Bryce orders us caramel twists and mugs of their pure hot chocolate. She gives coins to the workers.

Within a minute I'm staring at our tray of desserts, thinking I'm going to get a stomachache. I'm not used to eating sweets regularly, not since I was a High. Back then I ate them way too often. But after I fell to Low, I couldn't afford such luxuries. A serving of canned cake on the *Gladian* is usually the most I can handle.

Bryce leads us to a narrow staircase. We climb up the metal steps that rise to a platform that overlooks the shop. It's beautiful and quiet up here, with cozy nooks for people to tuck in and read or study.

I stare in amazement. Have the Middles always been this way? When I was a High, I didn't come here nearly as often as I'd have liked. As a Low, I wasn't exactly welcome, and I couldn't afford anything, anyway.

We pass a couple romantics who snuggle and whisper in their nook. Bryce leads us to small table surrounded by a padded bench covered in soft, warm pillows. The nearby frosty window gives us a glimpse of the winter sky and a passing skyship.

We sit. Bryce adjusts the pillows just the right way around her, and she smiles. The first time I've seen her smile tonight. She stirs her hot chocolate with the caramel twister. Then she cups her hands over the mug, lifts it to her lips, and closes her eyes. And she just grins and breathes.

"You were happy here," I say.

She looks at me over her mug.

I take a sip. It's incredibly sweet, but quite tasty, too.

"I've just never seen you happier," I say. "Drinking that chocolate and swimming in those pillows."

She goes quiet and glances around us. We're alone, far from the whispering workers below, the nuzzling romantics, and another couple holding hands by a fireplace.

"For all the Skylands' problems," she says, "it was nice coming Above. Studying, being with friends, looking at the stars. Learning."

I nod. Better than her life in the Below. "Still, you had to think about your mission."

"I put it out of my mind as much as possible." She takes another sip. "You should make a nest."

"What?"

"With your pillows. It's comfortable. Just tuck them around you."

"I'm not a bird, Bryce."

She snorts.

I grin a little, too. Then I reach for a pillow, but my side throbs with a sharp pain from my bruises. I seethe.

"What's the matter with you?" Bryce stares at me with concern. "Are you hurt?"

"I'm fine."

Her eyes narrow. "Just a few minutes ago, you were telling me that we needed to work on our communication." Her face becomes stern. "Are we going to work on it or not?"

"It's just—it's not a big deal."

She eyes me skeptically. And she's completely right that communication should fly both ways. But how am I supposed to tell her?

"Conrad, talk to me."

I breathe out and sip more of the chocolate. Father would tell me to keep my mouth shut. Or tell her that I fell or something. But then I meet her eyes and realize that I can't ask her to be honest with me if I can't be honest with her.

"I had a duel."

She lowers the mug. "What? With whom?"

"Uncle."

Her tongue seems to stop working. I take another sip of the chocolate. The warmth floods me, and somehow, my torso aches a little less.

"Conrad." She reaches over and rests her hand on mine. "Why did you duel?"

"It's not important."

"Stop being cryptic," she growls, "and just *talk*."

I breathe out, but not too hard because of my ribs. She's right. She's started sharing more with me, it's only fair I share more with her.

So I tell her the truth.

She's silent as she listens.

"You let him beat you up," she whispers, "so you could stay with the crew?"

I nod. "Like I said, it's not that big of a deal."

She squeezes my hand fiercely now. "You are better than this world, Conrad. Better. And"—she pauses, just to make sure no one can hear us—"your uncle is the worst of it."

Her grip is firm, reassuring. Something about talking to her, revealing things—it siphons some of the pain from me. Leaves me feeling less broken. I should talk to her. Mother would want me to talk to her.

After we finish our treats, I don't want this night to end because I'm thinking about how good it felt to talk and how I enjoyed her hand on mine. And that I kind of like this place she brought me to. It let me see another side of her I didn't know.

"Do you mind if we make another stop before going back?" I ask as we step out of the chocolate shop.

Bryce raises her collars. "Isn't it late?"

"I'm not tired if you're not."

She eyes me, then nods. "Okay. Where are we going?"

"To visit to an old friend."

I notice that she's walking a little closer to me than before. Maybe because I'm blocking a bit of the bitter wind. Or maybe . . .

Soon we're back on the lifeboat, soaring above the Middles. Now I'm the one pushing the navigation stick, and Bryce is seated directly next to me.

We keep flying until the Middles' crystal lights are gone and the endless shacks of the Lows splay out beneath us. A lucky few shacks have chimneys, and they puff smoke into the tender winter night. As we're gliding, I spot shadows scurrying along the icy alleys. Perhaps they're orphans—little children who lost their parents from duels. But there are shadows of bigger, more menacing people, too. The kind who will stick your gut because they like your shoes.

We soar over an area that cuts me. About ten months ago these Lows swelled under fire because gorgantauns attacked the island. As we fly over these alleys, a knot constricts my insides because I remember when I ran there, trying to get back to Mother.

"That's where we met," Bryce says, pointing. "I caught you by the collar and pulled you from a falling wall."

"Yes, thank you for that. What were you doing in the Lows that night, anyway?"

"I came to feed a little girl some bread," she says. "An orphan I found."

My mouth shuts. Bryce is better than this world, too. Meritocracy is awful. Innocents, including little children, have to suffer for things that have nothing to do with them.

"After the attack started on the island," Bryce says, "I tried to help whomever I could. But it was all chaos."

"What happened to the little girl?"

She goes quiet. "I couldn't find her."

We continue over the Lows. Smoke flitters into the sky. Bryce sits so close to me, her hips are warm against mine.

"We're here," I say.

I pull back on the navigating rod, stopping us directly above a small, wooden building. I kick a ladder over the edge, and it sinks to the icy roof. Once we hop off the ladder and land on the shingles, we grin at each other a little, realizing that the building below us is vibrating with dance and song.

"This was my home," I say. "It was destroyed in the attack, but McGill rebuilt it."

She laughs. "You lived above a tavern?"

"I've learned way too many inappropriate pub songs."

"You'll have to teach them to me sometime!"

I lock the ladder to a metal hook nestled between the bricks of the chimney, and Bryce and I follow the slight slope of the roof, our boots crunching snow. We approach a snowcapped dormer window that protrudes from the roof. These kind of windows are rare in the Lows—they let people step out onto the roof and potentially climb a ladder to a skyship. I scrape off the frost on the glass and cup my hands around my eyes to peer inside. It's all dark and quiet. Vacant. I slide the cold window upright and slip in. Bryce follows. Then we stare at the inside of the dusty, cold attic. It was rebuilt just the way it had been, although the dimensions seem off. It seems impossibly small now, but that could just be old memories.

My head's nearly touching the ceiling, the floorboards creak as we walk, and music plays beneath us. The fireplace is new—the stones are misshapen, not the way they were, but the mantle where I kept Father's cane looks exactly the same.

For several minutes, I'm sifting through memories of a place that's the same but isn't. I recall the times Mother tutored me on crystallic engineering before a meager fire or when, before she got sick, she taught me her way of the cane in the center of the room.

"This is where you lived after your exile," Bryce whispers.

I nod.

She slips her hand into mine. "Your mother would be proud of you."

Bryce's hand is coarse, like all Hunters, but warm and comforting. Her fingers weave between mine. I'm not sure how to respond to her comment, so I squeeze her hand. My heart thumps a little too much, too. Heat rises in my cheeks.

Mother would've liked Bryce. Bryce is tough as hell, gritty, and smart. Best of all, she calls me out on my birdshit. I'm afraid if I told Bryce how much I admire her, I'd scare her away.

"You are better than this world, too, Bryce."

She watches me.

My voice cracks a little because this is uncharted territory for me. And I don't know how she'll respond. But I have to say it. "Bryce, you came to the Skylands not to conquer, but to save lives. And when something threatened that goal, you flipped sides. You are the bravest person I've ever met."

Her cheeks redden a little. She meets my eyes again, locking me in place. Finally, she breaks eye contact and glances around the room again.

We stop at one last place. The place where Mother's bed used to be. Now it's storage for ale, grain, and potatoes. Mother told me, at this very spot, that kindness reciprocates, and she was right. Because the tavern owner, McGill, he brought us in. Let us live with him for years.

Well, it's time I pay him back.

"C'mon," I say.

She lets go of my hand, and we start down the creaky stairs. The dance and song intensifies. A couple Lows hiccup at the base of the stairs, their feet unsteady, unable to maintain their balance.

We step past them and enter a room full of tables and warmth. Full of laughter. McGill's Tavern has always been one of the happiest places in the Lows. An old man behind the bar fills another drink and a waiter hurries it to a table. A musician strums a dented guitar while drunk Lows sway to the rhythm.

Most of the people are too preoccupied to notice me or Bryce. But the man behind the bar does. His mouth falls, and he wipes his hands on a rag and hurries to hug me.

"Conrad!" McGill lets me go, then pats my cheek. "Look how strong you've become. Sturdy as a mashtaun!" He glances at Bryce and gives me a coy look. "And who is this?"

"This is Bryce," I say. "She's my friend."

He hugs her, too. She glances at me in surprise, then smiles and pats his back. Soon, with drunken music behind us, we enter the back kitchen area. McGill has potato and pea soup bubbling on the wood-burning stove. While he's stirring and adding salt to the soup, I reach into my jacket and pull a bag of coins from my pocket.

"McGill, you let me and my mother live here for free," I say. "This is yours."

McGill turns, sees the coins, and drops the ladle. "Conrad, that's . . . that's . . . I can't take that."

It's a bag so dense he could move away. He could hire guards to protect his tavern from thieves. Best of all, he's a Low. You can't challenge a Low for their status because there's no place for them to fall. This money would be his and would always remain his. So long as he kept it safe from thieves.

"I'm the Prince," I say. "And I say you must take it."

He laughs and rests his hands on his hips. "Well, you're still the same snot you always were."

I grin.

"McGill," I say, turning serious. "Please take it. I need you to take it."

He eyeballs me, scratches his gray neck, and exhales. "Fine, boy. Fine."

Afterward he offers us drinks and sits with us at a secluded table, laughing and listening as I tell him stories of the Gauntlet—rising to Captain, becoming Prince.

Bryce and I slurp the hot potato soup. It's hardly seasoned beyond the salt, but it's hearty. A great meal in the Lows.

McGill offers more, claims he has some meat he could cook. Expensive—well, expensive for him, but I raise a hand. I'd love to spend more time with him, but it's late. So, after giving him a final hug, Bryce and I go back up the stairs, climb out the window, and take the ladder to the lifeboat. Then we sail into the sky.

As we're soaring through the cold air beneath the crescent moon, Bryce scoots closer to me. I point out a few places in the Lows. The dueling pit, for instance, and I tell her a couple stories. She leans against my shoulder.

I pause, a little shocked that she's so close to me now, because when she opened her door for me on the *Gladian* a few hours ago, I'm pretty sure she wanted to murder me. This is the same girl who kicked the shit out of me in a duel once.

Everything between me and Bryce is complicated. Forbidden by Uncle, too. But something about her makes me feel like there's something right in the world—even when it's gone to birdshit. She sits up and smiles at me. And I notice her lips. My breaths grow a little tight.

I've dropped mountains on gorgantauns. I've fought Lantians to the death.

But I've never kissed a girl.

We approach the *Dreadnought.* I still don't want this night to end. I just like being next to her and forgetting about all the bad going on. And part of me wants her to continue leaning her head against my shoulder because for some reason, my heart flutters when she does that. But I don't want to keep her longer than I already have.

We get a message over the comm from the *Dreadnought*, and I identify myself. I almost wish they'd tell us to go away. But the hangar doors crack open, and soon we hop off the lifeboat and stand on the deck of the *Gladian*.

We're alone except for the people on the distant hangar platforms. The repairers have apparently gone to bed.

We stand a little awkwardly, looking at each other. Her lips part as if she's going to say something, but then she hesitates. My eyes lock on her lips again. This time I'm wondering, just a little, what they'd feel like against mine.

She notices me looking, and her skin flushes.

"Well, that was nice," she says.

I scratch the back of my neck. "Yeah, I had fun."

But now, she's watching my lips, too. And suddenly, my face is burning hot. Almost uncomfortably so. I don't even know what to do with myself right now. But I really want to kiss her. Does she feel the same?

No, of course not. Besides, even if she wanted to kiss me, we shouldn't. There are people moving about on the platforms of the hangar.

"Well, good night," I say.

I turn to walk away but she catches my hand. Our eyes meet, and . . . her eyes. Her beautiful blue eyes. I almost can't stand how much they make my stomach twist. She touches my cheek, and her touch is electric. Sparks my skin. And now I'm breathing quick breaths. She gently rests her hands on my forearms and rises on the tips of her toes.

We're almost eye level.

She wants to be closer to me—I'm not an idiot. I can tell. Well, I want to be close to her so much it burns. But Uncle . . .

Now her warm hands grip my neck. She pulls me down, and I nearly stumble into her. She clutches me tight, stabilizing me, grins a little, then presses her lips against mine. Holy hell. Her lips are like liquid fire. My breath shudders.

Her body's pressed against mine. Warm. Tender. Her lips part, so I do the same. I'm feeling her breath. This is so strange and incredible at the same time. My hands rise to touch her. Not sure where to put them. I settle with her shoulders, but that doesn't feel right, so I slide them down to her lower back.

She presses her lips fiercer against mine. Now she's hugging me close, her chest breathing against my stomach.

A warning fires in the back of my head. Telling me to stop. That Uncle's people are watching. Father's voice is practically shouting in my head to push her away. And maybe I should. But all I'm thinking about is this moment of joy.

And I pull her even closer.

CHAPTER 20

THE NEXT EVENING UNCLE, ELLA, SEVERINA, AND I SIT AROUND an ornate table in an Urwin Manor dining room. It's a cold silence. The others quietly dab their mouths after slivering off bites of gorgantaun Westley. The decadent dish, a buttery pastry filled with mushroom, ham, and a tender cut of gorgantaun, takes days to marinate and costs a fortune. But I can hardly eat more than a bite because of the room's atmosphere.

It's broken, uncaring. Unloving.

Worse, Uncle's scowling at me. "You have not listened to a word I've told you about that girl, Conrad."

"Who?"

"Don't play coy with me, *Nephew*."

"Bryce is none of your concern."

He throws down his napkin. "Who the Prince fraternizes with in public is entirely my concern."

Ella's eyes widen as she looks between us.

"People are whispering about her, Nephew. This is why she's not allowed on the island. She has value! Now word is spreading about a Lantian getting intimate with the Prince. Today alone I had to squash several rumors."

My mouth shuts.

"Whatever you two decide to do together, do it in private. Do you understand me?"

My skin burns hot, angry. This is none of his damned business! But I'd be a fool to tempt him to exert more power over me. He could take Bryce away. And more.

So I force the words out through gritted teeth. "I understand, *King*."

He stares at me.

"It will not happen again," I say.

He scowls, takes a sip of his water, and doesn't speak another word on it.

We eat in silence. Don't look at one another. The tension's so thick you could choke on it. I hate it here. I came back to Holmstead and to this manor hoping to be lost in memories, but home isn't home without the people you love.

Ella picks at her cauliflower mash. Is this the life she truly craves? Does she not remember when we sat at this table six years ago and Mother would tell us stories and make us laugh . . . ?

As much as Ella tries to hide it, I can tell she's uncomfortable. She keeps giving Severina suspicious glances. Severina's a total unknown. Suddenly, Uncle has a wife. In his early forties, and never married—until her. What makes her special?

Eventually, a pair of cooks brings in dessert. They slide small plates before us, and Uncle takes one bite of the chocolate froulee before pushing the custard cake away.

"I've heard a rather interesting report," he says.

Our heads raise.

"Ella has been carrying a dueling cane." His gaze upon Ella makes her shrivel. "Is this true?"

Ice climbs my back.

Ella bravely meets his eyes. "Yes, King. I have."

Uncle's voice goes soft with traumatizing disapproval. "You were supposed to get a cane that I had crafted specially for you. But your impatience—"

"It was my fault, King," I say. "I ga—"

Uncle raises a hand to silence me.

"Let me see the cane," he says to Ella.

"It's on the *Gladian*."

"Get it. Now."

Ella practically runs from the room. Her eyes full of fear. It's the same fear I felt around Father. You didn't argue. You just obeyed.

Uncle's fingers drum on the table as he waits. Severina continues eating slivers of her dessert, completely unconcerned with the whole affair. My heart attacks my ribs and my thoughts are spiraling, considering a way to salvage this. What will Uncle do? Five minutes pass. He stands and clasps his hands behind his back as he watches the city through the window.

Finally, Ella returns with Mother's white cane, and she's biting her trembling lip.

Uncle motions her toward him.

I swallow hard as she brings the cane for his inspection. He stares at it a moment, until his brow wrinkles with recognition.

"Ah," he says. Then he looks at her. "So, you carried the cane of a Low?"

I nearly explode. A Low? Elise of Hale? The former Lady of Holmstead?

"This cane is unbecoming of one of your status, Ella."

He stands over her. Going to hit her. How will I stop myself from attacking him when that happens? I'll lose my crew. My ship. Pound thinks I'd choose my sister over my crew. But I shouldn't have to choose.

Instead, something else appears on Uncle's face. Something I've never seen before, not since I was a young boy and he'd bring me sweets when he came to visit Urwin Manor.

He leans down to Ella's level and gently lifts her chin so she meets his eyes. It's a tender expression, and enough that Ella responds. Suddenly, I understand why she feels how she does about Uncle. It's pure manipulation. These tiny moments of love—they're enough to feed her. Drive her. Because she wants to impress him. Will do whatever it takes to get that one little smile. That one little shoulder squeeze.

My blood rages.

"Ella, I am disappointed."

Her head lowers. "I'm sorry, Father—King."

"Apologies are not for Urwins, Ella. Look at me. You are strong. Only the weak look down."

She takes a breath and forces herself to look him in the eye.

He smiles softly. "I understand your desire for a cane, and I appreciate your instincts. I've heard of your exploits aboard the *Gladian*. Is it true that you battled multiple Lantians in the corridor and defeated them by yourself?"

"Yes."

"You are impressive, Ella. Keep impressing me, and perhaps it'll be you who becomes the first heir."

Ella puffs up her chest, proud. But I fold my arms. Severina looks over her froulee at me, and the tiniest of grins creases her lips. Uncle's already trying to pit Ella and me against each other.

I want to throw my fork.

"You must earn my forgiveness," Uncle says. "You will receive your cane. The true cane that you are owed and deserve. But you must prove something to me first."

Ella nods eagerly. "Anything, King."

Uncle rises to full height and straightens his jacket. He lifts Mother's cane. "Destroy this thing. This impostor. This cane of the Low."

I lock up. Feel like a brick fell in my gut. *No, Ella!* I want to shout to her. *Don't do this. Don't destroy the one thing Mother left for you. Please don't. You don't need to prove to him that you are strong because you already* are *strong.*

Uncle holds out the white cane with the black stag of Hale to her.

Ella side-eyes me. Hesitating. But I know what she's going to do. What she must do because she's been manipulated. And I failed her. Couldn't get enough time with her.

I watch, horrified, as Ella grips Mother's cane. She lifts the cane above her head . . . and after a sharp exhale, her face sets with resolve. She bashes the end of it against the floor. Over and over. Each strike makes me jerk. The cane cracks, and splinters spread about the room.

But I'm not here anymore. I'm with Mother, and we're in the Low alleys, huddled together under a grimy blanket, trying to stay warm. Three Lows break through winter's haze, stomping toward us. Coming with horrible intentions.

Mother stands, sweeps me behind her, and extends her cane.

"Leave," she warns them.

They ignore her.

So she makes them leave.

Ella keeps slamming Mother's cane against the floor. Finally, the stag comes loose and rolls to my feet. The eyes of the animal look up at me, judging me for my failure.

I failed Ella. I failed Mother.

Once Ella's done, Uncle smiles and rests a hand on her shoulder. The closest to a hug I've ever seen him give. Then he leads her away, taking her to his office, where he will award her with another cane. One with an Urwin eagle.

Severina rises to join in on the family event, but I remain at the table. Staring in shock at the stag at my feet. I'm blinking back tears.

They don't even care that I don't follow.

The door shuts, and my hands shake as I grip Mother's stag. What would Mother feel now? This would've broken her like it has broken me. I know she'd want me to let Ella go her own way. It's not my responsibility to choose the winds she should follow. But this—the destruction of the one thing Mother left for her—is too much for me to bear.

Uncle has pushed any thought of Mother from Ella's mind.

He alone reigns in Ella's heart.

My teeth clench. My body trembles. But I won't forget Mother. I won't forget the powerful woman who did everything she could to teach me a better way.

I wipe my eyes and pick up the remaining pieces of her.

✦✦✦

A few days later, I stand on a platform, overlooking the repairs of the *Gladian*. My gloves squeak while the hangar fills with the echoes of shouts, tools, and the clangs of metal.

My ship must be ready as soon as possible. The giga is coming, and I can't be on this island anymore. Can't be anywhere near Ella, or Uncle. Or anything Urwin.

I'm done.

Sparks fly across my ship's deck and hull. The *Gladian's* coming back to life. Over the past several days, the holes in her metal have been patched. The deck repaired. The engine room rebuilt. The *Gladian* really is a beautiful ship. Silver-bodied with a sharp bow that cuts through clouds.

On a platform below me, a great man walks with an entourage toward a ship. He's enormous in stature, with wide shoulders and a huge back. His ship's a dusty-colored eastern flier, thin and swift but stocked with multiple turrets. The kind of ship that is used to face the acid-spitting beasts of the East.

My eyes narrow on the man. Recognize him from when he visited my father years ago. Sione of Niumatalolo.

A half dozen varieties of dueling weapons hang from either his hips or back. Batons, a cane, a staff, bracers, and even smooth throwing stones. Sione's bald head glistens under the crystal lights on the walkway.

My forehead wrinkles. What is the world's most famous dueler doing on the *Dreadnought*? Oh . . . My face wrinkles with bitterness. Uncle's acting like a lotcher again. As his power weakens, as the Skylands lose respect for him, he's rallying support from those the Skylands do respect.

Sione's never bothered rising above High. Despite ample opportunity. No, his joy, his desire, lies within the dueling arena. And it seems, based on his attire, he's trained in every dueling weapon of the Skylands. I've heard he uses the same dueling weapon as his opponent. Proving he can beat them at what they're best at.

The chains connecting his ship to the *Dreadnought* slide back into the hull, and soon his ship slips out the open hangar into blue sky.

Someone stops beside me, leans on the railing, and watches the ship disappear. A cold wind passes between us.

We say nothing for several minutes.

Her voice comes out gentler and less direct than usual. Perhaps because I haven't spoken to her in three days.

"Do you want to see my new cane?" she asks.

I don't answer.

She unclips it from her belt and holds it over the railing. Balancing it gently on the edges of her fingertips. Could easily drop it and lose it into the depths of the hangar, but her balance is practiced.

She twirls it once.

It's a lifeless, red rod topped with a steel-eyed eagle. Red, because Uncle claimed that was her color. Bold. Indomitable. Courageous.

I feel nauseous.

"Though, truth be told," she says, flipping the cane and catching it, "it doesn't have the same balance as Mother's."

I squeeze the railing.

"But I'll learn it," she says. "Today I'm dueling Severina. For practice, of course. Don't know how well she duels. Uncle says that she's incredible. Meds will be on hand. Do you want to watch? I'm eager to test out my cane and see how strong Severina is."

My teeth nearly bite my tongue. She's so proud of her little cane. So proud that she passed the Urwin rite of passage and now she's a true Urwin.

"Congratulations," I say.

Then I turn and walk away, leaving her standing on the platform.

✦✦✦

The following evening, my crew joins me in my suite on the *Dreadnought*. Since Bryce can't visit the manor, I arranged for everyone to return to the King's ship. My suite's a massive room filled with snacks.

Pound's in a terrible mood, and he's stuffing his face. Sad. Disappointed. Angry. Probably failed to convince his family to accept him again. Roderick joins him, eating an apple and joking that Keeton caught a fish that's bigger than he is, but all he could catch was a cold.

Pound doesn't react.

"Conrad," Keeton says, sidling up next to me. "You haven't eaten a bite."

"They're a test," I say.

Her brow wrinkles in confusion.

"Uncle leaves this food to tempt me," I say. "To see if I have the will to say no. A true Urwin has control over his desires."

"But you're not a true Urwin," she says. "Have some of these chocolate-covered appleberries."

I don't answer.

Bryce leans against the wall, arms folded, watching us. Still disappointed that she's been trapped on this ship for days. And worse, probably upset that I haven't visited her since we kissed. Not that I haven't wanted to, but I've had a lot on my mind since then.

Arika joins Keeton, Pound, and Roderick and samples all the delectable desserts. Even as she bites sweet things, she has a sour face, too. Seems few of us of have been impressed with our six days on Holmstead.

Exhausted, I lower onto a cushion, feeling as broken as Mother's cane.

I've hidden the remnants of it on the *Gladian*. Because if Uncle had it his way, he would've dropped them into the sky.

For several minutes my crew socializes—at least a little more than before. Arika opens a bag stocked with winter mushrooms she got in the Middles and shows them to Pound. Telling him all about the mushroom sauce she's planning on making for everyone once we're back on the *Gladian*. Roderick, meanwhile, rests his head on Keeton's lap and tries convincing her to hand-feed him some grapes, but she squeezes his nose instead.

Through it all, Bryce watches me. Finally, she lowers onto the cushion beside mine. And I can practically feel her thoughts. Almost like they're creeping inside my mind.

"So," she says, "we kiss, and then you disappear."

I exhale. "My uncle."

"Okay, so tell me. We're working on our communication, yes?"

All my instincts tell me to lock up. Just shut it all away and move on. But when I look at her and she gently nudges me, I know she's right.

And it's not just her that I have to communicate with.

Slowly, my mouth opens. And the tone of my voice, serious and morbid, gets all their attention. Roderick sits up. Keeton leans forward. Pound puts down the platter, and Arika's watching me with concerned eyes. Soon they're gathering around, and the words just spill out from me. I reveal everything—from the Lantian slaughter to the moment I dueled Uncle to keep the crew together.

Keeton gasps. Tries to hug me, but I grimace from my bruised ribs.

"Sorry, Conrad," Keeton says, lowering her hands to her side. "You're still in pain. You need meds."

"Uncle won't allow it."

Pound growls, "Since when have you listened to that horrible birdshit?"

"Since he gained the power to take all of you away from me."

They stare at me. Perhaps realizing my greatest weakness. Not myself—I will push myself to the brink of death. Run so hard that I'll vomit. Fight until I'm unconscious. My real weakness is those I care about.

They are the thing I'd chase to sky's end.

"You dueled him . . . for us?" Roderick says. "To keep us together?"

I meet his eyes. "I'd do anything for my family." The room goes quiet. "If you'll have me."

The sky turns pink with the fading sun. The whole room watching me.

"You dumb cuss," Roderick says. "Of course we will."

Bryce squeezes my hand. Keeton and Arika give me reassuring smiles. But I'm not done talking. The next revelation is more difficult, but Mother used to force me to talk. Not just because I was a guarded little birdshit, but because she knew if I kept things down, hidden from everyone, I'd be toxic inside. Hell, Mother even got Father to talk. She knew that Urwins, particularly the men, were terrible at expressing themselves in healthy ways.

"Ella," I say, "will no longer be part of our crew. I don't want her in my life, either." My face flushes angry. "She destroyed my mother's cane."

The room stares in horror. Shock. Then it twists into disgust. Keeton's brow furrows. Even Bryce understands this enormous sin.

Pound's hands ball into fists. "How dare she?!"

The destruction of one's dueling weapon is an offense almost greater than murder. Dueling weapons go with people—even if their status rises or lowers. And if someone dies with no one to carry on their legacy, they'll often have their weapon strapped to their body, falling together into the great sky.

The original Urwin left his behind for his line. And Mother left hers behind for Ella. But Ella's rejection of it is like spitting into the eye of the dead.

I pull the black stag of Hale from my pocket and lower it onto the coffee table before my friends.

"She's a birdshit," Pound says finally. "An Urwin. And you know what, Elise? My family abandoned me. Didn't even open their gates to me when I arrived at their new manor. I waited for days. Nothing. When someone shows you who they are, believe them."

"We're all abandoned people here," Bryce says.

Everyone goes quiet.

"Well, I'm not," Roderick says. "My family *loves* me. My mother still sends me cakes sometimes. They're delicious."

We stare at him. Keeton looks ready to kill him. But suddenly, Pound laughs. And his booming laughter infects the rest of us until we're all laughing so hard we're nearly crying.

Eventually, Arika pulls out a small device from her pocket and exposes a little crystal, like a comm gem.

Pound stares at it. "What's that?"

"Expensive," she says. "Listen."

She taps the crystal, and it plays gentle, strumming music. The soft notes curl between us and leave us quiet. It's a music that beckons peace and pushes away anger. Arika tells us that the device is a recorder gem. It replays sounds and voices. It's remarkable new tech created by the Scholars.

Suddenly, the music catches all of us in its tender notes, and Bryce pulls me to my feet, places my hands on her hips, and leads us in a dance.

Pound laughs at me.

But he's the only one.

Roderick and Keeton get up next and they dance, too. Leaving Arika and Pound watching us. Pound scratches the back of his bald head and glances at Arika. He's generally an aggressive brute. One who is afraid of nothing. But something about Arika . . .

She lifts his huge paw off his thigh and pulls him up. His face reddens. I'm expecting it to be a disaster. Him stumbling over his feet. Being completely lost. But despite the splotches on his neck, he dances smoothly. Perhaps dancing like he used to dance with his little sister, his nieces. All the young people in his family he no longer gets to see.

Together, with the sun dying, with the wind blowing gently against the window, and with the music strumming the air, we all dance.

Bryce curls her fingers behind my neck. Her touch is warm, and her blue eyes pull me deep into them.

I'm no dancer. But I follow her lead. And for a shining, glimmering moment, I forget about Ella. Forget about the gigataun, the Below, the war, and all the other birdshit going on.

My weakness is tunnel vision. Sometimes, I get so focused on my goals that nothing else matters. For so long that vision was focused on Ella. Now? All I want now is to keep these people safe. Because this crew? These people?

They make the Skylands better.

CHAPTER 21

THE NEXT DAY A HUNTER VESSEL DOCKS ON HOLMSTEAD and brings new crewmembers for the *Gladian.* Apparently, they were handpicked for my ship when we were on Venator, but the island was attacked before they could join us.

Now Bryce, Pound, Keeton, Arika, Roderick, and I greet the new members on the deck of our fully repaired ship.

The first, Yesenia of Alvarez, leans against the railing, arms folded, her black hair tied behind her head as she studies us. She's our new Navigator. Well, she's supposed to be anyway, but I'm not just going to award her that position. Even if she brought a letter of recommendation signed personally by Master Koko.

I won't forget that Uncle picked her for my crew.

I shake hands with her. "You will be given an opportunity to earn the *Gladian's* strings."

She glowers at this. Did she really expect to come here and immediately be the Navigator, third-in-command? A High on my ship?

Arika shifts uncomfortably at Yesenia's presence, as though they know each other. Pound looks at Arika for explanation.

"We used to be friends," Arika says.

"More," Yesenia says without emotion.

Arika shrugs. "Life changes."

I glance between them, realizing that Yesenia is the person Arika was close with at the Academy. "This won't be a problem, will it?"

"We are professionals," Arika says. "Isn't that right, Yez?"

Yesenia merely nods.

Bryce and I share a look. We can't deal with more drama, but we can trust Arika's judgment. If she's willing to let their past go, then it's none of our business.

My crew and I focus on our last new member, who has just climbed the gangway carrying his small bag of things. A tiny guy, really. He steps forward, and in a nervous, rehearsed tone, tells us who he is. We all stare at him, stunned. Otto of Selma's no more than thirteen. He stands a full head shorter than Bryce, and he's thin as a nail. But he's already got his wax tin clipped to his belt and a bundle of rags, too.

Uncle couldn't have chosen him for our crew. There's no way he would've picked him.

"My da' was a Low working on Ironside," Otto says to us. "He didn't make it. When I heard Hunter needed new Selections, even really young ones, I signed up. We went straight from Venator to here, after the Gauntlet got canceled."

Pound and I share an alarmed glance.

"But I knows how to clean, Your Highness," he says to me. "Real properly."

"Call me 'Captain.'"

"*Captain*," he says, a little flustered. "My da' cooked at a restaurant, 'n' I've waited the tables since I was six."

I stare at him. I understand lowering the age for Swabbies—it makes sense—but, on my ship, we're fighting in the war. And Otto . . . is so little.

"If you're going to be aboard the *Gladian*," I say, "then you have to prove something."

"Anythin', Your High—*Captain*."

I stride to center deck, tap a button, and soon the munitions platform rises through the floor, revealing countless harpoons and mobile launchers. I take one of the heavy launchers. Almost as big as Otto himself. Then lower it at his feet.

"Lift it."

"What is it?" Otto says, looking over the weapon.

Pound shakes his head and closes his eyes. "He's the best they could bring us?"

Otto's ears turn red, and he shuffles in his oversized boots.

"Pound, don't be such an ass," Bryce says.

Pound grumbles.

Although I'm skeptical, I'm not entirely opposed to Otto's arrival, especially after what happened with Declan.

Otto's face wrinkles with determination. He lifts the harpoon launcher and stumbles back in his big magboots. But still, he maintains his balance.

"Good," Pound says. "Now run with that on your shoulder. Pretend you're about to fire a harpoon at a class-six."

"Class-six?"

"A HUGE gorgantaun."

Otto runs. Then trips over his feet and tumbles into the deck. The launcher slides away. Otto stands, wincing and massaging his shoulder.

Pound closes his eyes.

Otto's eyes water. He's weak. Not ready for this. How can we count on him to help us when we're in danger?

But Bryce steps forward, leans down, and whispers something in the boy's ear. Otto tightens the straps of his magboots and stands again. He lifts the launcher and runs. This time, slower. He jogs the length of the ship, the launcher bouncing on his shoulder the whole time.

He turns back to look at me. Waiting. His ribs jut out a bit, and he carefully lowers the mobile launcher onto the munitions platform. Then he watches me, hopeful.

I gather my crew, except for Yesenia since we don't know her well enough yet, and step away. Otto chews his dirty fingernails.

"This is ridiculous," Pound says. "The fleet has plenty of capable Swabbies."

"Not so loud." Keeton hushes him.

"He's only the Swabbie," Bryce says. "I'm sure he can keep the ship clean."

"But can he fight?" Pound asks.

"He ran better the second time," Roderick says.

"There must be a better option out there," Pound says. "Eagerness doesn't replace experience."

"Pound," Keeton says, "you're being a bully."

"A bully?" Pound scoffs. "I'm trying to keep the boy alive."

"If he stays aboard," Bryce says, "we will *all* have to keep him alive."

Pound closes his mouth.

I look at Otto and see a young man ready to prove himself. He's motivated, and he seems to be an eager Swabbie. Besides, we've already got one spy on the ship. Yesenia's here because of Uncle. Is Otto? I doubt Uncle would agree to have a thirteen-year-old board my ship.

My gut's telling me that maybe we need someone like Otto. A person without an agenda, without drama. A person I'll never have to worry about starting a mutiny. A person who will follow orders. So despite my reservations, I walk to Otto and reach my hand out to him.

"Welcome to the *Gladian*."

Otto smiles the biggest grin I've ever seen.

✦✦✦

I latch up my luggage, leave my *Dreadnought* suite, and start down the corridor toward the hangar. The fleet's about to disembark, and the *Gladian's* ready to fly again. But I don't have freedom just yet. With the gigataun's return imminent, Uncle wants me to stay with the fleet to help fight. And if things go well against the giga, there's a possibility I'll never need to go on Uncle's mission at all.

I hurry down the corridor toward my ship. Oh, I can't wait to have the wind splash against my skin again. The *Dreadnought* stinks of Uncle. It's a cold, uncaring place.

After I turn the corner, I stop because Uncle's waiting for me.

"If I contact you over the comm," he says, "you respond immediately. No excuses."

"Understood."

"The fleet will be heading south within the hour."

"South?"

"Latest intel tells us that the giga will attack there. We will speak again soon. If there are any issues with your ship, inform the *Dreadnought*'s Captain."

With that, he turns on his heels and starts down the opposite corridor. A gang of advisers from Politics, Scholar, Order, and Hunter waits for him.

Soon I go down the elevator and step out into the hangar. Fresh winter wind flows through my hair. The open hangar door exposes a blue sky, and I breathe out a little. This time against the gigataun will go better than last time. The whole fleet is here, and we're ready to fight back with all we've got.

As I approach my ship, I almost smile. Almost—until I see the Urwin cutting off my path.

She stops me. "Are you leaving?"

I stride past her. "Yes."

"You don't have to leave yet."

"I've spent enough time on Holmstead, on this ship," I say, still walking. "The *Gladian* is repaired, and I'm taking her into the sky."

She hurries to follow alongside me. I'm moving briskly. Her new cane dangles from her hip. Then she studies the thing swaying from my neck. A little glass capsule.

"What's that?"

I push the necklace, a shard of Mother's cane, beneath my collar. Shouldn't let her see that. Shouldn't let anyone, especially not on the King's ship.

I keep walking.

"Conrad," she says. "I'm trying to talk to you."

I pause on the platform. Breathe out, but don't look at her. "You told me, Ella, that I usurped you. That I took everything from you."

Can almost feel her eyes boring into me.

"But everything I did," I say. "It was all for you."

Then before she can respond, I descend the stairs, leaving her behind.

The *Gladian* gangway wobbles beneath my feet. And soon I'm standing on the deck and exhaling a contented breath. My ship purrs beneath me. Oh, she's alive again. A group of dockworkers is aboard, making final preparations for our departure. There are people everywhere.

Yesenia stands atop the helm platform within the glass bubble. This is her trial. Her opportunity to prove herself. Her hands are attached to the golden strings. Pound and Roderick mark off our weapons inventory on the munitions platform. They give Bryce, the Quartermaster, the thumbs-up. She jots something onto her notepad.

The last of the food crates, carried by a towboat from the dock, descends onto my ship's supply platform. After Arika excitedly checks over the supplies, she also gives Bryce the thumbs-up. Then Arika presses the control panel button on the deck, and the crates of food lower into the ship.

I bring my comm gem to my mouth. "Status."

A series of reports comes in. Bryce states that the storage room has been restocked. Arika reports she has a month's worth of fresh food for the freeze box. Keeton says that she's finished her modifications to the new engine. And Otto tells me he has three brooms and a mop.

Pound booms with laughter.

Afterward Roderick tells me we have more than enough weapons for a dozen hunts.

We're ready.

I crank the magnetics dial on my belt to a low setting, walk to the bow, and give the signal.

Pound excitedly roars at the dockworkers. They hurry from the ship and detach the chains. He pulls up the gangway. I tap my comm, informing the *Dreadnought* that we are disembarking. Once we get their confirmation, I nod at Yesenia.

She gently pushes the strings forward. No idea of her flying abilities, but I'm giving her an opportunity. If she can't even properly disembark, she probably can't fly well enough under the duress of a gorgantaun hunt.

We pull away gently from the platforms. Suddenly, Mother's voice stabs into me, telling me that despite everything, I can't leave without waving farewell to Ella. What if something goes wrong when the giga comes? What if we never see each other again?

I turn back to the hangar, to the platform where Ella had been.

But she's gone.

I exhale. *I tried, Mother. I tried.*

Soon Yesenia guides the *Gladian* through the hangar doors. Once free, we're blasted by the wintry air of the North and feel the sun's heat on our foreheads.

Roderick smiles.

Okay. Yesenia can get us out of the *Dreadnought*. Now, how does she fly?

"Crank your magnetics," I say through the comm as I pull my wind goggles over my eyes. "Yesenia, push it."

Yesenia nods, and she shoves forward. The next instant we rocket through the clouds. *Whoa.* I catch the railing to stabilize myself as ships blur past. We shoot between two carriers and beneath their sparrows. Otto, gripping the railing, laughs. It's likely the first time he's been on a ship even close to this speed. We soar above a blanket of clouds shimmering golden with the sun. Then, once we're on the edge of the fleet, Yesenia deftly turns us, her left arm straightened.

Now we're facing the white mountain of Holmstead again. Hundreds of ships stand between us and the island.

Yesenia throws her hands forward. We launch toward the island and the fleet at full speed. Roderick's laughing. We approach a battlecruiser. Ready to slam into the enormous black hull.

"Dive!" Pound roars, "Dive, you madwoman!"

Roderick screams.

Yesenia deftly plunges us beneath the ship, and I instinctively duck. The battlecruiser's hull flies directly above us. Roderick's eyes bulge, and he glances back at me. Perhaps thinking the same thing I am. She's a smooth flier. The smoothest we've seen since Eldon of Bartemius was at the strings. Even better than Drake.

We curl around carriers and cruisers and swifters. Finally, after a few minutes of shooting throughout the fleet, Yesenia pulls back to slow the *Gladian*.

Roderick, Bryce, and Pound clap.

"You fly like you're rushing to the lavatory," Pound says, "but aren't sure you'll make it."

Roderick slaps his thigh and howls with laughter.

A bead of sweat trickles Yesenia's tan forehead, and she's breathing hard. Flying isn't just about accuracy, it's about endurance. Fighting against the resistance of the strings. You must have shoulder strength and perfect hand-eye coordination.

Seems Yesenia has plenty of both.

We glide to a stop within the protective ring of battlecruisers and carriers. Yesenia climbs off the helm tile, the bubble slides away, and she hops off the platform. For a few minutes, I listen to Keeton's report on the engine over the comm.

Yesenia walks to the stern and peers at the fleet through a spyglass.

After Keeton finishes her encouraging report, I pull off my wind goggles and approach Yesenia.

"You're a strong flier," I say.

She nods. "This ship flies remarkably well."

"Thank Keeton for that."

"I shall."

It's an awkward, stiff conversation. But I'm going to have to make it more awkward. Be direct and speak plainly.

"Yesenia, are you working for my uncle?"

She lowers the spyglass and peers at me through squinted eyes. "What makes you believe that?"

"Because he assigned you to my ship. Specifically."

"He assigned me to your ship, Prince, because I am the best flier in Hunter."

"Call me 'Captain,'" I say. "I've met some good fliers."

"Yeah? Well, I'm better, *Captain*. The King wants you alive. So he contacted Master Koko and asked her opinion. You don't even remember me, do you?"

"Should I?"

"Yes. If it weren't for this ship," she says, her voice edging on bitterness, "I would've won the Gauntlet. We were all celebrating as the sun fell. Only to hear the news that the *Gladian* had flown out of the heart of a class-eight gorgantaun."

My eyes widen. "You were on the *Calamus*?"

"I was their Navigator. We were a good crew. Our Captain,

Huifang of Xu, is destined for greatness. She brought us together. We didn't have infiltrators aboard or would-be murderers. We deserved to win." She pauses. "Still . . . I know not to underestimate you." She speaks with the tiniest hints of admiration. "You didn't just win, you overcame. So when I was told about this position, I jumped at the chance. I just hope that . . . this crew doesn't fight like it did in the Gauntlet."

"We're united."

"Time will tell."

Then she walks toward another part of the deck without having been dismissed. But I call out to her.

"Glad to have you aboard," I say, "*Navigator.*"

She pauses, then nods and keeps moving.

I appreciate her honesty and her flying ability, but I hope she's not difficult. I can't deal with more difficulties right now.

I look around my ship and notice Otto's sliding the mop around, eagerly cleaning up nonexistent spills. I watch him, a little amused. Fortunately, I think I can count on him not bringing extra drama.

✦✦✦

After a full day's travel south, the fleet's hanging under the bright moon and I'm walking toward my cabin, ready for a restful night. But as I'm about to open my cabin's door, Uncle sends a fleetwide comm.

"We've been misled," he says. "Alona misled us."

I pause.

"Goerner's not in the south at all." He pauses. Breathing hard. His angry voice betraying anxiety. "We have received word: the gigataun is coming."

My heart sinks. I knew this was inevitable, but it'd been so long that I almost grew comfortable.

"Set a course to the following coordinates," Uncle says. "May the winds flow with us. May we all rise."

Shouts echo from inside my ship. My panicked crew scrambles out of their beds, hurrying to get into the corridors and off to their assigned tasks. I don't even have to look on a map because I know the coordinates by heart.

Pound stomps around the corner, and we stare at each other in horrified, ominous silence.

The gigataun is coming for Holmstead.

CHAPTER 22

POUND AND I STAND AGAINST THE SNOWY WIND. OUR BREATHS mist, and our jackets flap. Storm clouds obscure the stars above us.

Pound squeezes the railing so hard, it almost bends. Holmstead's the home of our ancestors, where we were raised to become enemies. Where our family's rivalry grew bloody.

My comm gem has gone gray. I wanted to send a long-range comm to Holmstead, but Uncle banned all long-distance communication within the fleet. The Lantians can't know we're expecting them, but this means we can't send Holmstead a warning, either.

Yesenia shoves the strings, shooting us to the head of the fleet. Hundreds of lights fill the sky behind us, and a squadron of sparrows flanks our sides. The Stonefrost Armada just joined the fleet, too. It's a massive fleet of old but powerful ships, each bearing the lightning flag of the Duchess of Stonefrost.

Despite our numbers, double from when we last engaged the gigataun, a warning swells inside me. This is the critical flaw with

Meritocracy: we're a society built on a collection of individuals who are all concerned about their own desires. Their own rise.

We're not a collective. But the Below? They work together.

"Engine at two hundred percent," Keeton says over the comm. "I can't push it anymore or it'll burst under these temperatures. We can't maintain this for more than an hour."

"Good work, Keeton. We only need thirty minutes," I say. "Holmstead will be upon us soon."

Lightning and snow clashes in the distance. Pound glances at me, and my throat tightens. This is a rare kind of storm—foreboding. The ensuing rumble sends an ominous moan through the fleet. I grit my teeth. No, it's just weather. It means nothing. And the Skylands may not work as a group, but we have the toughest people alive.

We will not lose Holmstead. I'll die before my island falls.

Arika brings everyone egg-filled peppers stuffed with energy boosters. Once she gives me mine, she pats my arm gently.

"Thank you," I say.

She nods, stops at Pound, and stares at him a moment, but his gaze is dead set on the horizon. She touches his back, and he accepts breakfast without a word. Then she takes a belt of handheld explosives from the munitions platform and clips it around her waist.

Pound eats his pepper automatically, but my stomach's so warped I can hardly eat at a time like this. Still, I need energy. I stuff the whole thing into my mouth and force it down.

The snowfall increases, cresting my wind goggles.

Suddenly, another bolt of lightning blossoms, and my home island appears in the distance. Seeing it again, in this context, nearly rips me apart.

The gigataun can't be coming here.

Can't.

Icy flurries spray over the deck.

I pull my spyglass from my belt. The white roofs of Holmstead sparkle under the pillars of early dawn light. Heatglobes burn red through the windows of the Highs and the Middles. The Lows, as always, display the flickering flames of logwood fire among the many shacks.

Snow falls peacefully on the sleeping city.

As I take in the sight, I'm thinking of Father, of Mother. Of my adventures in the Urwin grounds. I'm thinking of McGill.

Holmstead continues to grow.

I suddenly realize my hands are trembling, and it's not from the cold. I grip the necklace of Mother's shard around my neck. I failed her. Couldn't truly rescue her daughter from Uncle's clutches. I've broken a lot of promises in my life, and I desperately want to promise that Holmstead won't fall. That I'll be able to do something to stop the giga.

But what if I can't?

My brow furrows, and I clench my jaw. No. Holmstead won't fall. I won't let it. This is my home. Here my family learned to rise in this world that doesn't care about anyone except for the most powerful.

Yesenia pulls back on the strings, and we glide to a stop only a mile from the island. The fleet assembles around us. The sky is full of ships and snow.

Some Holmsteaders begin exiting their homes, breathing warmth into their hands, perhaps on their way to the market. Or to go on an early-morning walk.

"Captain," Otto says, pointing a finger behind us. "More ships."

I turn and peer through the spyglass. And at first my heart drops, thinking the dozens of approaching ships might be Goerner. Instead, I breathe out with relief. Master Koko has arrived with her black ship, the *Archer*, and she's brought all the Hunter ships she could on short notice.

A bit of hope grows in me.

I've not seen Master Koko since Venator, and for a moment I consider tapping my comm. Just to hear her voice. Draw from her strength. But it's not necessary, because seconds after she comes in range, all our comms light up.

A Hunter-wide message.

"Holmstead is under threat," she says, her voice steady as usual. "The gigataun is coming. But we, the Hunters, are built of gorgantaun steel. We rush toward death while others flee. And if today's the day we meet our fall, we will do so in glorious fire. Hunters"—she pauses—"let's hunt."

The faint echo of hooting Hunters grows over the wind and travels to my deck. Roderick's the first to shout, then Bryce. At first I'm not sure I can muster anything more than a whimper. But I force it out—all the worrying angst caught inside me.

I roar.

Then the sky falls to silence, but for the wind.

The *Archer* soars ahead of us, joined by another ship, the *Henry*. My eyes widen. The *Henry's* a hundred-year-old ship, belonging to the person who taught me all about being a Hunter. The person who taught me that to rise and win the *Gladian*, I'd need to take down a gorgantaun by myself.

Madeline de Beaumont.

Madeline's crew of aged, retired veterans stands atop the wooden deck of her ship with mobile harpoons, flak cannons, and shoulder cannons at the ready. My former trainer glances my way and offers a wave; then her ship pulls back, deeper into the fleet. Her ancient ship will do best as a support vessel in this battle.

I walk to the munitions platform and consider our weapons. After a few seconds, Bryce joins me.

"Can you sense anything?" I ask her. "Without the symbion, I mean?"

"I could never sense creatures. Just people."

I nod and lift a mobile launcher from the munitions platform. The twenty-pound weight presses against my shoulder.

“Conrad, I—I’m sorry the war has come here.”

My mouth opens, but suddenly the whole fleet quakes. A tremendous roar nearly splits the world apart. Makes my bones rattle and my heart stop. Bryce’s face twists with alarm. Then, from beneath the acid clouds, two vessels rotate the clouds into a vortex, creating an opening large enough for a beast that’s nearly a mile long.

The gigataun is back.

CHAPTER 23

THE GIGATAUN BELLOWS AS IT SOARS THROUGH THE SNOWY sunrise.

Its body plumes in golden flames from the Omega cannons of Titanium-class vessels. Blazing fire gushes over a patch of the beast's red scales. The scales sear the giga's flesh, and the monster rumbles. Seconds later, the giga jettisons them. And they spin dangerously through the air.

"Yesenia!" I shout. "Dive!"

A scale the size of our ship rockets at us. Yesenia throws her hands down. We nose-dive, and my ribs slam into the railing.

Holy hell. The gigataun didn't jettison scales in the last battle. The hot scale soars past us and strikes another ship. Shredding through multiple decks and cleaving the ship in two. Screaming crewmembers tumble out of the ship, arms stretched away from their sides. Jackets flapping. My stomach knots as falling people beg for help over the comm.

But we can't help them. Holmstead has thousands counting on us. Hundreds of civilian ships rocket away from the island.

We zoom around the jettisoned scales, Yesenia's incredible coordination keeping us unscathed. But the scales are devastating the fleet. Maybe that's why the giga is ejecting them like a damned porcupine. The Below isn't worried about us being able to take down their weapon. They saw what happened at Ironside. All the firepower of the Skylands, and we hardly put a dent in it, scales or not.

My body tenses. This time will be different. It must be.

"Yesenia!" I shout. "Bring us closer!"

She throws her arms forward, and I lean back from the sudden rush of icy wind. We soar above the undulating form of the gigataun. Its gigantic metallic coils gleam against the early light. I peer down the reticule of my mobile launcher. Spot an exposed opening of white flesh, then squeeze the trigger. My shoulder buzzes as the harpoon launches. It blazes across the sky and sinks into the giga's flesh. But it's nothing more than a needle in a bear.

"Bring it down!" Master Koko roars into our gems. "Bring it down!"

We follow the *Archer* and spiral around the gigataun's coils like a vortex. Flying with ridiculous speed. And we unleash everything. Arika tosses handheld explosives. Bryce fires blasts from her shoulder cannon. Roderick squeezes the triggers on the repeater turret, sending harpoon after harpoon.

Even Otto's shooting harpoons. Pound kicks a lever and his turret barrels explosions onto the beast's scales.

Koko's ship and a team of other vessels encircle the gigataun's neck, firing spinning discs attached to chains. The sharp discs lodge into scales, and the gigataun roars.

The chains tighten, still attached to the decks of the Hunter ships. The ships circle around the gigataun at full speed. The discs cut deeper. But they're digging against hard scales, and the embedded discs grind down to nothing.

Koko roars over the comm, telling the ships to detach. The Hunters attack with enormous harpoons that stab the beast. Order sends explosions that make my toes tingle. Sparrows buzz around the beast's face, peppering its eyes.

"KILL IT!" Uncle roars over the comm. "KILL IT!"

I hurry to the munitions platform. Got to be something. Anything. I stuff another harpoon into my launcher and wrap a belt of mini explosives around the harpoon's end. I tie the belt down tight.

I won't give up. Maybe this harpoon will dig deep into the exposed flesh and the explosion will rupture a vital internal organ. Or maybe it'll puncture the gas sac that keeps the beast afloat.

I race to the railing. My calves burning from the magnetics in my heels. The wind flapping my jacket collars. I peer through the reticule and fire. My harpoon spears the sky. Pierces the exposed flesh of the giga and sinks in. I wait with bated breath. The explosion sends off a juicy chunk. But the monster rolls on like I just threw a rock at it.

My heart sinks.

A few ships fly too close to the giga and are crushed by the monstrosity's rolling coils. The creature's so massive, its lazy undulations send waves of wind throughout the fleet.

Koko brings her ships in for another run, attacking with giant harpoons that stick into the scales. The Titanium vessels abandon their Omega cannons, their huge harpoons, and firebomb the giga. More scales launch into the sky, whizzing through the fleet. Cutting down dozens of sparrows and Hunter ships.

Master Koko backs off.

We swerve around the spinning scales. The more scales the giga loses, the more vulnerable it is. Problem is, each time the scales fly out, ships sink.

"We're not doing enough damage!" Bryce shouts.

Roderick keeps alternating barrels and trying different weapons. A few ships zoom around the giga's eyes, sending flak. Making it roar and snap at them. They're like little flies.

"Attack the giga's exposed flesh!" Uncle roars. "EVERYTHING WE'VE GOT!"

A fresh wave of thousands of sparrows swarms the gigataun. There are so many that a few slam into one another. The sky is a mass of them. The sparrows pepper the giga's eyes with white rays. And our harpoons sink into the giga's flesh. One after the other, creating pores.

Meanwhile, the Order battlecruisers continue their bombardment. Chunks of meat splash the decks around ours, and white blood snows the air. The giga raises its coils, shielding itself. Blocking our attacks, forcing us to target a new row of scales. More scales jettison, and damaged ships spiral toward the black clouds.

These damned scales!

The massive firepower of the Skylands, together, is hurting the horrible beast. But we can't handle the scales.

The giga continues its slow undulations toward Holmstead even as pieces of it fall.

Pound roars in desperation, and Yesenia flies us alongside the giga's sharp spines. We pepper the beast and dodge crossfire from friendly ships.

Got to try something else.

"Yesenia!" I shout over the comm. "Fly ahead of its mouth."

Pound gives me a crazed, excited look. Maybe he knows what I'm thinking.

Yesenia throws her hands forward. We hurl ahead of the beast, the icy wind slamming against my chest. Now the incredible giga's head is behind us. Its mouth closed.

"Roderick, Pound," I roar. "Target the nostrils. Let's see if we can get this bastard to breathe in something special."

Pound laughs. "Aye!"

They rapid-fire harpoons. Dozens of them. But they're clinging away, just hitting the lip, the crest, around the eyes.

I race against the gales to the stern, the torrent threatening to fly me across the deck. I kick open the gate and wait. Finally, Roderick sends a harpoon flying right down the giga's nostril. The beast thrashes, and its mouth opens.

Yes!

I slam my shoulder into the huge barrels of explosives. Sending them into the sky. Yesenia pulls us away, and we watch as the barrels soar right into the monster's mouth. Hopefully down into that beast's infernal pit.

"No way it can survive this," Pound says. "No way."

Muffled explosions follow.

The gigataun coughs smoke . . . and flies on. The damned thing just flies on. I stare in horror. We all freeze. My entire body goes numb.

Yesenia lifts the strings, and we follow the beast above its undulating body. As we do, the *Dreadnought* launches an artillery assault. Blue-gold explosions mushroom along the scales. My feet sting from the aftershock of the massive eruptions.

I race to the bow. The beast moans and thrashes. Another wave of sparrows swoop in, and they stripe the gigataun's scales under white rays, searing streaks across it. And finally, the beast slows as smoke rises from its flesh.

"It's hurt!" Pound roars and laughs.

The giga turns, and for the first time, it loses focus of the island. Pound's excitement fades when the giga's massive head, eyes full of hatred, scowl at the ships around it. Its incredible mouth snaps at the passing ships. They dodge around the teeth. Escaping.

Until . . .

A gushing sound fills the air. And something about it, the sound, the way its mouth opens and eyes roll back. It fills me with dread.

"Yesenia!" Bryce yells. "Pull back."

"No. Not now," Pound says, firing harpoons "We're hurting it. We can—"

"NOW!"

Before Yesenia pulls back, the giga begins inhaling. Its body balloons, and a horrible vacuum starts pulling ships in from every direction. Toward its gaping maw. The pull snatches us. Horrifically yanks us back. I crank my magnetics to high. Holy hell! I'm going to be ripped right off the ship. I leap to lock my arms around the bow's railing. My feet are sucked and lifted from the deck. Weapons and crates tear away from the munitions platform and go flying.

"It's pulling us in!" Roderick shouts over the comm. "Yesenia!"

She can't even answer, she's fighting the strings so hard.

Ships caught in the vortex around us spin and collide with one another. My legs flap behind me. Otto's screaming, clutching onto Pound's leg. Pound holds the boy with one arm while firing harpoons with the other.

The gigataun continues inhaling. Entire cruisers spiral into its mouth like it's a drain. Hundreds of sparrows vanish into the black pit. The railing's metal digs into my bones. My vision sparkles with pain, until I'm pulled with such force that my grip slips to my hands. And then my fingers.

I can't hold this.

"Yesenia," I gasp. "Pull us away."

She's shouting from inside the helm bubble. Can't see her. Can't even look back, but I imagine she's shoving with everything she's got. Suddenly, Keeton starts crying over the comm—can't exactly hear what she's saying over the piercing wind. Something about the engine overheating. Probably won't be able to keep this up for long, even with her enhancements.

My fingers lose purchase, and I start slipping. *Can't let go. Won't.* But the pull's too damn strong. I slip off the metal. My arms make a desperate lunge to grab the railing, but I'm already sucked away. On toward the bottomless pit.

Bryce, hugging Roderick's turret, reaches for me as I zip past. Her fingers just miss. Then my heart's in my throat as I shoot across the deck. My hands desperately seek something to latch onto.

I shoot right past the helm bubble. Going to be in the sky. Then on toward a slow, agonizing death inside the beast. The worst kind of end.

Except—

I slam into the *Gladian's* railing net. No time to be relieved. My body's pulled taut against the elastic mesh. The net digs into my flesh, feels like I'll be diced into a thousand pieces.

Ough!

I clench my jaw, try to lift my arms, my legs. But I can't get a single part of me off the net. Every time I try, the vortex's pull snaps me back. Beside us, other ships fight against the torrent. But some of them sink away suddenly, their engines failing.

Yesenia fights the vacuum. Fights the strings. The *Gladian* shudders from the pressure. Like it'll splinter in two. But as hard as Yesenia pushes, we're still falling toward the steel cage of the giga's mouth.

A sudden explosion fills the air. The gigataun's inhalation stops, and I roll out of the net in stinging pain. Wincing. I lift onto all fours, my muscles an exhausted mess. The gigataun roars, but it's gargled with blood. I glance to the left, where Uncle's ship and a series of carriers fire another barrage at the interior of the creature's mouth. The giga thrashes its enormous head and lifts a coil to protect its face.

Yesenia rockets us away before the giga can do anything else. We're all in a stupor. Exhausted. We're insects compared to this thing.

"Conrad, it's going after Holmstead!" Pound says, pointing. "It's going again!"

But nothing can stop it.

Nothing.

I'm numb. Broken. On the verge of passing out. I grab the stern's railing to help me regain my feet. My whole body stings from the net. While I'm just trying to recover, Pound goes manic.

"C'mon, you birdshits, FIGHT!"

He slams his foot on the turret's lever, and the barrels rotate. Then he swivels and fires a clawgun turret. The chain ripples after the giga and hooks us to the beast.

"What the hell are you doing?!" Bryce shouts. "You're going to get us killed."

The hooked line goes taut, and we're jerked after the giga like a helpless doll. Pound unbuckles himself and stands. Seeming ready to leap onto the chain, perhaps climb his way across, and . . . I don't know the hell what. Fight it with his bare hands?

Bryce leaps onto him.

"Get off me!" he shouts.

The giga drags us. Otto leaps onto Pound, too. Same with Arika. Roderick unbuckles from his turret and follows me as I race to Pound's turret. Pound's fighting them all. I dodge his swinging punches and crank a lever on his turret. The hook detaches.

The giga rolls on, and we tumble to the deck. Pound roars. He's dragged off the turret and hits the deck. He shouts about betrayal. Bryce, Arika, and Roderick try to keep him down. But I'm on my knees, watching the sky because the beast undulates for Holmstead. My eyes grow warm. It's going after the place where Mother cradled me. Where Father promised me that I would inherit all that was his.

The fleet's still firing at the beast, but with less intensity.

Uncle says something over the comms. Can't even hear it. Can't hear anything or feel anything at all.

Suddenly, the beast's great head slams into Holmstead's rocky underside. Digging in, carving a hole on its way to the heart of my home. And I just watch it, feeling helpless. Pathetic. We hardly hurt this thing, and it's going to take down my home island.

"I repeat," Uncle's dejected voice echoes, "evacuate Holmstead. We have lost. We have lost."

Pound kicks Roderick off, then stands, his eyes filled with

desperation. His family's still on Holmstead. He shoves Bryce, even Arika, then leaps back onto the turret. He rotates it and aims a harpoon directly at the helm bubble.

"Yesenia, fly us at the beast!" he yells. "Now!"

"What the hell are you doing, Pound?" Roderick roars.

We're worn down, but we leap onto him again. Then, with the help of Roderick, we pull him, legs first, from the turret. He weighs a ton. Roderick and Bryce lie on his arms. Trying to keep him down for good. As he struggles lifting himself, his wild eyes meet mine.

"Conrad, we still have time," he says. "Please."

"IT'S OVER, POUND!" Roderick shouts.

"We have to rescue evacuees," Bryce says.

Pound watches me, and my head falls. Then a horrible anger turns his face purple. He catches Roderick by the collar and tosses him. He flings Bryce. He rises to stand and charges me like a raging bull.

"COWARDLY LOTCHER!"

I backpedal, but not before he throws a skull-rattling punch. I fly back and hit the deck in a daze. Head stinging. Vision blurring.

Arika and Otto are shouting at him. Too terrified to touch him.

He's lost it. He's lost it.

I wipe the blood from my lips. And my heart rages. This birdshit's going to attack me, my crew, when we need to save lives? The people of Holmstead need us. Now.

I'm exhausted. Hurt. But the next instant, I'm on my feet. Pound swipes his massive arms at me, but I duck away. And as I meet his enraged face, my own anger matches his. All my frustration, the fury at our futility against the gigataun, it all explodes out of me as I sweep out Pound's legs and extend my cane.

Pound hits the deck. His eyes narrow on my weapon, and he stares at me like he just realized our friendship was never real. That it came out of convenience because we hated someone else more. We could never be real friends. He was an Atwood. And I was an Urwin. We were born to hate each other.

He stands and charges me. "TRAITOR!"

He's ready to mash me into the deck. Take over the crew—by force, and maybe crash us into the giga. But I pivot around his huge feet. I'm not the same Low he used to beat in the alleys. He swings at me. Enormous fists striking the air. Each dangerously close to cracking my jaw. But I maneuver around him and pepper him with my cane. A swift jab with the Urwin eagle into the ribs. The sternum. The throat.

The crew's around us, shouting for us to stop. But I motion them away because I need to knock him out, and I don't want any of them hurt.

Each time I hit him, I try reasoning with him. But he keeps coming. And finally, he strikes me—right in the gut. Then he catches me, wrapping his arms over my ribs, and squeezes the air from me like a damned snake.

My muscles lock up. Feel like my eyes will burst from the pressure.

But I can't let him take the ship.

So I raise my cane, and with it gripped in both hands, bring it down on his forehead. Once. Twice. Three times. After the third strike, we plummet to the ground. I smack my shoulder and roll across the deck.

He hits the ground hard, unmoving, blood dribbling down his nose.

The crew scrambles after us. Arika checks Pound's pulse. Bryce and Roderick help me to my feet, and I stare at him, feeling broken in so many ways. My chest is a hollow husk. And I feel like screaming. Screaming at Pound for making me fight him while our island's about to drop. At the world because Holmstead will soon be gone.

"He's alive," Arika says.

We chain him to a turret. Then, after Yesenia finally brings us alongside the island, we kick down the gangway onto the Holmstead dock. This was the closest dock to us. We flew out of position when Pound lost it.

High refugees scramble up the gangway to our deck. And they're lotchers, of all people. People like Nathan and Clarissa of Haddock. People who'd never do the same for others. But our retreat and Pound's delay made it impossible for us to reach the Lows at the base of the island.

Still, we must rescue anyone we can, and the Highs had the closest open dock.

I am shattered as I stare at my island. We can't get to McGill. Can't get to that kind, selfless man.

My deck fills.

Pound stirs awake and searches the refugees aboard. "Where's my family? Elise, where is my family?" His arms bulge with veins as he struggles against the chains. "Go to another dock." He turns to me, breathless. "Please. My family."

His words bleed me—but the giga's burrowed deep into Holmstead's underside. And we only have minutes, maybe seconds, until Holmstead falls. There's no time.

"Disembark," I say to Yesenia.

"Conrad!" Pound says, face melting. "PLEASE."

"I'm sorry, Pound. Roderick, the—"

Pound screams. His face turns purple. He weeps and calls out the names of his family: Stagg. Rolly. Cephalia. Mother. Father. His cries become shrill as we pull away. Atwoods do not beg. They're a proud bunch—it's one of the things that I always respected about them. But while we fly into the open sky along with the other retreating ships, Pound begs me to turn back.

It's too late. Because after a sudden cry, Holmstead plummets.

The massive island drops toward the acid clouds in a blink. Like a boulder sinking into water. It hits the acid clouds, sending torrents of black puffs into the air. I stare, frozen, as the last thing I glimpse of Holmstead is the crown of the mountain. Urwin Manor.

A plume in the acid clouds grows, and the island's final lights vanish beneath the waves of black. The surrounding ships dodge a violent updraft of toxic clouds.

Seconds after the black engulfs my home, a horrible collision deafens the world as it crashes into the Below.

I sag to my knees.

The giga bellows, triumphant. Then it soars toward another opening in the acid clouds, one created by Lantian ships. The giga's off to return to its great sleep before it'll come back. Again, and again, and again.

The final thundering of Holmstead's fall echoes and fades, and a hush comes over my deck.

CHAPTER 24

THE *DREADNOUGHT'S* CONFERENCE CHAMBER FILLS WITH argument. My eyes are red and puffy, and everything hurts. Just breathing hurts. Losing my home island. McGill. The people I knew. Many of them treated me lower than dirt, but they didn't deserve this.

I'll never be able to return to Holmstead. That thought swallows me into a despondent embrace. Reminds me of my failure. And really, failure's all I've accomplished since I won the Gauntlet. Failure after failure after failure.

Several Masters, including Scholar, Politics, and Mercantile, jab angry fingers at Uncle.

My head lowers into my hands. We had months to prepare for the giga's return, and we fared little better than the first time.

I sit in the shadowed corner of the chamber, away from the King's platform and away from the Masters who joined us in person. Bryce grips my hand. But I don't squeeze back. Her touch is normally a comfort, but everything's dull.

Uncle was furious that I chose Bryce as my adviser, as were several of the Masters when they realized who she is. But I don't give a damn. Bryce knows about the Below, and she knows what I'm going through because she lost her home, too.

Besides, the Masters' real quarrel is with Uncle. And they let him have it. Shout at him. Blame him.

As difficult as this moment is for me, none of my pain compares to Pound's. After we deposited our refugees on Frozenvale, we unlocked the chains around Pound and stepped back as they fell to his boots.

He stood to full height, wiped the snot from his face, and scowled at me for several seconds. Then he stomped to the hatch and went belowdecks.

I haven't seen him since.

Roderick told me later that Pound tried contacting his family on the comm gem. But no one responded. Still, there's a chance some are alive and that they're on another island—planning their rise to Archduke—which may not be possible anymore with Holmstead gone anyway.

Bryce squeezes my hand again, pulling me back into the *Dreadnought's* conference chamber. The Masters are still shouting at Uncle. Bryce's warmth is the only thing that tethers me to reality. She makes me feel that I'm still alive. That there's still something good left.

Part of me wants to get up and leave and just crawl into a corner somewhere. Because I can't deal with this birdshit. Can't deal with knowing that I've failed thousands of Holmsteaders. Can't deal with what Pound and I have become.

Uncle watches his critics from his platform, his fingers delicately playing with the Urwin eagle at the end of his cane. He meets the eyes of any direct challenge.

"The Highest High is meant to be strong," the Master of Politics says to Uncle. "Your rule has been nothing of the sort."

"Are you suggesting there is someone else who should be leading?"

Uncle's voice is soft, dangerous. "Tell me who is better. I will meet their challenge. This instant."

Regina, the Politics Master, straightens her purple robes and makes a show of standing before Uncle. But Uncle's a world-renowned dueler. As a Master, she could challenge him to a duel for the right to steal all the power that the Urwin family wields, but her fingers are twitching. She's like any Politician: they talk loud. Make big boasts. But when the storm winds howl, they're the first to cower belowdecks.

Father always told me that Politics is the Trade for lotchers. Weaklings who have no actual power unless it is delegated to them by an island's ruler. They're the people who never accept responsibility and always look to take credit for the good and to blame others for the bad.

Uncle massages his eyes as the Masters continue ranting about the lack of progress in the war.

"What have we done to strike back?"

"How can *you* lead us to victory?"

Several gems light up on the table beneath the King's platform. Each colored to match the Trade, representing the Masters who are joining us from another location. Because after the war began, Uncle declared that all twelve Masters and the Highest High must not be in the same location at once. If something were to happen to the *Dreadnought*, the Skylands would lose all their leadership.

One Master suggests that the real reason Uncle doesn't want the Masters together is because it would be easier for them to vote.

"Have your damn vote, then," Uncle says. "If you are so weak that you don't believe anyone can beat me in a duel, then vote." He leans forward. "*Vote*."

A unified vote from all twelve Masters could unseat Uncle. But the Master of Agriculture mumbles some sort of excuse because he knows that Master Koko, who joins us remotely, is on our side.

Loyal not necessarily to Uncle, but to me. And she's not one of these finger-pointing lotchers. She recognizes that winning this war won't be as simple as changing leadership.

Suddenly, the door bangs open, and the Captain of the *Dreadnought* comes rushing in. She's got a roll of paper in her hands.

The King stands, and the Masters whisper as they rise to get a better glimpse of the Captain.

"What is the meaning of this?" Uncle hisses.

"Your Highness," the Captain says, "you must see this."

She climbs the platform, hands the paper to Uncle, then steps back. The room quiets as Uncle unravels the paper. He reads over it, his brow twitching.

Then tears it in half.

"What is it?" the Master of Mercentile asks.

"There will be no surrender," Uncle growls.

"The Lantian Council offered a truce?" Regina asks.

The Masters glance at one another. Perhaps thinking the same thing.

"Well," Regina says, "what did they offer?"

"For peace," Uncle says, "the Lantians want my head—and the Skylands' unconditional surrender. They also want my heirs."

The room goes quiet.

My head rises. Bryce squeezes my hand more fiercely than ever. Perhaps she realizes what I'm thinking. That I can't live through what happened at Holmstead again. Can't continue carrying the burden that I get to live while thousands have died.

Two islands gone, and we've shown no signs of being able to stop the gigataun or win this war. The giga will come again and again until we have nothing left. At what point do we give up? One more island. Two more? Ten?

Father taught me that only a lotcher would surrender. But Mother taught me that true leaders are the ones who lead because they're meant to.

I'm about to stand. We can negotiate with the Lantians. Uncle and I will go willingly. Maybe we can spare Ella. Then this war will end, and lives will be saved. But before I rise, the Master of Order, Addeline of Lewcrose, stands from her position across the chamber. She's tall, narrow, and strong in her Admiral uniform—decorated in various badges.

"King Ulrich, you will not surrender?"

Uncle's face turns venomous as he meets her eyes. "We do *not* surrender."

She nods. And I sense what she's about to say next. She straightens her white jacket and strides directly before the platform.

"Then, for the sake of the Skylands," she says, "I challenge you, King Ulrich of Urwin, to a duel. For status and right to the seat of the Highest High."

The room breaks out into chaos.

CHAPTER 25

WE ONLY HAVE TO WAIT THREE DAYS FOR THE DUEL.

Uncle's face is hardened granite as he exits the arena tunnel and steps under the pale light beneath snow clouds. A thousand spectators murmur as he marches. People from all over the Northern Isles have come to Frozenvale's High dueling arena to watch because it's rare for such an important duel to take place this far north. Many in the crowd of Lows, Mids, and Highs lean forward, waiting for Uncle's challenger.

I stand on the wet, heated ground of the square, and my eyes dance over the crowd. There's anguish above me. Anger, frustration, sadness, and a little fear, too. Holmstead is gone. These people, they haven't come just to watch a King's duel; they're here because they're looking for something to yell about. Something to make them feel like they still have some control. They're looking for someone to take the fall.

Uncle opened this duel to the public because he wants it to be a spectacle.

"The Skylands will remember the strength of Urwin," he told me over dinner last night.

Snow collects on my brow, chills my skin. Ella stands beside me, quiet and stoic, her red cane hanging from her hip. We haven't spoken about Holmstead, but when I first arrived and walked through the tunnel to the square, I found her in the shadows, leaning forward against her knees and breathing hard—like she was trying to let something out.

Maybe she'd been crying. But I couldn't tell because it was dark, and once she noticed me, she went rigid. She told me that today the Urwins would rise again; then she walked into the square in silence.

I glance at her, trying to think of something to say, but I'm still mad as hell at her.

Uncle stops inside the painted circle on the pavement. Only Severina joins him. It's strange seeing him accompanied by only one other person. No team of advisers from various Trades. But he's a sinking vessel. His popularity has not been helped by the whispers that he could be a traitor, that he eliminated King Ferdinand as a way of weakening the Skylands before the Lantian Republic attacked.

I hate Uncle, but that notion is preposterous.

Severina grips her cane, ready for a duel even though it's not her time. Then she looks at Uncle with admiration. I stare in amazement, realizing that there's actual love between them. For so long the women attached to Uncle's arm were the type who wanted him to carry them to the peak of High status.

Still, Severina and Uncle keep a distance between them. They nod at each other, and then she marches toward us, the falling snow cresting her hair.

Uncle meets my gaze, and I glimpse Father's face in his expression. His gaze is cold iron. As much as I hate Uncle, hate what he's done to me, we still share blood.

If we fall, we fall together.

The crowd silences as another figure appears in the mouth of the dark tunnel. Several people stand to get a better look. Addeline of Lewcrose is elegant, thin, and powerful. She wears the white uniform of Order. And she brings support. Multiple members of Order, wearing the same uniform, follow in her determined wake.

Addeline stops in the square across from Uncle and waves off her entourage.

No dueling official here. Not necessary—because a duel for Highest High has no points. The only judge is death.

Uncle's breath steams in the wintry air. He pops his neck, then lowers into his dueling stance.

Addeline carries a traditional Venatorian staff. She's the daughter of a previous Master of Hunter and, from what I've seen, has a smug but no-nonsense attitude. Her family was tested on gorgantauns, and her skin is pure steel. But she's also the leader of Order, and her posture displays the grace and decorum of the most respected Trade.

Addeline lowers into dueling position.

The crowd goes absolutely quiet. My heart thumps in my fingertips, and an icy scorpion skitters down my back. If Uncle falls, the Skylands will surrender, and Ella and I will be handed over to the Lantians.

Uncle's face is focused rage. He meets Addeline's eyes.

No one speaks.

Without warning he charges, and the duel begins.

Addeline raises her staff in a rigid, defensive posture. Streaks of water kick up from Uncle's boots. He sweeps past her defenses, his body spinning nimbly, and jabs her chin. She stumbles back, blood dripping from her jaw. Uncle keeps at her. She slides in retreat, blocking with her staff. Her face wild with fear.

And desperation.

She's immediately realizing what a horrible mistake she made.

Uncle and Father were trained by my brutal grandmother, Isabella of Urwin. Father told me stories of her. Isabella became ill and died well before her time. But though her years were short, they scorched the North.

"My mother broke my leg in a duel when I was six," Father had told me, "and locked me in a cellar for a week with only a bottle of water to make it through. She explained that our enemies will do worse to us. That there were Lows who would eat us if we let them. The only way to prepare ourselves, when we live in our rich, decadent mansion, was through challenge."

I'm glad I don't remember her.

Uncle trips Addeline, and her back slams into the earth. She coughs. He leaps over her, about to stab his cane into her eye socket.

But pulls back at the last second.

The crowd murmurs. Addeline stares at the end of his cane, eyes wide.

"Often," Father had explained, "your grandmother pitted me against my own brother. Ulrich was so much smaller than I. Several years younger. If she thought I was softening my attacks on him, she'd make me suffer. Neither of us got dinner until we both bled on the Urwin Square."

Uncle stands over Addeline. My brow knits with confusion. *You've got her. Finish her.* And then my heart starts hammering—realizing his plans.

"Mercy only gives our enemies opportunity," Father had said to me once as I cried beneath him in the Square, holding my bruised ribs. "You think I'll go soft on you because you are my son? What kind of father would I be to you, Conrad? I am not a lotcher. I will prepare you for this brutal world, for Meritocracy, and one day you will respect my teachings because they will keep you safe. They will keep the Urwin family safe."

Uncle stomps the Urwin eagle into Addeline's arm. A sickening crunch follows, and she cries out. He steps back smoothly, water spraying from his boots, then lowers into a defensive posture. Snow falls while he waves her toward him.

The disquieted crowd stares in horror.

Coughing, and shaking in pain, Addeline uses her staff to climb to her feet. Blood spills from a head wound down over her chest. But she rises into her Order-like stance. Then, despite her unsteady feet, she screams and charges Uncle. She swings wildly and nearly hits him.

But he nimbly sidesteps her attacks. When she jabs again, he thwacks her ribs.

She drops to her knees, wincing. Uncle glides back, effortlessly, and lowers into his defensive crouch again. My stomach twists with disgust. Even some of the strongest Highs above are looking away.

"Finish her," someone in the crowd yells.

Uncle remains in his defensive position, snow building on his shoulders.

I glance at Ella. She's studying the scene, and I'm not sure what she's thinking. Is that admiration on her face, or revulsion?

The duel continues for fifteen minutes as Uncle strategically breaks Addeline one bone at a time. Eventually, she's not even able to stand. Both legs shattered. Chest heaving, and her ruptured, bruised arms spread away from her body as snow melts on her purpled face.

The crowd's roaring at Uncle. "FINISH HER!"

But this isn't a lesson for Addeline; this is a lesson for the Skylands. And Uncle will remain patient in teaching it.

Addeline moans in a pitiful display, unable to even clutch her staff. The Master of Order, one of the most powerful people in the islands, laid Low by Uncle.

Her supporters watch with tears in their eyes as she lies flat. Is that her husband in the crowd? Her daughter? *Just finish her, Uncle. You've proved your point.*

He remains in position, the snow now clinging to his hair. When it becomes clear she cannot even move, he finally strides over to her. Doesn't even look at her. She's beneath him and not worthy of a final glance before death.

He steps onto her chest with one boot. Leans into it. Then he lifts the other onto her. And he stands, all his weight crushing her sternum. She groans. Tries to breathe. But he looks up at the audience, daring any challenger to meet his eyes. His weight compresses Addeline, suffocating her. She can't do more than squirm beneath him. Her broken, flailing arms hit his legs.

I look away. Even Ella does. Everything about this makes me sick. Uncle should win with dignity. With grace. Addeline's not his equal. He needn't punish her. He could've ended this duel within seconds.

She's only doing what Meritocracy taught us.

Once Addeline goes completely still, Uncle brushes the snow from his shoulders, steps off her, and glowers at the members of Order who supported her. Their heads lower, shamed. Then he marches around the square, looking up into the audience again.

"If there's anyone here who wishes to challenge me," he shouts, "to prove they are the strongest, then let them come down and face me."

He wants to secure his reign, today. Under Meritocratic law, a King or Queen only has to accept a challenge once every two months. Otherwise, they'd never have an opportunity to lead. But Uncle offers to break this rule.

Snow falls as people stare at him. A couple people drag Addeline's body from the square.

"Come!" Uncle raises his arms. "You blame me for the fall of Ironside, of Holmstead. Are you not stronger than I? Are you not ready to lead us in this time of war? Face me! Anyone, no matter your status, defeat me and become the Highest High of all the islands. Even the lowest Low may take my role."

No one moves.

Perhaps, before Uncle so thoroughly embarrassed Addeline and proved his strength, many would've leaped at this wild opportunity. But now?

"Are you all lotchers?!" he cries. "MEET ME IN THE SQUARE!"

Finally, a Low man with tattered clothes stands. The crowd turns to look, and a shock wave of disgust spreads. The man hobbles through the crowd and comes down the steps. Uncle watches the man, amused, but a High woman's mouth opens, aghast. If this Low man somehow defeats Uncle, he'll become King. Just like that. The crowd's whispers turn into soft boos that build into a crescendo of hisses and shouts.

"This Low man could become the King?"

"This isn't Meritocracy!"

They're right. There are steps to follow—Low to Middle to High to Duke or Duchess to Archduke or Archduchess. Only then has someone earned the right to challenge the King.

It's a right earned through blood.

The Low man carries twin dueling batons, cracked from many duels. Perhaps they're inherited. Maybe stolen. The Low man steps onto the square and dances in place to loosen his gaunt muscles. He flexes a couple times in a bizarre attempt at intimidation.

Then he squares against Uncle and roars. Ready to fight. Uncle stares at him, then kills him with a toss of his dueling cane. It punctures the man's trachea and sends him twitching onto the arena floor.

The silent crowd watches Uncle pull out his cane. It drips red into the snowmelt. Uncle looks up at the audience.

"WHO ELSE?"

All's quiet. Uncle meets the eyes of anyone who dares focus on him. The wind makes his graying black hair flutter. Sunlight, piercing through the clouds, crests upon his shoulders.

He is King.

Finally, Uncle turns toward the tunnel and starts making his exit. His strength is proven. His rule is absolute.

Except . . .

Someone stands.

Uncle doesn't notice at first, not until the murmurs in the crowd turn into gasps and applause. I squint toward the benches, and once I recognize the standing man, my heart stops. This man is perhaps the one person here who could legitimately pose a threat to Uncle.

"I accept your challenge, King Ulrich of Urwin, and I shall meet your cane with my own in honor."

Excitement explodes from the bleachers. Few knew Addeline well; she'd only been the Master of Order for a few months. But everyone knows this man.

Sione of Niumatalolo.

The crowd chants. "SIONE! SIONE! SIONE!"

His technique's famous, but more than that, he's well regarded for being a High who shares his training secrets with everyone. Father respected Sione because he doesn't waver from challenge. He is a true High—one who's willing to let others rise over him—if they can. He personally trained the Talbas and many other powerful families along the Eastern Rim.

Sione's bald, brown head shines as he exits the crowd. Uncle stops, and his eyes narrow on the thick man approaching the square. Sione dwarfs Uncle. His shoulders are thick and knotted with muscle. His legs are tree trunks. But rather than lowering into a dueling stance, Sione marches across the square and reaches out his hand to Uncle.

"To the end," he says.

Uncle squints at him, then takes the offer. Sione's hand practically swallows Uncle's. Sione steps away. Despite his height, he moves with smooth grace.

Sione removes his dueling weapons—all except a dueling cane. Then he unbuttons his jacket, rests it on the wet ground, and rolls up his white sleeves. Whatever respect he had for Uncle evaporates. His brow furrows, his eyes go wild, and he lowers in a dueling stance, his cane held by one hand.

Uncle studies him.

Duelers from the Eastern Rim are known for the blitz—an unorthodox assault that's wildly unpredictable and dangerous. It requires tremendous hand-eye coordination and focus. But when acted out properly, it's devastating and often leads to deaths—intentional or not.

Uncle lowers into his stance.

The crowd's buzz grows to a din.

And within a blink, the two world-class duelers are at each other. Uncle spins the cane, thwacking away at Sione's defenses. Shifting around counterattacks. Uncle's a magician with the cane. Whipping it around like a hissing propeller.

The crowd leaps to their feet, shouting with excitement.

Sione deflects everything Uncle throws at him, and Lows in the upper edges roar with approval.

Sione goes on the offensive. His eyes furious.

Uncle anticipates Sione's move, pivots, and swings a rib-crunching attack. Except Sione shifts away, and Uncle's assault merely grazes him. Sione slides back and smiles at Uncle. Actually smiles.

Uncle pauses, standing erect as he considers the taller man. Urwin duels are not meant to last long.

"Meet them. Beat them. Go home," Father used to say.

Sione, however, is a slow-burn dueler. He comes forward, pressing the cane like an annoying tick toward Uncle over and over until Uncle retreats.

"It's the eyes of the dueler you must focus on," Father once told me. "They give away everything. Moves. Emotion. Fear. Use their eyes to win."

But Sione's eyes only betray focus. I've never seen anyone chip away at Uncle like this. Uncle retreats, again and again. Their weapons making the arena thunder. Sione and Uncle meet for a moment, pressing their canes against each other, but Sione uses his weight to shove Uncle backward.

Uncle hits the ground, and the crowd loses it. They leap to their feet, hollering.

Severina keeps a hand on her tense stomach, a glimmer of fear in her eye. Ella nervously fiddles with her fingernails. I stand in shock, considering for the first time that my uncle might fall today and that I won't be the one who caused it.

Uncle rises, icy water dripping off him. Sione comes at him again—but this attack's different.

Ella grips my wrist. "The blitz."

Sione's incredible. His cane whirs and spins without any predictable pattern. The whole crowd quiets, awed at the sight. Attacks come at Uncle brutally quick. Uncle's eyes are pure concentration. Posture correct, but his balance teeters from the onslaught.

Finally, Sione strikes Uncle across the jaw, and Uncle goes spinning into the hard ground again.

The crowd roars. The Lows are jumping on one another, just a swarm of chaos.

My heart stops. Never once considered that someone could defeat Uncle. What does this mean for me? For Ella? Will Sione give us up to the Lantians . . . ? No, he won't want the power. He'll give it to someone else. I'll be entirely at their mercy.

Uncle lies motionless on the ground.

"Father," Ella murmurs. "FATHER!"

But suddenly, Uncle laughs. His palm hits the wet ground, and he pushes himself back to his feet. Sione watches him, perplexed. The crowd quiets, confused as Uncle laughs again.

Uncle reaches into his mouth, pulls out a loose tooth, and tosses it.

"My turn," he says.

Uncle charges. Sione lunges, but Uncle leaps and pirouettes around Sione's attack. Then, with both hands, he brings the Urwin eagle across Sione's face. The giant man falls. Uncle tucks into a roll, springs back to his feet, and whirls on Sione.

The larger man stands, wipes the blood from his cheek, then thumps his chest viciously. He rushes for Uncle and swings with such force, it'd split a boulder. But Uncle tucks into a slide and bashes his cane against Sione's knee.

A horrible crack follows.

I wince just watching it. The crowd is dead quiet.

Sione moans, his trembling fingers cupping his leg, but Uncle's at him. Attacking viciously with speed unknown to man. Sione tries to pivot away, but his balance falters on his bad knee. And now Uncle's the one carving Sione's statue. Sione stumbles backward, blocking, wincing, and hobbling from his injured knee. Finally, Uncle jabs the man in the belly, and Sione falls.

The crowd goes absolutely still. Not even the Lows whisper.

Uncle's on Sione like a starving prowlon on a deer. Attacks come left and right. Sione rolls and blocks until, suddenly, the Urwin eagle snaps Sione's cane in half.

The crack thunders through the arena.

The Niumatalolo cane. One that had been with Sione since his meteoric rise, one that had never seen a defeat. Pieces of it float in the puddles of ice water beside Sione's heaving body.

Uncle beats in Sione's ribs, mashing them with thunderous attacks. Sione becomes soggy, red pulp as he spatters on the arena floor. The snowmelt turns pink.

Sione, in desperation, kicks Uncle off. His chest is rising quickly. He struggles to stand. When he can't, he rolls over and crawls for the largest chunk of his cane.

Uncle follows him like a stalking predator. He needn't make

Sione's death a spectacle, not like Addeline's. She didn't have Sione's pedigree, and she lost Uncle's respect.

But Sione?

Uncle frowns as he stands over the man. A frown that says Uncle's almost disappointed knowing what he must do. Knowing that killing Sione will only weaken the Skylands.

But there's nothing Uncle won't do for power.

Uncle cuts off Sione's path. Sione rises to lean on his haunches, his stunned expression focusing on the man above him. He pulls in one noble last breath, then closes his eyes.

"To the end," he gasps.

"Yes. Yours."

Uncle grips his cane with both hands and swings the Urwin eagle directly into Sione's forehead with an agonizing crunch. Then the famous dueler from the Eastern Rim drops, motionless.

For a long while, the crowd is quieter than the snowfall. Uncle turns to the faces above and wipes his red mouth.

His voice is soft. Calm. "Anyone else?"

No one speaks. Breath mists from the dazed audience. But something else grows on the benches. The way the people look at Uncle now, it's changing. The disgust is gone, replaced by . . . admiration?

Suddenly, a woman stands, her gaze meets Uncle's eyes, and she raises her dueling cane.

"Hail, King Ulrich."

"HAIL!" the crowd chants in unison.

Without hesitation, the crowd bows in deference. Everyone from the Masters to the Highs to the Lows.

Uncle turns, and his jacket whips behind him as he storms from the arena. As he goes, he motions for Ella, Severina, and me to follow him into the tunnel's darkness.

Ella and I glance at each other as we pass Sione's broken body.

Uncle's not a good man, but he's a strong man. Maybe, to win a war against an enemy willing to murder countless innocents, you don't need a good man.

You need the one you fear.

The one you hate.

CHAPTER 26

UNCLE'S NEVER SATISFIED. PERHAPS THAT'S WHY HE IS the Highest High. And perhaps that's why, regardless of whatever happens during this war, I'm not sure he'll ever lose his position as King.

"Only a fool would think the duels yesterday did anything more than buy us a few months' time," Uncle says to me. "The challenges will continue so long as the giga remains a threat."

We're inside his office on the *Dreadnought.* His forehead is wrinkled with furious exhaustion as he watches his fleet through the window. We're flying south toward Central Skies.

"We are losing, Conrad."

He motions me to stand beside him. For several seconds, we watch the dozens of ships trailing behind us in the blue sky.

"You must embrace that inner Urwin fury," he says. "Because this is war, even if you do not want it. We will not wait around for the gigataun to return. When it comes back, we will be ready for it with a plan for its destruction." He pauses and looks at me. "You will bring glory to the Urwins. The wind will echo our name through every current from Dandun to Venator. It is our responsibility, Conrad, to ensure the legacy of Urwin is eternal."

I nearly laugh at the expectations he just lowered onto me. Make our name echo in the winds? This isn't a class-eight gorgantaun we're worried about. This is the damned gigataun! It's five thousand feet long!

"It is time for you to learn of the mission I have for you, Nephew." He strides to his desk and lowers into his seat. "You are the only one I can trust with this. The dirt-eaters sense our blood in the wind." He glances at the door, perhaps wondering if he should open it to ensure no one is listening, then motions toward the chair before him. "Sit."

Once I lower into the chair, he writes out a series of words on a paper and slides it over to me. I blink at the information, incredulous.

Order
Hunter
Scholar
Agriculture
Architect
Law
Politics
Disposal
Waterworks
Art
Explorer
Mercantile

"The Twelve Trades? Uncle, this is a lesson for six-year-olds."

"Look deeper. The roles, Conrad. The *roles*. What does each Trade do? What is their purpose?"

I sigh and recall the chants my tutors taught me as a child. *Law: to provide judgment and justice to the islands. Disposal: to dispose of or recycle the waste of the islands. Hunter: to hunt the beasts that harm the islands. Explorer: to seek out discoveries and secrets that will enrich the islands.*

"Each Trade's responsibilities are narrow," Uncle says. "Focused. They were designed by our forebearers to keep the Skylands safe. To protect us should the Below discover a way to bring war to us. But Order's responsibilities are broad. Not specific. Recite them."

"Uncle."

"Recite!"

I stare at him, unsure where he's going with this. "To provide order to the fluctuations of power, to police the masses, and to protect the islands."

Uncle stands. "Broad list."

"They're the most powerful Trade."

"Not in the beginning. Before Hunter."

My brow knits. "The beginning?"

He stares at me, almost excited that he's piqued my interest. Another Trade was more powerful?

Uncle presses his hands on the desk and leans forward. "Order's original role was not military supremacy—but ensuring the peaceful transfer of power among the Lows, Middles, and Highs. Order's strength only grew because of the Trade that betrayed the rest."

His words play in my head. Another Trade betrayed the rest? Who? And is this another one of Scholar's secrets, like when they hid the Below's existence? Or when they tried convincing the masses that steel-plated gorgantauns and prowlons were as natural as the elk?

Uncle's eyes meet mine. "This is the secret to our victory, Conrad." His gaze is deadly focused. "The original twelfth Trade."

I breathe out. "What Trade?"

"Weapon."

I pause. Something about the word chills the air. As if it has power. I blink, considering the word and its connotations.

"Three hundred years ago," Uncle says, "there was no Hunter.

Weapon's role was to protect the islands. But Weapon rebelled. It took a united Skylands and five years of war, but eventually, the Skylands won. We broke the propellers of Weapon's great flying machines, and Weapon's territory shrank until its home island was bombarded to dust. Nothing left but plants, ruptured buildings, and skeletons. After that, Order took on the additional role of protecting the Skylands, and Hunter was created to fight the beasts from the Below." He meets my eyes. "Conrad, this is your mission. You are going to Weapon's island. We have reason to believe that something there will turn the war in our favor."

"Like a weapon that can kill the gigataun?"

"That's the hope." He pauses. "However, the Lantians might be aware of this weapon, too. If they get to it before we do, the war will likely be over."

I sink back, letting the information digest. Thinking about the enormity of my task. "So, you're only sending me and my crew? Why don't we send the whole fleet?"

"The fleet must protect the Skylands," he says. "Besides, this mission must remain a secret. If the Lantians are not yet aware of the weapon, an enormous fleet could tip them off." He leans back. "You will not go to Weapon's island alone, however." He taps his comm gem and speaks through it. A second later a man in his early twenties appears in the doorway. "Nephew, may I introduce to you Magellan of Cabral—the star pupil of Explorer."

A brown-haired young man strolls into the room, dressed in a red jacket and the yellow uniform of his Trade. His shifty eyes calculate the room as if he's checking for enemies or places to hide.

His left arm has a blue claw that spins and taps its pincers. Almost like a nervous tic. I've heard rumors of mechanical arms—replacements for missing limbs—but never seen one. In Hunter, an artificial limb or hand is often just a blade or spear. Maybe his claw is something unique to Explorer. Then again, I've not met many Explorers. They're an odd and rare bunch. Isolated from the rest of the Skylands because they're off seeking discoveries, not settling down and raising a family.

"Please call me 'Mage,' Your Highness," the young man says to Uncle. His eyes, made huge by the thick lenses inside his golden goggles, travel to me. "Ah, *Prince*."

My face sours at the word.

"Conrad doesn't like being called anything but 'Conrad' or 'Captain,'" Uncle says.

Mage studies me, then nods. "And why wouldn't he? Conrad earned his ship in the Gauntlet. It wasn't given to him by his inheritance."

Uncle's eyes twinkle. "This is why I like Explorers. They understand people even better than Scholar Doctors. Mage's Trade, Conrad, specializes in uncovering secrets."

"Humans are not much different from a treasure map, I'm afraid," Mage says. His giant bug eyes watch me. "You just have to know how to read them."

I hate the way Mage looks at me. Like he thinks he knows who I am.

Explorer is the smallest of all the Trades. They only choose a handful of new Selections each year. Highly respected and coveted. When I was younger, I used to imagine the excitement of being an Explorer. Their adventures, finding treasures on islands long lost in the Western Skies or remote isles never touched by humans.

But, if rumors are true, it's not all fun and exciting. Not with pirates, gorgantauns, and acidons out there. Furthermore, Explorers have been known to steal one another's discoveries. To an Explorer, a discovery is everything. Probably something equivalent to a Hunter taking down a class-six gorgantaun.

"Conrad of Urwin," Mage says. "I mean to take you to the uncharted airs beyond the Eastern Rim to Far East."

"The Far East?" I stare at him. "Does that mean someone has made it beyond the cloudwall?"

Mage smiles coyly. "We leave tomorrow. You will follow my ship, the *Rimor.* Prepare your crew."

Before I can reply, he turns abruptly and slips from the room. Not even dismissed. And when I turn to Uncle, he's got an amused grin on the corner of his mouth.

Uncle opens a desk drawer and reveals a Hunter badge. He strolls around the desk and stops before me. I squint at the black badge in his palm, and then my eyes widen. It's nothing more than a stripe, but the significance is so much greater.

"Master Koko is busy planning for the next gigataun attack," he says. "But I asked that she provide this for you. This time it is *official.* You have been promoted to the rank of Hunter Lieutenant Commander."

I stare in shock. The last time I commanded multiple ships, people died. I lost ships. A colossal failure—Master Koko made that clear when I returned in disgrace to Venator. Koko certainly wouldn't do this without pressure from Uncle.

I almost step back. Everything I have in life must be earned. That's power. Strength. Proving that I should lead because I'm meant to lead.

But I haven't proven a damn thing.

"I haven't earned the right to lead other ships," I say.

Uncle is surprisingly patient with me. "You are true Urwin. You want to earn everything. But we all must make sacrifices, son. I cannot send you into the uncharted airs with ships that won't follow your command."

"It's not right. It goes against Meritocracy."

"You had a squadron before."

"And look what happened to them."

"Sometimes," he whispers, "we must go against Meritocracy to maintain our power. Without us, Conrad, the Skylands would fall. We are the strongest. The ones meant to lead." He looks to the window. At the various ships following us under the afternoon sun. "You will command multiple vessels. A larger squadron than before. Furthermore," he says, "That little ship of yours? It is now yours entirely."

"You paid off the *Gladian*?!"

No, he can't give it to me. I have to be the one to pay it off. *Me*.

He slides me a paper, emblazoned with the Hunter harpoon insignia and signed by Master Koko herself. I stare at it.

"Master Koko allowed it," he says, "considering the importance of this mission. Now no one can steal it from you in a mutiny."

"They never could, Uncle," I say. "I still have more than eight months free of mutiny because *I* won the Gauntlet."

"Again, I admire your desire to earn everything, Conrad. But sometimes you must accept a gift, too. You will not move forward if you have to check your back."

Paying off the *Gladian* was a goal I'd set for myself. An ambitious one, too, especially since I was splitting more of my earnings with my crew.

I sink deeper into my seat. Uncle reaches the paper toward me again, and I grudgingly stuff it inside my jacket.

"Will I command Mage?"

"Mage is likely to become the heir of Explorer, their next Master," Uncle says. "He only follows me or his Master. Furthermore, he's rather stubborn like you, so I doubt you'd have much success commanding him. But the rest of the ships joining you? You'll have two Order vessels. Four Hunter vessels. You'll even have a high-profile Scholar aboard the *Gladian*. This expedition," he says, "is where you will prove your Urwin leadership. Stand."

I consider ignoring his command. Storming away. This bastard has dictated so much of my life. But resisting means he'll apply pressure to me, and I won't risk my crew. This was the deal I made with him. I must do what he asks without question.

Once I'm up, Uncle brushes aside my jacket to expose my silver

Hunter unform. He pins the black stripe of Lieutenant Commander next to my other Hunter badges.

"Find Weapon," Uncle says, stepping back. "Discover their secrets, and bring us back what we need to defeat the gigataun."

"What if I can't find anything?"

He pauses, then meets my eyes. "Then there is no reason for you to come back at all. We are already dead."

CHAPTER 27

AS WE MAKE OUR FINAL PREPARATIONS FOR DEPARTURE from the *Dreadnought*, I stride across the *Gladian* deck, open the hatch, and slide down the ladder. Once I'm in the darkened corridors, my heart hammers because I'm thinking about what to say to Pound. How to repair our relationship. Perhaps there's nothing I can say, but I've got to try.

Pound's door is slightly ajar. I push inside and find a sparsely decorated room. In the past we didn't have our own rooms, but after the Gauntlet I used some of my winnings to upgrade the ship and turn some of the spare storage rooms into individual quarters. A poster displays the punching fist of Order. Pound told me he'd wanted to be in Order when he was younger. He dreamed of being an Order Commander and entering Skyfleet and winning Skywar.

Bringing honor to the Atwood family.

Beside the poster hangs a black-and-white flag with his family's emblem: the Rock of the Atwoods.

My eyes narrow on the open drawers, and a brick drops into my gut because on his desk, where he often scribbled out plans for our next gorgantaun hunt, is a letter addressed to me.

I don't feel I'm in my body as I approach it. My legs carry me forward. After a shuddering breath, I open the letter.

Elise,

I resign my position on the Gladian.

The letter shakes in my hand. Technically, Pound can't resign, not without my permission. The one exception for that is when there's an open Hunter draft. Still, Pound's never been one to ask for permission. And it'd be a mistake on my part to force someone like him to stay.

I lower onto his cot, and my body goes cold. Pound gone. Leaving at a time when things are broken between us. And now, leaving me without a Strategist and one of my fiercest allies.

I tap my comm gem, hoping he's close enough to send a message. The light remains on. He's nearby. Still on the *Gladian*? Doubtful. But maybe the *Dreadnought*. I escape into the corridor and run. My heart's panging in my chest. I race past Arika and Roderick, who shout questions after me.

Pound's my friend. We broke a generational feud with our friendship. He can't leave. Can't. We need him. *I* need him.

I'm back up the ladder, on the deck.

Keeton watches me, sees the worry in my expression. But I rush past her to the railing and peer over the *Dreadnought* hangar.

And then I find his bald head. On a distant walkway, his luggage gripped in his hand.

With his height and wide frame, he's hard to miss.

Pound's now hiking the gangway of another ship. It's an expensive passenger vessel that came to resupply. For a moment he looks our way, and his eyes find mine.

I raise my comm to my lips. Thinking how to convince him to

return. But as I see the frown on his face, I realize that there's nothing I can say.

For Pound, being on my ship was always temporary. Because he, like me, would chase his goals to sky's end. He'll never get to rise if he's stuck on my ship. Never get another opportunity to become Captain. More than that, though, despite his family being a bunch of assholes, they *are* his family. They disowned him. But he must win them back, and like me, he'd chase his family to his death.

He'd never rest without knowing if they're still out there, somewhere in the sky.

My wrist lowers from my mouth.

Pound pauses. A man behind him urges him to keep walking, but Pound turns on the man and squeezes his nose. The man winces and backs up. Then, slowly, Pound starts up the gangway.

Fear stabs me. This may be the last time I see him. Can't leave it like this.

"Pound . . . ," I say through the comm.

But I don't know what the hell to say. Once, I hated him almost as much as my uncle. He did awful things to me, hurt me in the alleys of the Lows. Stole medicine from me. But when we became allies, friends . . . Well, that was proof that everything wasn't all birdshit.

Proof that we could, in fact, be better than what the world had intended for us.

"Pound—Pound, I'm sorry."

He doesn't answer. Not that I expected him to. If there's one place you don't want to stand, it's between Pound and his family. But when we evacuated Holmstead, we had no choice.

Now he needs closure with the fate of his loved ones.

Perhaps he's headed to Stonefrost. We'd heard rumblings that some of the Atwoods might've gone there to challenge the Duchess. If any Atwoods are still alive, that's where they'll be.

After he finishes climbing the gangway and stands atop the deck, I tell him something different over the comm.

"You are not my friend," I say. He turns and watches me. "You are family—even if you're a colossal birdshit. Pound . . ." My mouth shuts. The words hesitate on the tip of my tongue, but I have to tell him. Have to. I'll regret it for the rest of my life if I don't. "I love you like a brother."

We watch each other. For a glimmer, his wrist rises a little, as if he'll reply. But he merely nods, and the comm goes gray.

My head falls. The *Gladian's* about to go into some of the deadliest airs in the sky, and my strongest warrior won't be with me.

The gangway on his passenger vessel slides up onto the deck. Pound turns away even before his ship disembarks. Then he steps onto a platform that lowers him inside the interior of the ship.

And he's gone.

I stand for several minutes, watching his ship, wishing that this war didn't exist. Wishing that Meritocracy didn't force us to split. Wishing that this crew could've stayed together forever. But the truth is, at some point, this crew will separate. Not just Pound. Keeton wants to become Captain. Arika wants to become a Cook on Venator.

In Meritocracy, sometimes the strong must go their separate ways in order to rise.

I breathe through the stitch in my chest and tap my gem again. And soon my crew gathers around me on the deck. I tell them the news about Pound.

My crew listens with wide eyes. Roderick takes it the hardest. His face splotches, and he keeps blinking hard, trying not to cry. Roderick doesn't understand the venoms of Meritocracy the way the rest of us do because he doesn't care about rising. He's happy being the Master Gunner. Furthermore, Pound became one of his best friends. Trash-talking brothers. Always making bets about who was the better shooter.

Pound didn't even say goodbye to him.

Arika's also quiet. And I wonder, with a bit more time, if she and Pound would've found a connection. Her brow furrows.

"He left without a word."

Bryce rubs Arika's back.

Pound wasn't always easy to work with, but the crew respected him. And he was the best damn Strategist I'd ever met. Even if his plans were always a little . . . crazy.

"Are we telling the King?" Bryce asks. "We need a new Strategist."

I rest my hands on my hips, consider for a moment, then shake my head. I'm not giving Uncle another opportunity to throw someone else loyal to him on my crew. Worse, there's no way anyone could stand in Pound's boots.

Not on my ship.

So I look at Keeton, and she understands. Because for a time, she was our Strategist. A good one, too. This is her chance to rise again. I take out the copper Strategist pin that Pound left with his resignation letter.

"Keeton will be the new Strategist as well as Mechanic."

I pin it to her chest next to her white Mechanic one.

Yesenia raises an eyebrow. "It seems that I've joined a very unique crew. I hope you understand, Captain, how strange it is."

I do.

Pound's vessel launches into the distant sky.

Roderick steps beside me at the railing. "Goodbye, you big ugly cuss." Then he lowers his voice, as if he's worried his mother will somehow overhear him. "You stupid *ass.*"

✦✦✦

The wind from the open, afternoon sky is in my hair again. I stand at the bow, directing my squadron.

The ships follow mine. Three Predator-class Hunter vessels: the

Ferrum, Telum, and *Jaculor.* All mirrorlike and sleek. Copies of the *Gladian*. Meanwhile, trailing behind them is the largest, most powerful ship in the fleet, a Hunter Titanium-class ship named the *Explosio.* The monstrosity has Omega cannons. Those things can hit targets from a mile away. Flanking our sides are two Order cruisers, the *Intrepid* and the *Dauntless.* These powerful midsize ships are smaller, smoother versions of the Order battlecruisers. Each carries twelve sparrows, two dozen Aviators, and short command towers from where Order Pilots operate their vessels.

Those ships are as white as the clouds.

The tiniest ship in the squadron zips ahead. It's composed of wood topped with a glass dome that exposes Magellan of Cabral inside. The *Rimor* is a blue Bee-class Explorer vessel. A class of vessels so rare that I've never seen one until today.

I can't help but feel a surge of excitement as the squadron moves toward the unknown blue sky. But that excitement's tempered by the memories of my failures. I lost three ships in my last squadron in a single week. Even losing one ship is a damned, horrible mistake. Now I've been given responsibility over even larger ships with larger crews. Those are Order cruisers! More than a hundred people in this fleet are counting on me getting them back to the Skylands and to their families. But not just them; the whole of the Skylands' fate may rest in my leadership of this mission.

How the hell am I going to get everyone through this?

Worse, if I tell anyone about any of my fears, they'll find me weak. Think that someone else should be leading the expedition. And I can't stop thinking that someone else *should* be leading this mission.

I exhale and grip the railing.

Where we're going, we won't be able to communicate with the King. So every decision falls on me. The success or failure of this mission is entirely mine.

I stand in silence for several minutes, the crisp wind numbing my cheeks. Soon though, the air will be hot and arid. Soon we'll be in the Eastern Skies.

Roderick stops beside me. "I've finished modifying all the turrets."

"I thought you were just giving them a tune-up."

"Wait, I didn't ask you first?"

I shake my head.

"Oh. Well, I had an idea for how to make the repeaters quicker. Sixty harpoons a minute."

My mouth practically drops. Talking to him relieves some of my tension. "You're a genius, Roderick."

"I know. Are you mad I didn't ask you first?"

"Yes."

He stares at me.

"I'm kidding."

"You're still bad at jokes," he says.

"At least I'm not ugly."

"Still not a good joke. Everyone knows I'm wicked handsome."

"Your mother's opinion doesn't count, Rod."

"That's better," he says. "You're improving. I'll teach you humor someday. Like you taught me how to duel."

"You're a terrible dueler."

"Eh. I was a hopeless cause, and you're a hopeless cause, too. So it works."

I smile, then meet his eyes. "Roderick, you have complete autonomy on my vessel, anything munitions-related. You don't even need to ask."

"Oh, I knew that. I just wanted to give you the illusion, make you feel like you were in control."

We laugh. But Roderick's face turns serious. He glances behind us, as if he's checking to see if the others are around.

"Conrad, I know you have a lot on your mind, but . . ." He breathes out. "This mission . . . Something doesn't smell right."

My eyes narrow. "Explain."

"I don't know," he says. "I guess I'm just nervous. We have a squadron here with us, but it's not a perfect one. If the Lantians discover—"

"They won't."

"Conrad, Sebastian knew about this mission."

I pause, forgetting I told him that. Sebastian has always had a way of discovering things. He's a little rodent that way.

"We are ready for anything," I say, pushing through the unease, forcing the words out, because I must remain strong and prove I'm the leader that I must be.

Roderick bites his lip. "Well, I've done my part. Our turrets are more powerful than ever, and I contacted the other Master Gunners in the fleet. I gave them detailed instructions so they can update their turrets as well."

"You shared your secrets with the other ships?"

"Of course."

I blink at him in amazement. Roderick's inventions, calibrations—they're his earned secrets. Ones that he could use to help him gain a higher status within the Trade or perhaps, one day, move on to be a Master Gunner for a famous vessel. Like Master Koko's ship.

Instead, he freely gives them away for the benefit of the squadron.

"You're a good person, Rod."

"You don't need to tell me."

Then he pats my shoulder and steps away. Presumably off to the munitions room below. Probably has other blueprints to work on. New inventions.

I glance around my ship. Otto's scrubbing the clean railings. Yesenia's pushing the strings with ease. Bryce is talking with Keeton about something—going over numbers on a notepad. And Arika—I think she's belowdecks, preparing lunch.

My crewmembers are each so unique, but as I consider them, another worry nags in the back of my mind. A fear. Still, I try shaking it off. Yes, we're going to the uncharted airs, but we're coming back. Every single one of us.

I'll not let anything happen to my family.

✦✦✦

Three days pass. As Lieutenant Commander and head of a squadron, I am almost never alone. I'm either meeting with the two Order Commanders or I'm meeting with the four Hunter Captains. Or I'm followed around everywhere by the Scholar adviser Uncle assigned me, Tara of Kyle. And I rarely get to savor moments with my friends.

Even though my crew's preoccupied by the Eastern Skies, we haven't gotten over Pound's absence. Pound always had a way of saying something bluntly that other people skirt around. But now, meals are quieter. Less funny. We all know we have a mission to focus on, but it's hard when you're missing someone as big as him.

Whenever I get a few minutes to myself, I take advantage. I lean against the bow's railing, just breathing and enjoying the warm breeze that flutters through my curls and splashes against my goggles. These airs are so much warmer. I don't even need my jacket.

As we've flown through this region, I've glimpsed arid desert islands. Some with a beautiful oasis among the dunes. Others with shiny, dome-covered buildings that create the skylines of the cities.

My Scholar adviser suddenly joins me.

I almost sigh.

Tara of Kyle is young—only a few years older than me. Maybe twenty. And she's already Philosopher. A rank only given to the Master of Scholar and to the Heir to Scholar.

Her red hair billows around her, and she stands barely taller than Otto. Hell, he might be taller than her in a couple months. She's no fighter. Likely will go belowdecks whenever our mission becomes dangerous. But this doesn't matter because her mind is her true power.

The red robes of her Trade flutter over the deck, and the emblem of Scholar, an open book, spreads across her chest.

Like every Scholar, she doesn't carry a dueling weapon. In fact, when she ate her first meal with us, she said that part of her initiation rights into Scholar was the destruction of her dueling cane.

Her Trade holds the philosophers, the educators, the medical healers. And the propagandists.

Tara stands beside me, and she doesn't even say a word. My head shakes with irritation. The *Gladian* is a big enough ship. *Go elsewhere, Tara. I need time to myself sometimes.*

Ahead of us, Mage of Cabral's ship, the *Rimor*, zooms around like a small blue insect. It really is an odd, orb-shaped ship. Roderick has been going on for the past two days about getting a look inside. He's even sent a couple comms to Mage asking for a tour.

But Mage hasn't responded.

Tara rests her small hands on the railing. And together we watch in silence as the first glimpse of the cloudwall appears.

Sky's Edge.

I stare in amazement. I've never been, although my maternal grandmother, Cheryl of Hale, used to be quite the traveler when she was young and told me about it. Sky's Edge is an enormous vertical wall of swirling clouds that behave like no other clouds in all the Skylands. With Mage's help, somehow we're going to fly though it.

"We Scholars," Tara says suddenly, "have studied Sky's Edge for generations. The cloudwall spans the distance of a part of the globe. If it were gone, people from Dandun could reach Venator in half the time. Scholar has an island, just south of here, that measures the cloudwall—and tracks its expansions."

"The cloudwall expands?"

"Sky's Edge always snaps back in place, but sometimes it grows enough that the neighboring islands must evacuate. The powerful winds will churn through cities, hurl people into the sky. Sometimes islands even disappear."

"Disappear? Where do they go?"

She raises a finger at the cloudwall. I blink, considering an island sucked into that storm and that we're going to have to fly through it.

"But our island is farther away, where the cloudwall's expansions don't swell with as much power," she continues. "We've carved tunnels deep inside the rock, all the way to the island's heart. Whenever Sky's Edge expands, we hide."

I stare at the angry, gray wall of clouds. "I don't understand how it exists. No clouds act this way."

"The likely theory is it originated from the Defector War."

I turn to her. She stares, her blue eyes studying the cloudwall as though if she peers hard enough, it'll spill all its secrets. But there's more she isn't telling me—her Trade is well-known for hiding their knowledge from the rest of the Skylands.

"Explain, Tara," I say.

She still focuses on Sky's Edge. "With defeat looming, Weapon became so desperate to protect the territory it had left, it tried to make a new barrier. Some within Scholar believe Weapon tried to duplicate the acidic wall below us, making it vertical to stop the pursuing Skylanders from coming for Weapon's islands. However, something went wrong, and instead of a wall of acid clouds, well . . ."

We pause and watch the torrential cloudwall that shoots straight up, high into the atmosphere. So high that the air's too thin, too cold, for anyone to fly over it.

"Why would Scholar keep this secret from the Skylands?" I say. "It makes no sense."

Tara meets my gaze. "This has been argued among Scholars a half dozen times. Winners write the history. Ultimately, it has been decided, in each case, that the masses don't need to know. Either for their protection or the protection of Meritocracy. Though, if you want my opinion, the Skylands were so furious over Weapon's betrayal that it wasn't enough to simply destroy them. No, they burned them from history."

We stand in silence a moment.

"It is impossible to traverse through Sky's Edge," Tara says suddenly. "Scholar has tried for years."

"Mage knows a way."

Her face scrunches, skeptical. "We will see. Of course, we will need to wear filtration masks. The cloudwall isn't acidic, but it has sucked up some of the black clouds."

If we survive, we might have some terrible rashes for a few days—even if we wear the special suits we brought. Mage claims he discovered a secret path six months ago, and he returned to the King's fleet to bear the news only a month ago.

Hence, our mission.

"It's foolish to blindly trust Mage," Tara says. "But seeing as how we do not have much of a choice, *and* that I will be stripped as heir to Scholar if I do not join you on this mission, well, we can only hope he is truthful."

I try imagining Uncle's displeasure if Mage of Cabral taken us all this way for absolutely nothing at all. But Mage must've taken evidence back with him. Something that would make Uncle willing to send me.

I'm about to contact the other ships, tell them that within minutes we'll need to get into protective suits before entering the cloudwall, but I get a special comm message.

My brow wrinkles. It's from the King.

I tap the gem, about to tell him where we are, but he goes first.

"There's been an attack," he breathes.

A knot ties itself around my heart. What kind of attack? The gigataun? But it's too early for the creature to come back. Uncle continues, explaining that more than a hundred gorgantauns came after the King's fleet in the night. A quarter of the fleet fell from the sky.

I shut my eyes.

Uncle pauses. "Something worse."

"What could be worse?"

"Conrad," he says, his voice strained. "Ella is missing."

My body sinks into ice.

"Is she alive?"

"Unknown."

I'm suddenly left with the thought that my sister might be dead. Or stolen. I'm thinking about living without her in the world, and that I turned my back on her in the end.

"Conrad, where are you presently?"

I swallow a breath and give him our coordinates.

"Then this will be our last communication for a while," he says.

"What about Ella?"

"You have a mission to concern yourself with."

"How can I focus . . . when my sister's missing? Maybe dead?"

"You don't have a choice."

My teeth grit. I hate this unfeeling man.

We speak for a few more minutes, but I'm tucking it away for later, because all I'm worried about is Ella. Finally, Uncle bids me good luck and disconnects.

Tara stares at me. "I do not understand why you are upset," she says. "Ella is gone. That's one less competitor for your way to the throne."

I suck down a breath to keep from shouting. She's absolutely not one of the healing Scholars. "Quiet."

She raises an eyebrow. "Oh. I did not realize you were close with your sister. I have heard the Urwins . . . are not a very loving family."

"I'm not just an Urwin."

"Of course," she says, nodding. "I will leave you a moment to compartmentalize this information. It always takes the mind a moment to adjust to shocking events. But do not spend too long. The King has a strict timeline for us to follow, and if we are destined to die today, we are supposed to die within the cloudwall."

Once she's gone, I growl and almost punch the railing.

What can I do for Ella? Maybe she was taken to Goerner's fleet. Maybe they're trying to make her flip sides.

My mind plays over my options, when a horrible thought tells me I can't go back for her. There's too much at stake. And Uncle knows it. Why the hell did he relay this information to me now? Right when it'd distract me before a dangerous mission?

My brow furrows, and I strangle the railing until my fists turn white. Urwins must face challenges. Always. It's not enough that I'm on a mission to penetrate the cloudwall; I need to be broken while it happens.

Because muscles, when torn, come back stronger.

I shove my concerns about Ella down deep. It's up to Uncle to find her.

I tap the comm on my sleeve and make the announcement to my squadron.

"Prepare to enter the cloudwall."

✦✦✦

My ships follow the *Rimor* toward Sky's Edge.

The cloudwall's intense winds threaten to rip me from the deck. Rain drenches my face, and the exterior of Sky's Edge is so misty it's like breathing water. Worst of all, I'm wearing a thick, rubber suit that's supposed to protect my skin from the black clouds' toxins caught in the torrent. We bought them from Scholar. Apparently, they wear these things when they're studying the cloudwall. A hood squeezes tight around my scalp, a glass visor covers my face, and the suit's so rigid that it squeaks when I move.

But Mage says these will help us get through without awful skin irritations.

I breathe through a filtration mask. It's suctioned to my skin, wrapped tight around the back of my skull. My squadron got a full complement of these for the mission. They're not perfect, but they'll prevent lung rot from the low levels of toxins caught in the cloudwall.

Unfortunately, the mask makes my face soggy as hell. And the suit's so muggy, my skin's soaked.

Another gust of windy rain slams the *Gladian's* hull.

"Lockdown!" Bryce shouts, her voice muffled by her mask.

She looks like a lake seal in her suit. In another circumstance, Roderick would probably laugh at how ridiculous we all look.

We grip the metal railing. I crank my belt, intensifying my mag-boots. Can hardly take a step with them set so high. Then I fiercely squeeze the safety belt that connects my torso to the railing.

Bryce grips her safety belt, too. Roderick's strapped to the turret, equally protected by his suit and mask. He's on deck just in case we run into anything inside the wall. Arika, Keeton, Tara, and Otto are belowdecks.

The fewer people above, the fewer chances for an accident.

Torrents spill toward us and crash against the the hull. And we haven't even entered the cloudwall yet. The wind flattens my suit against my chest. Another blast slams the ship, threatening to turn us or blow us off course. But Yesenia maintains her steel-eyed focus, her strong arms keeping us rigidly straight.

"Don't exert too much, Yez," Keeton says over the comm. "I've got the engine humming, but we might need the power if the storm rips us in the wrong direction."

"Understood," Yez says.

The *Rimor* leads us closer to the wall.

Another blast of wind shudders our underside. Yesenia's arms shake from within the helm bubble.

"My compass is off!" Bryce taps the compass strapped to her wrist. "It won't stop spinning!"

"We have to follow Mage," I roar. "He has his own instruments."

His ship bobs and weaves along the wind, as if it's riding a wave. It shoots ahead, leaving the rest of us behind.

"Mage!" I shout into my gem. "Stay with us."

"Other way around, Prince," Mage replies. "Stay with *me*. I know the way in."

I glance back at Yesenia. Rain slides over the helm bubble. Fortunately, the glass is coated in a water-repellant substance. Or she might as well be flying with her eyes closed.

"Follow him," I say over the comm.

Yez nods. "Aye."

We cut through the unpredictable gales. The other ships follow. The larger Order cruisers and the Hunter Titanium-class ship fare better under the winds. But Mage's vessel, the smallest by far, seems to have no trouble. It shoots forward, directly at a dark patch in Sky's Edge.

A sudden hail of rock and debris peppers the deck. A pebble stings my back, and I wince. "The hell?"

"Careful," Mage says over the comm. "The storm carries debris. Quickly now. We're almost to the entrance."

"We're going there?" Bryce says over the comm, jabbing a rubber finger at the dark patch in the cloudwall. "But that is the most intense part! If we go that way, we'll be pulverized."

"It's the only way in," Mage says calmly. "At least, if you want to keep your ship in one piece."

My teeth grind. We've come all this way, placing our faith in a strange Explorer. But we don't have a choice. There's no backing away now. I tap my gem to send a message to every ship.

"Launch. Right at the dark patch."

A series of confirmations follows. I stop, glance back at Bryce. Then Roderick, and my squadron. We're going to make it. We have to make it through.

Yesenia shoves her hands forward.

The wind punches my chest. Tries to tear me from the safety belt and scoop me overboard. Maybe I should've gone belowdecks, too. But it's almost impossible to give orders from the Captain's cabin.

Mage's ship dives into the dark patch and is swallowed up by churning clouds and jagged cracks of lightning.

Within two heartbeats, we crash into the black spot and slip into darkness. My skin itches like hell—even with the rubber suit. Already under attack by the tiny amount of acidic particles caught in the storm. Worse, I can't see a thing. The *Gladian* rumbles beneath me. And my stomach rises from all the jerking movements.

Sudden lightning illuminates the inside of the stormy tunnel around us before we fade into complete blackness again. The suit dulls my hearing, but I can breathe. The filtration mask keeps the water out.

I hang onto the safety belt. What about the other ships? What if Mage's ship was sucked away? My gut clenches.

"Status?!" I shout into my comm.

But there's no response. Maybe they can't hear me. Or maybe . . .

Suddenly, a glimmer of light appears through the wild blackness.

"There!" Bryce shouts. "Yesenia!"

"I see it!"

We rocket against the gales and suddenly, we burst from blackness through a wall of mist. The winds weaken to a gentle breeze and the air clears and brightens. Water drips off every part of me, but my skin's no longer stinging.

"Welcome to the calm inside the mist," Mage says.

A ray of sunlight pierces the mist, exposing this bright gray corridor caught between walls of furious gales. It's like a canyon of winds.

The *Rimor* floats ahead of us. I turn around, checking for the other ships. One by one, they escape the dark black patch of the clouds behind us and enter this . . . this place.

I wipe the foggy visor of my filtration mask. The narrow corridor of calm air leads to another thick wall of clouds that blocks the view beyond. Shadows dance among those clouds. Above, a thin layer of clouds forms a roof.

"What's going on up there?" Keeton yells over the comm. "Why have we stopped?"

"We're inside Sky's Edge," Bryce answers.

"It's calm inside?"

It's unbelievable.

Roderick's strapped in his repeater turret, all soggy and dripping. He's looking rather relieved to be alive. After tightening his mask, he adjusts the controls of the turret, and a stream of water ejects out the base. Then his eyes widen in shock, and he points over my shoulder. I spin around and gaze at the stormy wall directly before the bow. A sudden clash of lightning illuminates an enormous shadow beyond.

"What—what is that?" Yesenia blurts out.

Oba, the lead Order Commander, speaks over the comm. "Prince, we have a problem."

I don't even have to ask. I know what it is, but they're not supposed to be real. We weren't even trained on them as Hunters.

The wind suddenly picks up again. Not as explosive as before, but it makes me grip the railing. Harsh rain splatters the deck, peppers my skin.

"Octolon," Oba says.

"But they're a myth," a Hunter Captain says on the comm.

"Not a myth," Mage says. "Just incredibly rare. They live in storms. Travel in them."

As I stare, I recall a moment from when I was young. I'd heard Father and Mother getting debriefed about a storm that struck in the

Far North. It destroyed most of a city. One of the survivors, a ragged man who'd lost everything, claimed something in the storm had been alive. At first he'd thought it was a pod of gorgantauns. But then it had just vanished, all at once.

The wind calms inside the corridor again, and another clash of lightning exposes more of the beast's shadow. My adrenaline kicks in. Eight arms splay out from the octolon's great, bulbous head. Each coiling arm stretches as long as a class-three gorgantaun.

The damn thing's enormous.

I raise my gem and call out to the ships.

"Someone talk to me. Any suggestions for how we proceed from here?"

The comm goes quiet. These are all highly accomplished Hunters. Veterans who've been hunting for decades. And not one knows a thing. This is all going to fall on me.

"Bigger problem," Mage says suddenly, taking over the comms. "The octolon's blocking the exit. That is the only pathway through Sky's Edge."

"There has to be another path," I say.

"I mean, sure," Mage says. "There are plenty of paths we could take. But they'd all kill us."

I wipe the rain from my face and lean forward. Bryce, Yesenia, and Roderick watch me. The fate of eight ships, and their crews, depends on my decision. It's a ton of damn pressure. I could kill everyone and fail the Skylands.

"Mage," I say, "what can you tell me about the octolon? Can we kill it?"

He laughs. "I've got a single harpoon launcher on my ship, strictly for emergencies. This is your domain, *Hunter.*"

My skin flushes hot, almost embarrassed. But I've got to ask questions, even if I'm admitting I don't know what the hell I'm doing.

"Okay, *Mage*, how do we evade it?"

He laughs again. "Go really fast. If one of its arms gets in your way . . . turn."

I shake my head.

"We could have the Order cruisers and the Hunter Titanium send a barrage," Keeton suggests over the comm.

"That'll irritate it," Roderick says. "Make it come for us here in the corridor. Right now, it's just sort of . . . floating there behind the clouds."

I pull my spyglass from my belt. Try to squint my way through the mist. For the barest moment, one of the octolon's arms surfaces through the storm. And I see the long, gelatinous suckers. Metallic scales, like a gorgantaun's, protect the beast.

"It's probably better to try to get past it peacefully," I say. "If we attack, we're guaranteed to have a battle."

"It's your call," Mage says.

I glance at my comm gem. My hands feel clammy as we rest on the precipice before the gray clouds, before the octolon. It feels like we're about to tip over a cliff.

"We fly past the octolon," I say. "Peacefully."

"But Prince," another Hunter Captain, Kirsi of Rebekah, says over the gem, "do you really—"

"Battle stations," I command. "Arm your cannons and turrets. Have your deck personnel get in the spare toxic suits and come above. Just in case."

The comm line goes quiet. Until finally, a series of "aye ayes" comes across.

Roderick contacts Arika over the comm to suit up and come on deck. Otto's too small to come above. Tara would get ripped from the ship, and Keeton has to manage the engine.

"Ready when you are, Prince," Mage says over the comm.

A few minutes later, once people start arriving on the decks in their suits, Bryce squeezes my shoulder, hops onto Pound's turret, and kicks a lever, switching on the enhanced harpoon repeater.

I snatch a shoulder cannon from the munitions platform and clip back into my safety belt. My friends gently nod at me. Then I look over the other ships and the people standing on their decks, armed and prepared.

Arika arrives, snatches a weapon, and straps herself into a safety belt.

I let out a long exhale. Gathering my will to face this challenge with the survival of not just us but the whole Skylands hanging in the balance.

"We don't stop for anything," I say to the whole squadron. "If one of us is hit, we keep flying. Our mission's too important." I swallow a breath. "Let's fly."

CHAPTER 28

AFTER WE LAUNCH THROUGH THE CHURNING WALL OF VERtical clouds, we enter a stormy tunnel. But the torrential winds steer the squadron close to the sleeping octolon. It's just off our starboard side. I'm hardly breathing, not that the beast could hear me through the mask or over the powerful gusts anyway. My eyes adjust to the growing darkness. The octolon's a giant, bulging creature with flexible scales and thick, gorgantaun-sized tentacles. It hovers in midair, its tentacles flowing with the winds.

"Steady," I say over the comm to the ships. "Steady."

Mage's ship is well beyond the octolon now, waiting for us to join it near the tunnel's exit. Get there, and we're out.

My squadron's all armed and ready, just in case something goes wrong. But I don't want to fight this monster. Not when we know so little about it, not in this gloom, and certainly not in these winds that have slowed us to quarter speed.

Arika is deadly quiet as she watches the giant monster. We continue soaring near the octolon's tentacles. Just a few hundred feet from us. The tentacles rise and fall as it sleeps. A metal beak shines beneath its torso. This creature has a strange, dangerous beauty. Multicolored scales that seemingly mimic the storm around it, blending it in. It almost has a glowing hue.

"Yez," Arika says. "You're too close to the monster. Back off."

"The winds!" Yez grits her teeth while navigating the strings. "It's like we're being pulled toward it."

Another gust slams into my chest. Slowing us to a crawl.

"Keeton," I say over the comm, "can the engine handle—"

"No," she says. "It's at capacity."

The creature sleeps. But we're right on top of it, only a couple hundred feet separating us and the spiny ridges above its eyes. We just have to get past this thing. *C'mon.* My jaw clenches. *C'mon. Just a little farther.*

Another sudden burst of wind slams into us, and we slide across the sky. Only a few dozen feet away from the octolon now. Yez fights the strings. No one shouts or makes a noise, but Roderick's frantically throwing his hands in the air, urging us away from the monster.

Suddenly, the octolon's giant, black eye opens. I freeze. The massive pupil contracts, then dilates, inspecting the storm, until it stops directly on my ships.

"FLY!" I yell.

Yez throws her hands forward, but we don't launch because of these damned winds. The beast thrashes tentacles into the air and one slams into us. My vision spins, whole body rocks. And in the next moment, I'm blinking in disorientation because blood's rushing into my skull. My safety belt's digging into my body. My ankles strain from the pressure of my magnetized boots.

We're upside down.

Oh shit, we're upside down.

"Right the ship!" Roderick cries. "Yez, right the ship!"

My magnetics are holding. I flex my toes, hoping I don't slip from my boots. But my left foot's no good; I lost a pinkie toe to the cold when I was a Low on Holmstead. Just then, my whole left foot slides free.

Holy hell.

The veins on my hands bulge as I grip the safety belt. The winds intensify, and my sock flaps, threatening to tear loose from my foot. I try shoving my foot back into my boot stuck to the deck. But miss.

Yesenia shouts, and using all her strength, she twists the strings. Finally, the *Gladian* rights itself. I shove my foot back in the magboot. And tighten the damned straps so tight, they'll probably cut off my circulation.

"GET OUT OF THERE!" Mage cries over the comm.

"It's coming again!" Roderick squeezes the turret triggers, sending harpoons at an approaching tentacle.

The octolon snatches the *Intrepid.* We're supposed to not stop for anything. But I can't do that. We can't leave them.

"ATTACK!" I roar. "Save the *Intrepid*!"

The other ships encircle the octolon. Maneuver slowly against the gales and swerve around the tentacles. They spray the creature with explosions. The *Explosio* fires its Omega cannons, and the octolon's head ripples from the blast. The dark storm erupts in gold light. Suddenly, the *Intrepid* pulls free, part of its hull ripped away and stuck on a tentacle.

"This way!" Mage yells. "We must escape through the tunnel's exit."

We soar away after him, but the octolon tucks its limbs in and darts for us. Cutting through the winds like they aren't even there.

"Faster, Yez!" Roderick cries.

"I'm giving it all I've got," Yez snaps.

The octolon nears. We can't outrun it. Not against these winds. I reach for my shoulder cannon, but it's gone. Must've slipped off when we flipped.

Out of nowhere, a giant chunk of rock comes flying right at us.

"Duck!" Bryce shouts.

Yesenia pulls back. I slam into the railing and wince. The rock spins past us. Yez throws us forward, away from the rock and octolon.

"Where the cuss did that rock come from?" Roderick yells.

Arika jabs a panicked finger ahead, and I spin to look. Islands, a whole group of them trailing debris, are caught in a dark patch of the storm that swells on the portside. And more than that, ghost ships. Ships from every era. Some no more than rusted metal husks. They're caught in a horrifying wave that rolls toward us.

"Dive!" I yell.

A jagged metal hull flies at us. Yez shoves the strings downward and we plunge beneath it. Yez navigates us between pieces of earth and dead ships. A chunk of debris crashes into the railing beside me. And the *Gladian* groans from all the intense winds.

The octolon nears.

The *Intrepid* and *Dauntless* fire massive explosions into the monster. But the beast bursts through them like they're nothing. It comes for our stern. Ready to reel us in toward its snapping beak, until a careening island slams into the monster. The octolon screeches.

Yesenia fights the strings to create distance. Moving us toward the exit. And Roderick sends thick harpoons at the octolon. Each one spears into the tentacles. The octolon catches sections of an island and hurls them. The storm breaks apart the larger pieces, but I duck and cover my head as small rocks pepper the deck.

"Ah!" Roderick cries. He clutches his shoulder after a rock smacks him, then roars as he swivels on the turret and starts shooting again. "EAT YOUR DINNER!"

Harpoons and golden explosions fill the sky. Bryce squeezes her triggers. The harpoons stick better than they ever do with large gorgantauns. Arika fires a harpoon, and it sinks into the octolon's head. Even so, our projectiles are pine needles compared to this thing. Not even the giant harpoons from the *Explosio* are causing enough damage.

We keep on toward Mage. Getting closer to the exit. But the octolon soars overhead and overtakes us.

My skin crawls. It's blocking our path. We'll have to fight our way out.

"KILL IT!" I roar over the comm.

My squadron encircles the monstrosity and attacks. Yesenia deftly navigates us around angry tentacles. We dip and swerve. Bryce switches her turret to explosives. She fires, and her shot hits the closest tentacle, sending waves up its body.

I can only watch. I'm unarmed and feeling so useless. But I can't risk rushing across the deck to the munitions platform. Not with these winds.

A deadly thought crawls into my mind. We'll have no way to reload the turrets once they run dry. It's too dangerous to run across the deck right now.

The octolon soars beside us, its left eye tracking our every move. Roderick rotates the turret, peers down the barrel, and fires. His harpoon cuts through the gale and stabs the monster's eye. It shrieks, and white blood sprays into the storm.

"CAN'T SEE US NOW, CAN YOU?!"

Roderick fires again, but the octolon raises a tentacle to protect itself, then launches all the other tentacles at us.

"Yesenia! Get us—"

But the tentacles sweep in from all directions. Within a blink, blackness surrounds the *Gladian*. The tentacles block the storm, and everything becomes eerily still. Panic pools inside me. We're engulfed by approaching tentacles. Roderick and Keeton desperately fire explosions and harpoons. The explosions sting my eyes and ring my ears. With each blast, we get glimpses of the advancing suckers. Worse, we see the octolon's silver beak. Just a few dozen feet away from the starboard side. It's eagerly snapping, waiting for us to be pulled to it.

I stand in place, horrified. I got us killed. All my friends. The ship.

Suddenly, an explosion erupts from outside the tentacles. The *Explosio's* Omega cannon? The octolon shrieks. Stormy light grows in my eyes, and a narrow opening appears between two retracting tentacles.

"GO!" I cry. "GO YEZ!"

She shoves with all she's got. We rip forward, and I squeeze the railing. Willing us to make it between the passage. *C'mon. C'mon.* Just before the octolon's tentacles close the path, we rocket between the gap and plunge back into the fierce winds.

I breathe out.

We can't kill this thing. We can only hope to outmaneuver it. Now we have a free path to the exit.

"RETREAT!" I shout over the comm. "FOLLOW THE *RIMOR* TO THE EXIT."

The squadron launches through the gales. The retreating Order cruisers continue firing their powerful cannons at the beast. The *Explosio* fires another ray blast from its Omega cannons. Just hoping to slow it down. Each sends rippling vibrations up the octolon.

"I'm low on harpoons!" Roderick yells.

Bryce and Arika confirm they're low on ammunition, too.

"Conserve," I say. "Emergency use only."

We're starting to approach the *Rimor.* Just a few thousand feet.

"This way, Prince," Mage says over the comm. "We must continue through the corridor. Quickly. Before it closes."

"It *closes*?" Bryce shouts over the comm. "You could've mentioned that before we entered!"

"Yes, well, I didn't think we'd dither around the octolon all day," Mage says.

"Dither?!" Roderick roars. "The thing cut us off!"

Yez's arms are shaking, tired. The wind comes at us from everywhere. My body shakes as I hold on. Behind us, the full squadron follows. The Order cruisers fire another volley into the octolon's head as it shoves an island aside. The beast lifts its giant tentacles to block the attacks, and the ensuing explosion lights up its scales.

“Wait,” Bryce says. “The octolon . . . It has some kind of camouflaging system.”

I stare in horror as the beast’s body shifts colors. Grayish-blue ripples flash across its body until suddenly, the creature’s gone. Invisible amid the gloom.

“It camouflaged itself!” Oba yells over the comm.

“Flak!” I yell to the squadron. “Fill the damned sky with it!”

Golden sparkles shoot into the storm. But the descending twinkles are ripped away and extinguished by the fierce winds.

A giant shadow swipes through the squadron. And an invisible force suddenly sends the *Telum* spinning. The Order vessels veer apart while the *Jaculor’s* turrets send harpoons right into us. Digging into our hull.

“Ceasefire!” I cry as I duck. “CEASEFIRE!”

The *Gladian* shudders from the *Jaculor’s* harpoons. A single one could puncture our gas pipes. Make us sink.

Yesenia struggles against the strings. She’s on the brink. Thoroughly exhausted. But we can’t replace her in the middle of this storm.

“We’re almost there, Yez,” I say. “Just a little longer.”

Her brow furrows with determination.

The octolon’s shadowy figure moves through the haze, illuminated whenever a flash of lightning spreads across its tendrils. The beast reappears and attacks, sending tentacles at us before it vanishes once more.

“It’s too fast,” Arika says. “It moves in this storm like it commands it.”

We fly hard after the *Rimor.* Every ship. But the octolon’s tentacles slash through the middle of the ships. Roderick shouts in terror as a tentacle coils around the *Dauntless.*

“NO!”

The Order cruiser's yanked, pulled like a toy boat in a bath, and sucked backward. My whole body prickles.

"Leave them," Mage says over the comm. "We have to get out."

"We can't!" I yell. "Fire!" I roar over the comm to the squadron. "FIRE!"

We attack with all we've got. Despite the storm and winds, and the fact that it's stupid as hell, I unclip from the safety belt. Then clench my jaw as I race to the munitions platform. The wind crashes into me. Threatening to lift me right off. But I dive to catch a crate of weapons. While grimacing, I lift a mobile launcher and attack the beast's head. Roderick squeezes the triggers, sending harpoons until his turret whines on empty. And Bryce peppers the beast until her turret runs out, too.

My squadron sends everything.

The octolon glows orange from the assault. Harpoons dig into it. Explosions make its body ripple. Gushes of flame from another Hunter ship blacken the beast's suckers. The storm flashes under the attack.

Even so, the *Dauntless* is pulled deeper into the tentacles.

"More," I say, hugging the munitions platform. "We've got to free the *Dauntless*."

"Prince," Mage says quietly. "They are gone. You said we wouldn't stop for anything. The corridor is closing."

I hesitate. It's one thing to say we won't stop for anything. It's another to leave people to their deaths.

Suddenly, the *Gladian* jerks. Yesenia tumbles, her dangling arms held up by the strings. Passed out, likely from sheer exhaustion. Her feet slide off the helm tile. The strings slip away, and the helm bubble opens and slides into the deck. Yesenia drops off the platform and tumbles across the ship, landing in a railing net.

"YEZ!" Arika cries.

Roderick and Bryce shout in panic.

Shit.

I lower the magnetics in my boots and run for the railing. The winds attack me. Threaten to rip me off. But my hands catch the metal. Yez's body lolls in the net. A fierce gale pushes her out, and just before she flies across the deck, I snatch her hand, pull her back into the net, and attach a safety belt around her waist.

"Conrad!" Roderick points.

I look back and can only stare as the octolon pulls the *Dauntless* to its beak. Nothing . . . nothing we can do. Just like I could do nothing for the people of Holmstead. For my other ships. For Pound. For Ella.

Bryce leaps onto the helm bubble, attaches the strings, and rotates us away from the *Dauntless*. I don't have the energy to tell her to go back. We can't go back. We're low on weapons; our best flier is unconscious; and we'd be risking everything.

I shut my eyes. We must leave them.

"Help us!" the *Dauntless's* crew begs. "Please!"

My throat tightens. I promised myself I wouldn't lose ships again, or people. And now an entire crew's going to vanish.

My head sags. "I'm sorry."

"Please," someone on the *Dauntless* begs. "I have a family. I have—"

I suck a long breath and reluctantly turn away.

"Follow Mage's ship," I say to the squadron. "We must escape, or all is lost."

Pleading voices cry after me, and I almost reach to shut off my comm. But no. I won't. I'll stay with them. I'll listen so I'll never forget.

Bryce launches us. And as we're rocketing away, the octolon's giant beak begins to crunch into the *Dauntless*' deck. The ship's crew fights for their lives. They shoot explosive blasts into the tender underside of the octolon. The beast roars, then expels some type of black gas that spreads along the deck. And within an instant, all the soldiers tumble to the ground. Paralyzed.

The octolon brings its tentacles close, crushing the ship. A series of metal and glass tubes—escape pods—shoot from the *Dauntless*.

Then the cruiser collapses under the weight. Squashed like a paper ball.

The octolon catches several escape pods in its suckers. The wind steals others. One pod slams into a chunk of rock.

People inside them shout for us, but we keep flying. Can't slow down. The *Dauntless's* sacrifice gave us time to escape. If we stop, their deaths mean nothing.

Miraculously, one escape pod manages to launch farther than all the others. Close enough that Roderick launches the clawgun after it. The chain ripples through the air until it *shunk*s onto the pod. He cranks the pod in, toward our deck.

Finally, we reach Mage's ship and follow it into a stormy tunnel leading toward calmer skies.

Bitter rain wets my lips, and my heart beats hollow. Even over the howling winds, the crunching of the octolon's beak is audible. We continue in somber silence, until we at last burst from the cloudwall, abandoning the living dead to the octolon.

It makes me sick.

CHAPTER 29

ARIKA UNSTRAPS YESENIA, AND RODERICK LIFTS HER FROM the railing's net. They rip off her rubber helmet. Yez is pale and dazed as she leans against him. We're about to gather around her, but we stop at the sight before us.

Our mouths fall.

"Welcome," Mage says from his ship directly above us, "to the uncharted airs."

Pink skies, gorgeous puffy clouds, and countless unknown creatures surround us. Multicolored birds, scaled in metal, squawk in orchestrated loops. Beyond them, a group of enormous animals float in the distance. The breathing holes above their heads make gushing noises, and they release low rumbling moans—almost in baritone song.

But the beauty of this new world barely registers on my weary heart because I'm haunted by the pleading voices of the *Dauntless* crew.

I pull off my rubber helmet, and the wind's cool on my skin.

Otto climbs atop the deck and hurries to the railing.

"What is this place?" he says. "We made it?"

Around the giant, gentle singing creatures, every manner of pishon zooms in their schools like golden dust in the wind. Tara and Keeton come above, too. Keeton hugs Roderick, then checks on Bryce and Yesenia. But Tara marches toward me, staring at this untouched ecosystem. She says something about some hypothesis, but I can't listen to some Scholar theory right now.

Yesenia leans forward and vomits.

"Oh, Yez," Arika says, holding Yesenia's hair back. "You probably have a concussion. I'm taking you below."

Yez's eyes are dilated, and she leans woozily on Arika for support. The two take the storage platform belowdecks rather than testing the hatch's ladder.

Otto unhooks multiple rags from his belt and hurries to clean the mess. But he screams and nearly trips because suddenly, one of those singing creatures, as thick and long as a class-two gorgantaun, rises from beneath our ship. Its humid breath gusts from its breathing hole, and several of its friends join it, their enormous blue eyes studying us. Like *we're* the strange thing in the sky.

Roderick hops onto a turret and raises the barrel, his fingers close to the triggers.

"Rod!" Keeton raises a hand to stop him. "Stop."

"What? It might attack us."

"A gorgantaun would already be eating our hull."

He hesitates before his grip relaxes.

I turn away from the bizarre creatures and focus on the cloudwall. The rest of the squadron floats outside it. I've been so preoccupied that I didn't even think to check their status. Dents and holes cover the ships. Many of the crews have come above to find debris, broken rocks, and even chunks of old ships lodged into their decks.

"Status?" I call over the comm.

A series of reports comes in. I breathe out with relief when I learn none of the ships lost crewmembers. Unfortunately, there are numerous injuries. Broken bones and filled medical rooms.

I stare at the empty space where the *Dauntless* would be. My eyes grow warm, and I don't know what to do, what to say. So I raise my comm gem and start to sing.

My crew looks at me.

"The Song of Falling" slips from my lips. The sorrowful notes hit me with power. Constrict my chest and make my voice quiver. But I must be strong, in front of everyone. Can't show weakness. Despite my best efforts, my voice won't stop shaking. Keeton and Bryce join my side and sing.

My voice strengthens.

The comm fills with song. Hardened soldiers from the other ships join in. Finally, the last note trails from our lips, caught in the wind, taken off with the dead.

Keeton stares at me, frowning. And the words are there, but she won't say them aloud, not here.

She'd tell me it wasn't my fault. Like Drake's death wasn't my fault. Like Holmstead wasn't my fault.

Even if none of these things are my fault, what kind of leader am I if I can't do a single thing to prevent them?

Suddenly, the escape pod that Roderick cranked in hisses open. We turn around, and just as the pod's glass bubble slides away, I freeze.

Bryce gasps.

We all stand in complete silence, staring at the person stumbling out of the pod. He's dressed in the garb of an Order soldier. But he's no Order soldier. He's only a boy in appearance. Dark black bangs drape over his face, partially obscuring his yellow smile. And seeing him fills my heart with dread.

Sebastian of Abel.

✦✦✦

"*You*," I say, unclipping my dueling cane and stomping toward him. "What the hell are you doing here?"

Sebastian backs up, hands out. "I've come to save my best friend: Conrad of Urwin."

I catch him by the neck, my skin burning hot, and push him until his back's braced against the railing. I'm ready to squeeze his throat. This little bastard's back on my ship! How? Why?

"Physical conflict isn't the Hunter way, Captain," Sebastian says.

"We're not in Skylands territory anymore," I snarl.

Sebastian cackles. "So does that mean I don't have to follow your orders, Your *Highness*?"

My friends gather around me, coaxing me to release Sebastian. But once Bryce gets close to him, he yips.

"Don't touch me!" he whines. "You Lantian traitor. Murderous dirt-eater from below the acid clouds. BACK! BACK!"

Bryce stares at him, her eye twitching.

Once she moves away, Sebastian relaxes and straightens his dirtied Order jacket. Seems like he's been rolling around in some type of gunk. Then he smiles that unhinged smile of his. I breathe with unease. Sebastian's the darkest side of Meritocracy—the side that warps people into something demented and wrong.

"You're probably wondering what I was doing on the *Dauntless*," Sebastian says.

I scowl.

He grins. Loving his audience. It's best to ignore him, but we need to know how he got here . . . and why he was on an Order vessel.

"It was a simple thing, really," Sebastian says, looking over his filthy fingers, then wiping them on Roderick's suit. "I infiltrated Order so I could join this mission."

"You *infiltrated* Order?" Bryce folds her arms. "That simple?"

"Yes. Quite like you, dirt-eater, I *infiltrated*. It wasn't too difficult. Only had to kill an Order guard and steal his papers. I pressed his eyeballs into his skull."

He chuckles.

My hands ball into fists. With Sebastian it's impossible to separate a truth from a lie. Sometimes he says things just to get a rise.

"Your Royal *Highness*," he says to me, "I warned you not to come on this mission. That this mission would break you. But you've always been stubborn, so I came to save you."

Oh, how I want to beat that smile off his face. Hurl him over the railing to be eaten by the black clouds. But I won't become a murderer, not even for him. I tap my comm and explain we have an infiltrator to the other Captains and Commanders.

"We have plenty of space in our brigs," says Oba, the Order Commander. "We shall take him."

"Don't tell me our grand reunion will be so short-lived, Prince." Sebastian pouts. "I was hoping we could catch up." Without warning, he taps his comm gem. "The Prince is broken. He will doom you all."

Roderick slams him into the deck.

Sebastian grunts, then laughs. "Rod, you've been eating your protein."

Keeton rips Sebastian's comm gem away.

I growl. Can't believe this snake is back. And I have to deal with him again. If I don't, his venom will spread just like it did in the Gauntlet. He could turn the other ships against me. Losing the *Dauntless* will probably make it even easier for him. He's a venomous serpent.

Sebastian touches the back of his head and shows us the slip of blood. "I thought Pound was supposed to be the uncontrollable, physical one. Speaking of which, where is our big, ugly friend?"

My lips twitch.

Sebastian watches me, studying my face. Then he starts laughing. Laughing so hard that he's wiping his eyes. He tries to lean on Roderick's leg to steady his balance, but Roderick steps back.

"It's funny," Sebastian says, regaining his composure and rising to stand. "For a while I thought this crew was special. Full of people who had risen above Meritocracy. Thought they cared more about one another than their own rise."

"He left for his family," Roderick says through pursed lips.

"His family? The ones who abandoned him? The ones who all died on Holmstead?"

"Have you no feeling at all?" Roderick says, his face red. "That was your home island, too."

Sebastian yawns. "Yes, well, it treated me lower than dirt. Good riddance, I say. Eh, Prince?"

He nudges me, but I snap. My fist plunges into his gut, crumpling him over. He falls onto his knees, wheezing, trying to will air back into his lungs. And once he breathes again, holding his stomach, he laughs.

Oba's cruiser, the *Intrepid*, pulls alongside us. Several Order guards run across their gangway. They shove Sebastian to the ground. At first he flops around, not resisting. But I see something cross his face. The same look when he broke Samantha's neck in the duel at the Academy.

"Get back!" I shout.

But I'm too late. Sebastian throws a quick punch into a guard's throat. Strategic. The man snaps back. Holding his throat. Eyes wide. Unable to breathe.

Sebastian broke the man's trachea.

"Meds!" Keeton shouts.

I slam my cane into Sebastian's face, and he falls. Meanwhile, his victim flails on the ground, mouth opening and closing silently as he kicks his legs.

Everyone's shouting.

Sebastian woozily watches the scene. But he's cognizant enough to grin. Evil little birdshit. A Scholar Doctor rushes over to provide aid and meds.

The other guards swarm Sebastian. Kick him. Make him bleed. They cuff him and lift him roughly. He sags forward slightly, his hair draped over his face. He blows the bangs away, showing me his purpled face.

"I will not stop," Sebastian whispers to me. "Good things are in store now that I'm here. Don't you worry, Prince."

Then he's dragged across the gangway onto the Order cruiser. The injured guard is carried across, too.

I stomp away, my skin hot. Sebastian's return can't be a coincidence. He's up to something, but I don't have time to figure out what.

✦✦✦

My boots rattle on the darkened floor of the *Gladian's* corridors. I'm out of the rubber suit and back in my Hunter uniform. Even though it's been hours, my skin's still clammy from that rubber thing. And I'm itchy despite the protection the rubber suit gave me from the toxins. Arika told me, and everyone else, that we all will likely have rashes. But the medicinal cream should clear it up overnight. Hopefully.

My wind goggles bounce against my chest, and my black Hunter jacket whips behind me. We've anchored tightly against the gray rocks of an island for the evening to recuperate.

The *Intrepid* will be on watch duty tonight.

My body's running on adrenaline. I need nothing more than to sleep in my warm bed. My legs slog beneath me like heavy stumps. Suddenly, Keeton and Roderick appear around the corner, stopping me. Roderick's biting his lip, anxious, but Keeton's eyes are determined steel.

"Conrad, about Sebastian being back . . . ," Keeton says. "He can't be trusted. Do you remember what he did to this crew? He lied and manipulated his way to becoming Captain. When he lost the role, he tried to murder people. Including you."

I say nothing.

"Get rid of him," Keeton says.

I raise an eyebrow. "How?"

Roderick scratches the back of his head, but Keeton's got an edge about her. Fighting a war will do that to you. Fighting for your life will do that.

"Maybe not kill him," she says. "Not directly. But we've left prisoners on islands before . . ."

"We can give him supplies," Roderick says.

"When this is all over," Keeton says, "we'll send someone for him. The longer we keep him around, the more likely he'll enact some plan." She steps closer to me. "Because we all know that birdshit always has plans."

Roderick pats my shoulder. "We'll support you, whatever you decide. But please consider it. He'll hurt us if he stays."

Then they leave me standing in the darkness of the corridor.

I exhale and lean against the wall. Mother would want me to be merciful, but could she have ever predicted someone like Sebastian?

Father's voice invades my mind.

When mercy overwhelms you, think only hate.

Well, I hate Sebastian with a fierce passion. But leaving him out here, on an island by himself? This is certain death. It *is* murder. How likely is anyone to return from beyond Sky's Edge? Outside of Mage, we're the first to be here since the end of the Defector War.

I continue down the corridor, trying to purge Sebastian from my thoughts and finally get some damn sleep. But just before I enter my cabin, my gem lights up. My eyes shut. It's from Tara. Never a moment's rest. The more important you become, the less time you have.

I could ignore her, but it's better to get it over with.

I head to the third level and stand in the doorway of her immaculate room. She waves me in while speaking about the uncharted airs into a recorder gem like the one Arika has. I glance around her room.

Her books are organized alphabetically along a wide bookshelf, held in place by a retention bar. Above her steel desk, magnetic pens stick to the walls, and the papers on her desk are filled with notes. She even has a crude map she's working on—tracking everything we're doing.

Tara's dressed in casual wear—well, casual for a Scholar, that is. Her red hair's tied back, and she's in a loose crimson uniform with Scholar's emblem of an open book on her chest.

Uncle's portrait hangs from her wall. She stops recording and catches me looking at the portrait, perhaps thinking I'm impressed.

"Your uncle is a great man."

I say nothing.

"Many do not understand what he has done to reach his status. But his steady leadership is what makes me believe we have a chance."

"I didn't realize you were such a supporter."

"I support those with strength," she says. "As should all in Meritocracy. Are there many stronger than him?"

I don't answer. It's interesting that she's the heir to Scholar because her Master, Cheng of Lee, does not provide much support to my uncle.

I swallow down my distaste for Uncle's image and meet her eyes. "You wanted to speak with me?"

"Oh, yes Prince." Then she pauses, a slight hesitation in her voice. "This is something you must consider. It is vitally important for the welfare of the islands."

"What is it?"

"The Sky's Edge hypothesis."

"The what?"

"Within Scholar, it is theorized that the cloudwall protected an entire ecosystem from the gorgantaun threat. These creatures"—she says, motioning to the crude drawings she's tacked on the walls—"the Below created them to be part of the gorgantauns' food source."

This is the last thing on my mind right now, but Tara plows ahead, regardless.

"The cloudwall has been a protective barrier. Now . . ." She pauses. "It appears these creatures have adapted to life up here. They are . . . thriving. This is likely a strategy the Lantians had hoped would work. Build a self-sustaining ecosystem for the gorgantauns that would weaken the Skylands without a single Lantian death." She breathes out. "The creatures of the uncharted airs must all be destroyed."

"Well, as far as we know, they're entirely peaceful."

"True. But if these creatures were able to escape, if Sky's Edge ever falls, they could spread across the skies and feed the gorgantauns. If we were concerned about the pods before, imagine what would happen if they had more of their 'natural' prey to hunt. Predator levels rise and lower depending on the scarcity of food."

"It would be years before they'd be able to spread throughout the Skylands."

"We've seen what happens when invasive species are introduced. The Skylands didn't always have gorgantauns, or blobons, or acidons."

I stare at her.

"You can be like the other generations before you," she says. "The ones that pass it on because it's not an immediate problem. Or you could be proactive and solve it before it becomes one."

I exhale and wipe my face. "Tara, even if you're right, we don't have the supplies. We must ration our ammo and weapons."

"Well, somehow, they must be destroyed. Do not let your emotions get the better of you, Prince. We must have no mercy."

The familiarity of the message annoys me. "Is there anything else you wanted to discuss?"

"That is all."

I say good night, then step back into the hall. I'm irritated that she brought this information to me now, right after we lost the *Dauntless* and right after Sebastian returned and broke a man's trachea. She's worried about things that are ten steps ahead. And worse, I'm frustrated that she added more to my pile of worries.

Why am I the one mercy or death always falls upon? Should I destroy a whole ecosystem simply because it's the food of something more dangerous? Should I throw Sebastian onto an island to fend for himself?

I *finally* push open the door into my cabin, kick off my magboots, pull off my wind goggles from my neck, and gently slip out from my Hunter jacket. My skin's still itchy from the toxic air, so I uncap Arika's medicinal cream and slather it over my neck where I itch the most. Oh, my stomach feels warped. I leave my comm gem on the desk, thinking I'll soon slip under my blanket and doze for as long as possible. But as I start toward my bed at the end of the hall, I find someone on the couch. See her out of the corner of my eye.

"Bryce?"

I turn to glimpse the figure and realize it's not Bryce at all. My whole body tingles. Can't believe it. It's impossible.

"Hello, Brother," she says.

CHAPTER 30

NOT SURE WHETHER TO HUG ELLA OR SCOLD HER. FOR SEVeral seconds, I just stare at her. Disbelieving that she's even here. It doesn't make sense. How did she get here? Why?

"Uncle is looking for you," I say finally. "He thinks you were captured."

"I stowed away here. No hello?"

I blink. "Ella, these are the uncharted airs. It's dangerous." I pause. "There's a strong chance we won't get back to Skylands territory."

"We will. We are Urwin."

I'm not in the mood for that Urwin birdshit. "We are *not* invincible. And the comms won't penetrate the cloudwall. Uncle's spending resources looking for you. Resources that could be spent on the war. Why—why did you come?"

She pauses. Mouth opening and shutting. Hesitating because she's been taught to hide emotions. Still, her face betrays her. There's an admission there that maybe, just maybe, something I've told her connected with her.

"I don't trust Severina," she says.

"You stowed away because of that?"

She goes quiet. "She . . . she is ruining everything."

"I'm not interested in Uncle's wife, Ella. Look, you've come all this way." I need to communicate in a way she understands. "It shows strength to speak plainly, and honestly."

She meets my eyes, unconvinced, but she unclips her cane, the ugly red thing Uncle gave her. The blank one without a story. Then she pulls a necklace from her collar. It's a light chain with an emblem of the Urwin eagle and our initials, *CoU & EoU*, etched in the back of a hanging pendant. It's the same gold necklace I gave her years ago when I promised we'd be together forever.

"I'm here for Mother," she says.

She exposes a new capsule at the end of her necklace, a little fragment of Mother's cane inside. Just like mine.

"This chip was all I could find," she says. "I went back for the rest of her cane, but I couldn't find it. Uncle threw it out. He must've tossed the stag out the window."

Something about this revelation cracks me. Guilt. Ella did something because of Uncle's pressure, but she regretted it almost immediately.

I open my desk drawer and pull out something that glistens under the light of the crystal lamp. Ella stares at the black stag of Hale with relief. There's sincerity in my sister's eyes. But it doesn't make sense. Ella's stubborn as hell. There's no way she flipped this easily.

"You destroyed Mother's cane . . . ," I whisper. "Ella, you broke the legacy she left for you."

"I'm stuck," she says.

My eyes narrow. "What?"

"I'm stuck," she repeats, visibly chewing on a thought she can't quite get out. "Like . . . Uncle's part of me, but Mother is, too. I'm stuck between them. Pulled in two directions." She nibbles her lip again. "Does . . . does that make any sense?"

I know this feeling better than most, but I don't know what to say. Her face is wrinkled with conflict. I deal with this all the time, being pulled in two different directions. But I try to be myself. The problem is, I don't think Ella even knows who she is yet.

I sink into my seat behind the desk. She watches me, and her fingers nervously twitch.

What am I supposed to do with her? Send her back with one of my ships, with no guarantee they can cross safely through Sky's Edge without someone like Mage to guide them? Weaken my squadron to protect her? What message would I be sending if I push her away now that she's finally reached out to me?

"So, am I staying?" she asks.

I meet her eyes. Even though I'm not convinced about why she returned to me, I make a decision. One that I hope I won't regret.

"You're staying."

Uncle can search in vain. I don't give a damn.

✦✦✦

I wait until morning to reintroduce Ella to my crew. Roderick and Keeton are speechless. Bryce blinks in utter amazement. Yesenia folds her arms and looks Ella up and down. But Otto . . . His face flushes pink as he glimpses my sister.

Something about that look makes my brow furrow.

Arika's the only one who smiles at Ella. She offers her a tray of breakfast. While my crew eats and asks Ella how she managed to stow away, I walk to the window and contact the other ships to inform them of the situation.

"We are willing to take the Princess back to the Skylands," Oba answers.

"We can't lose another ship," I say. "Besides, if you go back, you may have to face the octolon alone. Worse, you'll need Mage, and we can't spare him."

"We will do whatever you decide, Your Highness."

"She will remain with us," I say.

The comm goes quiet for a moment. Oba's voice returns. "As you wish, Prince."

"I can assure everyone in the squadron that none of you will be blamed for this unexpected arrival," I say. "I will bear full responsibility." I shift the subject. "Mage?"

His voice comes over the gem. "Yes?"

"We should depart soon. How long will it take us to get to Weapon's island from here?"

"Uh," he says, voice hesitating. "May we speak in person?"

Something about his tone fills me with unease. "In person?"

"Yes, I have . . . information for your ears only."

My brow wrinkles. I can't deal with another surprise. We've had too many. Bryce and Keeton watch me as they eat their eggboat toast.

"Better make it quick, Magellan of Cabral," I say, forcing my voice to remain calm. "We have a sky of people to save."

A few minutes later, Mage stands in the doorway of the *Gladian's* command room, staring at Bryce, Roderick, Keeton, Arika, and my sister. Roderick picks at the warm potato puffs and dips them in lemon sauce. The others brought their breakfast, too.

"Prince . . ." Mage hesitates. "I was under the impression we'd be alone." His blue robotic pincers fiddle with his jacket's buttons.

"I changed my mind," I say.

He remains standing in the doorway.

"My crew would discover the truth either way, Mage." I lean forward, hands on the desk. "I'm assuming you're here with bad news?"

"Well, I—I haven't been entirely honest."

I exhale. "Tell me."

He blinks at my crew. Feet shifting.

"I trust everyone here, Mage."

"That's the thing, Prince. *I* don't."

"You don't have a choice. This mission hinges on you. My crew will hear about it from me now or later. Might as well be now."

He eyes Bryce. "I only speak if she is gone."

Bryce's arms fold. Keeton and Roderick place supportive hands on her shoulders.

"I trust Bryce," I say.

"She is a Lantian."

"We are all aware," Keeton says, a bite in her voice. "She's still here. That should tell you something, *Explorer*."

Mage blinks and enters, careful to shut the door behind him. Soon he's sitting opposite me. And it's strange that now, he looks so small. Narrow shoulders. A jaw that could crack from a single punch. The first time we met, he seemed to be able to read me. Had an obscene amount of confidence. But now I'm realizing that although he's great at uncovering secrets, his eccentricities, the way he talks and laughs—it's all a mask.

Deep down, this Mage of Cabral is a bit of a coward.

"How did you lose your arm, Mage?" Ella asks.

He shifts. "A mashtaun."

"Mashtaun?" Roderick says. "How the cuss did you tangle with one of those?"

"Well, that brings me to the reason I'm here."

We stare at him.

He breathes out. "I should've given this information to the King, but I was protecting my discoveries." His face splotches with heat. "I didn't recently find a way through the cloudwall. I've been navigating these uncharted airs for two years."

We go silent.

"I wanted to be a Traveler. It's the highest rank in my Trade."

"So," I say, leaning back, "you were hoarding the discoveries."

He clears his throat and nods. This damned Meritocracy, making people selfish even when the fate of the islands themselves is at stake. In his Trade, there's no greater honor than being the one to uncover new secrets. The discovery of gold is worth more than the gold itself.

"But the uncharted airs have changed," Mage says. "It wasn't like this two years ago. The Below . . . I think they're here."

I shut my eyes. Uncle said that was possible. But perhaps if Mage had really emphasized this to Uncle before we left on the mission, then maybe we'd have more ships.

"Are you taking us to Weapon's island or not?" Bryce asks.

"That's the thing . . . It's not that simple. I've made some discoveries." Mage looks like he'd rather jump overboard, but he forces the words out. "We need to go to another island first." The room falls silent. "In my travels here, I've discovered that Weapon had a secret island called Celentus."

Keeton and Roderick glance at each other.

"I have mapped out seven islands in these airs," Mage says. "Made numerous discoveries. All with the hope that when I revealed them all at once, I'd become a Traveler."

"You haven't revealed this to your Master?" I say.

"Marian knows I found a way in through Sky's Edge," he says. "She credited me with the discovery. Then she made me come before King Ulrich. But I didn't tell her everything because I'm not done yet. The next discovery could put me in the history books. It's just—I need your help with Celentus."

"So, we're going on some errand of yours to help you become famous?" Arika scoffs. "Isn't our mission to save the Skylands?"

"Of course we're here to save the Skylands," Mage says, irritated. "But I deserve credit. Now," he says, "Weapon created something. A device of unimaginable destruction. This is information I told the King. Conrad knows this, too."

I say nothing.

"But this next discovery, no one knows except me." He slides out a tattered journal from his jacket. The pages are frayed and partially rotted. "The journal of the Master of Weapon."

He lowers the leather-bound book on the table.

We lean forward and stare in amazement. In these uncharted airs, a massive, wide-open space, Mage managed to find a journal that belonged to the final Master of Weapon. He might be dishonest and selfish, but that doesn't mean he isn't exceptionally skilled at his Trade.

"I'm guessing," I say, "you have a whole set of discoveries aboard your vessel?"

"And I'm guessing," Roderick says, stuffing another sauce-covered potato puff into his mouth, "that's why you haven't let me tour your ship."

"Yes," Mage says.

Roderick chews and grumbles.

Mage flips open the journal. "The thing is, the Master of Weapon, Brone of Atlan, planned to use his weapon against the Skylands and reverse the war. But Brone grew tired, old. When his weapon was finally operational, he realized that if he used it, it would change the world forever. He says here"—Mage flips open the journal and points at a line—"'What's the point of winning a war if there's nothing left remaining?'"

An icy tendril coils inside me. What kind of weapon did Brone create?

"Seeing as the Skylander Armada had defeated the last of Weapon's flying monstrosities," Mage continues, "it was too late for Brone to destroy his weapon. So he locked it in a vault on Perditio—Weapon's home island."

"But Perditio was blown to dust," I say.

"The city was destroyed, yes. But the tunnels below the island's surface are intact," Mage says.

"Okay, so why do we need to go to Celentus?" Bryce asks. "Let's head straight to Perditio."

"Not that simple. Yes, the vault is on Perditio, but Brone? He buried himself with the key to the vault on Celentus. Unfortunately, Celentus is flooded with mashtauns."

We stare at him, mouths gaped.

"That's how you lost your arm," Ella says. "And that's also the moment when you turned into a coward."

Mage turns scarlet.

Roderick gives me a wary glance. Mashtauns. Giant, steel-plated gorillas. We've fought the beasts of the air, but mashtauns are the rulers of the islands. Not even prowlons take on mashtauns.

"Can't we just break through the vault on Perditio?" Keeton asks.

"It has a destruction mechanism attached to it," Mage says. "Tamper with it, and all the contents inside will be destroyed, including the weapon."

Keeton swears and sinks back.

"Wait, did you say that Brone *buried* himself?" Arika says, confused. "What do you mean when you say he buried himself?"

"Meaning his body rests underground," Mage says.

Roderick and Keeton share a strange, confused look.

Bryce suddenly gasps. "He *buried* himself."

We look at her, perplexed.

She taps her chin. "If Brone buried himself, it might mean that the last Master of Weapon . . . wasn't from the sky."

The room falls silent.

We turn to Mage for confirmation. He reluctantly nods. "Brone was a Lantian."

And we sit, blinking at this information. Realizing the Defector War was actually a Lantian attack on the Skylands. Not even Bryce knew this. This war really has waged for centuries.

"So," I say, "we need to go to Celentus, find Brone's body, and collect this key of his."

Mage nods.

"Can you give me the coordinates to Celentus, Mage?" I ask. "Draw it on the map for us?"

"*No*," Mage says, a sudden forcefulness in his voice. "This is the right of an Explorer. I'm not required by anyone, not even *you*, to reveal my discoveries. You will have to follow me."

My eyes narrow on him. Annoyed. "Fine, Mage. Set a course, and we will follow."

He nods and stands. "Celentus is dangerous, Prince. The mashtauns there are . . . abnormal. I suggest you prepare your people accordingly."

He leaves before I can respond.

CHAPTER 31

I LEAN OVER MY BEDSIDE, UNABLE TO SLEEP.

I must know why that little birdshit infiltrated the *Dauntless* and came here. So I slip on my boots and contact the *Intrepid*, and soon I'm crossing the gangway with the cool night wind at my back. The Order Commander, Oba of Abdullani, waits for me. He's a barrel-chested man with brown skin, a thin mustache, and bushy eyebrows. He bows as I drop onto the white deck of his ship.

The *Intrepid* stretches twice as long as the *Gladian*. It's covered with mountable cannons and other weaponry. Guards bow as we pass them. Oba and I climb the ivory command tower's stairs and enter a small room encased in glass. Inside, the Order Pilot stands near the ship's strings, studying a map. And beside him is the Order Protector, the woman in charge of the *Intrepid's* security and defenses.

On Order ships, every position has at least one assistant or junior officer, besides the Commander or Captain and the Lieutenant, because Order ships must always be ready. In Order, one person will rest while the other is on duty. Except for in times of battle—then everyone's on deck.

Oba guides me to a platform at the back, and after tapping a button, we descend into the musty ship.

He takes me down a corridor far narrower than any on my ship. We pass a mess hall, where a couple off-duty soldiers enjoy a coffee in a windowless, lifeless room. Next, we pass an exercise room filled with weights and a short track, where a few sparrow Aviators jog.

Finally, we approach the munitions locker. The Munitions Expert stands behind a glass case. Behind him is a locker filled with Order weaponry: auto-muskets, explosives, and even a few electric spears that have been swiped from the Lantians.

"Are you sure you'd like to meet with him, Your Highness?" Oba asks me.

I nod.

"Very well." He takes me left, and two men stand at the end of the hall, guarding a single door.

"Would you like me to join you in the interrogation?" he asks.

"I can handle Sebastian."

We stop at the door. Oba looks me up and down, considering—perhaps even skeptical. But he doesn't really have a say in the matter. So he motions the guards aside then stuffs a key into the lock.

"When you are ready to leave, knock twice."

He pulls open the door, and I step into a familiar, acrid smell. It's only been a couple days, but it takes me back to the Gauntlet, when he marinated in his own sweat in our brig. Sebastian has never been hygienic—but that issue is exacerbated when he's trapped in a cramped, contained space.

Sebastian rises from his cot as I enter.

The door shuts behind me. The room's sparse. A sink, toilet, and a cot. But it does have a small library of books. Several of which, it appears, Sebastian tore up in boredom, leaving tattered pieces about.

"Prince!" Sebastian says, grinning widely and raising his arms as if to hug me. "I feared you'd never come."

He approaches me. Perhaps expecting me to flinch or step back. When I don't, he stops a foot from me.

"What can I do for you, Your *Highness*?"

"Why are you here?"

"Always so blunt, Prince. We have so much catching up to do. I bet you enjoy being the Prince. Telling others what to do."

"Just answer the question."

Sebastian chuckles. "I told you! I came to save the Skylands from certain extermination. When I realized you'd accepted this mission, despite my warnings, I knew I had to come and save you."

I stare at him.

"It's funny," he says, strolling away and lowering to sit on the cot. He crosses his legs. "You should be concerned with how easily I managed to infiltrate the *Dauntless*. Real lackluster security on your ships, Prince."

"You should be concerned with what happens to you at your next Hunter Tribunal," I say. "Next time when I provide testimony, I won't tell them to spare you."

"That was *you* who told them I shouldn't be killed?" He pauses and presses a hand against his chest. "Prince, I'm touched."

Oh, I hate him. "You attacked an Order guard, Sebastian. Nearly killed him. Not even I have the authority to step in and protect you from the Tribunal."

He shrugs, unconcerned. "Enough of me. I haven't expressed my congratulations to you yet."

I stare at him. "Congratulations?"

"Your new stepmother, of course! What's her name? Severina?"

"Sebastian, why are you really here?"

"Severina's a strange one, you know," he says very conversationally. "Powerful. A High on her island. Some were thinking she might challenge the Duchess of Rootland. Samantha of Talba's mother."

I stare at him. Disgusted that he'd mention Samantha.

"You remember Samantha, yes?" Then he lowers his voice as if he's sharing a secret. "That stupid girl whose neck I broke in the Day of Duels." He laughs. "Underestimate me at your peril, Prince."

"I know perfectly well what you're capable of."

He wags a finger at me. "But you don't know what I know about Severina."

There's no point in engaging him. It is his game, and I won't play.

Sebastian, bored that I don't take the bait, uncrosses his legs and slaps his thighs. "This mission is doomed to fail. The thing is, *Prince*, the Below has been in this area for quite a while. Months, in fact."

I squint at him. Trying not to give away what I know. "How would you know that?"

"Connections."

"Uh-huh. Like your aunt?"

"My dear aunt is merely Master Koko's assistant, Captain. She doesn't know everything. Though maybe her connections will grow someday."

"Okay, so you have connections and don't want to share them. Fine."

"You're not going to dig more?" he asks. "I have all sorts of information. All you must do is ask." He pauses and meets my eyes. "You didn't have to come see me, you know. But your curiosity got the better of you." He laughs. "It's late, and instead of sleeping, you're here with me. We're like young lovers."

Just can't with this bastard. Sick of looking at him. Sick of smelling him.

"How's your sister?" he says. "I'd love to meet her."

My hands ball into fists and my gloves squeak.

"Overheard the guards talking," he says, waiting for my reaction. "You're complaining about me not being forthright?" He chuckles. "Communication goes two ways, Conrad."

"*Prince*," I say.

He laughs. "Look at you—sounding more like an Urwin every day.

You've always seemed like the type who would only appreciate something if you earned it. But I suppose I was wrong. Soon you'll be just like your uncle." He laughs again. "The thing is, *Conrad*, I exposed how weak your ships are by infiltrating one. Now you are stuck behind the cloudwall, outmanned. Outgunned."

"Why didn't you report what you know about the Below being here to a superior? Your aunt has easy access to Master Koko," I say. "If you believe your connection, that is?"

He just smiles.

My teeth grit. "I'm considering leaving you on an island. Speak honestly."

"Conrad, I'll give you one bit of information. Something, I think, that shouldn't come as a surprise considering how easily I managed to stow away on here. Someone aboard these vessels has a symbion."

My eyes narrow. "Who?"

"Free me, and I'll tell you."

Won't even consider that. I'd rather rub sand in my eyes than free someone like him. Still, I must substantiate his claims—even if they are coming from him.

I tap my gem, connecting it with all the Captains and Commanders—and their seconds-in-command, just in case—and advise them of the report.

Sebastian walks around the cell, humming while we wait. He plays the drums on his thighs for a moment, listening for the results to pour in.

My heart thuds as the other ships check the necks of everyone in my fleet. But it's not long until I'm getting all-clear messages from all the Captains and all the Commanders.

Sebastian just laughs. Knowing that I woke everyone up for nothing but his amusement.

The bastard.

I tap the door twice, and the guards let me out. Sebastian's still laughing as I stomp away. Talking with him is always complete waste of time.

"Cut his rations," I say to Oba, "in half."

✦✦✦

The morning breeze makes my jacket flap. The wind comes from multiple directions at once. One of the drafts is warmer—more active and consistent—while the other is gentle, sporadic, and cool.

The *Rimor* shoots ahead.

Bryce stands beside me.

A cloud of tiny flying creatures—crablike with tails—zooms past us. One stops to land on Bryce's shoulder. She laughs. When she reaches to touch it, the creature jets backward, then joins the rest of its kind.

"Do you know anything about this place?" I ask her.

She shakes her head. "I wasn't around the Designers. This is all new to me."

"Minlons," Tara says, suddenly. Standing behind us. She's got a notepad out, and she's quickly sketching the creatures. Giving credit to Mage for the discovery but taking the chance to name them herself. "That's what I'm calling them. They will require further research, but I believe they are of the same genus as the sheltauns."

I watch her. If Scholar knew how to get through Sky's Edge earlier, they'd have immediately dispatched their academic ships to record everything. But the responsibility falls entirely to Tara. I imagine she wants to record the existence of these creatures now because she believes that they all ought to be destroyed.

A trio of balenons—also named by Tara—the singing beasts with the breathing holes atop their heads, bursts through the white clouds beneath us. Their wide mouths open and the minlons scatter, but not before the balenons suck the little critters into their mouths.

"Well, I know about these creatures," Bryce says. "The balenons, as Tara calls them; we called them 'sky whales.'"

"Sky what?" I say.

"*Whales*. We have them below—in the ocean."

Tara's listening. Intrigued.

"But we were told the sky whales were a failed creation," Bryce continues. "That they died out."

"Perhaps the Lantians are not aware of them then?" Tara asks.

"I doubt it. Goerner has something on his ship that allows him to control every Designed creature."

"That must be how he controls the gigataun."

She shakes her head. "Well, he and the Lantian Council. They have to be able to control the beast in the Below, too; otherwise, it'd destroy the colonies whenever it wakes after its long slumber. Plus, the Lantian Council knows that if Goerner were the only one with control, we'd only have to destroy his ship."

Tara's no longer drawing. I suddenly wonder whether she might have one of her recorder gems in her pocket. So I send her off. She steps away, irritated. But not even the heir to Scholar dares go against a Prince.

Bryce and I stand alone, the wind in our faces. I look over the edge of the ship, at the swirling black clouds that blanket the sky.

"How did you come to the Above?" I ask.

"Remind me another time, and I'll show you."

"It's strange that we cut your symbion, but it still works."

"My experiences are still in it." She shrugs. "It just doesn't transmit or tell me when other Lantians are around. Not without touching them."

We go quiet. Enjoying the beauty of this strange place, and a moment of peace. I glance at her. Remember the moment when we kissed. And recall the joy and excited twist in my chest.

"What?" she says.

"Nothing."

"You're thinking something."

"Just reminiscing."

"Oh yeah?" She smiles coyly. "About what?"

"I was wondering . . . if you could show me that first kiss we shared—from your perspective."

Her skin flushes. "I'd rather you not know what I was thinking at that moment."

"Was I bad?" I ask.

"Was *I*?"

"No."

"Well, neither were you."

"If I said you were bad, would you have said I was bad?"

She laughs. "Yes."

We stand close together, our hands almost touching, and gaze out at the sky. As we watch some type of metallic bird rest atop a balenon, my pinky grazes hers. Gentle enough to make it seem an accident. But when she doesn't move away, I bring the rest of my hand onto hers.

She meets my eyes. Her blue ones always managing to drown me. My heart thuds anxious energy, and my stomach does a backflip. She opens her mouth to speak, but I'm afraid that if she does, I'll have to respond, and my voice will shake.

"What are you two looking at?" Ella steps between us. "Oh, I've never seen creatures like this."

Bryce and I glance at each other over Ella's head and frown.

Ella unclips her spyglass and peers at the distance.

"Captain," Bryce says, clearing her throat and straightening her jacket, "I have duties to perform. Let me know when Celentus comes into view."

I nod, a little disappointed.

Once she's gone, Ella turns to look up at me. And her face is serious. "Conrad, Bryce is a *Lantian*."

My eyes narrow.

"You are the Prince of the Skylands," she says. "The Skylands will never accept her. If you get too close, they'll accuse you of being a traitor."

I want to argue, but her words cut because of their truth. Whatever's growing between Bryce and me—it's dangerous out in the open. Part of me doesn't give a damn. Let the world think what they want. But we're at war, and the Skylands have already been challenging my family. Furthermore, there's no telling what my support is like on the other ships.

We've already lost the *Dauntless*. What if ships keep falling?

I shut my mouth. Despite how I feel about Bryce, I must keep it buried. Deep inside. And not let it out.

CHAPTER 32

CELENTUS APPEARS IN THE DISTANCE, FLOATING AMONG A bed of thick, fluffy clouds.

Tara studies the island through her spyglass. Her eyes are wide, wild even. Her previous formality and decorum gone. Now all she can do is frantically document her observations about the creatures, the strange winds, and the erratic island behavior of these airs.

Celentus is a rainbow of colors. Blue leaves wave under the wind. Red grass flitters. And white tree trunks blanket the yellow hills.

"Strange place," I say.

"Indeed," Tara says excitedly, hastily adding new sketches to her notebook. "It is likely the Below's Designers created not just fauna, but flora to support their gorgantaun ecosystem." She stops drawing and looks at me. "Whatever their plan was, they never completed it—since this is all isolated behind the cloudwall."

"Trapped here for hundreds of years."

"Yes, and it has done quite well. It is remarkable."

I look at her. "You admire their work?"

"Of course. How could any academic not be impressed with what the Below accomplished here? If not for Weapon's erecting Sky's Edge, this ecosystem would have spread throughout the Skylands. Brone of Atlan's cloudwall inadvertently saved the Skylands, but it was not enough to save himself." She pauses, slides her pencil into her notebook, and meets my eyes. "Your Highness, have you considered what I told you about these beasts?"

I shut my mouth. I'm a Hunter; I've killed many creatures created by the Lantians. But thus far, they've all been creatures bred for death and destruction. Here, nothing has tried to attack us since the octolon.

"I will inform the King of the ecosystem when we return to the Skylands." Uncle can decide what to do with them later. Right now I need to focus on the mission.

She nods. "Thank you, Prince. That is wise."

"Yesenia," I say, turning back to the helm bubble, "bring us to Celentus."

"Aye."

She pushes the strings, and we soar for the island. The other ships follow. As we approach Celentus, tiny metallic lizards dive off orange bushes and scurry into the red grass. Somewhere among the waving white trees and dark shadows of the blue forest, something moans. It's a low, threatening rumble. Ominous.

My jaw sets.

I faced a prowlon alone on an island when I was ten. Killed it, too. But even prowlons flee from what faces us here. Everything on land does.

My fleet hovers above the island, but not too close. Mashtauns are known to hurl boulders at passing ships. Or leap onto them.

Then again, Mage mentioned these beasts are different from the ones we know in the Skylands. Perhaps they've evolved or changed. This is part of the reason we cannot simply drop into the jungle near the burial location. It's too dense there, and we'd be dropping in blind. So we find a clearing—wide and open with plenty of light. Just a few miles from Brone's supposed location. We hover high enough—hopefully—that nothing can reach us.

"If you don't mind," Mage says to me over the gem, "I'd prefer to follow the team while floating in the *Rimor.* Just above, you know. Safe distance."

"Impossible," I say. "You'd lose track of us."

"But—"

"If you want to be credited with any discovery here, Mage," I say, "then you must be present, in person."

He goes quiet. "I understand."

Roderick kicks a roped ladder over the *Gladian's* edge, and it drops into Celentus red grass. Around me, my crew scurries about the deck. Collecting weapons, ammunition. I hoist a mobile harpoon launcher, drop it onto the weapon crate near the pulley system, and stomp toward the helm bubble.

"Yesenia," I say. "You have command. No one leaves the ship. Understood?"

"Yes, Captain."

I'd prefer to leave command with Arika. I just know her better, but it'd go against Meritocracy. Arika is the Cook, a Low. And as Navigator, Yesenia will be the only remaining High on the ship after my group drops onto the island.

I walk toward the ladder, but a small figure stops me. Her arms folded and a determined look on her face.

"Take me with you," she says.

"Ella, we can't have both heirs on this island. We don't know what dangers Celentus holds."

"Well, we still don't know what dangers the uncharted airs hold, and we're together now."

"We're together now because of a choice you made, Sister. But now, we have a choice."

Her face sours. "Apparently, I don't."

I pat her shoulder. "I'm sorry, Ella."

She scowls, then marches away.

Men and women from Order and Hunter climb down the roped ladders of their ships. I step out through the open gate in the railing and climb onto the ladder. The wind makes my jacket flutter, and the ladder sways as I descend. I hop off and squish soft mud beneath my boots.

The muggy air's so thick I could drink it.

I squint from the sunlight as the others join me in the clearing. Tara watches me from the railing above, her head shaking. Earlier today she tried to convince me that it wasn't logical for the Prince to go on such a dangerous mission. But I'm a Hunter. A good one, too. And I'd never force my friends to do something I wouldn't do myself.

Roderick, Bryce, and Keeton drop beside me. Arika, Yesenia, Otto, Tara, and Ella will remain aboard the *Gladian.* I directed every Captain and Commander to leave behind enough people to operate their ships in case of an emergency.

Roderick stares at the shadowed jungle ahead of us and clutches his shoulder cannon tight.

"Mashtauns," he murmurs. "Everyone ready to go die?"

He laughs, but no one else does.

Hunters from the *Explosio, Telum,* and *Ferrum* join my crew. They're seasoned people; some have had limbs replaced with sharp, gorgantaun-steel blades. Their eyes, like their bodies, have seen too much.

Yesenia and Otto use the rope and pulley system to lower our chosen weapons on a crate. Arika's not helping them, though. She's belowdecks, preparing a meal for when we return. Something special, she'd said. My gut tells me, after what we're about to do, we'll need some comfort food.

Keeton and I snag the mobile launchers, while Bryce collects a flak cannon. We have a good balance of weapons.

Finally, Mage descends from the *Rimor*, his gangly, uncoordinated feet nearly missing each bar of the ladder. He slips the last few feet and lands on his back. He stands quickly and straightens his jacket like nothing happened.

A few Hunters chuckle at him.

Mage approaches me, marching through the grass, his pincer claw twisting as he glances at the harpoon's point in my mobile launcher.

"Captain," he says.

"You know the way?"

He pulls the journal from his pocket and taps it.

"Could the journal lead us to a trap?" Bryce asks.

"Doubtful," he says. "This journal was meant to be found by Lantians. Brone wanted them and no one else to recover the key. Guess he didn't expect me to show up. We all ready?"

Everyone's geared up. A band of fifty people or more.

"Let's go," I say.

Mage nods and points us toward the jungle. Kirsi of Rebekah, Captain of the *Explosio*, and her crew head out first, using blades to cut through the red grass. They have the most island-hunting experience.

Mage follows them.

The ground squishes beneath us. A thin layer of fog hovers above the plants. As we crush grass, metallic insects roll into balls and shoot away. A faint odor lingers in the wind—like decaying flesh and corroded metal. We quietly enter the jungle's shadows. Trees fly up hundreds of feet and the canopy above sways, dappled with bits of sunlight.

The odor grows.

We trudge through the undergrowth, mostly in hushed whispers.

A small arachnon, just a few inches across, scurries along the bark. It hisses, then pounces at us. Roderick yelps and leaps back, but Keeton backhands it and squashes it beneath her boot. We watch her use a stick to free the squished metal spider from her heel.

She shrugs and moves on.

"Those things are so poisonous," Roderick whispers to me.

We all watch the tree bark a little more closely. The stench in the air intensifies.

Eventually, we splash across a narrow stream and chilly water numbs my toes. A few silver fish with golden eyes watch us from beneath the water. Suddenly, a burst of squawking birds jets over us. Mage jumps in panic. The birds soar through the canopy before landing on the branches, and they watch us. Their little eyes shining, their metal beaks clicking.

The jungle grows darker, denser. And shadows dance among the vine-covered trunks.

"This place is so creepy," Rod mutters.

Mage taps the comm on his wrist. His voice comes in, soft and low. "Quietly now. We're entering their territory."

Everyone slows. The odor's so pervasive, it's stinging my nostrils. Roderick's breathing through his mouth.

"Ugh," Rod says. "What's that stench?"

"Them," Mage says.

Rod clutches his shoulder cannon a little tighter.

Kirsi of Rebekah steps beside me. She's well over six feet tall. Square shoulders, powerful legs, and built like a bear. Her head is shaved except for a single black ponytail. She carries a harpoon like it's a spear.

"Your Highness," Kirsi whispers, looking down at me. "We should recap the tactical brief for the ranks."

I nod. I'd asked her to be my adviser for this trek, and I spent a few hours last night studying her notes from her many mashtaun hunts.

"Mashtauns are intelligent and dangerous," she whispers into her gem to the group. "The armor on their shoulders, their back, and their foreheads is as thick as the scales of a class-two gorgantaun. Aim for the armpit, the forehead, and just below the sternum. A well-placed harpoon is all it takes. But"—she pauses as a cool breeze rattles the trees—"they move fast. Faster than anything that big ought to move."

An Order guard beside me clears his throat and squeezes his auto-musket.

"Can we avoid them?" Roderick whispers, following behind us with Keeton.

"No, we can't avoid them," Kirsi says. "They likely know we're here. Mashtauns communicate on a high level."

"Like, they talk?" Roderick's brow wrinkles. "Why didn't you send us notes about that?"

She stares at him. "I *did*."

Rod's face reddens.

Keeton nudges his side and hisses, "I told you to read them."

I shake my head. A little irritated. Roderick's an incredible Master Gunner, but it's just like him to not read her notes. Back in the Hunter Academy, he spent more time eating desserts and ogling girls than studying the flight manuals and engineering textbooks.

Suddenly, the *Explosio* Hunters raise their fists, signaling us to stop. A strange silence has swept over the jungle, and the smell burns my eyes.

My finger reaches toward the trigger on my launcher.

Beside me Mage fiddles with his jacket buttons again.

Then we hear it. Barely audible over the flowing wind. It's low—like gruff whispers—but not any language I've heard. Grunts.

"Prince," Mage whispers in a panic. "I'd really like to be on my ship for this."

"Quiet," I mutter.

Kirsi motions her hand, telling us to lower. We all kneel. The sharp grass stabs into my thighs, and tiny metallic insects scurry away and dig into the dirt.

Suddenly, the grunting whispers stop.

We wait several minutes, listening to the soft crushing of vegetation in the darkness. Bryce kneels on my left, her eyes intently focused on the jungle. Something hisses to my left, and Kirsi jabs her harpoon. We all jerk, ready to fight. But Kirsi's pressing her boot against the skull of a fifteen-foot anguon—a metal snake—and dislodges her harpoon from its head.

"Lucky it was a baby," she whispers. Blood drips from the end of her weapon. She raises her comm. "Keep moving. Quietly."

We stand and continue.

"Mashtauns are clever, but they're still animals," Kirsi whispers to me. "They'll spring traps and communicate, but they are not *us*. Our brains remain our greatest advantage."

Mage points out the raised, rocky formation at the apex of a hill before us. A series of caverns awaits, veiled with purple vines.

"There," he whispers. "Brone's buried in that range."

"About a twenty-minute walk," Bryce whispers.

We enter denser foliage. Bushes and branches claw at me. Insects with tiny, sharp pincers bite at my exposed flesh where my sleeves are rolled up. I swat them away, scowl at the bumps growing on me, and correct my sleeves. Bryce smashes another aggressive arachnon with the butt of her flak cannon. Until now, the uncharted airs have been peaceful. Celentus seems to have everything. I wouldn't be shocked if it had prowlons, boarlons, and lupons, too. It makes sense that Brone would leave the key here. Who in their right mind would explore this place?

I glance at Mage and his robotic arm.

We continue for ten minutes, approaching the slope that leads up toward the rocky ridge. The grass grows like trees here and Kirsi's Hunters go to war on it, slicing a path for us. Finally, we start up the incline toward Brone's rock formation.

The canopy darkens so much, it's like we stepped into night. And the horrible stench returns. Sharp and overly sweet. My throat goes dry. The neighboring Order guards activate the crystals on their auto-muskets. And several of the Hunters tap their comm gems to light them up.

I squeeze the grip of my launcher. If I were looking to ambush my prey, this would be the perfect place.

"Keep moving," Kirsi whispers. "Don't stop."

The incline burns my calves, makes my forehead perspire. The weight of my launcher digs into my shoulder. And the damn bugs keep biting me.

"They're everywhere." Roderick slaps the back of his neck. Then he coughs and spits. "Eugh! I got one in my mouth."

"Shh!" Keeton hisses.

We glimpse a break in the canopy. It exposes a clearing among the trees. I'm about to point us in that direction, but Kirsi grips my shoulder.

"Stop," she whispers over the comm to the group. "Not another step."

Everyone freezes.

She points, and almost completely hidden in the darkness is a slight hint of silver. It's a chest—thick and powerful—and three times as wide as the strongest man's.

The whispers among the trees come again. Gruff.

Bryce, Keeton, and Roderick bunch closer to me, inside the ring of Order guards. We're all supposed to be these tough bastards. People who've hunted the most terrible beasts in the sky. Yet we're shivering like children.

The guards grip their muskets. One blinks rapidly, probably

because she's sweating into her eyes. Mage's face has turned a special shade of pale.

A stick snaps behind us. We whirl around.

"Shit," Krisi whispers.

"What?" Roderick asks.

"We're walking into a trap."

Mage moans.

Kirsi nods toward the clearing. "They want to lure us there. A band of them waits in the darkness. But they don't know we've seen them."

Another stick snaps behind us. Then another and another. Gruff whispers follow—as well as the sudden beating of a chest.

"Stand your ground," Kirsi whispers over the comm. "Everyone, stand—"

"AAGGH!"

A Hunter is ripped away, his fingers scraping the dirt. He cries out desperately as a long, silver hand drags him into the darkness.

The Hunters panic. Stumbling over one another. We fire into the jungle. The air echoes with explosions and harpoons twang against trees. The jungle swells with golden blasts. More people are dragged into the darkness, screaming.

Kirsi roars, "STOP!"

The jungle darkens again. My entire body's trembling as I reload from the hovering crate behind us. *Holy damn hell!*

We go quiet. And listen. The stolen Hunters shout in the distance, pleading for help. But their pleas turn to screams and then to the sickening sound of snapping bones.

"Look out!" Roderick shouts.

Something flies toward me. I dive into the grass and a second later, a man's mangled corpse hits the ground inches from me. His body bent backward.

"MOVE!" Kirsi cries.

We run. More corpses fly into our ranks, hitting some of us, and steering the rest toward the clearing. That's where the beasts want us.

Kirsi redirects us each time.

I stare at the dead bodies as we run, wishing Madeline de Beaumont trained me more on mashtauns. Wishing I didn't feel so helpless and didn't have to rely on Kirsi. People are dying. But I can't operate on instinct when I know so little. I've no choice but to trust that Kirsi knows what she's doing.

Suddenly, another Hunter cries as he's dragged into the jungle. Pleading with us to help him. But we can't, and it cuts me.

We come together in a tighter formation and run up the hill, away from the clearing. The mashtauns crack branches and trees around us. Still trying to spook us into the clearing. But as we hike higher, I realize that the clearing's actually encircled by tall rocks—hidden in the darkness. Only one way in or out. We would've been trapped.

Finally, we slow to a walk but stay in tight formation. We're all breathing hard. My hands feel sticky on the grip of my mobile launcher. Heart hammers. My back's wet, and I wipe my forehead with my sleeve. Keeton reloads her launcher from the hovering crate.

Something whispers in the trees, and the Order guard beside me panics. He squeezes the trigger of his auto-musket. His blasts spray the branches. The attack exposes, for a blink, the deformed metal face of a giant beast only thirty feet away.

Mage was right. These mashtauns are different. They're misshapen, with long, thin arms and faces like melted wax.

The beast thuds its horrible chest. But Kirsi shouts for us to face the other direction. Despite it going against every instinct in my body, I force myself to turn away from the mashtaun. And sure enough, while the one thuds its chest in our rear, three other beasts appear on the other side of us. Ready to break through our ranks and rip us to pieces.

But we're ready for them.

"FIRE!" I roar.

Our harpoons whistle as they stick into the mashtauns. Cutting through the thin scales under their sternums and their armpits. Roderick squeezes the trigger of his shoulder cannon, blasting the metal off a mashtaun's shoulder. These beasts are smart bastards, but their armor's not impenetrable.

One falls dead, and white blood sprays over us.

Bryce shoots the flak cannon, making the space glow. Revealing not one or two more mashtauns, but a whole pack. They're thumping the ground, and their awful, misshapen bodies bounce around the trees.

Kirsi's eyes widen. "Run."

Then she takes off. Deeper into the forest, up the incline, and into the darkest parts of the jungle. I save my harpoon. And I just run. People behind us shout, scream as the mashtauns charge after us. The beasts catch more of our party, pulling their limbs off. Hurling their bloodied torsos into our ranks.

My exhausted legs beg for a break.

"Ahh!" Bryce shouts.

My breaths stop. Bryce? I glance back in terror, but I'm squinting through darkness. The Order guards grab my arms.

"Keep moving, Your Highness."

"No. Where's Bryce? Where is she?"

Kirsi's shouting ahead. "C'mon!"

Mage's crying.

"Bryce!" I shout as I struggle against the thick arms tugging me with them. "BRYCE!"

Keeton and Roderick turn back, too, but a mashtaun charges them. Roderick fires a blast into the beast's drooping face—shooting its head right off. Roderick falls back from the explosion, and Keeton helps him up.

"C'mon!" she shouts.

More mashtauns snort and charge. Their giant fists grinding the earth as they dash on all fours. Their wild eyes full of hungry hate.

The Order guards urge me on. One fires his auto-musket as a mashtaun leaps ahead of us. His pellets ding off its face, except for one that penetrates the beast's eye. The creature falls forward, dead, and crushes the undergrowth.

Mage shouts about a tunnel ahead—the opening into the burial site.

"We can make it!" he cries. "Just a little farther."

"Bryce!" I shout.

Can't leave her. Won't let her die here. I rip free of the guards' grip. Force myself to turn back and run toward where I heard her yell.

The Order guards chase me. Roderick, too. They're shouting, calling me a crazed idiot. Suddenly, a mashtaun bursts from the trees to my left. Its eyes glowing with glee as it chases something. My breath stops, because ahead of the beast is Bryce. She's hobbling toward me. Her flak cannon gone. Blood trickling down her arm.

The mashtaun's malformed face grins. One eye bigger than the other. It's fifteen feet tall, and it raises its enormous silver fists. Ready to pummel Bryce into the ground.

I suck a breath, peer down the reticule of my launcher, and squeeze the trigger. My harpoon launches. The mashtaun's about to break every bone in Bryce's body. But my harpoon spears the creature directly beneath its sternum. Right into the heart. The beast freezes, a puzzled expression on its ugly face before it tumbles backward.

The Order guards finally yank me back and into the tunnel with them. Seconds after I fall inside, coughing in a misty, dark place, Bryce tumbles in and lands next to me.

She's wincing as she holds her bleeding arm.

"Bryce," I groan. "Are you okay?"

She doesn't have time to answer because mashtauns roar around the narrow tunnel's opening. Their giant arms reach inside. Mangled fingers digging around, sharp claws scraping the rock, creating sparks.

We scramble away into the darkness, our hearts in our throats. But the beasts can't squeeze inside.

We made it. We got away.

I want to laugh with relief, but then I see the shock on Bryce's face and hold her tight, realizing just how close I was to losing her.

CHAPTER 33

FIFTEEN.

That's how many the mashtauns killed. Fifteen people chosen specifically for this world-saving mission. And they're gone. We have no immediate way to replace them.

My responsibility. Mine.

I massage my forehead as we're using the crystals at the end our weapons to expose the tunnel's craggy walls. The humid air's like a warm lake, and it stinks of ancient dirt. Fortunately, without the sour stench of mashtauns.

Water trickles in through the cracks in the tunnel. Fluorescent mushrooms grow in the corners, and a few insects and other strange animals scurry away as we march. Every few minutes, someone squishes an arachnon.

"There were too many mashtauns," Kirsi whispers.

She has gone extra quiet because it was her ship that suffered the most losses. Her crew. My stomach twists with guilt—too many people have died under my leadership.

I breathe out. Their sacrifice will mean nothing if we don't give it value. We sing softly for the dead, but the notes are just another guilty reminder. The lyrics honor them, but the best thing we can do for them is to find the Master of Weapon's remains and finish this damn mission.

Our steps echo. Occasionally something huffs in the distance, but Mage claims there's no way the mashtauns can get in. Unless the tunnels have changed since the Master of Weapon drew his maps.

I clutch my launcher. Hundreds of years is a long time.

We come to a fork in the tunnel. Mage stops us, shining a crystal on the journal. His eyes squint in concentration. I step to stand over his shoulder, but my eyebrows rise as I realize the journal has no map at all; rather, it's a series of random numbers.

Mage squints at me through the thick lenses of his golden goggles. "You didn't think he actually drew a map, did you?"

"Well . . ."

"You have to decode it," he says. "They're a list of directions that correspond with drawn illustrations later in the journal. It took me a very, *very* long time to figure that out."

"What if you got the numbers wrong?"

His huge bug eyes narrow. "Prince, I am an *Explorer.* We are discoverers. Not just in the airs—but in all flights of life."

"Okay," I say, backing off. "So, which way?"

"Let me determine where we are first."

I leave him be.

Down the tunnel, Kirsi's leaning against a wall, away from the others, her eyes closed. I swallow a breath and stop before her. We're silent for a few seconds.

"You never get used to it," she says finally, not opening her eyes. "Remembering the dead. Your mistakes. But the dead are not numbers. People are *not* numbers." She opens her eyes, and rolls up her sleeve, showing dozens of marks that streak her arm. Fifteen new cuts stripe her skin in bloody lines.

"Never forget," she says.

I stare at her. Despite Kirsi's experience, she still mourns the dead. She hasn't become desensitized.

"Do you . . ." I glance around me to make sure I'm not overheard. "Do you ever feel so guilty you can't sleep?"

She peers at me, then slides down her sleeve. "When I was a young Captain, yes. But then I realized the guilt didn't make me a better leader. It made me worse. I second-guessed myself at every turn. Slept terribly. Over the years my crews mutinied several times, and I fell to various positions. Then I rose to Captain again, a decade ago, and I've not lost the position since."

"How?"

"People die under every Captain. It's a fact of life in Hunter. But I realized that if I wasn't leading, someone worse would, and even more would perish."

I consider her words. Am I saving lives by being Prince? How can I say that someone else would've done a worse job when the tally of the dead keeps growing beneath my watch?

"We have to get the key," Kirsi says. "There are people in the squadron who will be quite displeased when they find out how many we've lost. If we come back with nothing, this whole mission will fall apart."

My body tightens at this revelation. "What people?"

She shrugs. "We're not going to fail, so what does it matter? If that bridge drops, we'll cross it then."

I exhale. People aren't going to risk their lives without a good reason. We must get the key.

"You saved us, Kirsi."

"No." She shakes her head. "The dead did."

I go quiet, considering her words. Thinking back to when we had to abandon the *Dauntless* to get past the octolon. Their deaths allowed the mission to continue.

In another world, maybe I'd just be leading the *Gladian* crew. We'd be hunting together, clearing the skies, and I'd be working to pay off the ship. I wouldn't be thinking about any war. Wouldn't be shouldering the burdens I am now.

I never wanted to be Prince. I didn't earn it. But I *am* Prince. Maybe I just need to accept that it's part of who I am now.

And do everything I can to rise to the occasion.

Kirsi pushes off the wall, nods at me, then after a steady breath, she heads to speak with her crew. Perhaps give them comfort.

I search for my own people. Mage's still deciphering the map. Roderick sits and calibrates his shoulder cannon. Keeton leans against him as he works. Bryce rests behind them while an Order guard bandages her arm. She seethes, her expression pained.

I stop in front of my friends.

Roderick looks up. "Well, that was a disaster."

"It could've been worse," Keeton mutters. "If not for Kirsi, we might've run into that clearing."

"Maybe we should've listened to Mage," Roderick says gruffly, emptying gunk that got into the shoulder cannon's ammo tray. "We should've had the *Explosio* send a barrage onto the island."

"That would have been a bad idea," Bryce says, nodding at the guard who just finished her bandage. "It might've destroyed the burial site."

"Besides, we didn't know where the beasts were," Keeton says, pushing her black locs behind her shoulders. "This is a big island, and the *Explosio* has only so much ammunition. What if we need it later?"

Roderick frowns and shuts his eyes. "I'm just tired of watching people die."

We go silent for a moment.

"I miss when it was just us, on our ship, searching for gorgantauns," Keeton says. "Traveling the Hornthrow Isles together. Trading canned applesauce to the *Calamus* because Sebastian burned our beans."

Roderick chuckles. "Sebastian's food was disgusting. Remember when you were Cook, Conrad?"

"I was never Cook," I say.

"Yeah, but Pound forced you to make a meal," Keeton says.

"You were worse than Sebastian." Roderick smirks.

"I was not."

"Oh, absolutely you were," Bryce says, nodding vigorously. "After that first meal, the whole crew had an intervention with Pound."

I blink at them. "What?"

"We told him that if you made another meal, none of us would work," Keeton says.

They all laugh.

My face cracks with a grin, and I shake my head. "Stupid asses."

"There's that smile," Roderick says, patting me.

I want to keep laughing with my friends. It helps relieve me from the crushing weight in my chest, but Mage calls out to the group. Roderick frowns, and soon we're up, walking along a dark tunnel again.

At least this time, I'm feeling the comfort of my friends with me.

We continue for what seems like hours. Mage and Tara communicate over the comm. Her voice is slightly garbled since we're underground. Still, he gives her tiny details about the things we're seeing.

"Are you using the recorder gem?" she asks.

"Of course."

"Good. This is history. It must be remembered."

"Unfortunately, the gem does not record visuals."

Tara sighs. "Yes, perhaps I should have come."

Mage shakes his head. "Fifteen people are dead, Scholar."

She goes quiet after that.

The air grows cooler. Either it's night, or we've gone much deeper underground. Eventually, as we start to shiver, we come to a series of stairs carved into the earth. Glowing moss blankets their surface.

"What a strange place to leave your body," Roderick says.

"Brone didn't want to be found by anyone but the Lantians," Mage says.

"Then why didn't he give the key to them?"

"He couldn't," Mage says. "He was likely the last Lantian still above the clouds at that point. I don't believe Weapon even realized he was a Lantian. He mentioned in this journal that the other members of his Trade thought they had gone to war for power. To take over the Skylands. They didn't realize they were supporting the Below, but Brone had no additional support from the Below coming. At the end of his life, he realized that this weapon his Trade created shouldn't be in anyone's hands. But if it had to be possessed by someone, he preferred it to be his people."

We pass over rotted, weathered boards that bridge a stream and reach a rusted, sealed door. No way we'd be able to get it open, not even if we attached a chain to the handle and everyone pulled.

"Roderick," I say.

"Finally," he says. "My turn."

He and a couple other Master Gunners lace explosives around the door's hinges. Then, we all hurry up the stairs.

"This won't collapse the tunnels?" Mage asks.

Roderick pauses. "I didn't even think of that." Then he laughs and snaps the trigger mechanism. "Oops."

The door explodes. My ears ring, and I cough as dust falls from the ceiling. Smoke filters into my nostrils.

We wave our hands through the haze and travel back toward the door. It fell inward, exposing a dark room inside.

"A tomb," Bryce mutters.

We enter the tomb, coughing and breathing through our sleeves. A stone box rests in the center of the barren room. Bryce hurries ahead, Mage close behind. She brushes off the dirt that crests the coffin's lid. Her eyes narrow as she reads the words that are partially obscured by the tiny droplet of water that's been falling on the stone lid for ages. She squints at the words, deciphering them.

"What if," Roderick says, "we came all this way and find out that it's the tomb of a different dead guy?"

"Relax," Bryce says, glancing back at us. "It's Brone."

Roderick and several others use harpoons to pry off the stone lid. But as they're struggling, grunting, and swearing about how heavy it is, horrible thoughts cloud my mind.

What if someone got here before us? What if Brone changed his mind and put the key elsewhere?

The coffin lid slides off and hits the ground with a resounding boom. Once the dust settles, Mage steps toward the coffin and peers inside. He's quiet for several seconds. Enough that I start to approach, too. My heart hammering. But then he laughs because, shining under the light of his crystal, is a steel octagon.

The key.

CHAPTER 34

GETTING BRONE'S KEY WAS THE FIRST PROBLEM, BUT NOW we must get off Celentus alive. And even though the key's now dangling from my neck, everything has gone wrong since a mashtaun somehow got into the tunnel.

We're shouting as the beast slams into the narrow walls. The rocks glow from its shoulders' scraping and sparking along them.

"Oba!" I cry over the comm. "We need immediate evac!"

"What are your coordinates?"

The best I can give is a rough estimate.

Hunters shout behind me, firing harpoons. The weapons clang off the mashtaun's shoulders and elongated skull.

I'm running so hard that blood trickles down my throat. How the hell did the beast get inside? Roderick lags behind, but Keeton and Bryce pull him to keep up.

The beast chases us to an exit we're afraid to take because we know what's waiting for us.

But we don't have a choice.

We scramble out into the night. The stench is eye-watering. And from the surrounding, dark jungle comes a series of horrible roars. Bryce fires golden flak into the sky, signaling the fleet.

And then we're running through the jungle again. A mashtaun bursts from the trees. It catches a pair of men like they're mice. They squirm, legs kicking. The beast shows its mangled teeth in a wild smile and smashes the men's heads together.

"Oba!" I cry as we race through soggy dirt. "Send the ships. Now!"

Kirsi's shouting something at me. Her finger's raised in the air—when an enormous hand pummels her to the ground.

"Kirsi!" I roar.

I fire my last harpoon at the beast above her. It flies through the mashtaun's chest, and the creature tumbles sideways.

Kirsi lies on the jungle floor, a twitching, bleeding mess.

"Go," she sputters at me. "Go."

"But—"

Another pair of mashtauns erupts from the trees. Thumping their massive chests. Baring their crooked teeth. But I have nothing left to fight them.

"GO!" Kirsi bellows.

A mashtaun catches her legs and drags her into the shadows.

And I run. Like a damn coward, I run.

Bryce shouts to Oba, giving him a new set of coordinates. There's still a whole band of us survivors hugged close together. We're firing weapons into the trees. Mostly hitting nothing. Mage is panicking as though he's about to run off into the jungle alone. Roderick and Keeton catch his arms to keep him with us.

The moon peers in through the slits in the canopy. Insects buzz around us, and I feel like if I run any more, I'm going to throw up.

More mashtauns come thumping to our left.

Roderick squeezes the trigger of his cannon. A vomiting blast blooms across a beast's chest. The creature careens into a tree.

We finally exit the jungle and struggle through the tall grass. But without the trees, there's little to slow the mashtauns. They burst into the clearing, running on all fours. Great shoulders pumping. Long arms gliding them forward.

My people shout. Some fire their last harpoons.

But nothing will slow the beasts.

Suddenly, a shape zooms directly over us. The gust from its momentum sweeps the grass flat. The *Gladian!* Atop the deck—mounted in Roderick's repeater turret—is my little sister. Can't see much else or hear anything, but I imagine she's shouting as she squeezes the triggers.

The mashtauns leap, ready to crush us in a single bound. But Ella launches hell into them. Harpoon after harpoon flies into their torsos. Cutting through their silver armor as if it were nothing.

The beasts hit the ground with thundering quakes. One mashtaun falls at my boots. It breathes out a final whimper, then nothing. More mashtauns charge from the trees. But the other ships arrive and bombard the ground. The island quakes and flames gush.

Swarms of mashtauns keep coming.

"They never end!" Bryce says.

The *Gladian* smoothly glides to a stop directly above us. Otto drops a roped ladder. Ladders fall from the other ships, too, and panicked people clamber up.

"Come on!" I say, nodding to Bryce. "Up!"

"You first," Keeton says, breathless. "You're the Prince."

"I don't give a damn who I am. Get up there!"

"I don't care who you are, either," Mage says, pushing past us. He climbs first.

My friends scramble up the ladder as mashtauns barrel toward us. But Ella continues launching harpoons. The *Explosio* lights up the island with liquid flames, creating a firewall between us and the monsters. Blocking them off. The surviving mashtauns grind to a halt and beat their horrible chests. The fire glows in their hate-filled eyes.

I'm behind Keeton, halfway up the ladder, when the *Gladian's* repeater turret whines. Grinding on empty.

A mashtaun leaps over the firewall. The thing's missing an eye, and half its teeth are gone. It roars and leaps for me. Its disgusting mouth opens wide, ready to bite me free of the ladder. Just as it rises and nearly catches my boots, the *Gladian* elevates. The mashtaun's crooked fingers stretch. But the ship soars out of reach, and the mashtaun falls back to the island.

It screams an almost-human shout and tosses rocks. The others do, too. Giant boulders and stones. But we're well above their range.

My stomach lurches while the *Gladian* pulls away. And soon we're all dangling, shouting with exhilaration, as the *Gladian* sails.

Heavy wind makes the ladder sway. I take one careful bar at a time until Otto and Tara pull me onto the deck.

Then I roll over, the *Gladian's* cool metal against my back. My head is pounding from my heartbeat. But we made it. Somehow, we made it.

We're all smiling. Relieved and grateful to be alive. But once we're shooting away from Celentus, out into the open night skies, we look back at the island. And the deck falls silent as we all remember those who didn't make it.

The people we left behind.

Once we're at a safe distance from the island, the ships slow to a stop. And with the soft wind sliding between our hulls, our comm gems light the night. I can sense the hurt. The anguish. Some of them lost friends today. Some of them lost a Captain.

But we got the key.

CHAPTER 35

I WILL NOT BECOME DESENSITIZED TO EVERY DEATH I'VE witnessed.

If I'd known how to hunt mashtauns, I would've led us through Celentus, not Kirsi. If I'd had more experience, maybe she and many others would still be alive.

I'm alone, leaning on the starboard railing. The cool night wind splashes over me. All my ships hover above a bed of white clouds. We're resting in the dangerous open airs. Earlier we tried anchoring to a minor island, but the *Ferrum* spotted a prowlon skulking among the trees. So rather than risking it, we pulled away.

Everyone needs to rest, recover, and mourn.

Getting Brone's key should feel like a great victory, but how can I celebrate when thirty people have died on this mission? Thirty people counted on me to get them back to their families.

I'm a hollow pit.

The dead's cries haunt me. Their screams, as their fingers leave trails in the dirt. Kirsi's eyes, looking up at me, her body lying in bloody ruin.

You saved us, Kirsi.

No, the dead did.

My eyes clench shut. I try breathing away the images, the sounds. But they're part of me now.

I'm not the same boy I used to be—before all this responsibility. I used to be the one who fearlessly leaped into the sky to take down a gorgantaun. But that was back when I had nothing to lose. When I only counted on myself and risked everything for my own goals.

Suddenly, a gentle hand touches my arm. My head lifts and I find Bryce. Seeing her, just being beside her, gives me warmth. She smiles softly despite her bruised face. "We're all waiting for you in the cafeteria. Arika made something comforting."

"I'm not hungry."

She leans her head against my shoulder and wraps an arm around me. We remain standing, two warm bodies surrounded by cold nothing.

"Food will make you feel better."

"I can't eat."

"Neither can I, but we need to try."

"Bryce—"

She turns me toward her, and there's a fiery tenderness to her. "I know what you want to do, Conrad. You want to escape somewhere in the ship and tuck those emotions of yours deeper inside because you're afraid if someone notices you being human, they'll find you weak."

I say nothing.

"You're not the only one struggling. Your crew respects you. Loves you. You are their *friend*, and they need you."

Bryce's words flood into me. Kirsi warned me about feeling guilty. But I can't just push everything I'm feeling away. Can't just pretend it didn't happen.

"I need time," I say.

"What?"

"I need time to be alone."

She pulls away.

"That's not what I mean." I speak quickly. "I just—I need some time to deal with this in my own way."

She folds her arms and studies me.

"Bryce," I say firmly, "I need this."

She opens her mouth to argue, then heads to the hatch. Just as she's about to climb down, she stops and turns back to me.

"I'll miss you."

Oh, my gut twists. I'm so damn rotten sometimes, but I feel as if I'm caught in a room where the ceiling is slowly descending on me. Readying to crush me. I just need to breathe. Just fill my lungs and work through all this. Maybe if I were cruel and heartless—more like Uncle—those thirty deaths would mean little to me.

But Mother taught me better than that.

Sometimes, her voice returns to me, *you need to do what others won't because you are strong, and because you are good.*

An Order soldier watches me through the *Intrepid's* scopes. I grumble at the invasiveness and turn to the hatch. I head belowdecks, my boots hitting the base of the ladder. The corridor before me is dark, but it echoes from my crew in the cafeteria. Clinking knives, forks on plates, and hushed voices.

A pull tells me to go straight to the cafeteria. Surround myself with the people who give me strength. But when I take a step, Kirsi's mangled body flashes in my mind again. Then the crushed *Dauntless.* And Holmstead falling. I see Drake electrified. I see Pound leaving, stepping onto another ship without even saying goodbye.

I'm completely strangled. Can't escape this. I make a hard left away from the cafeteria. My steps echo down an empty, silent corridor and into the shadows where the crystal lights do not glow.

After entering the Captain's cabin, I lock the door and shut off my gem. Then, with a breeze hitting the window, I lean against the door and slide to the floor.

I just sit. Don't know for how long.

Mother's voice enters again, less defined. As though I'm forgetting what she sounds like. Forgetting her. *Never lock away your feelings, Conrad.*

And while I'm on the cold floor, my mind slips back to when I was younger and had started fighting in the Holmstead Low dueling pits without her permission. I did it for her. She was getting sicker by the day. Technically, at fourteen, I was too young to duel. But the gamblers didn't care, so long as I could fight and they could make money.

Each time Mother fell asleep, I'd snatch Father's cane and slip out McGill's attic window. After three weeks of fighting, I earned enough coin to trade for medicine. Oh, I was so excited. My heart sang golden, and I ran through the alleys with an extra spring in my heels. Whenever I got Mother meds, she was her old self for days at a time. She'd smile again. Laugh.

These type of meds could treat her symptoms, but they weren't powerful enough to heal her lung rot. But even having Mother back to her old self temporarily was enough joy in itself.

Unfortunately, on the way back to McGill's Tavern one night, three shadows cut me off. Stood over me as looming, horrible beasts.

The Atwoods.

Apparently, that night was the anniversary of when my paternal great-grandfather killed Steffan of Atwood in a duel. And these hulking monsters were there to exact vengeance for their family.

The ensuing struggle reddened the earth and left me whimpering on the alley floor. One of them clutched the back of my hair, but I jabbed him with my cane. Right in his groin. The Atwood bowled over, and then I ran, despite the blood trailing my skull. Ran despite my breaths stinging. Ran despite the crushed medicine capsule lying on the dirty ground.

They couldn't catch me.

After I climbed back through the window into the tavern's attic,

I hid Father's cane in the corner and, wincing in pain, approached the meager fire.

Mother was waiting for me.

"Where were you? What happened?"

"Nowhere."

I winced, holding my side as I lowered to rest before the fire's embers.

"Don't do that to me," she said. "You're bleeding and clutching your hand like it's broken. Speak."

Even though lung rot had weakened her, Mother had more strength then. Well, more than she did in her final days, anyway. She stepped off the decrepit bed and crouched in front of me, blocking my sight of the orange glow.

Her bony fingers raised my chin, forcing me to meet her eyes. Her white hair cascaded over her narrow shoulders. But her eyes held blazing strength.

Her voice stabbed me. "Speak. Now."

"Mother . . ."

"I didn't raise a lotcher," she said, irritated. "Are you so weak that you cannot tell the truth to your own mother?"

Father taught me all about meeting the eyes. Looking away is a sign of deference. Weakness. So I met her gaze. And once I did, I knew I couldn't keep what I'd locked inside away from her any longer.

My shoulders slouched, and I broke like a shattered window, pieces of me across the floor.

"I lost them. I lost your meds."

She touched my arm. Tender, but firm.

Then I explained everything.

My face burned, and tears trickled down my bruised cheek. Everything hurt. My body, my pride. The one victory I'd had in months snatched away because of family history I had nothing to do with.

Mother caught my shoulders, pulled me close, and hugged me.

"Never lock away your feelings, Conrad. They'll make you poison inside. Sit up. Look at me."

I wiped my nose on my dirty sleeve and rose.

"This world claims you need to hide your feelings because they make you weak." Her eyes were fire. "They are *wrong*."

"But, Mother—"

"Listen, Conrad. It's okay to be angry. It's okay to be sad. It's okay to let others know you're feeling these things. Promise me, Conrad, that you will speak to me. Promise me."

"Mother—"

Her voice gained an edge. "Promise me."

So I made her a promise, one of the many I broke. Like the night I slipped out into the snowstorm to return Ella to her. Instead, the gorgantauns came, and I never saw Mother alive again.

My head rises from my arms. Even with her gone, I can almost feel her warmth around me now, giving me strength. Willing me to stand and face my failures.

I'm no lotcher.

Master Koko on Venator told me that I won't be able to lead if I'm looking back. That people die in Hunter. Uncle said something similar. Kirsi told me guilt made her a worse leader. Maybe they're all correct. And Mother is right, too. I need to go to my friends and find strength in those I care about.

I will never forget the dead. Must always honor them. And I must always allow myself to be human and to feel. I stand slowly and move toward my desk. This is something I have to do for myself, and then I'll be done with it.

Then I'll look forward.

I pull the *Dauntless* crew manifest from my desk's files and read over the names of the dead. Adel of Robin. Cynthia of Heather. Alexandre de Georges. My fingers trace their names as if that'll tell me something about them.

When I finish, I slide envelopes from my drawer and write letters. I write until my wrist hurts. After I finish the *Dauntless*, I contact the other ships. Ask for the names of their casualties. And I keep writing.

These thirty names? They're thirty of my failures. But they will not just become numbers. Their deaths will not be in vain. I squeeze Brone's key. Our success will honor their sacrifice.

After I finish sealing the last letter, I head straight to the cafeteria. I'm not even sure if they're still awake. It's been well over an hour since they started eating. They wouldn't have waited this long for me, would they? Maybe they're elsewhere, the rec room. Or gone to bed. But I need to check.

When I enter, I almost grin with relief. They're still here, but the room's cold and quiet. Keeton and Roderick stand in the corner, speaking in hushed tones. Bryce stares out the window at the purple night. Ella's eating cookies and talking helm strings with Yesenia. Otto's sound asleep, snoring on a bench.

Arika bolts upright from a table. "Captain!"

The whole room turns. Keeton breathes out and hurries to pull me into a comforting embrace. "I was so worried about you."

Arika heads to the kitchen. "Are you hungry, Captain? Of course you are. Let me heat it up for you. I made a feast."

The others gather around me. Looking relieved. Shouldn't they be furious that I was gone for so long?

"Arika made a feast fit for Selection Day," Roderick says. "Honey-glazed gorgantaun."

Bryce stares at me, arms folded. "Where were you?"

I meet her eyes. An urge tells me to lock that information away. It makes me vulnerable, seem weak. And I'm suddenly conscious that my sister is watching. She's an Urwin. She despises showing weakness. Even so, I won't lock things away and be noxious. I will be the son Mother wanted me to be. So I open my mouth and explain.

"You wrote letters?" Bryce says, confused. "To whom?"

"The families of the dead."

The whole room goes silent. Everyone stares at me.

Roderick pauses, calculating the numbers. "You wrote *thirty* letters?"

I nod.

Then suddenly, Keeton steps closer to me. Her dark, warm eyes reading me like they always do. She touches my shoulder. "Conrad, what happened wasn't your fault."

"I am your leader," I say, straightening. "The responsibility is mine."

"Yours?" Roderick says. "Your responsibility?"

"Mine," I say.

Rod's cheery eyes vanish, and a hidden blaze ignites behind them. It's sudden and unexpected. "That's—that's—" He pauses, then forces the word out. "That's *birdshit*, Conrad."

I almost step back. Keeton's mouth falls. Otto stirs awake, and Arika nearly drops a spatula. Roderick only swears when he's furious. Everyone's watching him now, and I stare in utter bewilderment as he keeps after me.

His face is splotched with red. "You don't have to suffer through all of this by yourself, Conrad. We are with you. Have always been with you. You don't get to claim complete responsibility, not when we're out there bleeding with you."

I don't even know what to say.

"You have no problem giving us credit when we win as a crew. How can you take full credit when we lose?" Then his voice becomes firm. "We're all in this. All of us. TOGETHER."

Finally, Roderick exhales, hands on his hips. His eyes are a little wet.

"Rod's right, Conrad. We're in this with you," Keeton says gently.

I look between them, feeling incredibly foolish. Even so, Roderick steps forward and wraps me up in his thick Master Gunner arms. It's an angry hug. Rough. He's powerful enough to crack my back if he wanted. But his muscles loosen, and now his arms are those of a brother.

Bryce sweeps in next, and for an instant I think she's going to yell at me. But she urges Roderick off me and hugs me as tightly as she ever has.

"I'm sorry," I whisper to her.

"Don't lock me out again," she says.

"I—I won't."

Ella watches the whole thing. Silent.

Before long we're done wiping eyes, and we're smiling again. My crew, my friends. No, we haven't forgotten the dead, but we must keep moving forward and not always look back.

We sit around the cafeteria tables, and they eat dessert: moist, chocolate-drizzled cakes. And I'm feeling the warmth of their company, their smiles. Bryce sits close beside me. I squeeze her hand. Her eyes meet mine, and my stomach spins because that's what her eyes always do to me.

Arika brings out a giant tray of food for me, and despite all the horrible events of the day, I can't help but rub my hands together as she pours hot honey over my slab of gorgantaun.

I take a bite and almost shudder. The succulent meat melts on my tongue. The kick from spicy peppers leveled out by the tangy, sweet honey.

"Arika," I say, "this is—it's so damn good."

The Cook beams.

Ella lowers into the seat across from mine. She's enjoying her cake, and she's talking to Roderick now, complimenting him for his "top-notch" turret modifications. I watch her. Ella's grown so much as a member of this crew. When she first arrived, she took her meals in the cabin, alone, and wasn't part of any of the hunts. Now she's building connections. She's saved my ass multiple times already, too.

Arika wanders over to Yez. "Would you like dessert?"

"You know I don't have a sweet tooth." Yez pauses, recognizing her own irritated tone. "Apologies. I am a little tired after today."

"You don't need to explain," Arika says. "It's fine."

The two stare at each other. It's a little awkward, and I get the sense that whatever they had before, neither is willing to reengage it.

Yez breathes out. "Ari, I'll take some coffee if there's any left."

Arika smiles and hurries to retrieve a mug.

After the crew leaves to rest up for our departure to Perditio, and we're all out in the corridors, Bryce walks with me. And as I look over at her, I'm reminded of the first time I saw her on Holmstead, when she saved me. Her spikey hair was like golden fire.

She hugs me again, just us, in the shadows of the corridor, the engine thrumming under our feet. And while she brings my neck down to kiss me, a sudden stab of fear sinks into my heart. I clutch her so tight I have to relax my arms because I don't want to smother her.

Maybe this crew will rise or fall together, but my closest friends have escaped so many near-death experiences. That can't last forever, can it?

Sooner than I'd like, Bryce wishes me a good night's rest before stepping away. As her steps echo, I'm left alone, worrying about the dangers that lie ahead.

✦✦✦

The cool hand of Meritocracy strangles the balance of my squadron.

I stand on deck under the morning sun, my lips pursed and my gloved fists squeaking. Just twenty minutes ago, we were prepping to leave for Perditio. But then I got word that the *Explosio* hasn't been able to vote in a new Captain after losing Kirsi. They tried three times during the night. Worse, the gridlock turned violent and two people tried to kill each other.

I massage my temples.

Yez navigates the strings, bringing us to the port side of the *Explosio.* The Hunter ship is a Titanium-class with towering harpoon turrets and gorgantaun skulls painted on the hull. Its length is twice that of the *Gladian*, and it's three times as wide—this, to balance the ship from the incredibly powerful Omega cannons that rise over the deck.

We come to a stop, and Roderick slides a gangway over to the *Explosio*. I walk across with Bryce, Ella, and Roderick.

I can't believe two of the *Explosio's* crewmembers tried to stab each other. Physical conflict is not the Hunter way.

I step onto the ship's painted black deck. More than a dozen people bow as we walk past. They're rugged people without Hunter jackets, uniforms, or pins. They've got grungy, rolled-up sleeves and tough expressions. They're the support crew Kirsi must've hired to help manage such a large vessel. The actual Hunters, the crew, wait for me on a platform.

A tall, thin man with blond hair approaches me. The blue badge of Quartermaster waves with his black Hunter jacket under a burst of wind.

"Prince." He bows slightly. "I'm Jerome of Judith, the most experienced member of this crew. I've been with Kirsi for a decade and have earned the right to be Captain."

I stare at him in silence.

"I'd appreciate," he says, "if you'd endorse me."

"I am not here to choose sides," I say, "I'm here to ensure this resolves quickly so we can focus on saving the Skylands."

Jerome's face sours.

I step past him and move onto the platform.

We descend, and before long I'm seated inside the *Explosio's* command room. It's a wide space with a window that gives a glimpse of my ship. Bryce, Ella, and Roderick stay beside me. We've all brought our dueling weapons—because even though most of us are Hunters, we've learned to keep them with us.

My fingers tap the Urwin eagle as I listen to Miri of Octon, the

Explosio's Navigator, make her pitch for Captain. She hasn't spoken a word to me, not much more than a simple bow when I first stepped onto the platform.

Certainly less assertive than Jerome.

With Kirsi gone and two of its crew in the brig for fighting, the *Explosio* only has five Hunters eligible to vote. The problem is, all the votes are split between Miri, Jerome, and their Master Gunner, who keeps voting for himself.

I sit and listen to them make their pitches. But after an hour, my knees are bouncing, and I'm chewing on my tongue to keep from yelling at this crew because the mission's waiting on them.

Jerome shouts something about being owed a favor.

My head pounds with a furious headache. These echoing voices remind me of the Gauntlet, when my crew was constantly bickering about who should be Captain. In just a couple weeks, my crew had gone from Pound to Sebastian to myself and almost to Bryce. We were pretty much useless in the hunt until we finally settled on a Captain.

Ella watches the whole affair with her arms folded, disgusted.

The *Explosio* crewmembers are all puffing up their chests. A couple get in each other's faces, but Miri separates them.

The room falls silent. And I'm starting to think that we're just going to have to settle this on the go. If Miri won't fly the ship, I'll have someone else do it. Don't care that I don't own the *Explosio*, this damned mission is far more important than any of these eager people using Kirsi's death to rise.

But suddenly, their Swabbie starts speaking, and her words make me freeze. Bryce clutches my arm. Roderick gasps.

The Swabbie reveals the true reason why the crew's vote is split: one of the candidates wants to take the *Explosio* back to the Skylands. This candidate thinks I'm weak and will lead them all to their deaths. They don't believe Brone's key will work.

Shock fills me—until suddenly, my rage ignites. These selfish cowards. Kirsi warned me about people in the squadron wanting to abandon the mission. They were on her damned ship!

I shouldn't get involved. But we can't allow the *Explosio* to leave. Who knows what dangers lie ahead? And they're not getting through Sky's Edge alive without Mage. So I stand and make an endorsement for the woman who wants to see this mission through.

"Miri of Octon should be your Captain."

Jerome and his supporter whirl on me, irate. "How dare you interfere?!"

"Listen to these birdshits," Ella mutters. "Islands are falling, and all they care about is the pecking order of their insignificant ship."

"*Insignificant*?" Jerome says. "The *Explosio* is insignificant?"

I raise my hand to stop Ella, but she's already going.

"When you compare it to the fate of the Skylands? Yes. In fact, all of us are. Me. You. My brother."

Jerome scowls.

The *Explosio's* Master Gunner, who has also maintained that he should be Captain, stares at the floor, his face wrinkled in thought. Finally, he pushes off the wall. The whole room quiets. He's the one we've been waiting to flip.

"Due to off-ship interference," he says calmly, "I have reconsidered my position." I close my eyes and shake my head. The Master Gunner continues, "I will now vote for Jerome of Judith to become Captain."

Ella explodes. "You cowards! You're all going to die if you leave. You won't get past the cloudwall, and you might be dooming the Skylands."

Jerome's supporters ignore her because they're smiling about their victory. Miri throws her hands up in disgust. At least she recognizes the ridiculousness of Jerome's plans.

Jerome and his two supporters step toward me.

"Your Highness," Jerome says, "I am taking this ship, and we are leaving." He turns to Miri and her support. "You are welcome to resign and join another ship in the squadron if you'd like."

My voice is soft. "No."

Jerome looks back at me. "What?"

"You are not leaving."

His eyes squint. "These are the not the Skylands, Prince. You have no authority over me, here."

"We need your ship," I say. "If you want to leave so badly, we'll give you a lifeboat, a box of beans, and some water."

Jerome's face turns scarlet. He stomps up into my face and gets spittle on my cheek as he rages. "I challenge you to a duel."

The whole room goes silent. My eyes narrow, and my hand squeezes the Urwin eagle. But I breathe calmly. Meet his gaze dead-on.

"That would be a mistake."

"Are you too big of a lotcher to accept?"

Don't have to accept. Jerome doesn't have the status to challenge me or my authority. Not to mention we're Hunters. Physical conflict is not our way. But if this is how I'll keep the damned *Explosio* here, then so be it.

"The deck," I whisper. "Fifteen minutes."

"Conrad," Rod says. "You don't—"

"Yes, I do."

Then I storm from the room.

✦✦✦

The sun beats down on me. Hot. And the air is strangely calm. Each ship has closed in, per my orders, so everyone has a view of the *Explosio* deck if they choose to watch.

Uncle's tried to teach me lessons before. I didn't think I'd taken many of them to heart, but now here I am, meeting a challenger personally, just as he did with Addeline, with Sione. He wanted everyone to see the duel and know why it was fruitless to challenge him.

But I'm not fighting to prove I'm the best, or for my status. I'm fighting for the Skylands.

I unzip my Hunter jacket, and Roderick takes it.

"You sure you know what you're doing?" he asks.

I roll up my silver sleeves. "Yes."

The *Explosio* deck fills as other ships drop gangways. People step over to watch the duel. A couple ships hang a little above the *Explosio*, and crews ogle from over the edge of the railings. The worst part is, some are excited. Like this is a damned game and the Skylands aren't counting on us.

Tara's several feet away, holding a notepad and a recorder gem. Preparing to draw or document everything she's about to see. She'll likely report the results to Uncle when she can, especially if I lose.

At least Mage doesn't seem concerned at all. The *Rimor* hangs in the distance, alone. Not even sure he can see us from that far away.

Bryce and Ella approach me. I think maybe Bryce will try convincing me that I don't have to do this. Oba can force the *Explosio* to come along. Besides, Kirsi left enough of her paid people on the *Explosio* that we could run it with or without Jerome and his defectors.

Instead, Bryce meets my gaze, her expression fierce. "Beat his face in."

Ella is awed by Bryce's response and nods with vicious approval. Then Ella leans toward me. "Watch his eyes," she says. "The eyes will give away his moves, his feelings. They are betrayers."

Oh, she has no idea how much she is like Father, too.

Bryce takes my goggles from my neck but doesn't touch my arm or provide any comfort because she expects me to win. She steps away with Ella.

I scowl. It's ridiculous that even on this mission, where everyone was handpicked to help save the Skylands, lotchers have infiltrated some of the crews. I feel like snapping a harpoon in half.

Damned cowards.

Finally, Jerome and his support rise on the platform. He's carrying a dueling staff—one that looks seldom used.

We don't need any dueling officials here.

He stomps toward me, brow furrowed. Perhaps thinking because he's twice my age and slightly taller that he can somehow intimidate me.

Stupid birdshit.

A few of the crowd are smiling, excited about the duel. We're losing a war. We can't waste our time on trivial games like this.

I lick my teeth bitterly. My friends watch me. Tara starts sketching.

Then the duel begins.

Jerome screams and charges me, his staff raised. It's an untrained, wild attack that reeks of someone who hasn't dueled in ages.

A few people cheer, excited for the entertainment.

They'll find none.

I smack Jerome's staff away and dig my cane into his gut. He bowls over, coughing. My cane twirls, and the eagle slams into his cheek. A bloodied tooth flies from his mouth, and he hits the deck. He tries to push off the ground, but I throw two swift kicks into his ribs, then I roar and slam the cane on his damned skull.

He drops.

The audience falls silent. His supporters stare, stunned. One urges him to get up, but he's done.

I spit on him, furious that he wasted everyone's time.

He's fortunate to still be breathing.

If I were Uncle, I'd have him tossed overboard. He had no right to challenge me. But I am *not* Uncle. I will not eliminate my threats. He will be facing a Hunter Tribunal for instigating a duel when we return to the Skylands.

Jerome, and his supporters, can spend the rest of the mission in the brig. *Enjoy it, you birdshits.*

I tap my gem to the whole fleet. My voice is a low growl. "Set a course to Perditio."

Then I snatch my jacket from Roderick's arms, cut through the silent crowd, and follow the gangway back to the *Gladian.*

CHAPTER 36

AFTER A DAY OF FLIGHT TOWARD PERDITIO, THE FADING sun glows over the quiet decks of my ships. I disconnect the rings from my fingers and step off the helm tile. Yez needed a break, so I took the strings for the last few hours. The glass bubble slides away, exposing my moist skin to the air.

I breathe out. Feeling more relaxed than I have in days. Maybe I should ask Yez to let me fly more. Something about it . . .

After a few minutes of breathing in the cool sunset, I head down the hatch to look for my sister. It's been a while since we've talked. Just us.

I find her in the munitions room. She's alone, studying our stockpile of weapons. She eyeballs a miniature clawgun, one of Roderick's designs, then follows a wall of harpoons and stops to stare at the thickest ones.

My boots stop beside her. She doesn't turn to look at me.

"There's something that's keeping me awake at night," she says.

"Oh, you too?"

"What if Brone's weapon doesn't exist? Or what if it's not powerful enough? What if it doesn't even work anymore? It has been hundreds of years."

I shift a little. The Skylands would lose. But it wouldn't be quick because Skylanders will keep fighting until millions have died.

"We are fighting for a chance," I say. "And a hope."

She looks at me, perhaps pondering my words. But I'm not sure it relieves her of her fears. Don't blame her. Those same thoughts have swallowed me, too. But with all my other responsibilities, I just have to push them away.

She runs a finger along a harpoon. "It was kind of impulsive, stowing away here. But when you left to go onto this ship, I felt something." She pauses, perhaps struggling against the force inside her that tells her to lock everything away. "It was like this awful disconnect. Like, that if I let you go—we'd be broken forever."

"Ella, I—"

"You had a right to be angry with me. I wanted that cane so badly—I wanted to please Uncle so much—that I'd do anything for him. But after he left me with my new cane, and you weren't there to see it, I was empty. I tried to pretend I was proud. But inside, I was cracked."

I stare at her, amazed. And I so want to hug her, but she'd absolutely hate it.

"What's done is done," I say. "You have a cane. It is yours to forge a new story. Mother would want that."

She frowns and looks back at the wall of weapons. I'm not sure she's convinced. Maybe she's still stuck in the guilt, and maybe it's a good thing that she's suffering from it.

It means that she isn't Uncle.

"Conrad, your crew loves you."

"They're my friends, but it wasn't always that way. When we first met, I was too much like our father."

She almost nods at this. She's never had a hard time critiquing Father because Uncle's been whispering that in her ear for half her life.

"I've told you so much about Mother and how you need her." I touch her shoulder, only for a second because I know she doesn't need the comfort of touch. "But in Uncle, you only got the worst parts of Father."

She's quiet.

"My relationship with Father was complicated," I say, sighing. "Sometimes I hated the man. But now, looking back—he prepared me. Without Father, I would be dead. Without Father, I never would've been able to rise. You told me that you are split. Well, the truth is, I am, too. Always have been. And I've learned that I needed both our parents to be where I am."

She watches me, her face wrinkled with contemplation.

I shut my mouth. Something I've learned about Ella is, she won't accept an idea that's forced upon her. I have to be subtle, persistent, and patient. So I say good night and step away, letting her mull over these thoughts.

I'm just grateful I have her with me again . . . and that she chose me.

Chose us.

✦✦✦

"Captain," Yez calls over the comm. "We've reached Perditio. But you need to get up here."

Roderick and I are finishing a lunch of fried pishon sandwiches. I nod at Arika, thank her for the meal, then hurry down the corridor toward the ladder. Once I push open the hatch, I'm blasted with swirling, hot winds.

I climb to the deck, and a gust slams into my chest. Roderick follows me. This is a hell of a windstorm, but my brow wrinkles. I'm perplexed because the sky is clear.

Ahead of us hangs a giant, green island, filled with destroyed buildings overtaken by vines and vegetation.

I march to the bow, my jacket flapping, and remove my spyglass from my belt. Roderick follows me. The whole squadron has stopped, observing the island from afar.

Ancient buildings jut from Perditio Island like charred bones. Roderick nudges me and points at something beneath the island.

My eyes narrow. What the hell?

Something, some type of giant, metallic structure below the island, is the source of these fierce winds.

"I've never seen anything like it," Roderick mutters.

A windy vortex spins beneath the island, sucking up the acid clouds and exposing . . . the Below. A warning stabs my gut. That massive, ancient structure looks like a machine. Something that'd need to be turned on. It couldn't have been running for hundreds of years, could it?

"Mage," I say over the gem. "Was that vortex operating when you found Perditio?"

"No. Part of that structure was tucked into the island when I last visited."

"Bryce," I say. "We need you."

"Aye."

Roderick and I study the landscape beneath us. It's disorienting to see what is usually hidden below the black clouds. The Below is a barren desert landscape. Full of endless, golden dunes.

"They can come up," I say.

"What?" Roderick says.

"The Lantians. They might've been coming up for a while."

"Then the island"—Roderick says, breathless—"it's not abandoned. Someone must be there."

I send a message to every ship. "All ships on alert."

Roderick gives me a wary glance, pats my shoulder, and then hurries to buckle himself into the closest turret. I study the vortex though my spyglass. It really is a strange structure, with jutting spines that—

"Prince!" someone else yells over the comm. "Behind us."

I spin around, and in the distance, a dozen ships rocket our way. They appear from behind another, smaller island. They're huge, bloated battlecruisers. Worse, hundreds of sparrows fly at us. All launching to block off our narrow window of escape.

We were all so busy looking at the island, the vortex, that we didn't see them coming.

Roderick points back at Perditio, and another ship comes into view around the island. It's a ship like a black arrow. It's something the King has been desperately trying to find since the war began.

The *Golias*. Admiral Goerner's ship.

✦✦✦

"Magnetics to high! Lockdown!" I shout as another blast ripples against the *Gladian*.

We rock, and I grip the railing to maintain my balance. We're flying so damn quick that I can barely move. Can hardly get up my mobile launcher. I'm jerked to the left as Yez turns us.

Enemy sparrow fighters come at us again.

"Down!" Arika cries.

They zip over us, their hot blasts leaving streaks in the deck. I launch a harpoon, but the ship shudders and my attack hits nothing but sky. Roderick's turret clicks, whirling around. He squeezes the triggers, and his harpoons send several sparrows into a tailspin.

Otto, Arika, and Ella fire harpoons. Their attacks stab through the glass of a sparrow, striking the pilot. The sparrow loses control and slams into the *Explosio's* hull.

I load my launcher.

Another sparrow nose-dives after us, but Bryce lights it up with her turret's flame cannon. A trail of smoke follows the fiery sparrow. It zooms over our heads and crashes into a Lantian battlecruiser.

Explosions drum one after another in my ears. Yez throws her hands forward to launch us away from a flurry of sparrows.

"Torton!" Bryce shouts. "Port side!"

The creature opens its mouth and fires. But Yez shoves the strings again. I dive to lock my arms around the railing. My teeth grit. The wind goes to war on me, but I keep my hands on the railing. And we rocket away before the torton's lightning pierces us.

The damned sparrows come again, and my comm fills with panicked shouts. We've got no way to fight back against this many sparrows. Our sparrows fought like hell, but they've all sunk from the sky. Our ships are overwhelmed. And Mage flew off, leaving us.

"EAT IT!" Roderick cries, firing harpoons after a squadron of sparrows that sails past. "EAT IT, YOU CUSSES!"

Goerner's ship approaches us. It's a massive shadow, and I'm nearly flown backward when its enormous cannons threaten to rupture the sky. The blasts strike the *Telum*. My ears buzz. A great swell of golden death rises from the Hunter ship's deck, and several crew fly overboard.

I watch them, hesitating, then glance at the open sky behind the ships. A single shot from one of those battlecruisers could destroy us. But if we make it past them, we could escape.

Several crewmembers of the *Telum* fall.

"Save them, Yez!" I roar. "Save them!"

She's about to shove the strings forward, when the torton reappears right before our bow, blocking our path. Its mouth widens.

"DIE!" Bryce roars.

She squeezes flame onto the flying beast. It growls and turns away, camouflaging itself. But the damned thing distracted us long enough that the *Telum* crewmembers are out of reach, falling toward the exposed Below.

My mouth's dry as I watch them.

An explosion rocks the air, and my ribs slam into the railing. The *Gladian* wobbles. Yez fights the strings, straightening us before we flip.

I turn back and stare in horror as another Hunter ship glows like a giant fireball. The *Ferrum*.

Bryce fires flak into the next wave of sparrows. Roderick's squeezing the triggers. My squadron's desperately shooting everything we've got. But we don't have enough. I keep loading harpoons. Shooting sparrows.

They're relentless. They don't end.

We're only a squadron. This is a fleet we're fighting. They outnumber us five to one.

The *Explosio* launches a huge barrage from its Omega cannons. The explosions strike one of Goerner's cruisers. And the cruiser explodes, sending heat wafting into us. Goerner's fleet responds. Two battlecruisers fire their own blasts at the *Explosio*, destroying its cannons and making the deck smoke.

"Prince," Oba says to me over the comm. "You must retreat."

"We're not leaving."

"The battle is lost. We will hold them off. Go."

I bite my lip. I've left so many behind. And the survivors are dying now because I failed. I never should've assumed Perditio would still be dead. I should've sent a scout.

"Prince, NOW!"

My body stings, and I close my eyes. We have the key. We have no choice.

"FLY!" I shout. "YEZ! GET US OUT—"

Suddenly, we're rocked by something. My head hits the deck, my vision blurs.

"They hooked us!" Keeton yells over the comm. "Captain, they've shot a hook through the hull. I—I can't get it out."

I sit up, and the world seems to go still. All flames and smoke and harpoons and shoulder cannon blasts. And that's when I see Roderick. He's looking directly at me, and there's a resigned look on his face. The look fills me with dread. No. It goes against all my instincts. It's a look that's telling something I won't consider. Would never consider. I can't. Won't. There's not enough room.

"Go," he says over the comm.

"Roderick."

"Go, you *damn* cuss!"

He kicks a lever on the turret, making the barrel switch into his incredible repeater. And the next second, he's shouting and hammering the air with harpoons. He takes down three sparrows in three seconds. They go spinning wildly.

He keeps firing. Eyes set. Determined.

"I'll handle these bastards!" Roderick roars. "Go, Conrad!"

Can't leave him, but now Ella and Bryce are tugging me. Pulling me toward the hatch. This was the emergency plan. We prepared for it because we had the heirs of the Skylands aboard.

Finally, I start running, sparing one last glance at my best friend. Roderick is flames and fury as he brings war to the sparrows. He switches his barrels again and scorches the sky.

Ella, Bryce, and I slide down the hatch's ladder. The *Gladian's* corridors shake. We use the wall to keep our balance. Explosions pang against the hull.

Roderick comms Keeton. "How's the engine?"

"W-we're stuck."

His voice quiets. "How . . . how are you?"

"I'm coming up," she says, her voice breaking.

"It's too dangerous."

"I'm not leaving you up there alone, Rod."

My skin goes cold. The way they're talking—this is different. And I'm broken. Broken knowing that there's no room to get them off the ship, too.

"We're being boarded!" Arika yells.

Suddenly, Keeton, covered in coolant spills, emerges up the stairs. She races past us, her eyes wild with fear and panic.

"I'm coming, Roderick. I'm coming."

"Keeton!" Bryce cries.

But we can't go after her.

Ella, Bryce, and I reach the bottom level and we pull the tarp from our hidden escape pod. Bryce is breathless. She reaches to hug me, tears in her eyes threatening to spill over.

The pod's meant for one, but it's big enough for two. The King didn't account for Ella stowing away. Ella mashes the button, and the escape pod opens with a hiss. She jumps onto the only seat.

"C'mon, Conrad!"

I should've asked for more pods when this was installed on the *Dreadnought*. But we needed space for supplies. We didn't know how long we'd be in these airs.

Bryce's fingers dig into my back, and I feel her trembling fear.

She won't survive Goerner. She betrayed the Below. They'll torture her and throw her into the sky. My heart hurts at the thought of losing her. At the thought of abandoning my crew to death. But the Skylands need an heir in case something happens to Uncle.

Suddenly, Bryce touches her symbion scar and her hand sparks. She squeezes my hand, and in an instant, I'm pulled somewhere else, flooded with an experience.

✦✦✦

It's the time Bryce and I went on a walk back in the Hunter Academy. We stood together on a balcony and watched a moving constellation of golden fireflies. But now I'm feeling this moment through her eyes. Looking at myself the way she saw me. Feeling her excited pulse. The twist in her stomach. And noticing how her eyes focused on my lips for the briefest of moments.

She looked up at the stars. They peered at us between the clouds.

And they were so strange to her. So mysterious. Each one separated by so much space. All alone.

"Do you ever just look?" she asked me.

"At what?"

"The stars." She paused to breathe. "Where I'm from," she said quietly, doing her best to keep her tone neutral, "we don't see stars much."

I didn't know the feelings swirling inside her then. The loneliness. The connection with the stars going beyond their strange beauty. But feeling their isolation. Blinking out in a black canvas, unable to connect with one another.

She thought of her brother, Damon, then. Wishing he hadn't sacrificed himself for her. But she was going to do him proud. She was going to build support. Rise the right way in the Skylands' wicked Meritocracy and show that the Below didn't have to go to war with the Skylands. All she needed was my support.

That's how much she believed in me. From the beginning.

✦✦✦

I'm pulled from the memory.

The *Gladian* shudders again. I meet her eyes. I've got so much to say to her. My squadron's crying through the comm. Roderick and Keeton have gone quiet. My whole ship has. The battle's lost. The *Explosio* and the *Jaculor* have surrendered. Lantians have entered my ship and they're racing through the corridors, searching for us.

Won't be long.

"C'mon, Conrad," Ella says. "Get in the pod."

I grip Bryce by the back of the neck and kiss her. Feel her heart against mine. Her skin. Her heat. Her tears. And I don't want it to end. Don't want this to be the last time I hold her in my arms or feel her breath. But I shove her, hard as I can, because I know she'd never go willingly.

She trips into the escape pod.

Ella's eyes widen. "Conrad, no!"

I mash the button on the control panel, and the pod seals. A door slides open in the *Gladian's* hull. Behind me, Bryce and Ella stare in horrified shock, their hands banging on the glass.

"Conrad!" Bryce shouts over the comm. "No. Please. No. Conrad!"

"Stay alive," I say.

I tap the button, and their escape pod rockets into the sky. Blazing at a furious pace. Within a few blinks, it's beyond the enemy ships, shooting off toward the horizon. Once it exhausts its initial fuel, they'll be able to manually control it. Then they'll have to find an island, hide there, and hope Uncle comes.

But they have a chance.

By the time I turn around, Lantians have entered the storage room, carrying their electric spears. They're sneering, ugly monsters.

And from behind them steps someone who makes my stomach fall. My brow wrinkles, confused.

He parts their midst.

"Great work, everyone," he says. The Lantians cheer. Laughing about how they've captured the Prince of the Skylands. That they've bested me. That they think they have the key to the weapon that'll end the war. "We got him, and now we can turn him to our side."

The serpent comes toward me, smiling that yellow grin of his.

"You know, *Prince*," he says as he slithers closer, "I learned something from Bryce."

My eyes narrow, trying to piece everything together.

"If she could flip sides," he says, "then why couldn't I?"

Then Sebastian laughs.

And laughs.

CHAPTER 37

"I TOLD YOU THERE WAS A SYMBION IN YOUR SQUADRON," Sebastian says. "It was exposing your location. The entire time. But you didn't think to check on the little captive inside the *Intrepid*."

He's flanked by three angry-looking soldiers. One stomps forward with his electric spear. I instinctively reach for my cane, but I dropped that in the escape pod because I didn't want Father's legacy to get destroyed like Mother's.

I dodge the man's jabbing spear, hurl a wooden box at his face, and dive into him. I rip the spear from his hand and knock him unconscious. Then I'm up. My eyes narrowed on the Lantians. They're here to make me their prized prisoner, like last time. But it won't be like last time.

This is where I'll die. I'll not let them take me alive. And I'm bringing Sebastian along too because I've had it with that rat bastard.

I charge.

The other two Lantians intercept me, but I break them with the spear. As easily as a blade through grass. I fight like the heir of Urwin. Trained by Allred of Urwin and Elise of Hale.

Sebastian backpedals and dives before I can jab his heart. He shouts at the others who pile into the room. Maybe ten of them. I'm surrounded.

Don't give a damn.

After Uncle bested me so easily, I spent many evenings on the deck, practicing with the cane. Adjusting my balance and my defense.

Three more Lantians fall at my feet, locked in paralysis from the sparking spear in my hand. I'm blazing fury. They've taken my ship. Hurt my friends. And Sebastian betrayed the whole Skylands.

Sebastian squeezes behind the others, fear in his eyes.

I'm coming for you, you birdshit.

I storm toward him. Roar and slice through Lantians. More fall at my feet as others rush to meet my spear. They're shouting. Snapping at one another in frustration. I'm just one person. How hard can I be to bring down?

But I'm a cornered animal, like I was in the Holmstead Lows.

More Lantians arrive, this time carrying auto-muskets. But they stand on the stairs, unsure what to do, because clearly, they're meant to take me alive.

My heart rages. Body grows slick with sweat. More and more Lantians stuff the room. Another dozen.

I drop two more soldiers, leaving an opening to get to Sebastian.

The little bastard runs. I chase after him—my legs eating up space, carrying me across the room. In an instant I'll be on him. And I won't just send him into paralysis. No, I'll give him what he wants. He always wanted me to turn into a killer. *Well congratulations, you birdshit. Here's your damn prize.*

I lean the weapon toward him, about to get his back, when someone throws a spear, blunt end first. It slams into me and pounds my chest. I rock backward and hit the ground. And before I can stand, another Lantian jabs me with the electric tip of his spear. Volts of electricity jolt through me. My teeth clamp shut, nearly biting my tongue, and my body locks up.

Can't move. Not even my mouth.

All my fury, locked in electric paralysis.

Sebastian, surrounded by Lantians, returns to stand over me. He's grinning with relief. The rest are breathing hard, but they're looking at me with an admiration that makes me sick.

I'll kill him. I'll kill that bastard.

Sebastian bends down and pats my cheek. I want to gouge his eyes. Catch him by the back of his greasy neck and slam him into the ground.

"Don't worry, Captain," he says. "I'll make sure you're taken care of. You have my word."

And then he laughs as the Lantians lift me off the ground.

✦✦✦

I'm carried onto Perditio. The blue sky above me is empty as Lantians carry me like I'm a damned trophy. They're cheering as they pass through a line of soldiers.

The bastards holler.

I'm completely helpless. And as I'm drowning in their celebrations and hardly able to suck a breath, I suddenly realize how alone I am. No friends. No one to help me. Not even the voices of Mother or Father are with me.

Jerome of Judith was right to want to leave the mission. I got everyone killed.

The jubilation continues.

My heart collapses, and I'm haunted by the look Roderick gave me on the *Gladian's* deck before I ran like a lotcher. He knew that might be the last time he'd see me. Worse, I saw the panic in Keeton's eyes as she raced to him.

To be together in the end.

My eyes sting. I am nothing without my crew. If they're gone, it's all on me. All I ever wanted was to get my sister back. Instead, I got the weight of the Skylands and a war that I never wanted.

Mother told me the strong lead because they're meant to lead. Well, she was right about that. She just didn't realize that I wasn't one of them.

Uncle called me a rodent. That's what I am. A sniveling little thing that got lucky. That was able to form friendships with people better than me, who elevated me, made me look stronger.

The Lantians continue carrying me. The paralysis refuses to let me suck in a full breath. Won't be long until I suffocate.

A few minutes later, I'm looking at a ceiling of carved rock. We've entered a tunnel in the cool underbelly of the island. Makes sense that the Lantians would carve tunnels into the island—not unlike their colonies in the Below.

I recognize glowlons, the strange bug-like creatures from Bryce's memory, dashing around the ceiling. Their brightly illuminating carapaces burn my eyes. My vision goes splotchy. And my body's begging for just one lungful of air.

Finally, I'm brought through steel doors and dropped onto a soft rug in a warm room. The ceiling glows with tender glowlon light, and my slight breaths catch the scent of savory food.

Sebastian leans over me. Grinning. He turns my head to the side to whisper in my ear. "I told you I wouldn't kill you."

Then he spits, slowly filling my ear with hot foamy saliva. I'm stuck in place as it slithers deeper into my canal, muffling sounds. He grins a tartar-filled smile, his hot, fishy breath on my face.

"That's enough, Sebastian."

Sebastian stands and snaps to attention. "Yes, sir!"

"Did you bring the key?" Goerner asks.

Sebastian hesitates. "Well, here's the thing, sir . . . It seems that Conrad managed to send it off on his sister's neck."

Goerner's voice darkens. "And where *is* the sister?"

"We are in the process of trying to locate her now, sir."

Sebastian's saliva cools in my ear, still muffling the voices.

Can't believe Sebastian managed to reach any kind of significant status with the Lantians, but he's always been a manipulative bastard.

"Leave us," Goerner says, irritated.

Sebastian rotates on his heels and spares me a final, coy look before marching out with the Lantian soldiers.

Goerner stands above me, watching me for a few seconds. He kneels, lifts his black locs, and touches the back of his neck while his other hand sparks. Then he taps my chest. A jolt hits me. My body unlocks, and I suck in an enormous breath. I roll over and cough hard. Sebastian's spit slides from my ear, onto my cheek. I brush it with my shoulder, disgusted.

It's just me and Goerner. No guards. No weapons. Nothing. I'm not even tied up.

He frowns at the saliva slipping from my ear and drops a napkin onto the ground. Then, he strolls back to a table of food.

"Come," he says. "You're probably tired of eating ship rations. I'll introduce you to the delicacies of my people."

"I have a great Cook," I say, voice raspy.

"You are the Prince; I'm sure you do. Still, I believe you'd enjoy some of these dishes."

This bastard. I'd like nothing more than to charge and kill him. He dropped my island. Killed McGill. And he wants to talk about food? I clean my ear with the napkin, nearly gagging as I try to get it all out. Once I finish, I toss the napkin and stare at Goerner. But I notice his beasts, resting on their haunches near his feet at the table. They're silver creatures, four-legged, with steel spikes around their ears. And their red eyes stare at me as their pink tongues sag.

Lupons. Steel wolves.

Goerner's finger slides over the closest one's snout. It nuzzles up against his leg. Like it isn't a murderous beast that steals children from their beds.

I stand.

Goerner sits at the table before rows of meats—all white. The only produce is root vegetables: carrots, potatoes. Some mushrooms. But everything else is meat.

"Our Designers," he says, waving a hand over the display of food, "saved our colonies from starvation through the creation of meats that give us the nutrients a body needs. Meat infused with vitamins normally only provided by plants. As you are probably aware, we don't get nearly as many vegetables below. Not when the sun is blocked out by the death clouds."

I glance around the room. My brow knits in a little surprise because Goerner's kept all his Order medals, his Pilot pin, his Order Protector sash. And his walls are decorated with paintings of famous Order ships and past Order Admirals.

"Come," he says. "Try the leptaun."

He nods at a platter where a giant metal rabbit rests in its own juices with a Skylands apple in its mouth.

I stare at this meat. At this man. His lupons growl at me, perhaps impatient that I remain standing.

"Where are my people?" I say.

"Those who surrendered are in custody."

"And those who didn't?"

He frowns. "Sit." Then he adds with some restraint, "*Please.*"

My eyes narrow on him. I'd rather he not send his lupons at me, so I lower into the chair opposite to him. An empty plate sits before me, as well as a cool glass of water. I drink the water. Guzzle it in one go and wipe my face with my forearm. But I'm not touching the food.

Goerner leans back. "Last time we saw each other, well—"

"You were in the process of cutting my arms off."

"Yes, and to be perfectly frank, I'd be doing the same now, but the Lantian Council believes I should keep you alive. It is their command that I follow. I'm skeptical of their decision. You are a zealous Meritocrat."

"Zealous Meritocrat?"

"People whom we've determined are too risky and stubborn to ever mold into our future society. People who have manipulated the Skylands Meritocracy to such a degree that they're too dangerous to be part of us." He pauses. "But you do have something about you. A saving grace, so to speak."

I stare at him. This man acts civilized, but he ordered the deaths of countless innocents. And he will continue dropping islands with the giga until we have nothing left. Somehow, he has the audacity to talk about *me* being a risk?

"Our victory is inevitable, Prince," he says. "But we would prefer to stop the bloodshed. This is why we offered to negotiate the Skylands' surrender. But your uncle is the most stubborn man in the sky. It is his fault that so many have died and will continue to die. He has ignored multiple offers of ours that would bring peace."

I stare at Goerner and realize that something shifts under the sleeve of his left arm. Wriggling around.

Goerner reaches for the roasted leptaun leg. Peels off the metallic scales, and bites down into the soft flesh. He chews quietly, the juice dripping off his chin.

"If you assassinate the King, Conrad," he says, wiping his face with a napkin, "you will become King. Then our peoples can negotiate a true peace."

I laugh at the suggestion.

"You have a problem assassinating a man like him?" he says. "The King trusts you, and we know what he did to you. Murdering your father. Banishing you to Low. Letting your mother die."

"Your gorgantauns killed my mother."

"She never would've been there if it weren't for your uncle." He takes another disgusting, juicy bite. "You probably blame yourself for your current predicament, but it all goes back to your uncle, Conrad. It always has."

I say nothing. I won't defend my uncle. We both know I hate the man. But Uncle hasn't killed nearly as many as Goerner in his quest for victory. If Goerner's goal is to get me to blame Uncle for my failures and join the Lantians instead, I'm not buying it.

"The Council has decided you deserve the chance to make a choice. End this war." He scoops a bite of steaming potato. "We're willing to let you live in peace with your friends. I am told that is more important to you than anything. All your friends, including the traitor, Bryce."

His sleeve wriggles again.

"You needn't have sent Bryce away in that pod," he says, stabbing a carrot with a fork. "We would've spared her—so long as you were compliant."

I fill my glass with the pitcher. This man is a liar. He would say whatever it took to win the war.

Suddenly, a small, silver head appears out of his sleeve. Its eyes watch me while its forked tongue licks the air, almost like it's tasting my scent.

Goerner finishes chewing the carrot and notices me looking at his sleeve. "Ah, my cobron. Angh." He massages the underside of the serpent's neck. "Incredible creatures. One of the rarest of anything the Designers have created."

I say nothing.

Angh slithers back up his sleeve, out of sight.

Goerner wipes his mouth again and stands. "Prince, there is something I'd like to share with you." He approaches me. "Has Bryce introduced you to experiences of the symbion?"

I nod slowly.

"I thought so. Her tale is one shared by far too many Lantians. There aren't enough resources below."

"You'd have more resources," I say, "if your people didn't have to sacrifice their rations to feed your sleeping gigataun."

He pauses, then nods. "Sacrifices sometimes must be made to achieve victory." He stops before me. "If you will allow me, I'd like to share another experience with you. One that I think will change your entire view of the Below." He approaches me and reaches for his neck. "May I?"

He says it like it is an option.

"I share this with my apologies," he says. "Unfortunately, this experience is from back when the symbions were new. It suffers from the fogginess of typical human memory. It has been passed to me from another."

He shocks my hand.

✦✦✦

I'm no longer in the room with him. I'm someone else, some man I don't know, and I'm standing in a barren landscape that's devoid of life.

My heart's beating fast because I'm about to do something that hasn't been done in years. I'm about to enter a sealed capsule that'll shoot me into the sky, pass me safely through the death clouds so I can infiltrate the Skylands. I'll become a Skylander. I'll rise through their Meritocracy, become a High, and show them a better way.

My family surrounds me. I've already said goodbye to all but one. Mom comes to me, tears in her eyes, and collects me in her arms.

She pulls me close.

"Don't forget who you are." She points a finger into my chest. "The world above will try to break you. Make you forget humanity. But be better than what that world intends. Be better. Be the son I raised you to be."

I hold her tight—or he does. We're one now, and my heart's consumed with fear, knowing this will be the final time I'll see her. But I have a mission because we Lantians are starving. In the Below, only the people who live in the Zones away from the unControllables manage to live a bearable life. But the people above the death clouds—they have resources. Food. Comfort.

Mom squeezes me one last time, and I lower into the capsule. The chair's stiff and uncomfortable. Then the Lantian Council comes to me to wish me luck.

I'm their hope.

The capsule seals shut and tilts back, aimed toward the sky. I glimpse my family through the glass. They back up and watch me, holding one another. Their eyes red.

I press my palm against the glass. I'll not fail them. I'll show the world there's a better way.

Suddenly, with an incredible jolt, the capsule launches into the sky. My body shudders from the burst of speed, and wind slams against the glass. I'm traveling at such insane speeds that darkness swallows my vision. I bite down hard. Try to fight it, but before I know it, I fade from consciousness.

When I wake, my vision's blurred and vomit cakes my chest. I peer through the glass at the world of the sky. My pod . . . it broke through the acid clouds. Unbelievably, I made it. Now I'm soaring through a star-filled night, and the stars glitter with the most beautiful glow. I'm staring at the sight, awestruck. Disbelieving that this is what the sky looks like above the black. It can't be real.

My capsule arches and descends toward a frozen island crowned with shining mansions. It's remarkable. Beautiful. So many rich homes. My gut lurches as the pod sinks faster. Now I'm seeing smaller homes, then shacks. But I'm not close to the city. No, I'm plunging directly for the green-and-white forest. I grip the handholds. The capsule shudders, and the trees grow bigger in my vision. I stop breathing, then my capsule cracks through the trees and branches.

My head shakes violently, and my vision spins.

The pod crashes into the surface and glides over snow-crusted bushes. Finally, it comes to a grinding halt, sliding through stones and slushy, wet snow. My head's swimming with dizziness. I sit for several minutes, breathing away the disorientation until I press the eject button, and the domed roof shoots off the capsule.

Cold wind attacks my exposed skin and my wet chest. Makes me alert. I stumble from the pod and hit the frozen ground. Oooh. I feel horrible, and the snow's so bitter it stings my fingers.

Finally, I'm up, ambling through the snowy forest. I walk, hugging my arms against my chest until, through a parting of trunks, I glimpse the city that climbs up a white mountain. Smoke swirls from the shacks at the base of the city, while giant, glorious manors rise above all.

This island, I've learned from training, is one of the harshest, most brutal of all the Skylands.

If I can make it here, I can make it anywhere.

Holmstead Island.

✦✦✦

Goerner jolts me again, and I'm snapped back into the underground room with him. He stands over me. His lupons chew the bones of the metal rabbits.

My skin's hot. Flushed.

"You understand what I showed you?" Goerner says. "What that memory was?"

Don't even know what to think, but I meet Goerner's eyes, and my mouth opens, softly.

"My mother's father," I say, my heart thudding, body gone cold, "was a Lantian."

CHAPTER 38

OVER THE NEXT MONTH OF MY CAPTIVITY, ADMIRAL GOERNER meets with me constantly. He has continually assured me that my friends are safe and healthy and that they'll remain that way so long as I play along.

Furthermore, I've had a birthday, but I didn't tell Goerner that. I'm seventeen now. It's the first birthday I've had without Mother. Last year, with McGill's help, she brought me cherry ice cream and we ate it together while listening to tavern music.

I miss her so much that it hurts to breathe.

Without knowing it, Goerner has been giving me presents of his own: more experiences of my grandfather. Despite my hatred of the former High Admiral, I can't help but wake up each morning excited to learn more. And see the world through Grandfather's eyes. Live his emotions.

Apparently, Hale shared these experiences with other Lantians who infiltrated years after he did. They thought his experiences would help them blend in and live as a Skylander. Because even though my grandfather never ended up rising in the Skylands, he was successfully able to hide his identity for his whole life. Even from his wife and daughter.

Grandfather had no family name in the Above. He was simply Hale. And after dueling his way to become a Middle, he just stopped. He hated that to rise, he had to tear a family from their home and send them to Low.

Honestly, Hale could've risen higher through his capable dueling skills, or gone through the Selection, but he met someone, Cheryl of Thornton, and fell in love. She was a Low, the daughter of a pishon catcher who sometimes got to see the world. And because Hale was a Middle, she assumed his name. Cheryl of Hale. After that, my grandfather completely lost sight of his mission.

Hale was sent to conquer the Above without bloodshed and save the Below. But the reality is, he never cared about rising. The Lantians sent the wrong person. Hale didn't have the drive, but his daughter did.

Mother.

Through my grandfather's eyes, I watched as Mother grew up. I saw her first steps. Heard her laugh. She grew into a powerful person who would eventually lead Holmstead with Father.

Young Elise was stubborn as hell, not unlike Ella.

Despite Hale's objections, she became a fierce dueler. In her early twenties, she'd go to the Middle pits to compete in some of the island's most dangerous duels for extra money. And one day, after defeating a hulking man and celebrating with some cherry ice cream, she met someone.

Grandfather watched it all, heartbroken, realizing his daughter was slipping away from him.

The handsome young man who approached Elise had dark, intelligent eyes under tangles of brown curls. He wore a fine uniform, and a black cane topped with an eagle dangled from his hip. Seeing him was like looking at myself in a mirror.

Allred of Urwin was in his late twenties and was the heir to one of the most powerful families in the Skylands. And within two days of Allred meeting my mother, Hale caught them kissing under the moonlight outside his home. Grandfather did not trust my father. Every time Hale saw the young man, his skin would grow hot. The hair on the back of his neck would rise.

"Stay away from him," Hale scolded Elise one night after she returned home late. "He is broken, twisted. An Urwin."

"I'm twenty-two," Mother said. "I'm not a child."

"He is the worst parts of Meritocracy."

"There is goodness in him, Father. You just don't know him."

"There is no goodness in anyone like him."

Mother's face flushed. She flung back her white hair and met Hale's eyes dead-on. Then she stormed past him without another word.

My parents' romance was a forbidden one. Elise was a lifelong Middle, and Allred was the heir of power-hungry bastards.

Goerner shared an experience with me where Hale was butchering a deer in the shed behind his home. Footsteps approached outside, cutting through crispy snow.

Hale added a hock of meat to the pile but didn't look up at the young man who stepped into the shed.

"Hale," Father said, "I'd like to speak with you."

Hale stabbed the cleaver into the wooden table, wiped his hands on his apron, and looked up. "What, Urwin?"

My father paused, and though he hid it well, I recognized the nervousness in him. His fingers fiddled. Hale saw it, too, and it sank him into cold dread. He knew why Allred was anxious.

Father swallowed his breath and walked forward, regal. Straight-backed. Despite his obvious nerves, his eyes never wavered once from Grandfather's face.

"I am going to ask Elise to marry me."

Allred lifted the cleaver, squeezed it until the handle squeaked, and slammed it through a bone. "Do you expect my support?"

"I don't," Father said. "But I wanted you to be the first to know."

Hale cleaved off the deer's front leg. His breaths coming fast. My father stood for several seconds, waiting, then turned to leave.

Hale felt like swearing. But he breathed for several seconds, relaxing, and called out to him. "Do not corrupt my daughter, Urwin," he said. "Be better than this world. Be better than your family."

Father stared at him as if he were registering this statement. Then he stepped back out into the snow.

Mother and Father were married shortly afterward. But this was the turning point, because the wedding didn't take place in the beautiful High gardens of Holmstead, or in one of the ritzy plazas, or even on the Urwin grounds, where all the rich and famous would be invited to attend.

No, it was a small, private ceremony in the Middles. Father and Mother made their promises to each other and danced and sang with a close group of friends.

Not a single Urwin attended because Isabella of Urwin, the Archduchess, forbade it. Worse, she banished Father for marrying a Middle. It was after the ceremony, as Hale watched his daughter spin in the arms of the man she loved, that his heart cracked.

Their love was real.

After the wedding Hale asked the newlyweds to move with him and Grandmother to another island together. That way they'd be away from the Urwins' influence.

It didn't take much to convince Father. He clearly wanted to be away from his mother. So they went to Frozenvale, where they lived quietly, surviving off the land. They avoided conflict and duels. Still, Father trained with the cane every night, and Mother trained with him because in the Skylands, you always must be prepared for someone wanting what's yours.

The small family lived in peace until Father's past came back to him two years later. My paternal grandmother, Isabella of Urwin, found the Hales. She sat regally in the chair across from my grandfather, her narrowed, dark eyes scanning the quaint Middle home.

"Where is my son?" she whispered.

Hale folded his arms. He tried to keep his face stoic, but his stomach kept twisting. And he couldn't help glancing toward the door, hoping my parents wouldn't return early from their fishing trip.

"They went to another island," Hale said.

Isabella squinted at him through studying eyes. "Do not lie to me."

"When they come visit, I will be sure—"

Hale stopped because he heard the cheerful voices of my parents walking up the grassy path that led to the home. They were laughing, carrying bags of fish, and Mother's belly had a bump. A son was coming soon.

Cheryl tried to warn them, but Father was laughing about something, and when he entered the home, his smile shrank, and his face flushed. Isabella's eyes bore into him, ready to cut him into a thousand pieces.

But something happened that neither Hale nor Father expected. Isabella stepped past Cheryl, walked to her son, and wrapped her arms around him. The stiffest of hugs—but love behind it, too.

They stood quietly, Father's eyes wide, until finally his arms raised to hug his mother back.

Experiencing this moment through Hale's eyes nearly shattered me . . . because as Isabella hugged him, my father almost melted into her arms. Like this was something he'd desperately craved his whole life. I suddenly understood why Father was the way he was. Why he rarely hugged me.

His severity was a learned trait.

Isabella told Father to come back to Holmstead because her other son, Ulrich, would become the head of Urwin without him. She said

Ulrich was going too far with his ambition. Ulrich had plans to ensure the Urwins would never lose their power. A plan to cement his power forever and eliminate any threats that stood before him.

"Return to my side, Son," Isabella said, looking him in the eyes. "*Return.*"

But Allred couldn't make such a decision so easily. He needed time, so Isabella agreed to give him peace, and she left.

My grandparents couldn't let Allred return to Holmstead, to Urwin. Allred would be among serpents again. But they had no say in the matter.

Father considered his mother's offer for a day. When Isabella returned, he straightened his back, breathed out, and turned her down.

Isabella's face fell. She shut her eyes, lifted the collars of her jacket, then left. But she wasn't gone long, because she returned month after month, and at one point even broke a golden rule of Urwin: she begged.

She knelt before him, clasped his hands in hers, and looked him in the eyes. "Allred, I am dying."

Father's eyes widened.

"I have one year left, Son."

Father's voice shook. "But Scholar's meds—"

"Not even they can save me. We've tried."

"But I—" Father said.

"You *must* return to Holmstead. Bring your wife and raise your son there. The mantle must go to you and to you alone."

Father hesitated at this, but suddenly, the experience I'm seeing goes murky.

✦✦✦

My vision blurs as Goerner shocks me and brings me back in the room with him and his lupons. Goerner steps away, back to his side of the table, and lowers to sit. His shoulders slouch with exhaustion.

"What happened next?" I ask, leaning forward in my chair. "What about the rest?"

"We don't have all of Hale's experiences."

"That's it?"

"There's no more."

My heart sinks. I've started craving these memories. Relished seeing my parents in a different life. Seeing Father when he wasn't so callous. Seeing Mother when she was young and hopeful.

I want more. I wish there were more.

I slip into despondence because I'll not get to see them again. Any of them. Hale, Cheryl, Allred, Elise, and even Isabella. My vision goes warm, and I bite my lip to fight back the bitter tears. I'll not cry, not in front of Goerner. But it's like I just lost them again. I got to see them alive and happy. I got to hear their voices.

"We can surmise what happened afterward," Goerner whispers solemnly. "Allred accepted his responsibility and returned to Holmstead. Not much later he probably sang 'The Song of Falling' at his mother's funeral and released her body to the winds. After that it may have been only a couple years before your father started teaching you the ways of Urwin. Because from the time you were little, you were trained to become as brutal as necessary. Trained to become the strongest and prove that your family deserved to lead."

I sit in silence.

"For nearly a decade, your father led Holmstead, and the island prospered until one day, your uncle killed him and took over. When the Hales came to save you from the misery of the Lows—Ulrich killed them, too. Had their ship wiped from the sky. And just to make sure you and your mother could not inherit anything, he had the Hales' small home burned."

The tears threaten again. I play with the cup on the table before me.

"So, you must ask yourself, Conrad, Prince of the Skylands, who do you want to be? Your mother's side attempted to instill moral values in you. But the Urwin side of you demands power. Strength." He stands. "If you join us, we will give you your ship back. Your crew back. We will fly you to the Skylands, and we will give you this."

He pulls a tiny glass capsule from his pocket. A needle rests in a clear liquid.

"All you must do is prick your uncle with it. It's cobron poison from Angh. No antivenom exists. Once you kill him, you can end this war. You will become the King, but you will answer to your real people: the Lantian Republic. The Lantian Council and you will lead the Above and the Below into a new era of prosperity. You've seen the Vortex. Weapon created it to eat the death clouds. We learned how to turn it on shortly before you arrived here. We're going to use it, Conrad, to remove the barrier between our peoples. It will take years, maybe decades, but the world will be whole again."

I stir the bowl of meat before me. Don't feel like eating. Despite the excitement of seeing my family again, I haven't felt like eating much since I've been captured.

"I'd be a pawn," I say softly.

"No," Goerner says. "You will be the savior to many. I cannot think of a more important position."

I lift my fork and stare at the dangling white meat. "And if I say no?"

Goerner frowns. He doesn't have to say a word in response. He'll send me to see my family. And my crew? They've only been kept alive as an expression of goodwill.

He walks me back to my room and stands in the doorway. "You have until tomorrow to decide."

The door shuts behind me, leaving me in my cold, rocky room. But it's unlocked. Always is because Goerner wants me to have the illusion of being free down here.

Except, anytime I leave, I'm escorted by guards.

Every day for the last month, I've been told things about the Lantians. About their Council. About the people like Bryce, who wanted to show the world the better way. But Goerner has also told me what the Lantians think of the Skylanders. That they believe the islands have too many zealous Meritocrats. And they'd have to be eliminated for this plan of peace to work. The fact that the islands haven't surrendered after losing so many lives is proof that there are some whose stubbornness will be their execution.

I pace about my cell, moving past my desk, where I've been recording everything Goerner tells me each day. In many respects, Goerner's plan makes sense. It could bring about a new age of peace for the Skylands, and for the Below. We could work together. The war would be over.

But would I ever be truly safe? Or would they eliminate me once it became convenient to them? And can I really trust Goerner?

Uncle is a vile, cruel man, but he only killed Lantian infiltrators and soldiers. Goerner and the Lantian Council killed *innocents*. Children. Families. Civilians. How can I forget the terror in the eyes of those who fell with Holmstead and Ironside? How can I forget that this man's Designers created the beasts that killed my mother?

After weeks of listening to stories of the Below, of my grandfather, I know my mother and grandfather would never condone what Goerner or the Lantians have done.

I exhale and lower onto my small cot.

After a few minutes, I dress in Hunter's uniform. The Lantians took a spare one from the *Gladian* and gave it to me. I pull on the silver, form-fitting clothes with gloves, a black jacket, and magboots. Once I open the door, a trio of Lantian guards follows close by. Goerner claims they're for my protection against rogue Lantians, but I'm not an idiot.

I wander along the tunnels beneath Perditio. It's cold. Craggy rocks and scattering glowlons on the ceilings. Other bizarre creatures growl at me as I stride past. Men and women eye me with disgust, still furious with Goerner for inviting the Prince of the Skylands into their home.

Then I pause at the heart of the tunnels. The vault to Brone's weapon. It's a vast door of rusted metal. Goerner's been trying to open it since he got here, but he can't without the key. And he fears any further attempts might trigger the destruction mechanism.

A voice snakes into my ear. "Still making a decision?"

The hairs on the back of my neck rise. I turn. He's watching from the shadows, leaning against the wall. His black hair hangs over his pallid face.

"I don't want you to accept Goerner's offer," he says.

"Because we'd be on the same side?"

Sebastian laughs. "Yes."

He pushes off the wall and tries shooing the guards away, but they ignore him. Seems he doesn't have as much authority as he thinks. Or maybe he had more but lost it because he hasn't been able to locate Bryce and Ella.

"You realize," I say, "that you will never reach the power you seek with the Lantians? You will always be an 'other' to them."

"We'll see."

"Should've killed you when I had the chance."

"Probably. Your life would be easier. Goerner's fleet never would've known you were coming to this miserable island. You could've waited for an opportunity to sneak inside, or surprise them with an attack. May I share a symbion experience with you? It's rather new . . . and I'm quite fond of my symbion."

"No."

"Shame. I thought you would've liked to see me kill Roderick."

I stare at him. He's lying. But he grins with a simple innocence.

"I killed him in the corridors of the *Gladian*," he says. "When I escaped the *Intrepid*. It was quite the shot. Got him through the gut. He fell and cried like a little animal, too. Oh, you should've heard Keeton's wails. Tragic."

My jaw clenches. "Goerner told me my friends are still alive."

"Thought you were smarter than that, *Prince*." He tsks. "Goerner's wise enough to know that if your friends are dead, he'll lose leverage."

His words spark doubt in my mind.

"I'm in a conundrum myself," he says. "Because if you refuse Goerner's offer, you'll be dead, and I'll be left alone in this cruel, miserable world."

"You are broken."

"No. You complete me."

I scowl at him. My gloves squeak.

He starts toward the exit. "Make your decision quickly, Prince. The war is waiting, and from what I hear, the gigataun is getting hungry."

Then he cackles as he strolls beyond the guards, his shadow following his serpent form.

✦✦✦

Goerner stares at me, face blank, as I explain my decision.

His left eye twitches. Perhaps realizing that he spent so many resources on me for nothing. Suddenly, his eyes rage, and he punches me right across the jaw. His guards come at me, beat me into the ground.

Just like that.

Proving that once I resisted anything, they'd do this to me. I sink away into another place as the strikes come. Imagining my friends. Wishing that if they are still alive, I didn't just doom them.

But aligning myself with mass murderers? That's not what Mother meant when she told me to be better than what the world intended. I can't simply chase my friends to sky's end. Not when it comes at the expense of the Skylands.

Maybe I'm not the leader I'd hoped to be, but I think of Kirsi, and this time . . . this time I'm ready to be the one left behind for the good of the rest.

By the time my vision's blacking out, Goerner pushes his locs back and stands erect, taking a stabilizing breath. His cobron hisses at me, and for an instant I think it'll bite me. But it slithers up his arm.

"Return him to his room," Goerner commands. "Lock him in. Tomorrow morning we drop him into the sky. Afterward we move on Dandun, with or without Weapon's creation. It's almost time for the island eater to return."

CHAPTER 39

I'M LOCKED IN MY ROOM. NOT THAT IT MATTERS; I CAN hardly move. My face is swollen. The left side of my head throbs with pain. Think I've got a loose tooth. Bruises darken my torso, and blood trickles down the back of my throat.

Going to die soon. Not much can be done about that now.

After getting captured, I somehow managed an extra month of life. Through my grandfather's memories, I saw my parents before I was born. Watched Mother playfully dance for her parents. She looked so much like Ella, her white hair bouncing with every movement. And I got to see a younger, less hardened version of Father. He was a physical copy of me. Curly brown hair. Focused eyes. Tall and strong.

And his smile. So strange that when Father was away from his mother, he allowed himself to smile. But the world broke him and turned him into the thing he later became. If I weren't about to be executed, I'd worry that maybe this world would eventually break me, too.

I gently lower onto my bed and lean against the wall, trying to sip breaths through my aching lungs. Maybe Father and I aren't all that different. His mother made him into who he was.

Just like mine did.

I sink into blue sadness knowing I was robbed of meeting the happier version of him. Maybe if Uncle weren't a bastard, I would've had my true father. We would've lived as Middles on Frozenvale. Happy. I wouldn't have been raised under the shadow of Urwin and never would've been among the serpents.

But I got a very different father. The one I knew . . . his affection came with the cane and his desire to make me strong, to prepare me.

I drop my head into my arms, lost in one of my own memories of him. One that I've kept close to my heart.

After he left me to take down a prowlon by myself, I returned from the island to his skyship. I'd proved myself worthy, but I also stopped speaking to him. There are things you don't come back from. Like abandoning your child to potentially die on an island with a vicious beast.

One night we paused to rest from our flight back to Holmstead, and I lowered onto my bed in my small cabin. I stared at the wooden ceiling boards, stewing in hatred of my father. My eyes burned. Betrayal stung me. Shouldn't have believed him when he said we were going on a fishing trip. Father never did anything with me for enjoyment or affection. Usually the most I'd ever get from him was maybe a hand on the shoulder. And that was only after he'd beat me in a duel.

After I shut off the light crystal that evening, the door cracked open, and a shadow stood in the doorway. I shut my eyes, pretended to be asleep. *No, Father, I will not talk to you*. He stepped toward me and sat on the edge of my bed. Suddenly, his hands tenderly brushed my hair from my eyes. He leaned forward and kissed my forehead.

My lip almost quivered. My skin grew hot, and I desperately wanted to sob.

I needed him to say something to me. To tell me he loved me and that he was sorry for what he had to do, but he needed to make me strong. Because as powerful and mighty as he was, he couldn't stop Meritocracy.

He kissed my forehead again. Brought my blanket up to my neck and slid his fingers through my hair. His mouth cracked open, and two words came out. Soft and proud.

"My son."

When he left, I rolled over and cried until my stomach hurt.

After we returned to Holmstead, I saw Father only sparingly around the manor. He was more stressed than usual. Once, I'd overheard him arguing with Uncle about something I didn't understand. Then, on the day I was to get my own dueling cane from the Equilibrium, I went to his office with excitement in my heart. He'd promised me that since I survived the prowlon, I was now officially an Urwin.

We were going to get my dueling cane together.

But when I pushed open the door into his office, a flurry of papers flew into my face. The balcony door was open, blowing icy wind about the room. And I found Father, face down, lying in his own blood. A bag of coins in his hand.

Before a scream even left my lips, Uncle appeared behind me and stared in feigned horror. He shoved me aside. Held my father against his chest and roared. The rest of the Manor came running after that. Oh, Mother . . . when she saw Father, she dissolved into the ground. Her whole body trembling. She hugged me so tight I almost couldn't breathe.

I stood in shock, watching Uncle. His face was twisted in pain, his voice was hoarse, but not a single tear wetted his cheeks.

Order was called. Guards searched the room and found the note on the desk. Handwriting that matched Father's.

Suicide, they said.

But when I looked at Uncle, and his false pain, I knew they were wrong. He murdered Father to become the head of Urwin.

I push away that memory and roll onto my side, groaning from the pain of Goerner's beating, my eyes wet. I'm broken. Defeated. But I'll be with my family again soon. Tomorrow I'll drop into the sky, and the winds will carry me to the place it took my parents.

No matter how high we rise in life, in the end, we are all equal.

In the end, we all fall.

✦✦✦

Someone shouts outside my door, and an explosion follows. I shoot upright but immediately hold my side, seething. It's pitch-black.

Suddenly, boots scramble outside in the tunnels. The ground vibrates from another series of explosions. Dust rocks from the ceiling onto my face. Then my door bursts open, and four Lantian guards enter in a huff.

"What's happening?" I ask, blocking the sudden light with my hand.

One hits me with the butt of his spear. I fall back, vision shimmering. They collect me by my feet and yank me off the bed. At first I'm dazed. Then terror coils around my insides. They've come to kill me. Now that it's happening, I'm not ready to die. My hands desperately search for something to catch, but there's nothing except pebbles.

"We have to take him to the *Golias*," a guard says, as I'm pulled from my room.

The rocky ground cuts into my back as they drag me. Out in the tunnel, Lantians run for the exits. Some toward their ships. Others toward their turrets on the surface to fight back at whatever or whoever is attacking.

Another explosion buzzes my already spinning vision, and a guard dragging me tumbles to his knees.

"C'mon," another guard says, helping him up. "There's no time."

I grimace as the rocks slice me. Who's attacking? How'd they find the island? Could Ella and Bryce have gotten back to the Skylands and returned with help? My heart leaps at that thought. It gives me a little energy.

I'm dragged down a tunnel that leads toward a carved-out hangar. At the end I spot Goerner's black battlecruiser floating beside the dock, preparing to depart. Lantians are running everywhere.

Why don't they just kill me now and leave me?

Maybe Goerner doesn't actually intend to kill me right away. He could attempt to use me to negotiate with Uncle. Or perhaps he plans to publicly execute me in a place where Skylanders can see.

My teeth grit. Can't give up. Not when it's possible someone's come for me. I catch the leg of a running woman. She tumbles and smacks her head against the rock. And in the commotion, the guards lose their grip on me.

I seize the woman's spear and use it to push myself to unsteady feet.

But I have no strength. Nothing left in me. It was beaten out. I lean against the wall, breathing hard, my back bleeding. I'm about to topple to the ground when a voice, clear as the last time I saw him alive, enters my mind. Father made me duel in moments like this. In the Urwin Square, he beat me. Made me marinate in my own red.

Rise, Father whispers. *Rise like your ancestors, Conrad. Rise.*

He is with me. Father's with me.

And whatever's left inside me comes ablaze. I shout so hard that I nearly lose my voice. Don't know how I'm doing it, but I'm spinning the spear. Then I'm at the guards, cutting through them like the wind. Ignoring my pain. The sparking vision.

I send all four into electric paralysis.

Fortunately, everyone in the hangar's too busy preparing to disembark to notice.

I lean against the wall, blinking through the spots in my eyes. Suddenly, voices approach from around the corner. Shit. Adrenaline surges in me, and I snatch the closest unconscious guard. Then with gnashed teeth, I drag him into a room.

Once I slip him into the shadows, two people shout outside. Yelling about the fallen guards. I've got to work quickly. My fingers furiously rip the guard's uniform off. I stuff my legs into his pants. Strap on the boots.

The guards leap into my room, ready for a fight. But when they find me, I'm fully dressed in the Lantian's uniform, and I'm leaning against the wall for support. I've left the unclothed guard behind a crate of supplies.

"The bastard Prince," I say, stumbling forward and falling at their boots. "He attacked me and ran."

The men squint at me. Hopefully the bruises hide my face. They must know I don't have a symbion, but maybe not all of them have one. Bryce said getting a symbion is a special privilege.

One of the men grips his spear, and I expect the attack to come. I prepare myself for it. I'll have to fight them both. Somehow.

Instead, they catch me gently by the arms and lift me to my feet.

"We'll find the fussock," one says through bitter teeth. "Where'd he go?"

I cough to hide my relief. "The surface. He was headed to the surface."

"Trying to get away? That slippery bastard."

The left one speaks through his comm cube. Bringing an alert to the whole island that the Prince has escaped.

Goerner screams back, "Fine! Kill him on sight. I don't care how, just end that miserable shit's life."

"C'mon, soldier," they say to me. "We'll get him together."

"I've always wanted to gut a Meritocrat Prince," I say.

They laugh.

"Any meds?" I ask.

"Meds? Who do you think we are? Uptight Skylands Scholars?" he snorts. "C'mon."

We start out of the tunnel. And I lean on these idiots' shoulders.

Can't believe this. We move past rows of rushing Lantians. Many are arming themselves with weapons. Preparing to charge toward the tunnel's exit.

"You really want to fight in your condition?" one of the men asks me.

"I'd fight to my dying breath."

"Good man," he says. "For the Colonies."

"Yes. For the Colonies."

A smile creases my lips because now I can see the exit. For the first time in a month, I'm breathing air from the surface. A figure approaches from an opposing tunnel. Walks ahead of us. And my breath nearly stops. I'm hoping against hope that he doesn't look my way.

Why him? Why always *him*?

Suddenly, his gaze snaps directly toward me, and my heart falls. His eyes widen, and his mouth opens, stunned. For an instant he's clearly ready to shout. But then he starts laughing and laughing.

"What the hell is so funny?" one of my helpers asks the pallid boy.

"Nothing," Sebastian says, stepping aside to let us pass. "Absolutely nothing at all."

Sebastian is many things—but he truly believes we're linked, that we are meant to face each other. And he can't live without me.

It's probably the closest thing to love he's ever experienced.

I glance back at him, and his pink lips smile beneath his dark bangs before he turns and hurries deeper into the tunnels. No doubt on his way to Goerner's vessel or another ship.

Explosions rock above us. People shout. My ears ring from the assault. Whoever is attacking doesn't seem to care that they might crush me in the process. It's a wild sort of attack. One that you wouldn't expect from someone like Order.

So, who the hell came?

We continue toward the open door. Ahead, Lantian leaders are shouting at us, waving for us to get out there and kill the flying bastards.

My helpers let me go. "Can you walk?"

I nod, grimacing a little as I shift my weight to my better leg.

"Good luck," they say. "For the Colonies!"

Then they burst from the ruins and race for the turrets.

I hobble out into a war zone. It's pure bedlam. All around, Lantians launch weapons at the passing ships. The night sky glows with golden and blue flames. Explosions pop across Perditio's surface.

I duck behind some rubble. Stupid idea, coming above. Maybe I should've stayed below, but then again, someone might've taken me to a ship to recover. Or to a doctor. And eventually I'd be recognized.

The world around me is all fire and screams.

I rise over the slab of rubble, just enough to see the bombarding ships that circle the island. I squint, focusing on the flags and paintings that mark the hulls.

My mouth falls.

Can't be. How?

It's not the King's fleet. It's not Hunter. Not Order. No, the ships flying overhead, firing with reckless abandon, making me dive behind another crumbled wall to avoid a harpoon, they belong to an armada. One of the most powerful armadas in the sky. The one owned by the Duchess of Stonefrost.

Except, these ships don't carry the lightning flags of the Duchess of Stonefrost anymore. Ownership has changed. A new family has taken over Stonefrost. And they're flying black-and-white flags.

I glimpse someone on a ship that zooms past. His bald head shines under the golden light, and he's yelling at his family to keep firing. His family who are as numerous as they are terrible.

Pound.

Somehow that colossal birdshit brought a fleet of his whole damn family to Perditio.

CHAPTER 40

THE LANTIANS ON THE SURFACE HAVE GONE QUIET. SEVERAL of their ships have dropped from the sky, and only a dozen or so of them escaped with Goerner's ship, now flying in the distance with the sunrise.

Pound and his horrible family disembark from their massive ships and step onto the remnants of Perditio's rotten dock. But I'm pressed against the ground by a slab of wreckage. The thing fell on me during the attack and rests on my chest. My exhausted arms struggle to lift it. Can hardly breathe, let alone shout for help.

The Atwoods, followed by gangs of armed, hired helpers, walk among the field of the dead, ending any remaining Lantians without mercy.

I shove the slab with both hands again, but my shaking arms fall to my sides. Too weak, I feel like a little child.

"Help," I moan.

A massive figure crunches the gravel nearby and stabs a dying

Lantian with a harpoon. I groan. The huge person's head perks up, and when I see his face, terror grips me. The figure's eyes narrow. He stomps forward, then stares down his big nose at me.

His face scrunches in a scowl. "Urwin."

He's one of the Atwoods who used to beat me in the alleys with Pound. Stagg. He steps onto the slab, pressing it against my chest and raises his harpoon.

"Beg, you lotcher. Beg."

The pressure builds in my eyes. I gasp. Head feels like it's going to pop.

"Beg," he spits.

He leans forward and aims the pointed end of the harpoon at my face. "Going to stick you in the eye."

My hands desperately push against the slab. My legs kick. Suddenly, Stagg goes flying off the slab. He hits the ground, rolling, and grunts. Another bastard, even bigger than him, towers over me.

His voice booms. "What the hell are you doing, Stagg?"

My vision is splotchy, blood on my lips, and my chest's stinging. But I'm smiling because of the giant, bald-headed Asswood standing over Stagg.

"This is the Prince."

Stagg holds his side. "So?"

Pound kicks him twice with his giant boots. Stagg grunts and tries to stand, but Pound shoves him over again.

"Get my father, you ugly birdshit."

Pound punts Stagg's behind, sending him falling forward. Then, as Stagg stumbles away, Pound turns to me, and his rage softens. The dirt crunches under his massive boots.

"You're looking rather flat there, Elise."

"You mind"—I wheeze—"helping me?"

"But you look so comfortable."

He laughs with relief. Probably relief that I wasn't executed by the Lantians. Relief that when he left the *Gladian* to find his family, he didn't doom his friend.

He bends down, and together we push off the slab. I cough and suck down a full breath of air. For several seconds I lie on my back, just letting air in and massaging my chest. Finally, I sit up, wincing, and lean against rubble.

Pound stares at me, frowning. "You look terrible."

"Yes, well, when you stop complying with Goerner . . ."

"I'll mangle his neck personally." He looks back at the ancient, ruined city. "What is this place?"

"You don't know? This was the home of Weapon."

"The home of what?"

I stare at him. "How did you find this place if you don't even know what it is?"

"This eccentric weirdo led us here. Told us about you being captured, but he refused to say much else. He kept hamming on about how this would be his 'discovery.' He led us through the cloudwall. You wouldn't believe the ridiculous suits he made us wear."

I brighten. "Mage of Cabral?"

"Oh yeah, that's his name. Yippity little birdshit. Like any of us care about any 'discovery.' But I guess you should be grateful. He saved your life."

"Where is he?"

Pound shrugs. "Hiding on his baby ship until the fighting is over." He glances around at the quiet dead. "Still too dangerous, I assume."

"Not everyone's meant to be a Hunter."

"I suppose. Besides, my father wanted this to be an Atwood victory. Unassisted—outside of the ones we hired, of course. This victory will force your uncle to recognize us before the whole Skylands. He stopped recognizing this armada, rejected us from the King's fleet once we took over Stonefrost. For the last month, we've been in the

Eastern Skies, killing gorgantauns, searching for Lantians. Trying to help the Skylands. Then Mage suddenly showed up, telling us in a panic about what was happening beyond the cloudwall."

Pound bends down and hoists me to my feet. I topple forward, and his massive arm stabilizes me.

"Careful, Elise. You need meds. Always meds with you."

"If it weren't for meds," I say, "I'd probably have died a long time ago."

"You're expensive to keep alive."

"Worth it, though."

He eyes me, then laughs. "Debatable."

We stand there, me leaning against him as we stare over the massive men and women who go about, searching the dead.

Toddlers giggle from carriers on the backs of some of the Atwoods. I nearly shake my head. Since birth, these bastards are taught to be vicious and cruel. My family's the same way. Except, I don't think I was carried around by Mother during a battle. That's insane as hell.

Then again, being thrown onto an island alone with a prowlon is pretty damn crazy, too.

"Hey, you!" Pound shouts at a younger Atwood who's running around with a harpoon as a spear. "Get me some water."

"I'm killing things."

"I'll beat your face in. Go."

The boy glares, then runs back toward a ship. A few minutes later, he lugs a pitcher of water to us. Pound thwacks the boy's back in a bizarre sign of affection, and the boy races off—ready to stab something.

"Drink, Elise," Pound says.

He tips the water toward my lips, and I don't even care that it's spilling all over me. I pull the pitcher away from him. Hugging it like it's my life. It's damn cold but goes down smoothly. I swallow great gulps, not realizing how thirsty I was. Immediately, my body kicks into action and puts the water to use. Giving me energy. Clearing the haze in my head.

I belch and sit on the rubble.

"Got my family back," Pound says proudly, with his hands on his hips as he watches the shouting Atwoods kill stragglers under the morning sun.

I wipe my face with my arm. "You told me they were all 'assholes.'"

"Oh, that hasn't changed. But I love them."

"Even though they abandoned you?"

He shrugs. "I wasn't strong enough then. They appreciate strength, and I lost them everything."

"Why did they take you back?"

He exhales. "Well, after they rose back to High on Holmstead, they had aims to rise further. My father, Aggress, wanted to be a Duke. The whole family had left Holmstead weeks before the giga came and moved to Stonefrost."

"Fortunate timing," I say.

"Conrad," Pound says, suddenly going quiet. "I—when I thought my family died, I lost it."

I stare at him.

"The relief I felt when I found them on Stonefrost . . ." His lip almost trembles. "When I saw them alive again . . ."

"That was how I felt when I found Ella."

He blinks at me.

"Pound—" I pause, recalling the hurt on his face when I pulled my cane on him at the Battle of Holmstead. "I'm sorry about—"

"Shut your face, Elise. I would've got us killed. You saved the crew because—because I lose control sometimes."

"Well, what I did was shitty."

"No, what *I* did was shitty."

"Okay, a truce," I say. "We both did shitty things."

He eyes me, nods, then nudges my shoulder in a playful way.

Except I topple over and fall to the ground. He watches me struggle for a moment, being the big bastard he's always been, then offers me a hand up.

"Sorry," he says. "Didn't mean to knock you over."

I'm not sure he means it, but I deserved it. Still, neither of us was really responsible for what happened to Holmstead. It was Goerner and the damned gigataun. They were the reason Pound did what he did.

And I did what I had to do to protect the people I care about. Pound was only trying to do the same.

We stand together, reunited, watching his family storm about the battlefield. "So, you found them on Stonefrost?" I ask.

He nods. "Yeah, my father challenged the Duchess." He breathes proudly. "Going to Stonefrost was strategic because my family doesn't trust your uncle. We believe your uncle will try to exterminate us. The Duchess of Stonefrost was one of the few to have her own personal armada. One that she'd been using for years to protect her islands from gorgantaun attacks. Naturally, my father wanted it."

My head shakes. The Duchess of Stonefrost—both my father and uncle worried about her potentially challenging to become Archduchess of Holmstead. She was a fierce dueler.

But apparently, not fierce enough to beat Aggress.

Pound continues, "When I got to Stonefrost, I ran into my father while he was intimidating the people of his new island. And he ignored me, right? Well, I challenged him. Right then and there. In the middle of the Highs."

I look at him.

"It wasn't a formal dueling challenge or anything. I saw him up the street, speaking to groups of people. I raced up to him and started punching him."

"You just . . . started punching him?"

He nods.

"I had the upper hand," he says. "He fell at my feet, but then Stagg and Rolly, and like a half dozen of my cousins, nieces, and nephews, came running. Even a toddler. I knocked out four of them before they overwhelmed me." He pauses and looks at me. "Not the toddler. I didn't hit the toddler."

I'd laugh if it wasn't birdshit crazy, but he breathes the memory in like it's warm chocolate. "When I woke up, I was in their new manor on Stonefrost. As if I'd never been gone."

Heat flies up my neck. "That's all you had to do to get your family back? Just punch them? Unbelievable."

"I got a concussion, Elise."

"To get my family back, I had to win the Gauntlet," I say. "I ran the length of a class-five gorgantaun. You and I had to frame Sebastian just to get him off the ship. I stabbed myself in my own damn shoulder, Pound. I did all that just so Uncle would let me see my sister again."

He nods. "My family might be assholes, but they're not Urwins."

My mouth tastes bitter, and he pats my back with his enormous hand. A year ago there was no one, outside of Uncle, who I hated more than Pound. And now I sit beside him, more grateful than ever to be with him.

"Have you seen Sebastian?" I ask.

"Sebastian?" Pound raises an eyebrow. "Why would that little birdshit be here?"

He doesn't know. When I explain, Pound tosses a rock, and it crashes against the remains of an ancient building.

"Little traitorous vermin."

We go quiet, and I sit and use the water to wipe my face and tenderly dab around my wounds. Finally, Pound calls out to his terrible family.

"Stand up," he says. "Don't appear weaker than you really are."

"But . . ."

"Just do it, Elise. It's not that difficult."

"Bastard."

My legs wobble beneath me, so I gently lean against a broken wall and fold my arms, trying to look casual. Before long a whole gang of giant Atwoods surrounds us, including some of their hired hands. They stare at me with great disdain, and they're all hulking monsters. Giant women with massive shoulders and ugly men with bald heads. Their massive palms could envelop my skull. Their thick boots could collapse my lungs.

Can't help but swallow. I'm standing, mostly helpless, against the sworn enemy of the Urwins.

The widest of the Atwoods, the bearded head of the family, breaks through the monsters. He thunders forward, crushing the gravel beneath his incredible boots. The new Duke of Stonefrost, Aggress of Atwood, squints at me through his only eye. He wears a pair of wind goggles, one side blacked out to act as an eye patch. He's around fifty years old—and nearly as tall as Pound, but with an even meaner gaze. He stares down at me as though I'm more an insect than a Prince.

"You are Urwin," he says bitterly.

The Atwoods boo as if the word itself is venom.

Aggress stands, staring at me, his eye narrowed. He raises a sharp hand, and they all go quiet.

I push off the wall a little, trying to look powerful before him, despite the fact I'm covered in blood and bruises and my clothes are wet.

Uncle would never admit it, but if there's one person in the sky he has feared, it's Aggress. Uncle orchestrated duels in the surrounding isles, empowering Dukes and Duchesses who were aligned with his interests. Hoping they'd deter Aggress and others trying to rise.

"You ran a gorgantaun's back," Aggress says finally, in his deep voice.

I nod.

"And you ripped out its eye?"

"Yes."

He licks his teeth and glances at the others behind him. His awful progeny could hurl me off the island and blame the Lantians. Hell, they could leave me here and claim they never saw me. They're outlaws now, so why should they care if I'm the Prince?

A twisted smile grows on Aggress's face. "That poor gorgantaun."

I blink at him, perplexed.

"It lost an eye," he says. "Just like *me*."

Silence.

Then he laughs. It's a long, bellowing laugh. Deep from the gut. The whole group laughs, too. Until suddenly, he stops in a wild instant.

And so do they.

"Well, I hate you," he says, glowering at me. "You're the spawn of liars and cheaters. But—I respect what you've done."

Not sure what to say. My mouth opens, but Pound gives me a wary look.

"My son assures me that you're more Elise than Urwin," he says, "so I'll pretend, for now, that you aren't a traitorous, backstabbing lotcher. I'll pretend I don't have you at my mercy. I'll pretend this because we Atwoods are at war with the bastards who dropped Holmstead. And today, we'll have our victory over them."

The Atwoods roar.

Aggress stomps away, waving the others to follow him to the tunnels. "C'mon. Let's get these dirt-eaters."

When they go, I breathe out and nearly topple over. Pound catches me before I hit the ground.

"I'll find you meds."

He walks away, but I call out to him. "Do you know that happened to the others?"

He pauses, then laughs. "I probably should've told you earlier." He points at three figures approaching us. "Here they come."

It's Mage of Cabral.

But behind Mage come two other people who make my heart

sing. And the next instant, even though I'm broken, I'm hobbling toward them.

Bryce and Ella.

✦✦✦

The *Gladian's* still afloat inside the Perditio hangar, damaged, but apparently the Lantians were in the middle of repairing it before Goerner rushed to escape. The *Gladian's* a great ship. It makes sense that they wanted to use it for their own devices.

I sit on the couch of my cabin on the *Gladian*. The room's been ransacked. The Lantians likely sought secrets or the key to the vault.

Bryce injects me with meds.

Sudden warmth blossoms in my chest, and a tingling sensation immediately numbs all my wounds. Within a few minutes, I'm breathing easier. The meds soothe everything but the deepest of aches. Those will take time.

But we can't sit around for long; we must warn the Skylands. We must get beyond the cloudwall and send a message to Uncle that the giga's coming again. And this time, it's coming for the heart of the Skylands' knowledge.

Dandun, the home of Scholar.

Bryce lowers beside me and sinks into the couch, entirely and utterly exhausted.

"Are you okay?" I ask.

"Still pissed."

"Because I pushed you into the escape pod?"

"Yes."

Her head rests on my shoulder, and her hand slips into mine. Even though she's angry, it seems she's grateful that we're both alive. That we did get to see each other again.

Another person stops before us, her face stoic.

"Kept this for you," she says, reaching out my black cane to me.

I stare at it. The cane of the original Urwin. My fingers gently follow the wings of the Urwin eagle.

I lower the cane and focus on my sister. "Ella, are you—"

She punches me.

My head rocks and I fall back, grimacing as I massage my jaw.

"That's for sending us away without you," Ella says.

I wince a little. "Ella . . ."

"No. You had no right making that decision for us. Do you know what you put on us, Conrad?"

I close my mouth.

But I had to ensure their survival. I've failed as a leader, but I couldn't lose everyone to save myself. Ella needed to be safe. And Bryce would not be sitting with me right now if I had gone into the pod instead of her.

"Ella, I am sorry."

She folds her arms. "Urwins don't apologize."

"I do."

She lets out a long sigh and paces the room. "Uncle's going to murder me when we get back," she whispers. "I abandoned him. If I hadn't come along, you and Bryce could've escaped together. You never would've been captured in the first place."

"Uncle won't harm you. He needs you. You're an Urwin."

She bites her lip, not entirely convinced. But she breathes out, relaxing from her burst of anger.

"Ella . . ."

"What's done is done," she says. "Let's just move forward from now, okay?"

"Are you—"

"I do not repeat myself, Conrad."

I breathe out. "Okay, Ella. Okay."

Bryce squeezes my hand. "Do you know what happened to the others? The crew?"

The reminder of my friends shuts my mouth. I shake my head, and the room goes quiet.

"You had a birthday," Ella says suddenly to me, cutting the tension.

Bryce sits up. "You did?!"

"Oh yeah," I say, scratching the back of my head. "But Goerner and I already celebrated, so don't worry about it. We made a lot of good memories together."

They laugh. I don't want to make this a big deal. It's not, and honestly, thinking about my age and just how young I am reminds me how many years I may still have and how none of them will include my parents. But Bryce and Ella try to make me smile. They each give me a birthday wish. Bryce wishes that I'll see the end of the war, and Ella jokingly wishes that I stop being a stubborn, pushy brother, before wishing that I will find peace and happiness.

It'd be nice to have some peace and happiness, and savor our reunion a bit more, but I have to know what happened after they escaped.

Bryce and Ella explain that just before their escape pod ran out of fuel, they landed on an island several miles from here. They were alone together. Stuck for days. Worse, the Lantians found them and chased them through the jungle. While Ella and Bryce hid in the darkest parts, where perhaps prowlons roamed, they made a small fire.

The glow of the fire attracted a fleeing skyship: the *Rimor.*

"Mage saved you?" I say, staring at them.

"Well," Bryce says, "it took some convincing over the comm. Like, we had to agree to not touch anything on his ship."

"And sign a contract that we'd never speak of any of his 'discoveries,'" Ella says.

"But we had leverage, too: the key to the vault."

Watching Ella and Bryce talk—almost finishing each other's sentences—makes me wonder just how close they've grown. It'd make sense though. They had to survive together.

"Mage couldn't resist that," Ella says. "So he lowered the ladder."

"Roderick would be so jealous that you got to see the inside of the ship," I say.

Bryce laughs, but the reminder of our friend makes my smile shrink. We all go quiet, sinking in the memories of him and all the others. Arika and Keeton, and even the newcomers, Yez, Otto, and Tara.

I clear my throat. "Sebastian claims he killed Roderick."

Bryce stares at me. "He what?"

"Sebastian turned, Bryce. He has a symbion."

She scoffs. "Impossible."

"It's how the Lantians knew we were coming to Perditio," I say. "They tracked him. We flew right into a trap."

Her mouth shuts. "Why would the Lantian Republic ever give someone like him a symbion? He's not from the Below."

I shake my head, unsure. He's always been a weasel.

Ella's watching me, and I consider telling her the truth of our ancestry. But I don't think on it long because the more people I share this secret with, the more likely Uncle will find out. He'd never allow Lantian blood to taint the Urwins. We'd be banished. Maybe executed.

Worse, I'm just not sure how Ella would respond to this. Her whole life is built around being an Urwin.

I pause.

Can it actually remain a secret? The Below knows. Sebastian knows. They gave me an opportunity to turn to their side, and I can't help but consider that, once they find out Ella and I are still alive, they'll use it against us.

I breathe out. Can't think of that right now. So I push it down, deep away, a problem for another time. For now, I need to know what happened to the rest of my crew.

I tap my comm gem, hoping that Pound kept his Hunter one.

"Have you found any evidence of other prisoners?" I ask him. "Roderick?"

The gem stays lit, but it takes a moment for him to reply. "Bloody uniforms. That's all."

My eyes shut.

They can't be dead. Don't want to believe they're gone. But Sebastian's words about Roderick keep coming back to me. The pride in his voice. Ecstasy. He's always been a liar, but sometimes, there are glimpses of truth, too.

Bryce squeezes my hand. Neither of us says a thing. All we can do is hope our friends are alive somewhere and that they got away.

"We're finishing up our search of the tunnels," Pound says. "If they're here, we'll find them."

"And the other ships in my squadron?"

"Either destroyed or taken with Goerner."

I sink back. Deflated.

Still . . . we have a mission. The Skylands need us.

I stand, Brone's key dangling from my neck. My brow wrinkling with determination.

"I've failed so many people during this war," I say to Bryce and Ella. "People who have counted on me died. Simply because I wasn't ready for this. But I—*we* are not going to fail this time. The Skylands are at stake."

Then I snatch my cane and storm toward the door. Ella and Bryce follow me.

"Mage," I say, tapping on my comm gem. "Come to Perditio's tunnels. It's time to open the vault."

✦✦✦

We gather before the vault's giant metal door. Everyone, including the Atwoods. Mage steps forward with the key, his pincer twisting excitedly. He's the one who knows how to operate the lock mechanism—at least, that's the hope.

He stuffs the key into the lock and twists it. But nothing happens. We stand around, looking at one another. Pound scratches the back of his head.

Mage steps back, hands on his hips. Then he raises his finger with an idea. But before he can proceed, Aggress shoves him aside.

"Move, little man."

Aggress stomps to the space around the key, glares at it, then growls as he pushes the mechanism with both hands. Suddenly, the whole lock shoves into the door, a click sounds, and a loud boom echoes.

The huge Atwood retreats as the door, with a great bang, yawns open.

"I was going to do that," Mage says, irritated.

"Took too long," Aggress rumbles.

Bryce and I glance at each other, our hearts thudding, as ancient, dusty air blows into our faces. Fear slices my heart. The Master of Weapon hid this because he worried what it might do to the world. He didn't even want his own people to have it.

Once the air filters away, we step inside. The space is adorned with old insignias of crossing swords, which I presume was the emblem of Weapon. In the center of the room stands some type of hulking red device resembling a cannon.

An ominous warning, scrawled hastily across the length of the barrel, reads: NO TURNING BACK.

CHAPTER 41

AFTER SLEEPING FOR HOURS ON END, I CLIMB TO THE *Gladian's* deck. Just as I open the hatch into the morning sky, Aggress sends an order to the armada, and my ship comes to an abrupt halt. The whole armada stops, including Mage's wooden vessel.

I rise to my feet, "Why did—"

Then I freeze. The acid clouds beneath us . . . they're gone. There's a distinct trail exposing the surface below the black. It cuts right through the black clouds like a spear.

Bryce leaves the helm bubble and joins Ella and me to look over the railing.

"Goerner," Mage says over the comm. "He must've taken the Vortex machine from Perditio."

"What machine?" Aggress asks.

After Mage explains, Aggress rumbles, "Dirt-eaters."

"That machine ate up the black clouds," Mage says, "creating this trail."

"Goerner must've mounted it to the hull of the *Golias*," Bryce says.

A barren landscape splays out beneath us. A long stripe of mountainous terrain. We're dumbfounded, staring in amazement at how vast the Below is. I can't get accustomed to the feeling. I'm disoriented. Suddenly, the sky isn't open: we have a solid floor beneath us, and we're tethered to it no matter where we go.

Gazing farther ahead of us, I notice the landscape below as it changes to water that stretches on and on. The water moves in waves, larger and grander than any lake. Its movement is mesmerizing. We watch the white waves for several seconds, and it'd be easy to forget about what we're supposed to be doing, but we can't delay, so I raise my gem to my mouth to speak to the Atwood Armada.

"We need to keep moving."

Aggress's low voice rumbles back over the comm. "You don't give the orders to this armada, *Urwin*." He pauses. "We follow this trail. It'll lead us straight to Goerner. If the winds are on our side, we can beat him to Dandun."

A series of "ayes" follows.

Of course they wouldn't listen to me.

Bryce pats my back, then returns to the helm platform. My ship has a skeleton crew. Just me, Bryce, and Ella. No Roderick, Otto, Arika, Keeton, Yesenia, or even Tara. The *Gladian* feels so empty. Lonely.

I glance at Mage's blue vessel at the head of the armada. Just then, a comm comes to me only.

"It would seem that you are no longer in charge, Prince."

I growl. *Yes, thank you, Mage.* This is the first time we've spoken since before the ambush.

"Happy to hear you haven't changed, Mage."

There's a pause, and I think for a moment that Mage is going to say that he's sorry about what happened to the squadron. To the others. But then my comm goes gray.

I exhale.

In seconds the Atwood Armada launches. Bryce shoves the strings forward, and we shoot to the head with Mage's vessel. The Atwood Armada is composed of giant old metallic ships with powerful cannons. Not built for speed like the *Gladian*, but heavily protected and armed. Even with the wind, even with the distance, I can still hear some of the bastards laughing.

We need to get to Dandun quickly, and the *Gladian's* far swifter than the Atwood Armada. But we only have a skeleton crew aboard, and we have Brone's weapon with us. Leaving the safety of the armada would be a huge risk.

I crank my magnetics and approach the bow. Ella follows me, and we're quiet as we stare at the Below again. It's just so . . . alien to see what's beneath. Almost wrong.

"It's like finding out you had a secret basement," Ella says from beside me. "You really want to know what's down there. Why would Goerner suck up the acid clouds now?"

I shift a little, wondering that same question. Perhaps this is to let more Lantians come to the Above to help in the upcoming battle. Maybe it's because he wants to move to a post-acid-clouds world. Or maybe it's something else we're completely unaware of.

"I don't like it," Ella says.

I almost agree. Then I pause and glance back at Bryce. Thinking of all the people like her, the young people in the Lantian Colonies who just want to see the stars. They've been locked away, under earth, ever since the Ascension, when the Skylands tore from the surface and gravitated into the sky.

"Regardless of what happens at Dandun," I say, "everything is going to change."

Ella goes quiet.

The wind lashes against the hull. I glance to the ship trailing just behind on the port side. It's painted sky blue and dotted with rust marks. The *Dominion*. Pound's ship. It's an old Warship-class—a retired class of vessels from Order. It's crewed by a collection of Pound's relatives: Stagg, Rolly, and even his sister, Noose. They all have terrible names, but they're a terrible family, so it makes sense.

Pound stands at the bow. He glances my way and nods. He got command of the *Dominion* after apparently beating both Stagg and Rolly in a duel. Well, the way he described it to me, it sounded more like a brawl than a duel.

Atwoods reward strength.

Pound may never become the head of his family again, but he has a place with them. And even though his family is full of birdshits, I'm happy for him. Happy to see him looking whole again.

Still, his vessel is skyshit. The deck's covered with patches and wobbly metal. The engine makes a strange whirring noise, even over the wind. And it even has one of the old Chaos cannons attached at the bow. Those double-barreled cannons were banned by Order because they tended to blow up or overload the engine. Very powerful, but very dangerous.

Of course, Pound kept it.

I glance back at the new cannon on my deck, hidden under a flapping tarp. As dangerous as Pound's Chaos cannon is, mine might be much worse. We're not even sure what the hell Brone's weapon does. It took hours to transport it and get it bolted to the deck. At first, Aggress demanded we put the weapon on his ship, the *Bedlam*. But when I reminded him that the weapon could potentially destroy the world, he shut his mouth, thought about it for a minute, and said he'd rather an Urwin die using it first.

A cold breeze hits us, and I squint through my spyglass. A storm grows in the distance—giant, pluming clouds and a dash of lightning. We don't have time to go around, either.

"Magnetics up," I say to the armada. "This might get rough."

Not even they are stupid enough to argue about that.

"Conrad," Bryce says to me over the comm. "If Goerner has the

Vortex sucking up the acid clouds—what will happen when he reaches Sky's Edge?"

My eyes widen. Could the Vortex destroy the cloudwall? I'm reeling from that possibility. But we won't know the answer to that question for miles, when we finally reach the wall's coordinates.

Ella nudges me. "Ship."

"What?"

She points at the distance. "There."

Something dark floats in the growing storm clouds. I quickly peer through my spyglass, and my eyes widen. The ship's smoking. Panicked crewmembers fight a fire. Is it one of Goerner's ships? But why would they leave it behind?

When we draw closer, my heart leaps. It's not one of Goerner's ships. It's the *Intrepid*! And the crew fighting the fire? I shout with surprise. That's Yesenia. That's Otto, Tara, Arika. And Keeton! Golden joy surges through me. My friends got away—somehow, they got away.

Even though their ship's on fire, I'm cheering. I lift my arm, preparing to send a comm as we draw nearer, when something else appears among the storm clouds. Something that should be in the cloudwall.

✦✦✦

An octolon tentacle descends toward the *Gladian*. I drop my mobile launcher and run. It's going to crush us all.

"Bryce!" I shout.

"I see it!"

She throws her hands against the strings. Goes to absolute war with them. We rocket forward, blazing through the rainy winds. My ankles scream from the tension between my magboots and the storm trying to knock me off.

We soar past the tentacle into a patch of open, rainy sky. Bryce is sweating. She can't even wipe her forehead. And we're not done yet, not even close.

The octolon tucks in its legs and darts for the *Intrepid*, but not before Bryce shoves the strings. The wind howls against my body, and I crank my magboots to the max. Take one difficult step at a time until I reach the turret. I strap myself in as Ella leaps onto the other turret.

We fly past the octolon, cutting it off.

And Ella and I lay hell into its head. Filling it with dozens of harpoons in thirty seconds. Individually, each attack is nothing more than a pin needle. But all of them, sticking into the scales—that makes the octolon thrash in fury.

"We have to save the *Intrepid*." I yell over the comm. "Every ship, kill the damn monster!"

The Atwoods roar in response. Either because they agree, or they're furious I'm giving them orders again.

Bryce pulls us to a stop, squarely in the path of the darting octolon. It's coming straight at us. Ella and I keep squeezing the triggers. My body's trembling with rage and fear. Can't lose the *Intrepid*. Can't lose my friends again. The whole chair vibrates with each harpoon launch. *Swoosh! Swoosh! Swoosh!*

The octolon nears the *Intrepid*, and my mouth goes dry.

The *Intrepid* can hardly move. It's slow as hell right now. We have to keep the octolon away. So my boot slams on a lever, and my barrels rotate. Now I'm lighting up the bastard like a pyromaniac. Golden explosions plume along its metallic scales. Swells of fire rush up its side.

Ella continues with harpoon after harpoon. Some gliding through the scales, leaving jets of white blood spraying into the storm.

The octolon slows to a stop and flails its massive tentacles at us.

Luckily, the slower Atwood ships arrive. And they pepper the colossal creature with everything. Explosions, harpoons, cannons. The octolon thrashes and pulls back, away from us and the *Intrepid*.

I breathe a little easier.

But we're not done yet. We've got to take this thing down. It'd be simpler if we could just rescue the *Intrepid* and fly on. But the Atwood Armada is too damn slow. The octolon would overtake them.

We have to kill it.

"After it!" I roar.

"Stop giving us orders," Aggress rumbles.

I don't give a damn. He can mute me if he has to. I'm not losing another *Dauntless.*

Now the armada encircles the octolon. The creature's limbs lash out. A single one could crush multiple ships at once.

Bryce throws her hands again, and we launch after the octolon. I wipe the rain streaks from my goggles. The beast's tentacles flail around the armada. The Atwoods laugh over the comm, like this is a game. But Bryce is all fiery concentration. She swerves us over a tentacle and dives us below another, giving Ella and me another shot at the octolon's head.

Ella and I shout as we attack. The air's sparking with flak and smoke. Volleys of harpoons dig into the beast. Just one of those might take out its one remaining eye.

The octolon tucks its legs in again and retreats.

"Pound," I say over the comm, breathing hard. "Did you fight this thing in Sky's Edge?"

"No," he rumbles. "The thing was lucky we didn't see it."

While the octolon fights the Atwoods again, I reload the turret and glance back at the *Intrepid.* The *Intrepid's* crew has extinguished their fire, and their ship's limping away from the battle to a safer distance. Eventually, they stop near Mage's vessel, far off from us.

I raise my comm to contact them, but an explosion rings the air. Pound's on the Chaos cannon—squeezing the triggers and sending two enormous blasts at a time. The blasts make the air quake.

His ship groans. The hull of the *Dominion* ripples each time he sends a blast.

My eyes widen. That horrible cannon's going to destroy his ship.

Bryce throws her hands forward again, making us blast toward the *Dominion.*

"Pound," I shout. "Stop firing that c—"

One of the explosions strikes the octolon's tentacle and severs a sucker-covered chunk. I watch in shock as it falls. Pound's laughing triumphantly over the gem. Atwood ships zoom away from the enormous falling lump.

The octolon turns, its remaining eye narrowing on the *Dominion.* Then it throws all its tentacles at the ship.

"BRING IT!" Pound rumbles.

He fires again; his whole ship vibrates. It's breaking apart.

"POUND!" I yell.

The air thunders from his attack, and another part of the octolon falls. The octolon shrieks, rears back, and pulls its tentacles in defensively.

He squeezes the trigger again, but only smoke comes from his cannon's barrel. His brow furrows. He slams against the controls. And squeezes again.

"What the hell?!" he roars. "It's not responding."

The octolon must sense weakness because it unfurls its tentacles again. They soar for the *Dominion.* Bryce flies us to cut it off. *Shit! We're not going to make it in time.* I swivel my turret and unload harpoons. The attacks vibrate my whole body.

"Move, Pound!" Bryce yells over the comm.

He looks back at us, horrified. "We can't move."

"Your damn cannon fried the engine," I say.

Ella fires at the octolon. Shouting like she can get its attention. But it's focused entirely on the *Dominion* now, gliding toward it, furious.

Stagg and Rolly run for the *Dominion's* stern as the shadow grows over them. Noose struggles with the ship's strings from inside the small command tower. Urging the *Dominon* to move.

Bryce aims our bow toward the *Dominion* and launches us.

"Bryce," I cry, "What are you—?"

We slam into the *Dominion's* hull. The collision rocks us viciously. My head nearly hits the turret's controls. Metal grinds. The ships groan. Bryce yells, shoving again, willing us against the *Dominion.* Making both ships move.

Pound's eyes are wide with shock.

Bryce keeps it up until we pick up speed. Moving both ships away from the reaching tentacles. That gives the Atwood vessels time to catch up and pummel the octolon again.

Bryce's arms struggle against the strings' resistance. And finally, she pushes us safely away from the battle. The Atwood Armada sails around the beast's bulbous head.

Despite everything, we haven't done enough to the octolon. It's not going to go down.

"I'm extending a gangway to your ship," I say to Pound over the comm. "Get aboard."

"Go punch yourself," Pound says. "This is my ship. I'm not leaving it."

"It's dead, you idiot."

"Not yet," his sister, Noose, says over the comm. Then she leaves her station inside the command tower. Probably to check on the engine belowdecks.

I shake my head. Some ship he's running over there. People abandoning their stations and a cannon that destroyed the engine. Then again, it's not like I've been a glorious leader, either.

The war with the octolon continues. The octolon's arms fly through the Atwood ships. Nearly destroying two with a single swipe. But the old ships always manage to duck away. Little explosions ripple against the scales of the monster. Hardly doing any damage. The only thing that has managed to hurt it was Pound's stupid cannon.

I lick my lips. We could try flying away, but we'd be abandoning the Atwood Armada. I sit until a horrible thought fills me. Don't want to do this. Brone's ominous warning flashes in my mind.

No turning back.

"Prince," Mage says suddenly over the comm, as if he knows my thoughts. His ship has watched from the distance the entire time. "Hunting is your territory, but perhaps it is time to consider using that new weapon of yours?"

My skin crawls. There's no telling what it could do. Maybe it'd kill everyone in the area or destroy the whole world. Besides, we need to save it for the gigataun. There's no telling how many shots we'll have with it.

"Realistically, where the *Gladian* stands now, you are at a safe distance," Mage says. "But do what you think is best."

"We don't know what it'll do, Mage!" I shout.

"I imagine it will cause damage to the octolon."

"And the aftershock?"

"You have a fast ship. Fly away if necessary."

My brow furrows. My skin feels clammy. Pound's yelling at me to decide because it's his family out there.

I shut my eyes.

No turning back.

"I'm firing the weapon," I say to Pound over the comm.

He sends a warning to his family over the comm, but they keep circling the octolon.

My heart's thudding. Body numb as I unfasten the tarp and leap into the ancient weapon's seat. The aged leather cracks under my weight. I crank the wheel to make the barrel rise—we had to oil this rusty thing like hell—and peer down a foggy scope at the octolon. The beast's giant tentacles reach for the *Bedlam*, ready to bring down Aggress's ship.

My hands are shaking.

"Fire!" Pound roars over the comm.

I glance at Bryce. Take a breath. Then squeeze the trigger.

Nothing happens.

I try again.

"You have to hold it down," Mage says. "That's what the manual says. Hold it down until . . . well . . ."

"There's a manual?" I growl.

"Oh—yes. I took it. Didn't I mention that?"

Damned Explorer.

I swallow my spit and grip the aged triggers. They're rusted stiff. I press them down and hold. And as I'm squeezing, the *Gladian* quivers. Throbs from a steady, thrumming tremor. The weapon's been connected to our engine. Pulls energy from it. Suddenly, I'm nearly blinded as a beam of light, bright as the sun, dashes across the sky. It sears past the Atwood fleet and right into the bulbous, scaly head of the octolon. The intense beam leaves me blinking in splotches.

The light sinks into the octolon, and then . . . nothing happens. The beam just sort of vanishes.

"What the hell, Elise?" Pound roars. "That didn't do—"

BOOM!

The octolon shrieks as a swelling light appears in the center of its enormous head. A white void, like a tornado, sucks the beast into itself. The octolon's metal cracks. White blood spirals into a horrifying vortex of light.

I wince from the brightness.

Finally, the Atwood fleet jets away.

The octolon collapses in on itself. Its whole body, almost turning inside out, is sucked into a white nothing. The octolon's eye flashes in fear, its tentacles reaching out for anything, hoping to pull itself away. But it's sucked inside, and everything goes still.

Pound starts laughing until the octolon reappears all at once and explodes.

"Fly!" I shout. "Bryce, fly!"

She shoves against the *Dominion* again, pushing our ships away as chunks of metallic tentacles and suckers rain down. The other ships disperse, jerking between falling flesh and organs.

After the final pieces fall, the Atwoods raise their hands in triumph. Singing. Laughing. Pushing one another. But I sit, staring at the space where the octolon was. Then my eyes travel to the sizzling barrel of Brone's weapon. This thing—it could destroy islands. In one shot. An entire island could be wiped out.

"Now," Mage says quietly, "I understand its name."

"It has a name?" Bryce says.

"The Collapser."

White blood mists the air. Caught in the storm. It sprinkles the deck and dots my goggles. Pound marches up to the bow of his dead ship and points ahead of us.

"We're coming, giga." He laughs. "We're coming."

CHAPTER 42

I'D LOVE NOTHING MORE THAN TO GREET MY FRIENDS ON the deck. But I know that something must have happened to the cloudwall. That's why the octolon was out. Was the whole cloudwall destroyed? Impossible to know now. But at least part of it must be gone. And knowing this, before we pull alongside the *Intrepid*, I hurry to my cabin, hoping to send a message to Uncle. We're still miles from where Sky's Edge should be, so we have no way of knowing for sure.

I push into my cabin and squint from the window. We're back in the blue afternoon sky, away from the storm. I tap the special comm Uncle gave me, almost half expecting it to gray out. But the light stays glowing. My heart surges with relief.

"Conrad," Uncle says, almost breathless. "You're alive."

"The giga is coming," I say quickly. "To Dandun."

He pauses. "They're coming after the Scholars." He exhales, calculating what this information means. "My fleet's in the Central Skies. We're miles away." His voice gains an edge. "We have to beat Goerner there."

He sends an order to his fleet, his voice urgent and fierce. They're to set out immediately toward Dandun.

"Were you successful, Conrad? Did you get the weapon?"

"It's operational," I say. "And incredibly powerful. If we get a clean shot with the Collapser, we have a chance to take out the gigataun."

Uncle breathes out. "Good. Very good work, Conrad. How quickly can you make it to Dandun?"

I hesitate. Even after a month's time trapped on Perditio, the wound's still fresh. "My squadron's gone. Some of my crew's missing. We were ambushed."

He's quiet.

"We have an escort of other ships with us now, but they're old." I pause—realizing that he might ask who they are. I plow ahead quickly. "It will take us time."

"Then leave them," Uncle says.

"Goerner likely knows we're coming. We might get ambushed again and lose the weapon—the Collapser cannon."

Uncle pauses. "I see. Be as swift as possible."

"We're pushing every engine to the brink. We'll make it."

We go quiet, and my stomach knots because there's something else I need to tell him. Don't want to, but he's probably dedicating resources. Ships that could be helpful in a fight at Dandun. I sit, staring through the window at the wisps of white clouds. A huge pod of balenons flies beside us, likely heading toward where the cloudwall was.

"Ella's with me."

"What?"

No telling what he'd do with her. The punishment she might receive at his hands . . .

My pulse quickens. "I brought her with me against her will."

He's silent.

"It was a mistake, Uncle. You can't force someone to love you. I realize that now. But she's safe. She wasn't with you when your fleet was attacked by the gorgantauns. She's been aboard my vessel the whole time."

He still doesn't respond. I wipe my sweaty hands on my pants. Knead my knuckles against my thighs.

His voice starts, slow and stern. "You are stubborn, Conrad, and for this treasonous act, I should expel you from Urwin." He pauses, and I'm waiting for the punishment. "But if this Collapser device does what you say it can, the islands will praise our name."

I blink, suddenly realizing that maybe I'm getting off easy. He's not going to punish me so long as the weapon works. Of course. Uncle doesn't care about betrayal if he still has power. And he'll do anything, kill anyone, even family, for that power.

Suddenly, another thought creeps into my mind. I'm bringing the Collapser to Uncle. What would he do with something of that power? Assuming it works against the gigataun, what would he use it on next?

My chest tightens. Once I use the cannon, I must destroy it.

Uncle asks for a report on the uncharted airs. So I explain the hidden ecosystem and Tara's warning that it will feed the gorgantaun population if released.

"I'm not concerned about population theories at present," he says. "Get to Dandun and do not stop for anything. You fly. All day. All night. Do it in shifts. We must not let Dandun fall. We cannot lose the Scholars. We're *not* repeating the mistake of Holmstead; Dandun has an evacuation plan." He pauses. "I have preparations to make. We will await your arrival there. Understood?"

"Yes."

"Good."

He disconnects, and I hurry out of the cabin because I have other concerns—other people to meet with. The *Intrepid* had structural damage—a leak of gorgantaun gas, and it's only a matter of time before it falls from the sky. So everyone aboard that ship has spread among the Atwood Armada, including Oba and the remnants of his crew, to whom Aggress has given command of a small vessel.

I call for a reunion of friends in the cafeteria and jog there. But once inside, I pause because I catch Pound talking to Arika. I'm relieved to see her alive, and shocked to see that she's already cooking something. But there's an uncomfortable energy in the room.

"I'm sorry, Arika," Pound says. "I—had to go to my family."

Arika's back faces him. She's aggressively stirring something.

I backpedal until Arika spots me.

"Captain! It's so good to see you again! Have a seat. I'm cooking up a meal to recharge everyone and celebrate our reunion."

Arika steps around Pound, ignoring him, and comes straight for me. Pound's head lowers. She hugs me. It's a quick, fierce, and surprising thing. Then she drags me to a seat. Pound's following. Finally, once Arika forces me to sit, she whirls on Pound.

"I'm not upset because you went to find your family. I'm upset because you left without saying goodbye."

She sweeps past him, leaving him standing awkwardly. His face is splotchy red. And my own face is a little hot, too.

Pound grumbles and lowers next to me. For a moment I consider patting his back. But I'm certain he'd knock me unconscious. So I just sit, awkwardly, almost forgetting why I came here in the first place.

Yez and Tara are the next to enter. I'm not just relieved to see them but grateful to have someone else in the room. I stand and reach out to shake Yez's hand. Her grip's powerful. The hands of a Navigator who fights the strings. But she suffered burns on the *Intrepid*.

"Captain," Yez says, "I will fly the next shift."

I study her and her injuries. "You're sure?"

She eyes me, a little irritated. "If I weren't sure, I wouldn't have said it."

I almost grin. She's always had an edge, and I'm glad that hasn't changed. She sits at the end of the table, away from me and Pound, and unbundles a journal. Navigator charts. She jots a few things down. Like any good Navigator, she's been charting the uncharted airs.

Tara, meanwhile, eagerly asks me for as much information as I can provide on the Lantians and their strange creatures.

I tell Tara, quickly, about the glowlons and the leptauns. She eagerly writes them in her notebook. Asking for descriptions.

"What else?"

"Later," I say.

She frowns, irritated, but doesn't argue.

Otto enters and lowers a laundry bag in the corner. He appears to have grown an inch or two since I saw him last.

Ella pushes through the door, her red dueling cane dangling from her hip. She sits on the bench beside me. Pound nods at her, and Otto watches her.

Noose joins us next. Apparently, at least one of Pound's family came aboard. Stagg and Rolly, from what I've heard, went to another ship rather than serve under an Urwin. Noose's dark hair's tied in a ponytail. Oh, she's a fierce one. Remember her from Holmstead. Still, she's kinder than some of the Atwoods. One time, when Pound attacked me in the Lows, she told him to stop.

And he actually listened to her.

She's almost Ella's age, and when she looks for her brother, she finds Ella nearby. She scowls, gives my sister dagger eyes, and leans against the wall, arms folded.

Finally, Bryce steps in with someone I've been dying to speak with.

I stand. Hugging people doesn't come naturally to me, but I wrap Keeton in my arms. Pull her in close, just so grateful that we can be together again. One of my closest and fiercest friends. Keeton grips my back. Her body's shaking.

"Keeton," I say, pulling back. "What's wrong?"

"He's gone."

I blink, and then my heart drops. Realizing what she's saying. What Sebastian claimed. But he was lying. Sebastian is a liar. He didn't kill Roderick. Couldn't have.

"They took him," she says. "The Lantians took him."

"Wait, he's alive? But Sebastian told me—?"

Keeton licks her teeth bitterly. "He lied."

My stomach drowns in a mixture of relief and fear. Roderick alive. He's alive! But he's gone, and now I sink into horrible emptiness realizing that he's all alone. Maybe hurting, afraid, and missing all of us.

"I don't understand," Ella says. "Why would they take Roderick?"

"I know why," Pound thunders, his fist slamming against the table. "Because there's not a better Master Gunner in all the Skylands, and the Lantians are trying to win the war."

The room quiets.

I should be grateful knowing Rod's not dead. But how can I be? If Pound's right, Rod's being forced to create weapons for the enemy.

We all sit while Keeton tells us what happened back at Perditio. She explains that after I was captured, locked in paralysis, Roderick came to save me. He raced from the munitions room with weapons draping his massive shoulders.

"But Sebastian shot him," Keeton says bitterly. "The Lantians carried Rod away. We thought we were dead, until Oba's people regained control of the *Intrepid*. The *Intrepid* slammed into us, trying to save"—she pauses and meets my eyes—"you. When we couldn't get to you, or Roderick, we rocketed away on the *Intrepid*," Keeton says. "The Lantians didn't chase us because they had their prize. They had the heir. We've been struggling in the uncharted airs ever since. Trying to devise a way to save you from Perditio. Late last night, we saw Goerner's fleet shoot past, and not long later, a storm approached us with the octolon inside."

Keeton wipes her eyes, and Bryce and Arika hug her.

Pound thumps the table again, stands and walks to the window.

We watch him. His face red, splotched with heat and anger. For a long moment, he's quiet. Then he turns to face us, his eyes fiery.

"We're going to save the Skylands." He stomps to Keeton and catches her hand. "But I promise you, after we bring down that bastard gigataun, we will find Roderick. And when I get hold of Sebastian, I will lift him in the air, and I will yank out his serpent tongue and crush his spine."

No one says anything. No one quite knows what to say. But I'm with Pound. We have to save the Skylands first. Then we'll find Roderick.

We *will* find him.

✦✦✦

I enter Roderick's munitions room. It's a disheveled mess, partially because Roderick's a mess, but also because the Lantians raided it.

Blueprints rest on the floor. Creation is Roderick's joy. He's an artist of weapons. What would he say to me now, as I lift his papers? Call me a cuss for touching his things?

I stop and stare at a device sitting on his workbench. His mini clawgun that he originally dubbed "the Roderick." My fingers lift it and inspect the smooth metal and the straps. He's made several more versions of these. New and better iterations.

My chest is tight. Many people have given me credit for taking down the class-five gorgantaun by myself. It was the talk of the islands for a time. But the truth is, I never would've been able to kill that bull without Roderick's invention.

Without him, I never would've won over this crew. Never would've won the Gauntlet or reunited with Ella.

I owe Roderick everything.

I flip through a few scattered papers, past his diagrams of the repeater turret enhancement, and his calibrations for the flame turret. But my eyes narrow as I find another paper among the blueprints. Scratchy handwriting. It's titled:

Kid names.

My heart cracks. Roderick wrote out favorite names for future children. My eyes threaten to spill over as I read these little names. Because I know there's a strong chance I'll never see him again. That he'll never get to have these children because the enemy will kill him when he resists helping them.

Roderick's noble and good. The world's cruel to people like him. Cruel to the kind of people who just want to live—have a family. Be happy.

Baines. He wants a boy named Baines. And a girl named Olywn.

Baines of Madison. Olywn of Madison.

The paper shakes in my hand as I stare at it. My teeth grind. No, I'm not going to think as if he's already gone. Roderick will have his children one day, and they'll be sweet and weird and funny.

I fold the paper and gently place it in the interior pocket of my jacket. Don't want Keeton to see this. Won't let her see this.

It'll break her.

Then, as I'm walking from the munitions room and entering the corridor, I almost hear Sebastian's laugh slither into my ear. Almost see the triumph on his face again. And I remember him laughing as I escaped the Perditio tunnels.

Laughing because he tricked me about Roderick.

Laughing because he wants me to hate him.

Wants me to kill him.

Well, that rat bastard's got his wish. The next time I see him, I'm going to cut his symbion slowly from his neck, strap him to the bow of my ship, and let the birds peck at the wound. I'm not going to give him the honor of a Skylands death. No, I'll beat him, then drop whatever's left of him to rot on an island.

That bastard will regret his life.

CHAPTER 43

AS YESENIA SHOVES THE STRINGS THROUGHOUT THE NIGHT and rockets us into the Eastern Skies toward Dandun, it becomes clear that the Below's winning the war. Gorgantauns fill the sky. Almost everywhere we go, we pass islands bearing the scars of an attack. Retreating ships zoom past us, giving us dire warnings about what lies ahead.

We continue following the trail where Goerner's ship has eaten away at the black clouds, and we get the first reports about Dandun over the comm. And can only listen in horror to the desperate shouts.

The gigataun has returned.

My gem's connected with the King. He got to Dandun only an hour ago, and now he's screaming orders. Getting ships into formation. Telling them there will be no retreat. Dandun must not fall, and they must hold out until our arrival.

Yesenia has been flying for hours. I offer to take the strings, but she shakes her head. She's the best flier. Built for this. Still, we're moving too slow. The Atwood Armada's ships just don't have our speed.

"Conrad!" Pound shouts from a turret. "LOOK!"

My brow knits as fifteen forms appear in the distant sunrise, just before the islands that border Dandun. They undulate like long ribbons. Hundreds of feet long.

The hair on the back of my neck rises. These are the beasts the ships warned us about.

Mage's ship dives away and fires off into the distance. The coward. Tara shouts at him over the comm, but he doesn't answer. Not that he'd help us anyway. He's got his discoveries on his ship, and we let him keep Brone's key.

Fifteen gorgantauns charge toward us. All are class-six or class-seven. Our armada of old ships and the *Gladian* are no match for a pod of beasts this large. My skin tingles as the beasts bellow. But then I realize something about them while they're bathed under the orange sunrise. Something about their color as they get closer.

They're not silver.

They're red.

"Gigatauns!" Bryce yells over the comm. "Baby gigatauns!"

The Atwood comms fill with surprised shouts. We can't let them escape. These beasts aren't headed for Dandun. No, they're leaving to spread into the world. They will destroy the islands. But we don't have time to take them down, either. Not with their mother approaching Dandun. Uncle's shouting that it just destroyed a carrier.

"The weapon," Pound says. "Conrad, we need to use the weapon on these beasts."

"Another attack might fry the engine," Keeton says over the comm. "We almost destroyed it last time. I spent hours patching it up."

"Fine," Pound says, kicking a lever on Roderick's turret. "We'll do it the traditional way."

"No, Pound," Aggress says over the comm.

Pound pauses. "Father?"

"This," Aggress says, "is our duty to the Skylands. Conrad must get his ship to Dandun. We will create an opening."

"No!" Pound roars. "We're not leaving you."

"You will go, my son," Aggress says. "You will save the Skylands. ATWOOD ARMADA! FIRE!"

Explosions immediately heat the air—the aftershocks whip my hair back. The baby gigas bellow, their blue eyes narrowing on the Atwood ships.

"Go, Conrad," Aggress tells me. "GO."

And the armada veers off from us, firing at the gigas, attracting their attention.

"Don't you leave them!" Pound screams at me. "Conrad, don't you—"

"He has to." Noose touches his arm. "Pound, you have to trust your family."

Pound grimaces and shuts his mouth. He just got his family back, and now he can't help them in their time of need.

My heart sinks as the gigas turn toward the explosive blasts. They're enormous. And with all the other beasts from behind the cloudwall freed, they'll have plenty of energy to grow.

Hell, they might be fine just eating the gorgantauns.

It goes against my first instinct. Never run. Don't back down. Reminds me of Kirsi . . . and the *Dauntless*. But Uncle's screaming for me to hurry. His fleet's dying. And Goerner's ships and creatures are attacking the King's fleet, protecting the gigataun.

Don't have a choice.

"FLY!" I shout to Yesenia. "ON TO DANDUN!"

Pound watches in silence as his family engages the baby gigas. The ships weave in and around them. Shooting hot blasts into their thinner, juvenile scales. Yez shoves us downward, low enough that we should be hitting the acid clouds, but they're gone here.

"Engine at three hundred percent," Keeton says over the comm. "Give it all you've got, Yez."

Yesenia's brow furrows. Then she pushes against the golden strings. The sudden burst rocks me back, and we launch toward the battle that will decide the fate of the Skylands.

✦✦✦

We're flying around the dense group of islets surrounding Dandun. They block our line of sight of the horrific battle beyond.

"Acidons!" Arika shouts.

The snakelike creatures slip out of crevices in the islets, waiting in ambush. A whole swarm of them. Ten or more.

"Duck!" I shout as the acidons rear their frilled heads back and spit gelatinous globs of acid at us.

I dive to the deck. Yez yells and drops us into a nosedive. The wind flies across the hull. I clench my jaw, catch my mobile launcher, and pull on the railing net to regain my footing.

Yez pulls back, righting the ship. Now the acidons trail us, rearing their heads again. Pound and Bryce fire harpoons from the turrets. Though the brown-scaled acidons are each fifty feet in length, the slender beasts weave smoothly around the projectiles.

The golden-eyed creatures expose their long, silver fangs and spit acid again. Yez jerks us away while Pound and Bryce continue firing. Using Roderick's incredible repeater turret tech. And as swift as the acidons are, they're not perfect.

"BASTARDS!" Pound roars.

His harpoons decapitate several. The acidons thrash, their bodies dropping, acid raining. But one beast spits. The glowing glob flies directly for Ella at the stern. My heart climbs into my throat.

"Ella!"

Noose dives into my sister. They slam into the deck, and the green acid soars past them. It splashes against the deck and railing. Sizzling. Melting the metal. The railing sinks under the ooze. Ella and Noose stare at each other briefly. Then Noose grabs her shoulder cannon and fires, killing an acidon.

She gives Ella a pitying look, then stomps away.

Yez rockets us away from the other acidons. But when we pass another small island, more acidons slither out.

"PORT SIDE!" Arika cries. "THEY'RE EVERYWHERE!"

Damn these things! We're not even going to make it to Dandun.

Uncle cries over the comm for us. Telling us we're running out of time. But we can't make it. Not with these horrible creatures lying in wait for us. As if they're being orchestrated to do this.

My shoulder vibrates as I launch a harpoon. It spears through the throat of a hissing acidon—puncturing the acid glands and making them spill over the beast—melting its scales.

Six more acidons near. Dodging around Bryce's attacks. Getting close enough to spit.

Arika fires a shot that soars into nothing but sky. I hastily shove a harpoon into my launcher. Need a shoulder cannon. The acidons rear their heads. Pound roars, trying to switch his turret barrel to explosives.

Yez thrusts her arms forward. But it won't be enough. They're going to melt us.

That's when two ships suddenly zoom right above us. So close their winds almost knock me over. And I stand in amazement.

Pound roars in celebration.

It's the *Archer* and the *Henry*. Master Koko and Madeline de Beaumont.

"Thought you needed assistance," Master Koko says over the comm.

The two veteran Hunters go to war on the acidons. The *Henry's* ancient cannons pulverize chunks of rock in the islands. Exposing more hidden acidons. Then the *Archer*, with its incredible row of harpoon turrets, shreds the damn creatures before they can even escape from their lairs.

"Go!" Madeline tells me over the comm. "Save the Skylands."

"YEZ!" I roar.

We zip past as Madeline's and Koko's ships battle the dozens of creatures that keep slipping from the crevices. But we've got an opening now.

"WHERE THE HELL ARE YOU?!" Uncle roars.

"HERE!"

We rocket past the numerous islets and soar toward a horrific sight. It steals my breath. Dandun Island. The sky's complete pandemonium. Fire. Screams. Falling Order carriers. Shrieking tortons breathing death into ships. Sparrows spiraling toward the exposed surface below.

Beyond all that, the *Dreadnought* follows the most dangerous beast in the sky. Peppering the red scales with enormous, powerful cannons.

The gigataun.

The Skylands forces spiral in a cyclone around the five-thousand-foot beast. Firing everything they've got at the monster while ignoring the attacks coming from nearby gorgantauns. The giga's about to slam its head into Dandun's underside. We're still a few miles off and don't have a clear shot because a trio of orcons cuts us off.

Yesenia shoves the strings to avoid the orcons' ramming skulls. Otto and Arika fire at the creatures. Beyond them, another pair of orcons attacks a battlecruiser. They headbutt the hull, knocking screaming soldiers overboard. The orcons dive to scoop them into their mouths.

Yez swerves past them.

We all fight with everything we've got. Bryce, Arika, Ella, and I launch harpoons. Pound makes the air crack with explosives. His sister's firing flak into the eyes of neighboring orcons.

Suddenly, calamauns tuck their tentacles in and jet for our ship. One latches onto our hull, tentacles hitting the deck. Creating a wall around Pound's sister. Noose stabs the tentacle with harpoons. The calamaun comes closer, its eager beak snapping for her. Ready to bite her in half.

Ella pulls out a mini explosive. She shakes it fiercely, then hurls it directly into the calamaun's beak. A second later the beast explodes, and its tentacles slide free. This time, Ella gives Noose the pitying look.

In the distance, well out of reach from the battle, is Goerner's ship. Its tower is the thing controlling all these beasts. Lines of gorgantauns are shielding it from any blast.

A huge gorgantaun bull dives toward us.

"FIRE YOUR WEAPON!" Uncle cries. "CONRAD, NOW!"

"We can't! The beasts are everywhere!"

His voice projects over the whole fleet. "Protect the *Gladian*. At all costs."

Yesenia, arms shaking, pulls above the bull's mouth, and we loop through its coils. We've got one shot with the Collapser before it destroys our engine. But we need to get closer.

Pound swivels his turret and pellets our pursuing orcons with blasts that rip off their jaws. They careen into one another. Bryce attacks the gorgantaun bull.

Now a baby giga turns toward us. Blue eyes hungry.

I almost sink into despair as I fire again and again. No matter how many we kill, two more creatures always replace them.

Yez somehow jerks us to evade the ramming orcons and the chomping baby giga. Otto rushes to join Noose and Ella. He's lugging a big bag of mini explosives. Soon they're all frantically hurling the tiny barrels. When they detonate, the deck shimmers with golden light. The baby gigataun bellows. But its mouth comes after Pound.

Pound's laughing. Firing like mad.

"Get out of there!" Noose shouts at him.

But he keeps firing. One of his shots flies up the monster's nostril, opening its mouth. And at that exact moment, Otto rushes to Pound's side. Otto narrows his eyes, then hurls a mini explosive. It soars into the young beast's mouth and explodes.

It ruptures the baby giga's internal gas sac, and the beast moans as it plummets from the sky.

Pound glances at Otto with shocked glee. "I was wrong about you, Swabbie!"

Finally, the King's ship joins us, and we're flanked by a half dozen Order vessels, a pair of Predator-class vessels, and more. The *Archer* and the *Henry* reappear, too. Madeline and Master Koko. Together this convoy absolutely shreds the charging monsters and sends several orcons plummeting.

A surprise baby giga swoops beneath us, ready to swallow us whole—until the Order battlecruisers release all they've got into the beast. The air mists with its blood.

Now we're nearly within range of the mother gigataun. Suddenly, a gorgantaun, class-eight maybe, with rusted scales, charges after us. But our support fires everything into it at once. Harpoons, cannons, explosives. The beast thrashes its enormous head, confused. Allowing us to weave through its many coils and zip past its sharp, scimitar-like tail.

And then we're free. Got an open shot at the gigataun.

"FIRE!" Uncle roars. "CONRAD, FIRE!"

The giga, bellowing, slams its enormous head into Dandun's base. The desert dunes that surround the domes of the golden city shudder. Buildings topple. Hundreds of years of research held in those secret libraries. The creation of our medicine—all our understanding . . . not all of it could be evacuated, even with advance warning. There's just too much.

And it's all going to vanish.

I pull down my tinted goggles, leap onto the Collapser turret, and squeeze the triggers until a beam of light erupts from the barrel. Even with my tinted goggles, my eyes burn from the brightness. The beam travels across the sky. Right in line for the monstrous creature.

We've got it. We're going to get the damned monster!

Wait. I lean forward, squinting through the splotches in my vision. No—something's wrong. My shot—it targeted something else. Something swooped in our way, and the cannon locked onto it instead.

Dread pools through me.

An explosion fills the air. Pound roars in triumph—until realizing that the cannon locked onto a camouflaged torton that flew between us and the gigataun. The torton bellows as its body implodes inward, sucked into the Collapser's vortex.

Yesenia jerks us back to avoid the sucking storm. The other ships scatter. As we're zipping away, the torton vanishes, then reappears—its entrails and parts exploding into the sky.

No. Can't believe it. Our one shot wasted on a damn torton. A TORTON!

"What happened?!" Uncle bellows. "Conrad—"

We sit in stunned silence while the mother giga burrows into Dandun. Munching through rock. Going for the island's heart. The island has minutes, at most. My crew doesn't know what to say. I sit, blinking, staring. There must be more left in the engine. Something we can do. Anything.

"Keeton," I say over the comm. "Could we—"

"Our engine's crystal is spent. We need a new one."

"What if we fired again?"

"It won't work," she says. "If it did—" She pauses. "It'd kill us all. The ship would explode."

My skin tingles.

Uncle's still shouting at me. The fleet continues around my ship, fighting off attacks. We have no other option. No time, either. I glance at my friends and suck in a breath.

"Abandon ship."

"What?" Bryce says. "No, Conrad, you're not firing that thing again!"

"There's no other option," I say. "Get on the lifeboat."

For several seconds, they argue. Refuse to get off, but I am the Prince of the Skylands, and for once, I'm using that title to give orders. Pound tells me he doesn't give a damn, so I ask him as a friend.

His eyes water as he looks at me.

"Conrad, no!" Ella cries as Pound catches her and pulls her with him. "No. Please, Brother. Don't do this. Don't."

Bryce rushes to me. Her eyes spilling over as she leans in to kiss me. Her lips are soft, salty. And my heartbeat nearly goes still. Sooner than I'd like, she pulls away and races toward a lifeboat.

Ella's still begging me. Held back by Pound, and Keeton who just joined them. Arika, Noose, Yesenia, and Otto leap onto a lifeboat. Tara appears on deck. In her arms she's got a huge bag stuffed with books and papers. Yez and Noose help her aboard their boat.

Bryce hugs my struggling sister. My vision blurs as I raise my hand in farewell to them both.

Once the lifeboats lift off, soaring into the fray to join a neighboring vessel, I take a breath and stare down the aged reticule. My hands are numb, but strangely, my heart's calm.

The giga burrows deeper.

I swallow a breath, then narrow my eyes on the beast. This giant bastard dropped Ironside. Destroyed my home island. Killed McGill, and so, so many others.

Uncle may have handed me the title of Prince, but now it's time to earn it.

I squeeze the trigger, hoping my ship will give me one last thing. But the triggers merely click. Nothing happens. I swear and keep squeezing.

"C'MON, YOU PIECE OF SHIT!"

Gorgantauns charge after the ships protecting me. One coils around a battlecruiser and crushes the command tower. More orcons and tortons focus on us. The beasts are coming from all directions. A swarm of them.

Goerner knows what I'm trying to do. The air's filled with hellish blasts and shrieks that make me wince.

"FIRE, DAMMIT!"

I don't stop squeezing, until suddenly, the *Gladian* starts rumbling. Buzzing under my seat, vibrating my boots. I laugh. *IT'S WORKING! IT'S WORKING!* The *Gladian's* giving me the last of its life. A sudden jet of light blazes from the end of the cannon. And I'm cackling as the beam darts across the sky.

The beam connects with the enormous, red scales of the giga.

But my laughter fades as my ship trembles dangerously. The *Gladian* is going to explode. But I'm not dying if I can help it. I unclip from the belt, turn off my magboots, and race across the deck toward the munitions platform.

My one chance to get off this ship alive. I left them on the munitions platform, just in case. You never know.

The *Gladian* tremors again. It has only seconds.

My hands search in desperation. Where the hell did I put them? I dig around the harpoons, the explosives, the mobile launchers. Then I find one tucked inside a bag of mini explosives.

Oh, this is crazy as birdshit. But I've done crazier before.

An explosion thunders in my ears. Shakes my whole body like hell, and my knees slam into the deck. The *Gladian* growls, and the stern collapses. Suddenly, my ship begins to topple forward.

My stomach lurches as the wind howls. I lock one arm over a bar of the munitions platform and hastily strap my last chance to my wrist: a mini clawgun.

Maybe Roderick will save me one more time.

I crank my magnetics, stand, and run for the bow. Explosions break through the deck. Consume swathes of my ship. But I run against the wind. Against everything.

Pound's voice from the past echoes in my ears: *Fly, you ugly bastard. Fly!* And I leap overboard, boots first.

The sky is chaos. Harpoons, explosions, battling ships, roaring monsters, and sparkling flak. My jacket whips, and I fall past the battle and on toward nothing but an exposed, barren surface. None of the other ships are close enough. They probably don't even see me. I tap my gem to contact them, but I don't think anyone hears me over the blazing wind.

I continue falling. The gales slam against my goggles. My stomach lurches, until I hear a rumble. I glance to my side and—*HOLY BIRD-SHIT HELL!*

Fierce electric-blue eyes meet mine. A giant maw of death is chasing my fall. The baby giga readies to suck me into its acidic gut.

I'm a bug compared to it. But I laugh so hard, I feel like I'm going to throw up. Never thought I'd try this again.

My right arm struggles to rise against the winds, but I get it up, exposing "the Roderick" attached to my wrist. I aim past the baby giga's jaws at the underbelly of a coil. This needs to be one damn good shot, or I could accidentally launch myself right into its mouth.

I swallow a breath and squeeze the trigger. The chain ripples toward the beast. The scales better be thinner, or I'm dead.

And as my hooked claw fires across the sky, as it latches on to a scale, and as I'm suddenly yanked toward the baby, the whole world seems to explode with the scream of its mother.

The mother gigataun's torso rips inward, sucked into a Collapser vortex. *WE DID IT! We killed that giant birdshit!*

I'd cheer, except I'm being pulled right toward its offspring's mouth.

CHAPTER 44

I'M YANKED TOWARD THE BABY WITH UNBELIEVABLE SPEED. Can't even breathe. The baby's mouth widens, eagerly waiting for me to dive into it.

A giant, pink throat awaits.

I should be headed to the creature's underside, but the damned mouth—it's open so wide. I tighten up, close my eyes, and scream like hell. *Slam!* I crash into the creature's hard lip. My goggles fly off. Agony ripples through me. But I desperately kick away.

Can hardly see. Vision spins. But I'm zipping away from the angry, bellowing head and bound beneath the baby's chin.

Finally, I crash into the beast's underside. Pain erupts in my left shoulder. Might've broken something. Everything hurts, head soggy, eyesight blurred. I dangle from about two feet of slack in the chain. The baby's undulations make my stomach rise and fall. The claw-gun's strap pulls at my wrist, my skin. It's the only thing keeping me attached.

Got to climb the rest of the chain.

The giga's head coils around, eyes scanning for me. It'll pick me off like fruit from a tree.

I catch the chain, my shoulder crying, and start climbing the couple feet when a sudden, horrific blast spreads across the baby. The creature bellows. Surges of heat fly over me, and I dangle helplessly, shouting. *These damn Order idiots!*

I reach for my comm to send—no, my gem's shattered.

Have to get off this thing. Now. I take two quick breaths in and out. And despite my destroyed shoulder, bruises, and blurry vision, I climb. Several excruciating seconds later, my fingers slip into the cracks of the beast's scales.

Another explosion slams against the beast, this time toward the tail. Nearly shakes me free, too. But my magnetics are cranked to high. I detach the clawgun. Then, using my one good arm and magboots, I start up the side of the gigataun.

Never wanted to do this again. Even Pound would think it's crazy.

More explosions thunder against the monster. Now the baby's coiling its body, protecting itself from attack.

I ascend, one scale at a time. My teeth gnashing, my exhausted arms shaking. My heartbeat in my eyes. Finally, I reach the top of its flatter back, feeling as if my chest will burst. I want to lie down but can't.

I leap up and down, waving my arms at the massive Order vessels in the distance. "STOP FIRING, YOU—!"

Someone sees me. Far off. But it's too late; another massive ship fired. The volley soars in the air, approaching my position. *Shit. Shit. Shit.* I limp along the baby's back. Run as hard as I can.

BOOM!

The explosion rips the baby in half, and I'm jettisoned into the air. Golden fire swells around me. The monster shrieks. And now I'm falling back-first toward a patch of acidic clouds.

Two halves of the baby giga thrash above me, sinking. Blood spills into the sky.

My body goes cold with a tremoring finality. I'm going to die. At least, as far as deaths go, this is one hell of a way to go out.

Suddenly, something bursts from the smoke beside me. A ship. It's huge, blue. And then I grin because Keeton and Bryce are shouting from its deck, pointing toward me. But the ship's slow. A ship from the Trade of Waterworks, and it's covered in giant tanks of water. Used to put out fires on other ships.

They're too far away, and the giga's carcass blocks them.

I raise my arm, and point the clawgun, and fire. Just pure desperation. My chain ripples through the air. And before I can blink, my ruined shoulder's suddenly yanked fiercely from the socket. I roar in agony. It's like hot fire poured into me. But the shot hooked into something.

The falling giga.

Not what I planned, but dammit, I'm not done yet.

The clawgun reels me in, full speed. I hit the dead thing's snout feetfirst. My legs sting. The beast's head twitches under me. I crank my magboots again, detach the clawgun, and despite my raging heart, run like hell up the slope of its head toward the crest. As I'm running, the carcass falls past the deck of the Waterworks ship.

If I trip, I'll die. My legs are on fire. Ankles beg me to stop.

Only room for a few steps before I'll be out of reach of the Waterworks ship. So, with all my remaining strength, I leap atop the crest and jump into the sky. I aim the clawgun for the Waterworks ship and fire.

I can hardly see a damned thing because the wind's in my eyes. Feeling lightheaded. But the chain ripples in a straight line.

Then my chain connects with a glorious *shunk* just below the ship's railing.

I gnash my teeth and soar with incredible velocity toward the ship.

Oh, this is going to hurt. Or kill me. Maybe hurt and then kill me. I slam into the hull, and all goes black for a second before a wave of agonizing pain floods me. I dangle. Feeling like a lump of exhausted pain. Can't climb up. Can hardly even move. My left arm is completely broken, a bone protruding through the skin.

If I had any strength, all I'd have to do is climb a couple feet up the chain and I'd reach the railing.

The strap begins slipping from my wrist. My right arm weakly rises to hang on. But I've got nothing left. Nothing.

Suddenly, a giant, ham-sized hand reaches through the railing just as my wrist slips free. The huge hand catches mine and yanks me onto the ship.

I hit the deck in a daze. Blood in my throat. Body on the verge of passing out or death. Can't be sure. Then I recognize the person above me. He's grinning. The big, stupid birdshit is grinning. Why is it always him?

Pound crouches beside me and gently lifts me. And as I lie in his arms, leaning against him, the whole ship is cheering. No, not just the ship—my friends. They encircle me, laughing. The next few seconds are a blur.

But the celebration ends quickly because Goerner's ships are trying to escape.

Bryce squeezes my hand. Ella almost hugs me. Almost. Pound lowers me into a secluded place among the water tanks. And once there, I black out.

✦✦✦

When I come to, Bryce and Ella are holding me as a Scholar Doctor works on my arm. The Doctor mentions something about surgery. Can't use meds yet, or they'll heal my bones out of place. She says something else, but my ears are buzzing from the echoing celebrations.

Seems the whole world is cheering.

Bryce and Ella help me out from between the water tanks. I limp on one good leg, my broken, shattered arm tucked against my chest.

Pound's standing atop a railing and cheering. Thumping his chest as his shoulder cannon shoots a triumphant blast into empty sky.

"Goerner's ours!" he yells.

In the distance Master Koko's vessel, the *Archer*, is zooming around the *Golias* in victory. Apparently, her ship laid the shots that left the Lantian flagship smoking, engines destroyed, and its tower, where it commanded the beasts, burning.

I watch as boarding vessels, full of whooping Hunter and Order soldiers, launch after the Lantian flagship.

The beasts of the sky scatter. With Goerner's tower gone, they're no longer under his influence. The sky becomes a free-for-all. Some of the beasts shoot off in retreat, while others turn on Goerner's final forces.

Pound's laughing at the chaotic scene. It goes on for minutes, and I'm too weak to even stand. I lean against Bryce and Ella.

Then we hear the news.

Even over the wind, the Hunters aboard the *Golias* are whooping. They're lugging a bound Goerner like a prize above their heads.

I would cheer with the rest of my friends and the Waterworks crew.

Instead, I lean deeper against Bryce and Ella and sink into something not quite like sleep.

CHAPTER 45

TWO MONTHS HAVE PASSED SINCE THE VICTORY AT DANDUN. I've completely recovered following my surgery. Over these two months, I've stargazed with Bryce and spent mornings with Ella, just us, practicing our dueling skills. She's fast as hell—and is finally managing to hit me.

Many days I stand atop the hangar platform, watching the repairs to my ship. The *Gladian* wasn't destroyed. Apparently, when I was running along the baby giga, Uncle sent ships to save mine. They captured it with chained harpoons, stabbing into the hull before it crashed to the surface.

Master Koko told me that it would cost more to repair the *Gladian* than to build a new one. But I insisted. And so, she insisted that Hunter would pay for it. I killed the gigataun, and Hunter had been offering a Predator-class vessel to any Hunter who killed the beast. I'm grateful that I'll have my ship back soon. Except, I know why Uncle saved it. And it fills me with dread. My only hope is that the Collapser cannon is so damaged that Uncle will never be able to use it.

Some of the *Gladian* crew stayed aboard the *Dreadnought* with me. Arika's been working in the *Dreadnought's* enormous cafeteria, and Pound's been known to visit there for more reasons than just getting second and third helpings. Unfortunately, his sister, Noose, went back with her family. The good news is she had a family to return to. The Atwood Armada survived and destroyed the baby gigatauns, losing only a few ships in the process.

From what I heard, the Atwoods have traveled to the humid South. I suspect it won't be long until Pound leaves to reunite with them, but I think he's a little preoccupied with Arika.

Yesenia went stir-crazy here, so she requested a temporary transfer to a Hunter ship. I sent Otto with her. He needs to keep growing, keep learning and getting stronger if he wants to stay aboard my vessel when it's ready to fly again. And Keeton, having little to distract her from Roderick's absence—well, Bryce and I convinced her to follow Yesenia, too.

She needs the distraction of an engine before her.

We'll find Roderick. We'll find him.

The biggest news is the war. The fall of the giga halted any of the Below's momentum. They've lost their unstoppable weapon and their Admiral, and their fleet is in shambles.

At least, we hope so.

But we still don't know where Roderick is, and somehow Sebastian evaded capture. Fortunately, the war is waning. Without Goerner, without the gigataun, the Below has nothing except for their surviving beasts. And Uncle believes it won't be long until we can duplicate their technology and command the beasts for ourselves.

Victory, it seems, is entirely in our grasp.

But today I don't feel victorious as Ella and I stand before Uncle in his imperial office on the *Dreadnought*.

He's looking at us with deep disgust. Face wrinkled. That's the thing about Uncle; he'll never be satisfied. Never will stop until his power is total. After two months of torturing Goerner personally, he surveys us with absolute disdain.

Ella and I stand erect, meeting his eyes. Not arguing. Knowing how easily he could separate us again.

My skin tingles as he speaks because I know what he's going to say. He figured it out. Heat flushes my face. He comes forward and walks before us, his eyes narrowed on me, then Ella. His eyes bury deep into her and almost make her look away.

"You are not Urwin," he says.

My heart falls into my gut. Who told him? A thousand possibilities rush through my mind. Worse are the potential outcomes of this dangerous revelation. Uncle loves the Urwin blood as much as he loves power.

Ella blinks at him, confused. "What?"

"Goerner has lied before," Uncle hisses, "but this truth—he cannot manufacture. Not with his ability to transmit experiences through that creature in his neck. You both—your maternal grandfather, Hale, was a damn dirt-eater!"

Ella's head shakes. She looks at me, expecting me to push back. But when my head falls, she retreats. "No. That's impossible."

"You little birdshits!" he roars. "No wonder I've had so much trouble with you. You've always been vermin. I wasted all this time, *years* of my life, trying to mold you. Make you rise. Become strong. Instead, I was coddling the progeny of my enemy."

"No," Ella says. "Father—"

"How dare you?!" he spits. "How dare you call me that. I am *not* your father. You are the descendants of dirt-eaters. Disgusting rodents."

Her mouth clamps shut, and her eyes water.

I feel I'm somewhere else. All this time I've spent trying to win back my place as an Urwin, and once I do it, it's undermined by something outside of my control.

Uncle speaks over the comm. I'm expecting him to call the guards. Haul us away to be executed. Or perhaps tortured—as if we're spies, even though we know nothing. We've done everything he asked. We brought him back the weapon.

We saved the Skylands.

But that's not enough for Uncle. It'll never be enough. Not if we captured all the winds in our palms and held them out to him in offering. Because to him, blood is everything.

And ours is tainted.

Uncle doesn't call the guards. He calls someone else. The door opens a few seconds later, and she enters. Her long, black hair pulled back. Her eyes severe. Haven't seen her since before Sky's Edge. More than three and a half months. She's carrying a bundle in her arms.

Severina strides past us, elegant. Quiet.

For the first time I can remember, Uncle's expression softens as Severina walks to him, because in her arms, she's holding something that Uncle dreamed of having for years. The reason why he went through so many women.

A baby.

I almost sink into the floor.

"This," Uncle says, gently taking the cooing infant into his arms, "is Thaddeus of Urwin. And he is *true* Urwin."

A tuft of blond crowns Thaddeus's head. Maybe a few weeks old, he's draped in expensive red blankets.

Perhaps, in a family of love, we all would've smiled and gathered around the baby. Held him in our arms. Said hello and let his tiny fingers hold ours. We'd look into the bright blue sky together and recognize that it wouldn't be long until the Lantians surrender. The war would be over.

And with us in command of the Skylands, we could lead. We could show the world there's a better way. We could rebuild the surface. Repair old wounds. Reunite, even.

Instead, the weight in this unloving room bears down on my shoulders. Pushes me into the ground.

"Thaddeus," Uncle says, "is the true heir of Urwin."

Ella bites her lip to stifle a sob. But I stare at Uncle, my brow darkening. This bastard. Again. Taking away what is mine.

"You two," Uncle says, meeting our gaze with dark foreboding, "will have to do everything I say for the rest of your miserable lives. You are fortunate," he says, "that you are *part* Urwin. That we are so few in this world. But if the Skylands ever discover the secret truth of your origins, I will take you to the most populated island, fill the auditorium with Highs and Lows alike . . . and execute you both myself."

He carries Thaddeus toward the door before pausing and looking back. "Soon we will finally announce Thaddeus's birth, and then I will do what no Urwin has ever done. I will ensure that our power is absolute. Today the Urwins rise forever." He looks ready to spit at our feet. "Be grateful that a fraction of that greatness still runs in your blood."

CHAPTER 46

SEVERAL DAYS LATER, ELLA AND I STAND ON THE UPPERMOST platform of the hangar and watch the Masters of the Twelve Trades board the *Dreadnought*. But it's not just them. Many of the Archdukes and Archduchesses from every region have come, too, all to discuss the next step of the war, because according to Uncle, the Lantian Council has refused to surrender.

Uncle's next step is invasion.

He walks out from the corridor below us, accompanied by his advisers, and every person in the hangar stops to cheer. The popular King. The tales about him have already changed. It was he who recognized the weakness in King Ferdinand and unseated him just in time for war. It was he who, despite dissent, demanded that the Skylands not give in. That they fight until the last person.

It was he who met the challenge of anyone in the arena. And he defeated them all, including the great Sione of Niumatalolo.

Uncle raises a hand to silence them.

Everyone obeys.

He waits as the Masters of the Twelve Trades approach. Now that the war's so firmly in our favor, Uncle claims it's safe to gather all the Skylands' most powerful together again. Most arrive, but not all.

The distinguished guests start up the stairs and follow Uncle down the corridor. Off to the conference chamber. Uncle said I must be present for this monumental occasion. He claims it will be the moment that will secure the Urwins' place forever. Our plan for victory over the Below will be set.

I plan on joining them, but first someone waits for me on the platform. She looks up at me in her silver Hunter robes.

I pat Ella on the shoulder. She's been broken ever since discovering who Uncle truly is. And that she is only part Urwin. It has left her a fragment of her former self. Our duels have had less strength. Less desire. She finally understands that with Uncle, our safety is never guaranteed, no matter how dutifully we obey, how much we prove our strength. But we can't escape. He'd have us both killed the minute we cease to be useful. Right now we need to focus on finishing this war. Then maybe Ella and I can leave. Go off together—just us, maybe some of my friends—and not let Uncle know.

Get away from all the birdshit of this world.

There are always islands that care less about rising. Maybe the arctic North or the pirates' isles. Places where maybe Uncle would leave us alone. He has his heir. What he wants. He can mold that poor baby into his image.

I leave Ella, slide down several ladders, and stand before Master Koko. She grins faintly at me.

"You have always been so resourceful," she says, her voice softer than I recall. "The King's taking all the credit, but it was *you* who went into the uncharted airs."

"Wasn't just me."

She nods. "Yes, you have an ego, but when it comes to your friends, you're always so modest."

"They deserve the same credit I do."

She pats my cheek. "Today I am offering my resignation."

I almost step back. "What? But Master—"

"I have spent my life in service of Hunter, and I've done all I can. I feel at peace, knowing the war is in our favor. At the adjourning of the meeting with the King, I will offer my resignation."

"Master—"

"You should be the new Master of Hunter, Conrad."

My mouth stops working. I think I murmur a strange sound.

"I'll propose it to your uncle," she says. "Though, he'll never allow it because you are the heir." She doesn't know about the baby yet. No one does. That's part of Uncle's announcement in the conference chamber today. "But I'm going to try. With your permission, of course."

My heart sings as I stand before her. Maybe Uncle would actually allow me to be the Master of Hunter. He might like the idea of an Urwin—well, part of an Urwin—reaching the status of Master. With Thaddeus as the sole heir, there's a chance Uncle will say yes.

Something tells me that's wishful thinking, though.

I was given Prince, but my life as a Hunter? That's something I earned. Something I'm proud of. My crew. My ship. We won the Gauntlet together. We destroyed the greatest threat the Skylands had ever faced together. It wasn't easy. I lost so many.

But I am a Hunter. Always will be.

"Yes," I say, fighting through the choke in my voice. "I'd be honored to become the Master of Hunter."

Then I hug her. Gently. When I pull away, she stares at me in surprise.

"I didn't think Urwins were huggers."

"Yes, well, I've never really been an Urwin anyway."

She laughs. "I don't know about that. Outside of your uncle, I'm not sure I've met anyone more driven to succeed."

She catches my arm in hers, and I recognize there's a frailty to her now. As though this war caught up to her. Life caught up to her. "Would you mind if I lean on your arm as we go to the conference chamber? I injured my leg in the battle, and it just hasn't gotten better."

She would've had meds, of course, but not even meds can fix age.

I hold out my arm, and she grins and takes it. And I'm so grateful to have met someone like her. Someone powerful, who knows how to rise in this world but who also lifts up and supports others. Helps them feel whole. She is someone I can respect, whose praise I will fight to earn.

After my mother's death, she's come the closest to filling that void. And it hurts knowing that not even she can beat time.

In the end we all fall.

We walk together, and she listens intently as I tell her about all the incredible beasts we saw in the far-off skies. We speak of the continuing threats posed by the surviving gorgantauns, all fed with a fresh stock of prey now that Sky's Edge is open.

Worse, there are rumors that a few baby gigatauns survived. And some believe the strange, stormy weather as of late is a result of migrating octolons.

"Seems," she says, "you'll have immediate responsibilities as the Master of Hunter."

"I'd never do as well as you would."

"True," she says, laughing.

She pats my arm, and I smile at her.

We're the last ones in the conference chamber. Suddenly, the door slams behind us, making me jump. Then my smile shrinks, and a chill slithers down my back as I take in the scene. Uncle stands above everyone on his platform, his fingers tapping on his cane, while his other arm cradles the new heir of Urwin.

Every Master, every Archduke and Archduchess, has their hands in the air. Each Master is faced by a person dressed in the same uniform as theirs. Their protégées. And they all hold an auto-pistol, trained on their superior. The only Master who stands without a protegee, without a weapon trained on her, is Marian of Sandoval. The Master of Explorer. She's nearer to the King, watching the scene with a stoic face.

The Master of Disposal raises his voice. "King Ulrich, what is the meaning of—"

Ariana of Alcose pistol-whips him. Herm hits the ground and wipes the blood from his mouth.

"Ari," he says, looking up at his protégée. "Why?"

"Because if I'm going to live a life as a shit cleaner," she hisses, disgusted, "I better be the one in charge."

A pair of huge guards yanks me away from Master Koko. They carry me to the corner.

"No!" I try to rip free, but their massive biceps curl around my arms.

Another person steps before Master Koko. I almost stop breathing. It's her longtime assistant, Teresa of Abel. Sebastian's aunt. She's dressed in the same Master robes as Koko. Teresa points an auto-pistol at her boss' head.

Uncle raises a hand to silence the panicked room. "Seven years ago my brother stood in the way of my right to rule. He was weak. Couldn't do what was necessary. But now you all have the chance to prove that you are not weak, like my brother was. You can prove that you have earned the right to rule."

"We are *not* weak," Master Koko spits.

"That was not directed at *you*." Uncle's eyes fall upon the people holding the auto-pistols. "Prove your strength. Prove you will do what is necessary, and the power you've always dreamed of will entirely be yours."

"Uncle!" I shout. "Don't do this."

The guards clamp their hands over my mouth. Uncle's face breaks into a slight grin as he locks eyes with me. And for a moment, I consider that if Thaddeus were old enough, he'd be standing before me, too, holding an auto-pistol.

"Who will be my most loyal supporter?" Uncle says, turning back to the people below him. "Show me."

The leaders of the Skylands shout at their protégées. The Master of Politics falls to her knees, begging. Cheng of Lee, the Master of Scholar, stares quietly at his protégée. And my heart sinks in horror at who is facing him.

Tara of Kyle.

Her pistol's shaking. She's smart. She must understand the ramifications of this coup of Meritocracy. What it'll mean for the Skylands. But the pull of power is strong. She grits her teeth. Meets Cheng's eyes.

Then squeezes the trigger.

Cheng falls.

No.

The room becomes chaos. An Archduke tries to remove his dueling staff, but he falls, dead. The Master of Order charges his foe before his legs buckle beneath him, a hole bleeding in his skull. Ariana shoots next, and Herm of Decloos, the Master of Disposal, falls to the ground, his brown robes turning red.

In seconds the leaders of the Skylands are dead, all except Master Koko and Marian of Sandoval. Marian is silent. Her loyalty to King Ulrich is clear.

Master Koko stares at Teresa. Her eyes full of sincerity. "Teresa, you are my friend. We have been friends for decades."

"You were giving Master to someone else," Teresa says coldly. "You ignored me. Always ignored me."

"Teresa, listen—"

But Teresa squeezes the trigger.

And I feel I'm no longer present. I'm back to when I first landed on Venator and Master Koko came from the jungle, the torchlight on her face. She told us that she would teach us how to rise in Hunter.

She did . . . and now, she falls.

The bloody sight glows in Uncle's triumphant eyes. He's done it. He has surrounded himself entirely with people loyal to him. His power is unbreakable.

I'm sick. I'm shouting. And crying. I rip free from the guards and bolt to Master Koko, catch her in my arms. She's breathing quickly. A hole in her chest. Her scarred face, hardened from years of hunting, softens as she sees me. Recognizes me.

Then her body goes limp.

Uncle stands above this room of death, victorious. His will to rise unmatched. His power solidified, never to be challenged again.

CHAPTER 47

I SIT ON THE BENCHES THAT SURROUND THE FAMOUS SCHOLAR Debate Square. Dandun's hot air dries my skin. The sandy concrete grits under my boots as my knee bounces. This is the place where the most renowned duels of Scholarly wit have ever occurred. This is the way Scholars rise—through their ability to appeal to ethos, pathos, and logos.

Not the way Tara did. Murdering her own Master.

Uncle stands on a raised platform at the base of the amphitheater, addressing an angry crowd. They're all shaking their fists. News regarding the deaths of many of the Masters and Archdukes and Archduchesses has spread. The public thinks the Lantians are responsible, but they don't know that minutes after the slaughter in the conference chamber, Uncle gave the order for the *Dreadnought* to self-destruct. Because it wouldn't have been believable that the Below managed to assassinate each of them individually.

Something had to be sacrificed.

Uncle knows all about making sacrifices to empower himself.

I barely had time to get Arika, Pound, and Ella off with me and was fortunate that the *Gladian* was ready to fly again. Hundreds of others on the King's ship were not so lucky.

"The dirt-eaters destroyed my ship!" Uncle cries to the enraged crowd. "They're not finished! Now they attack our very way of life—our Meritocracy. Before she died in the explosion, the Master of Hunter," he says, his softened voice eliciting an emotional response from the crowd, "was planning on retiring that day."

The crowd cries out, horrified.

My hands ball into fists as I stare at this sadistic, cruel man above me.

Uncle tells the crowd it was fortunate he wasn't on the *Dreadnought*, or we'd have no leadership. He tells us he had to personally pick new Masters because he is the only one we can trust.

"They are here now," he says, waving his hand over the crowd.

The Masters arrive on cue, entering through the tunnels on either side of the amphitheater, all dressed in the garbs and colors of their Trade. Tara of Kyle leads the way, followed by the one Master spared by Uncle, Marian of Sandoval.

The crowd hollers in support for them.

Uncle raises his hand to silence the audience.

"This war is not over, Skylanders. We shall have vengeance against the dirt-eaters for their heinous assault. To accomplish this, I am personally sending my nephew, Conrad of Urwin, to lead the invasion of the Below. He has volunteered to go to the front of the lines. To fight and bring to justice all the vermin who murdered the Master of his Trade."

The crowd turns and claps for me.

My skin burns hot, and my gut squeezes with nausea. I feel like screaming out the truth, but Uncle has all the power. How easily he could reveal my true heritage. And even without him, that rumor might spread anyway. Sending me to invade the Lantian colonies is Uncle's way of getting rid of me. There will be some accident down there. I'll die. But Uncle has his heir, anyway.

Maybe he'll let Ella live. If she's compliant.

Uncle continues speaking.

Sand collects on my lashes as I scowl at him. This bastard sent me to save the Skylands. And that's exactly what I did. He's going to take everything away from me again.

I stand as the people clap for him. My sister rises next. Then we turn away and start up the amphitheater stairs. The wind splashes through my hair, heating my agitated skin. Kirsi of Rebekah told me to not hang on to the dead, or they'll leave me with guilt. I'm not sure I agree. Master Koko's death doesn't fill me with guilt. It fills me with rage. And it will be the thing that propels me to my rise over my damned uncle.

He calls me Urwin, but my name is Conrad of *Elise*.

Once I've finished off this damn war below, I'll return. I will meet him at his perch on the Highest High. And Uncle will tremble like the little boy I once was. He'll watch, helpless, as I break his cane and leave him begging at my feet.

Soon, I will be his downfall.

ACKNOWLEDGMENTS

Phew.

Writing a sequel for the first time was like flying through the uncharted airs, but thankfully, except for some setbacks—looking at you, the forty thousand words that took the story in the wrong direction—I had an absolute blast writing this one.

I set out to write *Among Serpents* with a few goals in mind. First, I wanted to write something I'd be proud of, and second, I desperately needed to answer how Conrad and company would triumph over the horrifying gigataun. Finally, I absolutely had to find a way to focus the story back on Uncle.

Accomplishing these things was incredibly gratifying, and I hope you, the reader, are geared up for the epic conclusion to the Above the Black trilogy.

Creating *Among Serpents* would not have been possible without the support of my amazing and patient wife. In fact, while I was working on this book, she surprised me with a gift. She took the guest room in our basement and turned it into a writing office, complete with a brand-new writing desk. Ashley, I love you, and I'm so grateful that you're pushing me to chase my dreams.

Alongside her support, I also cannot thank my agent, Heather Cashman, enough. She read *Among Serpents* for the first time in a whole weekend. Her highly complimentary letter told me I was on the right track, giving me the confidence I needed to make necessary changes before presenting it to my publisher.

Furthermore, I'd like to thank my editor, Jonah Heller, who again demonstrated a complete understanding of what I was trying to do. His diligent guidance helped me elevate *Among Serpents* to the clouds. Without him, this series would not be what it is. Thank you, Jonah. I am so privileged and fortunate that I've been able to work with you these last couple years. There are many people behind the scenes who make a book become what it is. A special thank-you to my copy editor, Pam Glauber, who has helped me through two books to maintain the timeline and consistency. Additional thanks to my proofreader, Manu Shadow Velasco, for having such an incredible eye. Thank you, Pam and Manu.

I'd also like to thank my amazing and weird and funny children. I love you with all I have. I wish you'd stay young forever. Your boisterous laughs fill our home with life even when I'm feeling overwhelmed and stressed with teaching and writing deadlines.

I'd also like to thank my students. My magnificent young humans whose relentless enthusiasm for *Sky's End* told me I'd tapped into something people wanted. Reading your book reports on *Sky's End* was one of the most surreal and amazing moments of my teaching career.

Among Serpents also had a slew of readers who gave me valuable feedback to help me make the book the best it could be. My wife, my colleague Anna Alger, and my dear friend Brandon Michie—thank you. I'm not sure where I'd get the courage to keep writing without your continued cheerleading.

I'd like to thank Amir Zand for another incredible illustration and Lily Steele for their amazing cover design. Also, I'm so fortunate my books landed with such a supportive publisher. A special thank-you to Sara DiSalvo, Mary Joyce Perry, Michelle Montague, Elyse Vincenty, Derek Stordahl, Terry Borzumato-Greenberg, Farah Géhy, Kathy Landwehr, and Bob Higgins, and to everyone else who helped rocket this trilogy onto bookshelves.

Finally, I'd like to thank you, reader, for joining Conrad on the next step in his journey. I hope you enjoyed connecting with these characters and the Skylands all over again, and I hope you're eagerly anticipating the final book.

Together we will rise, or together we will fall.

—MJG

Photo credit: Ashley Gregson

ABOUT THE AUTHOR

MARC J GREGSON is a *New York Times* bestselling author. He attended the University of Utah, where he received his bachelor of arts in English teaching. Marc's pursuit of learning has led him into the classroom, where he teaches middle school English. He believes in the power of words and that stories can unite people from all origins. Above the Black is his first fantasy trilogy for teens.

The

ABOVE THE BLACK

fantasy trilogy surges toward bloodthirsty battles of epic proportion in

DOWNFALL

3

Coming Spring 2026